Zigzag Girl

First published in 2026
by The Black Spring Press Group
London, United Kingdom

Cover design by Matt Broughton
Typeset by Edwin Smet

ISBN 9781917788038

Printed in Canada

BLACKSPRINGPRESSGROUP.COM

Zigzag Girl

a novel

Ruth Knafo Setton

THE **BLACK SPRING**
PRESS GROUP

To the magicians

Atlantic City, you'll be the death of me
Whoa, Atlantic City, you'll be the death of me.

—'Atlantic City Blues,'
The High Toppers

Atlantic City is like Dracula – you can't kill it,
no matter how hard you try.

—JIM WHELAN
(former mayor of Atlantic City, 1990-2001)

Pine Barrens, New Jersey

'Tonight you're going to become a man,' growled Big Nick. 'Any questions?'

Little Nick wasn't stupid enough to ask questions.

While they walked through the field, his grandfather Big Nick hacked weeds with his saw, and the poor sad lady humped over his shoulder flopped like a rag doll. She drooped with sadness – from her dark limp hair to her mouth to her scrawny shoulders. Even her voice drooped.

Earlier, in the cabin, she'd asked his name.

'Little Nick.' He might have had another name once, but he'd long since forgot it.

'How old are you?'

'Eleven.' *Almost.*

'That's a big boy, yet you sleep in a Sawing Box.' Her voice was smudgy with tears. 'Did you know that magicians saw women in half in those boxes?' She touched his hair with pale, fluttering fingers. A memory had trembled through him – a woman's warm hand stroking his head. A sweet voice telling him he was her good boy.

The sad lady had given him something of hers that burned red-hot in his pocket. Sweat dripped down his face and chest. Even his eyes were sweating so hard they scorched like tears.

'What kinda man you gonna be?' growled Big Nick. 'A real man or a sissy-man?'

The glowing orange ball in the sky was covered with black patches like a hundred eyes, every last one glaring at him. 'A real man.'

'A real man never lets others see him sweat. He does the deed and moves on.'

At the riverbank, Little Nick swept off the sedge and grass that hid the sneak boat. Low and light with a canvas apron that shielded them from winds, the boat always reminded him of one of the old man's backless slippers. They squeezed in tight, side by side, the woman at their feet. He and his grandfather dragged an oar through the water and glided as smooth as pelicans over the Mullica toward the colonial ghost town and the haunted graveyard.

Before they even docked the sneak boat at Clarks Landing, the stink of evil rose. Once upon a time this had been a real town with a church and houses. Now, all that remained was dead bodies and the smell of witchery. A long time ago they'd lynched Black men here. There was even a Hanging Tree nearby. Scariest of all, the Jersey Devil hid in the old tombs. He'd lay there hugging a corpse till his fifty-year sleep was over, then up he shot like a rocket, to attack again. The Devil had a horse face, bat wings, and goat hooves, and the only thing he wanted to do was kill. He'd butcher an entire family all at once, burp, and go back into hiding for another fifty years.

He and Big Nick took turns digging open an ancient grave.

'Open your eyes, boy!'

His eyes shot open.

'It's deep enough. Time to prove you're a man.'

*

When it was over, they rowed up the Mullica back to Joe Mulliner Road, followed by the moon with its hundred eyes. 'Bones to bones, ashes to ashes, dirt to dirt,' chanted Big Nick. 'She'll mingle with the other bones.' Happy now, he clapped his hands. 'Goodbye, Blackbird. That's one more gone for good.'

For the first time Little Nick dared to wonder if the old man might be wrong about the blackbirds being dead and gone for good. After all, in magic, you could rip a bill to shreds and put it back together. You could vanish a coin and make it reappear. You could saw a woman in halves, thirds, even fourths, slice off her head, and bury her with the Devil, and still you'd know that sure as there are ticks in summer, the next day or week or month, she'd press her cold hand to the back of your neck and whisper words that clinked like ice.

No matter how many times you killed her.

PART ONE
ROSE

1

Atlantic City

Wednesday October 17

24 years later

Nine minutes to the finale.

Hand me a flower and I'll transform it into a dove.

Shoot me from a cannon and I'll come out smiling.

But lock me in the box and saw me in half, and I'll scream bloody murder.

Unheard of for a Moon – a member of America's most famous magic family – to be terrified of that creaky old standard, the sawing box. But you're hearing it now.

In exactly nine minutes, Charlie, our production manager, and Van, my friend and co-star, are supposed to reenact the famous Sawing a Woman in Half illusion as it was performed by Magnificent Morelli and his assistant Cleo West in this theatre during World War Two.

The classic poster hangs in the dressing room: a man with slick black hair and a thin moustache gesturing to a pretty strawberry-blonde who holds a Statue of Liberty torch.

Between them is the infamous sawing box. Black letters slash across the top of the poster:

MAGNIFICENT MORELLI!

MAN OF MYSTERY

At the bottom:

NIGHTLY IN THE SCARLET ROOM
WORLD-FAMOUS ATLANTIC CITY
BOARDWALK

There's one problem. Van should have been here two hours ago.

My best friend and other co-star, Stormie, and I managed to get through the show to this point because we're used to working together and because even in the midst of frenzy, Charlie is an oasis of calm. We call it the Charlie effect. He quickly redesigned the order of illusions to make up for Van's absence.

But Van still hasn't shown up, so Charlie will saw *me* in half in Cleo's original sawing box. This is not the contemporary sleek or transparent sawing box you see on a Vegas stage, but the real thing. Pure old-school; a deep, long wooden container that resembles a coffin. No openings for head or feet. No clamps for neck or ankles. The kind of box in which the magician's assistant is completely locked inside, head to toe. If that's not horrifying enough, this is the same box in which Cleo's murderer placed her body.

Good publicity for a haunted theatre on Halloween, says Charlie.

At five-seven, I'm two inches shorter than the box.

Stormie, coming in at a fraction under six feet and 190 pounds, can't even squeeze inside.

Hanging right next to Morelli is our poster:

HALLOWEEN THRILLS, CHILLS
& BLACK MAGICK!
REBEL MAGIC
STORMIE, VAN, & LUCY
BLACK WIDOW THEATRE, 13TH FLOOR –
IF YOU DARE!
MIDNIGHT CASINO, OCT 17 – NOV 10

Van and I flank Stormie – a magical version of *Charlie's Angels*. As if instead of fighting crime, we resolve to change the world, one trick at a time. In the middle, Stormie towers over Van and me in an orange and black dashiki gown, enormous hoop earrings glinting through her copper-black hair that falls in long ropelike locks. On Stormie's left is Van, a tiny silvery futuristic superhero who sometimes bills herself as 'Kickass Korean Babe' – spiked hair, jumpsuit, thigh-high boots with four-inch heels, and a gleaming knife in each hand. On Stormie's right, I sparkle in my red-hot Miss Scarlett dress and stilettos. That's me, on the corner of woo-woo and fuggedaboutit – a magic wand in one hand, a cannoli in the other.

Tonight is our opening night, and it means something big to all three of us: our breakthrough as sisters of magic, an opportunity to make our name in the good old boys' world of magic, and for me, a chance to make *my* name without the Moons holding me up on stage.

Van wouldn't miss this for the world.

Her silver jumpsuit is hanging on the wheeled rack, her knives ready for action.

She's not answering her phone, but during the intermission, she left Stormie and me a message: Emergency. Start without me.

Stormie's golden-brown eyes were huge, her olive skin sallow, making the freckles stand out. 'Emergency?' Her voice was shrill. 'That is not a Van word.'

'An accident?'

'She'd tell us. No, it's MLD.'

For the past couple weeks, Van has kept her new boyfriend on the lowdown. Boyfriend is normal – Van juggles men like her knives. Keeping him secret is not. Stormie calls him, 'MLD,' short for Mysterious Loner Dude.

'Van would not miss our opening night for a guy, no matter

who he is.'

'Then where is she?' Stormie shook her fingers in my face. 'Look at my hand. The girl's giving me *shpilkes.*' Whenever she's emotional, Stormie brings out the Yiddish words her Jewish Nana taught her.

'If by *shpilkes,* you mean bad vibes, I've got 'em too.'

Stormie Weather is my sister in all ways but blood. Half-Black, half-Jewish and, as she says, 'all chutzpah', she's been my best friend since sixth grade.

I tapped a message: What's wrong? Need help. Call me.

Earlier tonight, before I left the house, my aunt grasped my wrist.

'Remember, darlin', we're in the season of Samhain.' Auntie Maze's voice, a marriage of Irish lilt and hoarse smoker, evokes both fey spirits and cozy pubs. 'The time of year when the doors between worlds are open. Messages flow back and forth between the dead and the living. Tonight, Nellie and I heard a woman callin' to you from the other side.'

Auntie Maze communes on and off stage with the first Moon witch, Nellie Moon, who brings her messages from the dead.

'I believe it's your mother. Do you hear her?'

'No, I don't hear anything.'

But I suddenly wonder if the woman Auntie Maze heard calling to me is not my mother, but Van. Ferocious, reckless Van, who's been going out night after night with a man no one knows. Van, who'd never miss her opening night, not in a million years, not unless something or someone prevented her.

2

Seven minutes to the finale.

Backstage, hands trembling, I tug on Cleo West's very own Stars n' Stripes gown, slithering into the shimmering satin. Too short for me. Seams fraying – it's been let out and tightened more than once. Cleo must have gained and lost weight during the war years.

I sit at the vanity, tightly clip my hair and pull on a long reddish-blonde wig. I hate wigs, they suffocate me and give me an instant headache.

Trapped, wrapped and bundled inside the constraints of hair and layers of fabric, my heart staccatos. When did the theatre get so cold? The scent of lavender crawls over my flesh, the sign that the Widow's resident ghost, Cleo, is in the house. When you grow up with an Irish witch as an aunt, you accept the presence of ghosts. Doesn't mean you like them, but you come to terms with sharing the space. According to Auntie Maze, 'Cleo wants us to see the cracks and stains left behind by the past. When she slams doors or turns off lights, she's saying, "Look! There's something you're not seeing!"'

I add final touch-ups to my stage make-up and check my reflection from every angle. I glimpse pinpricks of light in the mirror. Next to my reflection a woman's face appears, rippling as if she's underwater. Her fiery-gold hair wavers. Ice-pale eyes meet mine. Two Cleos in the mirror.

I grab the edge of the table. This is the first time she's shown herself to me! Just in case she's really there and I'm not losing my mind, I whisper, 'You're not real, Cleo. You're dead. Look, I'm just pretending to be you for an hour, okay? Now please go away.'

She stares at me through the glass. Her lips move. I lean forward, press my face to the mirror, straining to hear.

Cleo disappears, and a large black figure looms in the mirror. Moves closer.

I jolt to my feet and whip around.

A man wearing a black hoodie. At least he's real, not a ghost. He pushes back the hood. Dark hair falls past his chin.

'What's going on here?' he demands.

Shifting on my feet, I keep my hands low at my sides, ready to punch. 'You need to leave now.'

He steps closer. He's half a foot taller, his strong-boned face scowling, his eyes bitter as black coffee. 'Where's Van?'

'Not here.'

'She said I could come backstage.'

'Who are you?' Is he Van's mysterious guy?

Stormie arrives, breathless. 'You're on in five,' she says to me, and then slits her eyes at the stranger. 'Elvis Jones! What are you doing here?'

This is Elvis Jones? Definitely not the cheesy overweight Elvis impersonator in a white jumpsuit I imagined when I saw his poster:

ELVIS JONES

MAGIC IN HELL

MIDNIGHT SHOW

No one will be admitted after the door is shut.

I found the poster pretentious and, on principle, refused to see his show. If I'd known what he looks like, I might have taken a chance. He watches me with a sardonic grin as if he knows what I'm thinking.

'Hi, Stormie,' he says. 'I'm looking for Van.'

'She hasn't arrived. Yet.'

He retreats toward the door. 'I'm outta here.'

Stormie and I watch him leave, and she mutters, 'What the hell has that girl been up to?'

'I'm scared for her.' I hear the words and wish I hadn't said them.

'Maybe her phone died, and she's stuck somewhere. She's gonna show up.'

3

Four minutes to the finale.

Stormie and I move to the wings near heavy coiled ropes – seaman's ropes that balance the red stage curtains.

While I smooth Cleo's gown over my hips, Stormie adjusts my wig. 'You know you're a dead ringer for Cleo.'

'That does not make me feel good.'

I peek out at the theatre and catch snatches of Charlie's intro: 'Tonight, we have a one-time special finale in honour of the veterans of Camp Boardwalk. Lucy and I will perform the sawing box illusion, exactly as Magnificent Morelli and Cleo West performed it on this very stage.'

I nudge Stormie. 'How does sawing a woman in half honour anyone?'

Charlie goes on, 'I want to thank Jinx Faust, who organised tonight's reunion and donated the sawing box. It's an Eddie Garland original, co-designed by Cleo.'

He gestures to the woman in the front row. 'Let's give Jinx a hand.'

'What a dame,' mutters Stormie.

Jinx waves her jewelled cane. 'Can you believe it's been seventy-five years?' Her inimitable voice rings out, husky and seductive, decades younger than whatever age she is – anywhere from ninety to one hundred. With her black bob wig and lined map of a face, she occupies her seat like an ancient pharaoh. A Pulitzer Prize-winning journalist and local celebrity, she covered Atlantic City's murders and corruption in 'The Noir Beat,' her column for *The Atlantic City News*, from World War Two to the early twenty-first century.

Charlie's voice rises. 'If you're visiting Black Widow Theatre for the first time, you may not know that you're in the Old Tower, the historic centre of Midnight. For our Camp Boardwalk visitors, this theatre, and even the hotel, must be very familiar. When the US Army took over Atlantic City in 1943, they converted many boardwalk hotels into Army offices, centres, and residences. This hotel was transformed into Thomas England General Hospital, a military hospital for wounded soldiers, and this theatre was known as the Scarlet Room. It was open during the war but went through a dark period after the Great Atlantic Hurricane of 1944.'

'September 14th,' cries Jinx.

Charlie nods. 'That night, nine people were killed, and 390 wounded. One victim was Cleo West, Magnificent Morelli's fiancée and assistant in his magic show. Jinx, you saw his show, didn't you?'

'Oh yes,' says Jinx. 'Many times. They performed amazing illusions like the Blooming Tree and Mysterious Connections, but their standout was the Sawing a Woman in Half trick.'

'That night,' says Charlie, 'the night of the hurricane, a soldier named Frank Weir shot Cleo to death and placed her body in the very sawing box you are about to see.'

A stagehand wheels Cleo's sawing box onstage. My heart thumps, wild and frantic.

The audience rustles with anticipation. Charlie was right: there's a bloodthirsty excitement at the prospect of the same box being used.

Stormie murmurs, 'You'll get through this.'

'All I wanted is to make it as Lucy, and now I'm going to screw up Lucy and shame the Moons. Why why why isn't Van here?' I hate the whiny note in my voice, but I can feel a panic attack starting.

'We'll figure that out later, but girl, you need to chill.'

'It's supposed to be Van, not me.'

Charlie crooks his finger at me.

It's too soon. I'm not ready. 'Storm! This is the box which held Cleo's dead body! And I'm supposed to get in like nothing happened.'

Stormie frowns. 'Listen to me. Remember who you are. You're Lucy Fucking Moon. You *are* magic. Now go out there and knock 'em dead.'

4

Two minutes before the finale.

The stagehands have pulled down a screen on which they've superimposed the classic poster of Morelli and Cleo.

Charlie and I take our places behind the screen.

My gaze goes immediately to the box, waiting for me to enter.

Charlie reaches for my hand. 'Lucy. You okay?'

I twist around. We're face to face. Dark gold hair gleaming, he adjusts his bowtie and peers at me through tortoiseshell glasses. First time Van saw him, she pressed her hand to her heart and said, 'Oh please, let those glasses be real and not a prop.'

Tonight, carrying a top hat and wearing a tux in honour of the Camp Boardwalk survivors' reunion, Charlie is ridiculously beautiful and elegant, like a star from Hollywood's golden era.

He stares at me, lips parted. He breathes a word: 'Remember?'

I don't answer, but I grip his hand like a lifeline.

I have never told this to anyone. Not even to Da, Auntie Maze, or Stormie, and they know all my secrets. But this... this is too strange and eerie. Last summer, Charlie and I were backstage in the Orange Room, gathering props for a Moon Magick show, when Cleo's lavender wind swept in and rustled under our skin. We heard 'I'll Be Seeing You,' a big band song, coming from nowhere – the air, the ceiling, the wind. The room grew icy, and Charlie and I clung to each other. We danced, and when the music stopped, we kissed with a raw desperation as if we'd been deprived of each other for years.

We wrenched free and gaped at each other with a mixture of desire and shock.

The way we're looking at each other now.

We've never talked about it, but when we see each other, our faces heat up, and it's excruciating and weird. Something happened between us. We know it. We both know it.

He releases my hand. 'Ten seconds.'

I shut my eyes and feel myself swaying. I'm going to die in this box. 'Charlie!'

But my cry is muffled by the creak of the screen rising.

5

F*inale.*

As the screen rises, Magnificent Morelli and Cleo West are revealed in the exact position they are in the poster: Charlie in his tux and me in Cleo's wig and Stars n' Stripes gown.

I lift the unlit Statue of Liberty torch. A hard breath, and I echo Cleo's words: 'I like my coffee red-hot, my magic blazing, and my men so rich they set my fingers on fire.' My voice is soft, but I can't go louder.

I blow on my fingers and touch the torch. It flames.

Over applause and whistles, one of the veterans says, 'Aw, hell, Cleo's back in town!'

'So are we!' cries another one, in a wheelchair.

A cheer goes up, 'The Army's back in town!'

'Still alive and kicking!' says a woman with a white froth of hair.

Charlie steps to the edge of the stage. 'I'll need a volunteer to help me saw my lovely assistant in half.' Hands go up, and he says, 'Let me see...'

The great thing about live performance, especially in a small theatre, is seeing the expressions on the audience's faces and feeling the enthusiasm of their responses. Atlantic City audiences are not shy about letting you know what they think. Despite having only three hundred and thirty-five red-velvet seats, the Widow is grand. Chandeliers drip diamond-lights from an intricately carved sky filled with Nordic gods. And it feels spacious because there are two walls of windows – four on each side, rising about twelve feet. When I perform in sunlight, I see seagulls, waves, a slash of boardwalk. It's like performing on the deck of a ship for an audience of birds and mermaids.

Usually, at night, Charlie shuts the curtains but tonight the mottled-orange blood moon shines through the black glass.

I've been too anxious about Van to really look at the audience, but maybe someone is watching for a reaction to her absence. The front row is occupied by Jinx and the veterans of Camp Boardwalk surrounded by their wheelchairs, walkers, and canes.

Behind them sit Midnight's high rollers, their tickets comped.

My girls are here too: a half-dozen rainbow-haired, inked teens I teach cardistry to at Dante Hall.

The rest of the audience is the usual motley Atlantic City crowd, old and young, spiked hair and shaved heads, pale Goths and middle-aged hipsters.

Midway up the back wall, behind the seats, is a carved square like an open window: the booth, where Gus, our lighting director, adjusts his oversized, red-framed glasses and grimaces, his version of a smile.

My gaze locks on a man in the third row, his eyes boring through me. The seat next to him is empty. No reason that should unsettle me. It's the look of him: hard, hungry eyes fixed on me, lips twisted in a thin smile as if he knows something the rest of us don't. Short dark hair, ruddy face – was he there during the whole show? How did I not notice?

Elvis Jones leaps down the aisle and bounds onstage. What the hell? Charlie and I exchange glances.

'Hey, Elvis!' A woman's voice. 'You can saw me in half anytime!'

'Take *me* to Hell, Jones!'

Over titters and scattered applause, Elvis Jones strides to my side.

'Jones,' mutters Charlie. 'What are you doing?'

Jones ignores him. 'Why are you playing Van's part?' he asks me. 'Where is she?'

What is wrong with this man? Magicians don't volunteer for

other magicians. Unless there's a reason he came up here. Maybe he knows something. Trembling, I reach for my throat. My neck prickles, the curve between throat and shoulder. Tiny bugs under the flesh demanding I scratch. My self-defence trainer calls it spider-sense and tells me, 'It's the only thing you can trust.' But I don't need a warning signal to tell me something is wrong. Van is not here, and I'm about to enter a sawing box where a woman's murdered body was found.

Under the spotlight, the sawing box resembles a mummy case for an Egyptian goddess. On the wooden lid, Cleo stands on a boat. Her face is in profile, but one silver-pale eye stares up with disturbing intimacy. Over her red-gold hair unfurls a sail with hieroglyph-like letters: *Cleo of the Nile.*

The colours are fresh and bright, as if they were painted yesterday. Eddie Garland's artistry, with touches by Cleo West. Undeniably beautiful. And deadly.

The smell of Cleo's lavender whirls around me, an ice-cold wind. Terror claws at my throat. The same unreasoning terror that grips me each time I climb into the box. No matter that I know its inner workings and that my father has patiently walked me through its history. My rational mind knows it's not a coffin, I'm not suffocating, it's a trick.

But this box has already seen death. A dead woman was inside it.

Cleo's eye – that single silver painted Egyptian eye – stares full-on at me. She *sees* me. Through time. Impossible. But fire blazes through the eye. At me. She's furious at me. The torch slips from my hand.

Someone catches it the split-second before it hits the floor.

Elvis Jones. Peering in my face with dead-cold eyes. 'What's wrong? You high?'

'No,' I choke out.

He seizes my hand. Squeezes till it hurts. I jolt.

'Breathe with me. Deep and slow...'

I breathe. It helps. A little. My tongue is so gritty I can't lick my lips. My eyes so dry I can't blink. I must fight this. I lift my head.

Stormie watches from the wings. Her lips move: *You can do this, you can do this.*

'Miss Cleo, get over here. It's time to teach you a lesson!' Charlie recites Morelli's patter.

I missed my cue.

'Not the box, Morelli,' I whisper.

He gives me a reassuring smile, then turns to the audience. 'She refuses to listen!'

'If that ain't a woman!' yells a veteran.

Jones releases my hand.

Step by step, I cross the tormented sea of the stage.

Charlie and Jones lift the lid of the sawing box. Charlie recites the patter, but both men eye me suspiciously.

'I don't...' The words trap in my throat. The entire stage burns with rage. *Blood-red female rage.* Don't Charlie and Jones feel it? Cleo does not want me to enter the sawing box where her body was found.

The two men stand behind me, blocking me. Too late. I missed my chance. Weaving side to side, I grip the edge of the box and look inside.

This can't be real. My panic is making me see things.

I close my eyes.

And look inside again.

6

A man's voice carries traces of wind and salt, like waves rocking. I lean into the voice as if I'm on a boat deep in the ocean. He's calling my name.

Slowly I open my heavy eyes.

I'm sprawled on the stage. Elvis Jones supports my head. 'You fainted.'

I open my mouth to tell him that I never faint, but a cough cracks in my throat. He wraps his arm around me, helps me sit up and tilts a small water bottle at my mouth. I swallow. Another gulp of water.

We're onstage, the velvet curtains closed, shutting us in with the sawing box. The lid is still open. And I see her again.

A glimpse of blazing orange. A woman's body, naked and crumpled. The expressive face that always mirrors her emotions is paper-white, swollen. Van! My girl Van.

A slit of light shone through her eyes as if she saw me trembling over her. Between her lips, a black flutter, moth-like. Petals of a black rose.

I'll never unsee her.

Nausea twists my stomach.

'That wig looks tight.' Elvis Jones's voice comes from far away. 'I'm going to take it off, okay?'

His hands tug on the wig and pull it off. I sigh in relief. The wig constricted my breath as well as my head. I manage a soft 'thank you'.

His eyes probe me. 'How did you know Van was in the sawing box?'

'How did I...' I blink. 'What?'

'How did you know?' Black coffee eyes. Bitter cold.

'Are you out of your mind?'

'Am I? You didn't want to look inside. You knew what you'd find.'

I squirm out of his hold. Fighting dizziness, I stumble to my feet. I need to get away from him. He rises too, extending his arm to catch me or prevent me from running away. Every inch of my body trembles, even my teeth clack against each other. 'Who. Are. You?'

'You know who I am,' Elvis says. 'Who are *you*, Lucy Moon?'

Only the most terrifying question in the world. I feel his suspicious gaze following me to the edge of the stage.

*

Hours have passed since I discovered Van in the sawing box, but I'm still mind-fogged and unsteady. The detective in charge, Daisy Torres, organised a task force almost as soon as she set foot on the scene. The Widow swarmed with cops who cordoned off the theatre, took statements and IDs from audience members, photographed and videotaped, and examined the entire theatre including backstage. Behind the curtains onstage, the forensic team – a medical examiner, photographer, and technicians in white – examined and recorded evidence while Van lay on a sheet of tarpaulin.

Watching Detective Torres, I'm impressed by how cool and efficient she is. About forty, tough and compact, with flashing eyes and a ponytail scraped back so tightly it gives *me* a migraine. I met her a couple years ago when I accompanied Da to a cold reading workshop he conducted for police and investigators, instructing them on how to obtain information about a person by analysing verbal and nonverbal cues: the way they speak, gesture, move, and dress. In magic we use it to 'read minds,' but investigators can use the techniques to discern lies from truth.

While Da and the cops watched, I played the suspect that Daisy Torres questioned. Afterwards she and I talked a little. I asked her what it was like being a female cop.

'Add Puerto Rican and a mother, and maybe you get the picture,' she said.

'I'm not Puerto Rican or a mother,' I admitted, 'but I'm a woman in a man's field too.'

After the workshop, over coffee, she showed me a photo of her eight-year-old son. Her ponytail wasn't so tight then. And we're no longer playing pretend. Now, it's the real thing.

She and her partner, Detective Wax, set up a command post in the casino manager's office on the fourteenth floor to interview witnesses. When it's my turn to be questioned, I face them across the large desk. Behind them hangs an enormous painting of Midnight looming over the boardwalk like Dracula's Castle. Before we start, I ask Detective Torres if she remembers me.

'Of course. You're Lucy, Declan Moon's daughter. The cold reading demo two years ago.' She studies me while Detective Wax sets up a tape recorder on the desk. 'I know you had a difficult night,' she says. 'Discovering your friend and magic partner. It will be hard to talk about her, but anything you can tell us will help us find the person who did this. Do you understand?'

'Yes.'

Torres's partner, Detective Wax, is a weary middle-aged man with Resting Cop Face – hooded eyes that only let in bits of light and pursed thin lips as if he tastes something sour. But when he speaks, his voice is quiet, flat. No judgment.

'Walk us through tonight,' he says.

Two cops watching me, tape recorder between us, and my girl Van is gone. Tonight is a living nightmare.

'Go ahead,' says Torres. 'Tell us everything you remember.

Don't worry if it seems unimportant. Just talk.'

It comes out in a jumble of memories, impressions, and dread. Stormie and me phoning and texting Van between each effect, Elvis Jones's backstage visit, the man in the third row's hard gaze and secret smile, Cleo's red rage as I approached the sawing box...

'Cleo,' says Torres. 'You're talking about the magician? Didn't she die in World War Two?'

Her interruption returns me back to the casino manager's office, the cops facing me, the tape recorder whirling on. 'Yes. But. She haunts the Widow.'

Their expressions are carefully blank.

I add, 'Not everyone senses her presence.'

Wax clears his throat. 'So Cleo is a ghost?' When I nod, he says, 'And you're saying the ghost was mad?'

It sounds ridiculous in his flat voice. 'I think she was mad because I was pretending to be her, wearing her wig and dress, and about to enter the sawing box where her body was found.'

A moment of silence.

Torres nods. 'Okay, Cleo the ghost was mad at you. What happened next?'

'I looked inside the box.' A wave of horror sweeps over me. 'I saw–' My voice breaks. 'I saw Van.'

My hand goes to my neck. The panic I can't explain. As if I sensed that one day, I'd open the sawing box and find a dead woman inside. My nightmares warned me. I hear my father: *Don't let a wooden cabinet get the best of you. You're stronger than that.*

I'm not stronger, Da. I'm scared, and I was right to be scared. But I thought the woman inside was going to be me.

Torres stares pointedly at my neck. I'm clutching my throat as if my head will fall off. My tell. I lower my hand and tuck it under my butt. 'She... was naked. My... the orange scarf I gave her for her thirtieth birthday was... around her neck.'

They're watching me, not unkindly. I won't mention the rose unless they do. Maybe the shock made me imagine it.

'What else did you see?'

'That's all I remember. I think I screamed. And fainted.' I add, 'First time in my life.'

After a moment Detective Wax asks, 'What's your relationship to Vanessa Kim?'

I draw in my breath. Oh, God, I *love* that girl. We met three years ago at FISM – the International Federation of Magic Societies. We competed in the Close-Up Magic category, and we both lost, but that night we got drunk together and formed a mutual admiration society: she loved my take on the old TV show *Bewitched,* a witch mixing up her spells – more like ditzy Aunt Clara than clever Samantha. I adored Van's hilarious, foul-mouthed routine that featured magic about her 'girl parts,' while judges and audiences watched in horrified silence.

They're waiting. I let out my breath. 'She's my friend. It's because of me that she's here. I invited her to do the show with Stormie and me.'

'Where did she live?'

'Las Vegas.'

'Alone?'

'Yes.'

'Does she have family?'

'She's second-generation Korean American. Her dad died when she was a kid. She was raised in San Jose by her mom, and then by her older sister, who wanted her to study law. She did, for a while. Then she met up with magicians and did sideshow stunts – walking on nails, swallowing needles and fire, and hurling knives. She loved it. When her sister died two years ago, she was totally on her own.'

'No family members to contact?'

I shake my head. 'She created her own family – me, Stormie, and whatever boyfriend she had at the time.'

Torres and Wax exchange looks.

'So she had many boyfriends?'

Wax's tone makes me wince. How to describe Van? 'When she enters a room, the lights go on. I mean, she's the light. She attracts people – men, women, everyone.'

'Lucy.' Torres leans across the desk, and I notice a scar that curves from the edge of her mouth to her ear, a slightly raised half-moon. A scar that wasn't there two years ago. My eyes burn again. We're all so vulnerable. No matter how strong we think we are.

'Who was she seeing?'

'There was a casino manager at the Borgata, but that ended fast.' My mouth is sand-dry. I grab the bottle of water from my magic bag and drink. 'Then the mystery guy. She didn't tell us his name. Stormie and I called him MLD, short for Mystery Loner Dude.'

Torres scowls, emphasising the scar. 'What do you know about him?'

'Nothing! The three of us – Stormie, me, and Van – were supposed to have dinner last night but he messaged her, and she went to meet him. She promised to bring him to the Widow tomorrow – I mean today – to meet us.'

'Why do you think she kept the new boyfriend secret?'

'Maybe he's involved in something rough or illegal. Or he's married. Or we know him, and she didn't want to admit she was seeing him.'

Wax grunts. 'Maybe he's a stranger she hooked up with at the Speakeasy.'

Startled, I jerk back. Someone must have told them that Van loved to hang out at the retro bar on the boardwalk.

'Is that something she would do?'

'Well, yes, but–'

'She lived high-risk.' He strokes his huge chin.

'Van takes chances, but she's not stupid. Far from it. She sees through people. She has the best bullshit detector of anyone I know.'

'Was she having any problems?' Torres's voice is gentle, and I realise I spoke about Van in the present tense. I blink back tears.

'Not that I know.'

'Did she complain about anyone or anything?'

'No. This was the happiest I ever saw her.' My throat tightens, the sand-grit choking me. 'She loved Atlantic City. She, Stormie, and I were going to move in together. And she was in love. At least she believed she was.'

Wax's pouched eyes and Torres's dark eyes lock on me.

'Did she recently express fears about anyone in particular?' asks Wax.

'No.'

'Did you get the feeling she might have been in danger?'

'No.'

When they finish with me, I get to my feet and sling my magic bag over my shoulder.

'You're not leaving town, are you?' asks Torres. When I shake my head, she says, 'Good. We may need to ask you more questions about Van.'

Wax walks me to the door. With all his size and bulk, he's gentle, a comforting presence. 'Will you be okay?' he asks.

I nod.

'Do you need a ride home?'

I shake my head.

'If you remember anything else, let us know.'

7

I stumble out of the office, stagger down the hall past a couple of officers and wait for the elevator. As soon as the doors open, my stomach tightens. It's a box. A suffocating box with doors that close on you. I'll go down the stairs instead. Stormie is waiting in her room on the sixth floor, but I take a deep shuddering breath and grip the staircase railing.

Alone for the first time since I found Van.

The theatre must be crammed with cops, the police tape marking it as a crime scene. But even in my fuzzy state, I know he didn't kill Van there. He carried her into the Widow. How did he get her inside the theatre without anyone noticing? He could have placed her body in a large bag or container and wheeled her as if he were carrying theatrical props or cleaning supplies.

I go down another flight of stairs to the twelfth floor. No cops here. Not yet. Charlie will tell them about the back entrance to the theatre. I try the door. Locked. Back in the day, performers used it as an extra dressing room. These days it's used for storage. Stagehands carry props and equipment up.

Earlier tonight this door was unlocked, and I climbed the stairs to the thirteenth floor and entered the Widow from backstage. I always prefer entering a place from the back. When you enter a theatre from the front, you see the stage, the beautiful auditorium – you see the mask. But when you enter backstage, you see the true face of the building. The soul, the secrets, the spirits of the place. The place where the *real* magic happens. That's how you get the full picture: face and mask.

Very few people know about this room, and the hidden route to the theatre. I bet the killer knows. But even if he knows, he needs the keys. Charlie and Gus have keys because they work in various venues throughout Midnight. Elvis Jones works in Hell, Midnight's black box theatre. Performers don't usually get keys. I was the one who showed this room and the back staircase to Van. Maybe she showed it to Elvis Jones. That's how he got backstage without anyone stopping him.

Oh, Van. I lean against the locked door, wishing I could find the key to unlock her secret.

I climb one flight of stairs to the thirteenth floor. One summer an old-timer took me under his wing and showed me through the Old Tower – the historic heart of Midnight. That's when I first learned the building had been known as Chalfont-Haddon Hall, and later, during World War Two, as Thomas England General Hospital, a military hospital for wounded soldiers.

One of the many reasons I love Midnight is that instead of destroying the Old Tower, they built around it, keeping traces of history alive. Like a haunted theatre on the thirteenth floor and a lighting booth on the 13½ floor. I often wonder what Gus hides up there. As I approach, I see Gus the lighting director standing in front of the door marked 13½ with Charlie and his girlfriend, Misty.

A cop guarding the wooden doors to the Widow watches them. I take a moment to catch my breath. The night's events are a nightmare you wake from only to realise the terror is real.

Charlie glances up. His dark blonde hair is spiked with sweat, glasses crooked. 'Lucy. I was about to call you. How are you?'

'Hanging in. You?'

Before he answers, Misty hugs me. Soft and curvy, she smells of vanilla and innocence. With her rosy cheeks, summer-sky eyes, and breathless voice, she seems like a girl on the verge of leaping into womanhood. Makes no sense, I know. Instead of dancing for leering men, she should be starring in Hallmark Christmas movies.

'You and Van were so close. Ah Lucy, I'm so sorry.'

'Thanks, Misty.'

Gus lowers his large, red-framed glasses and squints at me. The greenish tinge of his face gives him a vampirish glow. He imagines himself the hero of every tale, but I picture him lurking in shadows, creeping through the underworld. He even looks like he dressed in the dark. His shirts are often buttoned wrong, and his trousers hang on his narrow hips. Tonight his long greyish-blond hair hangs in a fraying rope over one shoulder. His only redeeming quality is Diablo, the small black terrier dog in his arms.

Diablo is the surprise star of my Making Mr. Right illusion, in which I create my own Prince Charming out of bits and pieces, call on witches and mages to give me a lover who's kind and courageous, stir a foaming pot, and up bursts Diablo.

Gus leans one skinny hip against the door that leads to his lighting booth. 'Exciting, isn't it?'

I recoil, and Misty gasps.

He lowers his large, red-framed glasses and licks his lips. 'Ooh, did I say that out loud?' A sly smile creeps up his cheek. 'Don't whitewash Van just 'cause she's dead. Girl went out on the edge. That's what made her who she was.'

Charlie groans. 'Gus.'

He shrugs. 'Go ahead, Charlie, tell Lucy what you did.'

'It was a bit of a fight.'

'A bit?' Gus snorts. 'Becker just did the impossible.'

A faint flush rises up Charlie's cheeks. 'You know the drill: no one ever dies in a casino. So the management wants us to carry on as usual with tomorrow night's show, but I said...'

My jaw drops. 'You didn't!' As the production manager overseeing the shows in Midnight's five venues, Charlie enjoys a degree of power in the casino hierarchy, but even my father would have a hard time convincing the management to cancel a show.

Charlie's lips curve in a smile. 'They just needed to be convinced.'

'Oh, Charlie, thank you.'

'Before Friday night's show we'll hold a memorial for Van. Maybe you can do the ceremony when a magician dies?'

'The Broken Wand. I've never seen a woman do it.'

'Then it's about time,' he says. 'Sunset on the beach on Friday. Spread the word, all of you.'

'Okay,' says Misty. 'I need to go. Still a show to do tonight.'

She's looking at Charlie. 'Dinner tomorrow night?' At his nod, she murmurs, 'This time don't be late, babe.'

We watch her wiggle away in a vanilla cloud.

Gus clears his throat. 'I wouldn't keep that chick waiting.'

'Not my fault. Dead Men Rising and their demands.'

A heavy metal band, they are set to appear in Midnight's largest auditorium, the Crypt, this weekend.

Gus smirks. 'I heard about them.'

'Their manager is a pain in the ass.'

'Listen, guys, did either of you notice a guy in the third row? Short dark hair, black leather.'

Charlie shakes his head.

'No,' says Gus. 'But I noticed how Jones jumped onstage.'

'That was strange,' says Charlie.

'More than strange,' I say. 'There must be a reason he did that. Maybe he knows something about Van.'

Charlie rubs his forehead. 'You know, I saw him last night–'

'Becker!' The cop guarding the Widow points to Charlie. 'They want to see you in there.'

At my questioning look, Charlie says, 'They want to know about the layout, entrance and exit routes, backstage. Go home and get some rest. I'll see you at the memorial. Spread the word, guys.'

After the theatre doors shut behind Charlie, Gus and I linger.

'Guess who I saw with Van last night.'

My heart stutters. 'Elvis Jones?'

He gestures to the theatre's wooden doors, shut again. 'Our man, Charlie. They were arguing.'

'About what?'

'Dead Men Rising. Sex. Who knows? But she wasn't happy.' He lowers his glasses. 'Don't get mad at me for telling the truth. Van was at the Speakeasy almost every night, and she went there to get laid. I'm not gonna turn her into a victim because she's dead.' When I look at him with distaste, he shrugs. 'You stray, you pay. That's how it works.'

My ex, Amazing André, often complained that my pale eyes spooked him. I move closer, stare at Gus full force. 'So you saw her there last night?'

'Yeah.' He smiles. 'I was with my girlfriend. But don't let that stop you. I got more than enough to go around.'

He walks toward the elevator, his ponytail hanging down his back like a dead squirrel, Diablo trotting at his heels.

8

The ghosts of Midnight wander from the Old Tower's basement to the thirteenth floor, often stopping to spook hotel guests on the sixth floor. Frequent complaints about lights flickering on and off, sudden icy temperatures, and TVs blaring in the middle of the night led the management to install most performers (except superstars) on the sixth floor. Tomorrow night I'd planned to move into 607, next to Stormie. But I don't know what will happen. They may cancel our show. I can't imagine going back on stage. And tonight, I need to go back home to my room at home. I texted Da and Auntie Maze to tell them about Van, and they're waiting for me.

I knock on Stormie's door. The instant I enter, she opens her arms, and I walk in. We hug for a long time, leaning against each other the way we have since we were twelve. I've watched her light Yahrzeit candles for her dad who died in a car crash when she was thirteen and Shabbat candles with her mum and Nana. We used to play dress-up in Red Light Vintage, their clothing shop at the edge of Tanger Outlets. My Da and Auntie Maze taught us magic. Her favourite quote is by Ray Charles: 'If someone besides a Black ever sings the real gut bucket blues, it'll be a Jew.'

When we pull apart, we're both teary. I always tell her she has autumn eyes, rich brown flecked with gold, but tonight they make me think of winter – haunted and ringed with red. She took off her makeup, clipped her long coils of hair into a large bun and changed into her favourite pink sweats.

'You know what that detective Wax told me?' she says. '"Your friend took a walk on the wild side." The cops think this was a hookup gone wrong.'

I rub my eyes. 'Gus said Van picked up guys at the Speakeasy.

Maybe one of them got mad at her and attacked.'

She punches my arm.

'Ouch! What was that for?'

'Two words. Black rose.'

'It's not about me.'

She raises her eyes to the ceiling, imploring the noir gods of Midnight. 'You never think it's about you.'

'Because it never is.'

'Did you tell them about your mother?'

'She has nothing to do with Van.'

With a theatrical sigh, she tugs me to the edge of her bed and reaches for the bottle of Espolòn Tequila Blanco on the bedside table. She tilts her head back and drinks, then passes it to me. 'I know it's not Irish whiskey, but tequila does the job.'

I drink and immediately the earthy, slightly sweet vanilla and pineapple taste brings me back to the six months I spent last year touring in a Mexican circus with Van.

'One more hit,' she says. 'For Van. You rest in peace, sweetheart. We're going to find him, don't you worry.' She drank again.

My turn. 'For Van. If you can hear us, give us a clue. We love you.'

I pass it back to her. 'Tell me what happened after I looked in the box.'

'When you screamed, I thought someone was hiding inside with a knife. And when you fell, I ran. Jones got to you first.'

I press my palm to my chest. I *hear* the pounding. 'Where was Charlie?'

'He pulled the curtains shut. Called the cops. Calmed the audience. Did his Charlie shtick.'

Her fingers stroke the Star of David necklace her Nana gave her. Stormie's sign that she's stressed and worried. Her fingernails are painted with the same intricate Ace of Hearts manicure she gave Van and me. My breath hitches again. 'Remember when you did our manicures?'

Her full lips twist. 'He cut her nails.' At my blank look, she says, 'I noticed. She must have struggled. Fought him. Maybe she had blood under her nails... Okay... We can keep crying or we can try to find out what happened to her. It's gotta be us. No one else cares enough. It's time to bring back the Moon and Weather Detective Agency.'

'Ah, jeez, we were fifteen!' The two of us riding our bikes through town, searching for mysteries and following suspicious characters – including Tal, my secretive Krav Maga trainer. The fact that we both crushed on him made it more embarrassing when he caught us snooping.

She pulls me to my feet. 'Girl, time to call on your Moon connections. We need to search Van's room before the cops take everything away.'

'Maybe they already did.'

'Even if they did, they don't know where to look. They don't know our girl the way we do. How the hell can we get into her room?'

I clear my throat. 'I think I can manage that.'

'Ah. See why it pays to be Lucy Moon? People bend over backwards for you.'

'Not for me. For my dad.'

But her excitement is contagious. Anything to keep from sitting here crying and looking into the void. I call the old-timer who used to take me around the historic parts of the Old Tower. Fifteen minutes later Stormie and I enter Room 642.

9

I choke back a cry. Van's dresses, sweaters, and scarves are strewn on the queen bed – swaths of cloth, crumples of colour. The scent of her sharp, tangy black-pepper perfume permeates the room. One of her silver high heels is tipped over on the carpet, waiting for her to slide it on. Her presence is so strong – Storm and I lean against each other for a minute to take it in.

She sighs. 'I can't believe she's really gone.'

'Me neither.'

'Look at this stuff. What are we going to do with it?'

'She has no family.'

'There must be someone we can call.'

I swallow. 'We'll give the clothing to one of the shelters and store the knives and magic props at the Widow.'

Stormie opens the closet and kneels to poke inside.

I search the dresser. As I examine Van's jewellery box – all costume pieces – a thought strikes me. 'Storm. There was a hungry-eyed guy in the third row. Did you see him?'

She glances over her shoulder. 'No. Why?'

'Something about him creeped me out.'

'You think he might be MLD?'

'He's older, not really her type. And yet...' The ruddy face and thin lips, the compact muscular body, feet on the ground. Van and I are both drawn to people who appeared to be rooted, the kind you can lean on. Like Stormie. But we can get fooled, like me with Amazing André. 'He looks solid.'

She sits back on her heels. 'If it was him, he wasn't really looking for Van. He already knew she was dead.'

'Whoever did this must have known I'd take her place in the finale. And the moment of biggest impact would be the reveal when I was about to enter the box. Who knew tonight's program?'

'Everyone working on the show.' She sighs. 'Charlie and Gus, of course. The stagehands, sound guy...'

'Whoever killed Van needed access to the Widow. Not just to-night. Last night.' A sick feeling spread through me. 'Charlie and Gus have keys to the Widow.'

'Didn't Gus make a pass at Van?' she asks, her voice muffled from the closet.

'And you. And me.' I open the top dresser drawer. Van's under-wear. Tiny wisps of lace. A silk nightgown. I squeeze my eyes to keep from crying. She bought these for someone. The secret guy. Was it the man with the hungry eyes? Did she bring him to this room?

Stormie emerges from the closet, arms full of clothing. 'Gus told me he has a new girlfriend.'

'Made of rubber.'

She snorts. 'What do you think he hides in that lighting booth?'

'Weird porn.'

The first time Stormie met Gus, she told me, 'That man defines the ick factor.' She'd heard rumours about him being rough with women. His green-pale face is on every dating site from Tinder to the sleaziest, and according to Stormie – who hears everything at the beauty salon – he often changes his profile information.

'I just remembered something Van said.'

Stormie throws the clothes on the bed. 'Go on.'

'She said Gus was showing her the real Atlantic City.'

Stormie snorts. 'I wonder what else he was showing her.'

'She also said he's a great dancer.'

'He's such a weird guy. You just know he's hiding something.'

I search the second and third drawers. I unfold and shake out tank tops, sweaters, leggings. I bring them to the bed while

Stormie carries more clothing from the closet. I examine each piece carefully, then fold and place it in Van's silver suitcase on the bed.

'What do you know about Elvis Jones?' Saying his name aloud conjures up his bitter-eyed presence.

'He came into the Widow while we were rehearsing and gave us tickets to his show.' Stormie pokes her head out from the closet. 'Van and I went.'

'Where was I?'

'New York.'

The night I'd attended my friend Allie Katt's opening and stayed in her apartment. 'How was his show?'

She hesitates. 'Not what you'd expect.'

'Why so mysterious? What does he do?'

'See for yourself.' She sticks out her jaw, meaning she won't tell me anything else.

'What happened after his show?'

'I left. Van lingered.'

'Lingered as in...?'

'As in Jones is man-sexy and Van liked him. A lot.' She shakes her head. 'His show is in Hell, in the basement. He doesn't have the keys to the Widow.'

'He could have climbed the stairs from the twelfth floor. The back entrance.'

'That door is locked, isn't it?'

'Not always. Not when we leave it open to carry up props. During a show there's a good chance the door will be unlocked.'

'Not everyone knows that,' she protests. 'Only someone who knows the Widow the way you do. And Charlie, Gus, and the crew.'

'Clearly Jones knows it too. He works at Midnight. Why did he come into the Widow while you were rehearsing?'

'There's something uncanny about him,' Stormie says slowly,

as if words are being dragged out of her. 'Like your Auntie Maze. He goes over the edge. Way over the edge.'

She returns to the closet and fills her arms with Van's shoes. Size four. Mostly spike heels. Van adored heels, the higher the better. Stormie drops the shoes on the bed. 'I don't think we know the killer. He's the secret boyfriend, the shady guy.'

We search the entire room, even under the bed. Even the tiny fridge that contains snacks and mini-bottles of booze. No laptop. No purse or phone. No address book, no paper trail. Not even a scrap on which she scribbled a helpful name and number.

Stormie holds out her hands. 'Her killer took every clue. Phone, computer... God, I hope he left his DNA on her.'

'I guess we'll find out after the autopsy. Let's search the bathroom.'

The counter next to the sink holds Van's make-up and creams. I spray her pepper perfume on my wrist and sniff, feeling her presence. *Help us, Van. Help us find your murderer.*

Stormie's face appears in the mirror behind me. Her eyes are huge, her freckles stark. Everything about losing Van is terrible, but at least Stormie and I are going through it together.

Two overflowing cosmetic pouches sit on the counter. Van loved girly-girly stuff – makeup, dresses, heels. I empty the pouches on the counter. Stormie watches me examine a box of loose powder, half a dozen brushes, two sets of false eyelashes, mascaras, eyebrow pencils, liners, lipsticks, tubes of foundation and blush, and...

I slowly lift a tiny cardboard box. The kind I've seen in Da's study. He collects vintage matchboxes from India, Japan, Spain, England, wherever Moon Magick tours take us. The covers are decorated with exotic dancers, political figures, mystical symbols, and legendary nightclubs. The box I hold shows a red lollipop against a black background. Blood-red letters advertise: *The Lollipop Club, Atlantic City.*

10

'I know only one Lollipop,' I say.

'The one on Black Horse Pike. What the hell would Van be doing in a strip club?'

'A side hustle as a stripper?' Even saying it sounds crazy.

'Meeting her secret guy there?'

Stormie and I stare at our reflections in the mirror. I imagine Van between us the way we posed for our REBEL MAGIC poster. Rebels was Van's idea. Magician was already carved in stone, its symbol a man in a top hat pulling a rabbit out of a hat. She wanted us to create a new kind of magic.

'We need to hurry before the cops decide to search this room.'

'Wait!' cries Stormie. 'Do you think she posted anything online?'

Back in Stormie's bedroom I grab my phone and follow her to the window. An actual window, the kind that opens and closes, not hermetically sealed to keep out the world. One of the many reasons I love the Old Tower. The view is Midnight's outdoor parking lot, and beyond that, a slash of boardwalk, sky, beach.

Stormie watches over my shoulder while I check Van's Instagram photos on my phone. Van posted images of nature and darkly comic situations with half her face at one end of the shot, often obscured with a hat. She considered herself an observer of life's absurdities. For the first time I notice how rarely she posted selfies in which you see her whole face. And not a single picture of a guy since she arrived in Atlantic City. She'd been uncharacteristically quiet for the past few weeks. A few photos of the boardwalk, a shot of our poster.

We stare at it until with a cry Stormie grabs my phone and moves to the next photo. Ruby, the boardwalk singer, crooning from her wheelchair near the Speakeasy.

My heart jolts at the last photo she posted. A view from the top of the Absecon Lighthouse.

I stare out the window at the parking lot, but I see Van and me yesterday morning. After we climbed the 228 steps of the lighthouse, we caught our breath and joked with Buddy, the ninety-something caretaker, a local legend who climbs those steps every day. We walked around and looked out through the railings at the breathtaking views of the Atlantic City skyline, the ocean, and the South Jersey shore. Late October winds blew in from the south, and I breathed in the fresh salt air.

Van asked me about the Pine Barrens. 'Is it as wild as they say?'

'Some parts are haunted, but there are normal towns and businesses.' I told her it's vast, at least a million acres of Pinelands.

She took photos of the view with her phone. 'But if you look hard, I bet you can see the ghost towns, the swamps and cabins.'

'Why? Do you want to go there?'

'Just curious. It's like another world, but it's right here. A world under this one.'

With a laugh she pressed back against the railings and took a selfie of us. A picture I never saw. She didn't post it. But I can imagine our faces tilted to the sky. And me sniffing her, as usual. It's more than fearlessness – it's the dark of an autumn night when you're eighteen and going out with your friends and all dressed up and giggling because you're young and anything can happen and the sky is starry and moony and crackling with freedom and hope, and even though you can't see what lies ahead you plunge through because this is your time, your moment, your *now*, and you're going to seize it. That's my girl Van's dark. It whistles with excitement like her knives. It promises more.

Even when there's nothing more.

I turn to Stormie. 'Van asked me about the Pine Barrens yesterday.'

She draws in her breath. 'The Lollipop Club is on the outskirts of the Barrens. Do you think there's a connection?'

'We'll find out.'

'That's a promise,' says Stormie. 'And we'll find him.'

11

Back home, I get out of my car. The Moon house is a three-story pink framed house. The third-floor window blinds are shut. The silver moon sculpture in the front yard gleams. Auntie Maze's candles and large rock crystals diffuse pink-orange light over the living room windowsill where she painted turnips like jack-o-lanterns. 'We didn't have pumpkins in Ireland,' she explains. 'And this reminds me of home.'

Home. Who we are, who we love. The mistakes we make. The secrets we keep. The person who walks out the door, and the ones we leave behind.

I need to gather my strength before facing my father and aunt. I sit on the porch and picture Van. Not how I last saw her, but yesterday evening, with Stormie and me on the boardwalk in front of Midnight. We'd finished our final dress rehearsal and planned to go to DiBruni's for pizza followed by a drink at the Speakeasy.

Van looked up from checking her phone. She was dressed like Halloween – orange-tipped spikes in her hair, the long orange scarf I gave her looped around her neck, tiny leather skirt, and black tights. 'Sorry, you guys. I can't do dinner.'

'MLD again?' asked Stormie.

I nudged Van. 'Come on, this is our last night before opening.'

She tapped a quick text message, then looked up. 'This isn't about me choosing a guy over my friends. It's just... this guy blows my heart wide open.'

We stared at her.

Van, who never blushes, turned fiery red. 'Hey, I've kissed my share of frogs.'

'Who hasn't?' Stormie asked. 'Exhibit A: Peter Browne.' The obscenely wealthy white man-sized toddler who wanted Stormie to mother him. She continued, 'Exhibit B: Amazing Asshole.'

Amazing Asshole is what they call Amazing André, a frog by any standard. 'Bring your guy to dinner,' I told Van. 'We won't bite.'

'I know, but tonight is a game-changer.' Van grinned, her wide reckless smile. 'I'm going to surprise him.'

'How?' asks Stormie.

'I'll let you know. If it works out, I'll bring him for dinner tomorrow. C'mere, my loves.'

She held up her phone and took a selfie of us. She's a foot shorter than Stormie and half a foot shorter than me, and though she held the phone high I'm certain she cut off the top of our heads. The point of focus is her smile, so infectious it's hard to look without smiling back.

Stormie and I took a few steps, but I looked back over my shoulder.

Van stood alone, motionless, as if the boardwalk was filled with hidden landmines. One step and she'd sink between the rafters. For a moment she looked like a figure outlined in black in a stained-glass window. A shiver jagged through me.

I stared until I saw something I'd never seen in her.

Fear.

'What's going on?' asked Stormie.

'One minute.'

I hurried toward Van. I'd insist she tell me more about this guy and where she was going with him.

A drunk stumbled out of Midnight's gargoyle-encrusted doors, setting off dogs howling through a loudspeaker and blocking her from view. When he shuffled away, Van was gone. A vanishing act. Just like magic. Except that magic promises you'll see her again.

12

The comforting smell of steak and Guinness pie welcomes me inside. My father and aunt sit in front of the TV in the living room, their backs to me, greying-auburn heads leaning toward each other over their armchairs. Between them a small round table holds a bottle of Jameson and two shot glasses. I called a few hours ago to tell them about Van. I shouldn't be surprised they waited up for me but the sight of them kicks me in the chest. Da's green-black velvet cape and Auntie Maze's layers of pale green silk and gauze, the two of them windblown as if they just stepped off the Irish moors, dressed for action in case I need them.

A rare chance to watch these two hyper-aware dynamos without their knowledge. Memories and artifacts of their lives surround them. A long-ago black-and-white photo of their mother, Isobel – my Granny Moon – flying with angel wings around her husband, the dashing Artagan. Publicity shots of Moon Magick – the troupe from Ireland and the States performing on the stage of a cruise ship, in the White House, on the street of Philadelphia's Italian Market, on a Vegas stage, on the Atlantic City boardwalk. Photos of Da – receiving award after award, plaques, and honours. Auntie Maze framed and put them up. He never would. The classic shot of him holding out his hand to help his wife, the ethereal Teddie, out of the sawing box.

They don't hear me enter, but Aidell, Auntie Maze's black cat, approaches, sniffs me and stalks away. Named for an Irish queen, Aidell is as haughty as royalty. I wonder if she smells the presence of death.

'Too many dead girls...' A gruff voice.

With a start, I focus on the TV screen where a woman in Army camouflage crouches at the edge of a large dirt pit and rests her hand on a large grey and white Australian Shepherd.

The pink and black polka dot ribbon threaded through her grown-out pumpkin-orange mullet looks incongruous, particularly in such a grisly setting.

'At first, investigators believed this might have been a ceremonial place where bodies were decapitated, then interred, maybe for religious reasons. Details of the latest discovery, a female we're calling Jane Doe, have led to speculation she was murdered by a different hand, more recently than the others.'

Pam Woodson, a perky blonde newswoman from Atlantic City who has covered many Moon Magick events, leans toward her. 'Dr. Lose, what can you tell us about Jane Doe?'

The carrot-haired woman grunts with satisfaction. 'We're lucky with her. We have almost an entire skeleton. The skull, hipbones, and pelvis tell us she was a Caucasian female, five feet four inches tall, probably in her forties. There was trauma at the time of death. Probably homicide. We're investigating samples from the soil, fragments of clothing, and dental records.'

Pam says, 'Now I see why they call you a Bone Whisperer.'

'I'm a forensic anthropologist,' she says, brisk. 'I read bones. I listen to them. They tell a story.'

'Thank you, Dr. Lose.' Pam turns to a policeman. 'This is Lieutenant Martini of the New Jersey State Police. Do you have anything to add about this... death pit?'

Lieutenant Martini digs his thumb into his grizzled grey chin. 'We're working on this case, and we will get to the bottom of it. The Pines have been used as a dumping ground for bodies long enough. If you have information relating to this crime scene, please call the hotline. We ask for help from the Pine Barrens community as well as surrounding areas from Philadelphia to Atlantic City.'

A phone number flashes on the bottom of the screen.

My chest tightens. The Pine Barrens again. Is it a coincidence?

'We will find out who did this,' says Lieutenant Martini. 'We will find out who Jane Doe was and give her a name. Every human being deserves a name.' He moves closer to the camera, his pouched, weary eyes staring directly at me. 'We'll give her murderer a name too. We will find you. Yes, I'm talking to you. Don't think you can bury the past. Trust me: it will rise up and bite you.'

Every human being deserves a name.

'Lucy!'

Da comes toward me, his arms wide.

'Don't, Da. I must smell of death. I should shower.'

'You're the breath of life, a *cushla*.'

When Da calls me his wee heart in Irish, I wish I could stay a little girl safe in the circle of his arms.

Auntie Maze shuts off the TV and glides toward us. 'Your friend is still with you. Don't rush to wash her off.'

The three of us hug. When we release each other, Auntie Maze grips my arm, her seeing eyes clouded like sea mist. 'I heard her callin' to you again. I do believe it's your mother. Be careful, child.'

She releases my arm and looks at Da.

'Come with Maze and me tomorrow,' he says. 'I'll get you a ticket.'

They're flying to Las Vegas so Da can receive the International Brotherhood of Magic's Lifetime Achievement Award, which has been presented a mere six times in the society's hundred-year history.

'The police want me to stay in town.'

'Then I won't go!' Da tugs his short, burnished beard, his sign of anxiety. 'I don't want to leave you here alone.'

'For the love of God, this ceremony is for you. You have to go! Look, I'll move to Midnight, near Stormie.'

'Midnight!' cries Da. 'The killer has a connection to Midnight. You discovered Van on the Widow stage. With a black rose. People have limited access to the theatre.'

I shouldn't have told them.

Auntie Maze sighs. 'I don't like the idea of you at Midnight or alone in the house. Won't you please come with us?'

'I can't! Charlie cancelled tomorrow night's show, but we go back on Friday night. And we're holding a memorial for Van. Charlie asked me to do the Broken Wand. And the police told me not to leave town. They want to ask me more questions about Van. And I... I can't keep hiding all my life!'

'I'll ask Tal to stay here with you.'

Tal, my self-defence trainer and sometimes bodyguard. 'Da! I'm not a child, and he doesn't work for you anymore.'

'A killer is on the loose.'

Auntie Maze adds, 'A killer with a black rose.'

Da glares at me. 'He may be back, and that means you're in danger.'

13

I trudge upstairs and shut the door to my room. Drop my magic bag to the floor. Cosmetics strewn on the dresser, clothes draped over the bed, posters of Ionia the Enchantress and Adelaide Herrmann on the wall. Books, decks of cards, a shivering pyramid of white, yellow, and pink roses – origami, crepe paper, polyester. When I'm stressed, I either riff with cards or make roses. This room is my tiny refuge, my place of dreams, my own box that has kept me safe all these years. The blinds closed, as always. Another precaution that has become second nature.

I strip in the dark and pull on a large T-shirt. Then I kneel at the closet, reach for a small wooden chest on the floor in back, buried under a mound of clothes. I push it towards me.

Touch it.

Jerk my hand back as if I've been burned.

I reach for it again.

No. I can't do this. I shove the box back and bury it under clothes again.

I pace the room, gripping the walls, a wild animal trapped. But there's nowhere to go. I press my face and body against the blinds.

I turn and sink to the floor, my back to the window. So many things I didn't tell Torres and Wax. Not just about the black rose and me, but about Van. The way she squints one eye shut when she laughs. The smell of her sharp pepper perfume and fearlessness. The way her eyes glow like two flares when she hurls knives. The only time I saw her cry: when she found out her sister died. *That's it,* she told me. *No one left in my tribe but me.*

A storm begins in the soles of my feet and gathers force as it rages through me and bursts up my throat and through my parted lips: a cry so wild and lost it terrifies me. I let out the only word that makes any sense: 'Mama!'

Hours pass, minutes.

I stretch out on the floor, arms and legs star-like, and open my eyes. It's dark but faint glimmers of light shine through the blinds. Between night and dawn. Between darkness and light. This is the point of intersection – between ghosts and the living. For the first time I come close to understanding Samhain and our need to rip the veils separating us from the dead.

*

Hours later, still awake, I stare at the ceiling.

I get up and tiptoe back down the steps, avoiding the creaking boards. I enter Da's study, what I call the Temple of Magic, and go directly to the glass cabinet that holds Da's magic wands. They're lined up inside like rifles. Feeling like Goldilocks in the House of the Three Bears, I examine the wands and discard one after another – too heavy, too long, too small – until I find one that is just right: sleek and black with a silver tip at each end. I hold it up, twirl it like a baton, throw it in the air and catch it. It's light yet balanced.

Tomorrow morning I'll study the template for the Broken Wand ceremony, recite it at the memorial, break the wand, and afterwards, finally cry for my kick-ass, funny, vibrant friend.

14

Thursday October 18

A knock on the door wakes me. Auntie Maze enters my room. 'You've slept half the day, child, and we don't want to leave without seeing you.'

I sit up and rub my eyes. 'No, of course not. I can't believe I slept so long.'

She sits on the edge of my bed. 'You lost your friend, and you're gashed in the heart. Magic heals our wounds. *True* magic. When it is used with pure intentions.'

'Auntie Maze–' I begin, but she holds up her hand. 'It's time to see what you keep hidden from everyone, including yourself.'

I meet her fey silver-green eyes. 'I told you I don't have the sight! I don't see anything!'

'Remember the island?'

She's talking about a long-ago day on Achill Island, in County Mayo, off the western coast of Ireland. I trailed mischievous Moon cousins through the fairy trail of forest, fields, the haunted cemetery at Kildavnet, and the famous deserted village. I could barely see them through the thick grey fog. We ran to the coast, waves pounding against the shore, sand humming beneath our feet. The water smelled so sour and bitter I clutched my stomach. One of the cousins pointed to the ocean. 'Here's where they drowned Nellie Moon. She won't let anyone forget.'

Granny Moon and Auntie Maze had told me the story. When Nellie Moon was accused of being a witch, the leaders of her village tied her up, locked her in a wooden chest, and threw her into the sea to undergo the 'ordeal of water'.

If the chest floated: the water had rejected her, which meant she was guilty, and thereby condemned to death.

If she sank: the water had accepted her, which meant she was innocent.

Well, the wooden chest sank, and Nellie drowned. Which proved she was innocent. But it was too late to do anything about it because she was dead. However, her illegitimate daughter survived, and according to legend, since that day, one Moon female in every generation inherits the witch powers. Granny Isobel Moon was the witch of her generation. She passed the torch to her daughter, Maze.

As I clutched my stomach and tried to keep my balance on the trembling sand, I saw a pale red-haired woman rising from the water.

I gasped, and a moment later, Auntie Maze appeared at my side. 'Our Nellie is welcoming you.'

'Can she see me?' I asked.

'Yes. The way you see her – with the sight. This is how we connect across time and space. She died in 1864, but you see her, and she sees you.' Auntie Maze took my hand in hers. 'We're standing on one of the *caol áit* – thin places – where borders between worlds are malleable and porous, sometimes crumbling. Not everyone can sense them. You have to be a bit porous too.'

While the sand hummed beneath my feet, Auntie Maze smiled at me. 'Ah darlin', Nellie let you see her. It's a gift, the seeing. Don't be denying it.'

Now, Auntie Maze grips my hands in hers. Her hands radiate heat that rises up my arms to my shoulders and the prickle point in the curve of my neck. 'You're walking backwards is what you're doing. Your mother is callin' to you, but your heart is shut and you don't hear her.'

'You can't shut a heart.'

'Can't you? You're scared, darlin', but it's only by facing the fear that you can move forward. You have to open your eyes and ears and heart to let the past in.'

She releases my hands, but the heat remains.

'Your fear of the box? It's a ghost-memory. Your body remembers being locked in the Box of Death. Same as Nellie.'

'A wooden box can't hold our Lucy.' Da stands in the doorway. 'She's a Moon is what she is.'

Auntie Maze stares at me with her seeing eyes. 'A Moon is more than one thing. A part of you is suffocating. Coming up for air. She needs air. Listen to her.'

Da says, 'Come with us, love. We have a birthday gift for you.'

I follow them into my father's study. I bypass the armour, swords, books, and masks to stop before a tall, red-draped cabinet in the centre of the room. With a flourish, Da removes the drape and reveals a wooden Zigzag Girl, the paint so fresh it glows. *Please don't let this be my birthday present.*

'Happy Birthday!' Da and Auntie Maze cry together.

'Thank you,' I say faintly.

'Twenty-eight,' says Da, his eyes tearing. 'I can't believe it.'

The Zigzag Girl is a vertical Sawing a Woman in Half illusion. The magician inserts two large metallic blades through the cabinet, dividing the cabinet and the assistant in thirds. He pulls out her midsection, giving her a zigzag shape. It has often been called the perfect illusion.

There are four openings through which you can see the assistant's face, hands, and left foot. The assistant can breathe through the openings. She's upright, not on her back. Eye to eye with the magician. Of all sawing boxes, this is the only one I can tolerate.

But not today. Not after Van. Maybe not ever again.

'Do with it what you will,' says Da. 'We had the Zigzag Girl made months ago, long before Van's death. We know it must seem like a strange gift to you, in the aftermath. But please remember that it was made for you with love.'

'I know that.' My heart catches. These two. They love me without limits and yet cannot get it through their heads that I loathe the sawing box, no matter how beautiful it is. Neither one can accept the fact that maybe, just maybe, I hate the idea of a woman in a box.

Can't they just give me perfume or a new dress like other families?

Da says eagerly, 'The Zigzag differs from other sawing boxes. You run the show. You create the story.'

That's the secret reason I can tolerate this box. The power is in the assistant's hands.

Auntie Maze gestures. 'Look at the front of the Zigzag Girl, darlin'! Your father designed it, and Marcus Lincoln built it by hand.'

Years ago, when Da first witnessed my terror of the box, he took me to Marcus Lincoln's workshop in Philadelphia. A master inventor and designer of large-scale magic props, Marcus showed us a few sawing boxes he'd built that allowed for variations. He informed me that under special circumstances, he inserted a hidden hinge the assistant could control from inside. I liked plump, bearded Marcus and his obvious pride in his work.

On our way home, Da said, 'The secret apparatus Marcus talked about puts the control in the assistant's hands. Do you want me to have Marcus install one for you?'

I shook my head. My terror went deeper than a secret apparatus, deeper than the box itself. How could I explain what I didn't understand? Maybe Auntie Maze is right, and it's a ghost-memory that Nellie Moon passed it to me.

'It's your own fear locking you in the box, not the container itself,' Da says now. 'Won't you at least give it a try?'

His voice slices at me – yearning, yet not wanting to show how much it matters. I can't bear to hurt the man who taught me that magic is another word for love.

The Zigzag Girl's hair reflects the reds and purples of a desert sunset, just like mine. Chin-length waves frame the empty carved oval where a face should be. At her side is an open book from which butterflies fly. The Book of Wonder, an illusion I perform for kids at the Children's Hospital in Philly. Da really did design her just for me.

'Remember,' he says, 'you hold the key to your freedom, no one else.'

I enter the Zigzag to give her a face and fill her void. I dangle a red scarf from one hand while Da saws me in thirds, and my midsection juts far to one side, and yes, I can breathe inside, and it is elegant and truly brilliant and ingenious, and as long as I don't gain an ounce, I'll be fine. I even joke that having my belly disappear does funny things to my digestion, and I thank them, and we eat the caramel-apple cake with a splash of Jameson that Auntie Maze bakes for my birthday each year, and I blow out the candles.

We drink a toast to Van, but I picture my girl in the box, staring at me through slitted eyes. *Find him,* she says. *Find the one who put me here.*

15

My father, aunt, and I come to a decision: I'll stay at home tonight and tomorrow. If the show continues after Friday night, I'll move to Midnight. If it doesn't, I'll join them in Vegas.

An Uber arrives to drive them to the airport. I kiss them goodbye and watch them get into the car. At the door Auntie Maze turns. 'Do you hear her? The woman is still callin' to you.'

'Is it my mother? Is it Van?'

Her eyes shine with tears. In a moment her freckled face is wet. 'Remember, love: trust the sudden knowing. You know what you don't know you know.'

Another of my aunt's cryptic comments. What do I know that I don't know I know?

The car disappears around the corner, and an arrow of pain pierces my chest. I know that I don't know when someone will be ripped from my life.

In my room I yank up the blinds and open the window. I kneel on the floor and lean on the sill. The sun shines. Ocean wind blows in. Seagulls caw. The world is carrying on as if nothing has changed. But something has changed. The sky should roar, waves rage, birds shriek. A brilliant young woman with promise, talent, and heart has been murdered.

*

The night sky is blue-black and winter-bleak, as if the mild October afternoon was a farewell to golden fall, and we've turned a corner. Waves pound the shore, the moon glows, stars blink signals. Stormie and I sit on the beach a few minutes from my house.

We press against each other, knees up, shoulder to shoulder, and wrap an afghan around us.

She unscrews the top of that old standard, Wilens Blackberry Premium #49, and glances at me. 'So sue me, I like cheap wine.'

She supplied the drink, I brought dark chocolate and a box of tissues.

'If anything can make this worse, it's Wilens,' I tell her.

A wobbly smile through her tears. 'Van wouldn't want us getting drunk on expensive booze.'

'The hangover we're gonna have tomorrow...' She knows. 'I forgot to bring glasses.'

'Girl, what's wrong with you? This rich brew needs to be drunk straight from the bottle.'

Stormie slugs it back and hands me the bottle. Sick-sweet, definitely potent.

'Slides down easy,' I admit. Brings memories of double dates, parked cars, making out by moonlight. Summer nights on the beach, someone strumming a guitar, Stormie singing along, joints and bottles passed around while we waited for the sun to rise.

While she's drinking, I ask, 'Can you imagine Peter Browne drinking Wilens?'

She chokes, wipes her mouth, and pushes the bottle at me. 'Hell, no. Moshulu.'

Moshulu. A single word that evokes a night of reckoning for Stormie and me. It began a year and half ago at an Atlantic City fundraiser event held at the Borgata, the night Stormie met Peter Browne of the Philly Brownes. Yes, the Brownes who came over on the Mayflower and endowed so many chairs in Philly they'll never lack a place to sit. The ultimate WASP banker and a mixed-race magician whose side-hustle is styling hair, they paced around each other like tigers in a cage. The attraction was fierce on both sides. Peter's mother didn't approve. Neither did Stormie's mom and Nana: he's not Black or Jewish, and he has thin lips: 'the sign of a stingy man.' But Stormie confided, 'He talks dirty to me: mergers, portfolios, acquisitions...'

On a summer evening Amazing André and I joined Peter and Stormie on Moshulu, a four-masted ship docked on Penn's Landing that Peter had rented for the night. The Delaware River, lights of Philly, my best friend and me, and our lovers. It should have been heavenly, but the sky cracked, and an unexpected storm exploded, drenching us in an instant. Stormie and I laughed. André ran inside without asking if I wanted to join him and Peter burst into a tantrum. How dare it rain when he'd planned the perfect evening? Everything was ruined. He was right about that. Later that night, André proposed. The proposal from hell. Even before she heard about it, Stormie said, 'Hey, babe, about your guy... Watch out. He wants to be Mr. Lucy Fucking Moon.'

Dead-on. I should have listened.

I throw back my head and drink.

Stormie sighs. 'Peter was looking for a mother, not a girlfriend. How could I be so blind?'

I hand her the bottle. 'Well, you and Van told me straight-off that André wanted to marry my father, not me.'

Her elbow pokes into my side. 'You know what bothers me? How the hell did MLD get past her? That man in the third row. Maybe you met him before?'

I picture his hard gaze fixed on me. 'I don't think so. I'd remember.' I finish the last drops of wine. 'Whoever he is, he'll be at the memorial tomorrow.'

'The cops will be there. Don't you think he'll stay away?'

I stare at the midnight swirls of sky and ocean. 'He's a showman. The way he set the stage, knowing I'd find Van in the sawing box. He needs the audience's reaction. He'll be there.'

16

Friday October 19

The same nightmare I've had since I was a kid. A masked man shoves me into a sawing box and fastens the clamps around my neck and ankles. Behind the mask, he laughs – shrill, more animal than human. He lowers the lid and locks me in. Flames sift through the wood. No one hears me scream. I choke on smoke and ashes until the box explodes with me in it. The last thing I hear is his laugh.

I used to wake myself, screaming. Still smelling the fire. Some nights I felt a soft spray on my face, a sweet breeze soft as a caress. I open my eyes. It's morning, light squeezing through the blinds. For as long as I can remember, my dreams have burned through my mind – flaming fragments of a horror movie that follow me into the day.

Last night Da and Auntie Maze arrived in Vegas. This evening is Van's memorial, and tonight, somehow, Stormie and I must return to the Widow stage and perform.

I pull on a T-shirt and leggings and message Tal: I need a workout.

Within thirty seconds, he responds: Come.

I ride my bike to his gym about a mile away on Arctic Avenue in Ducktown, one of my favourite areas in Atlantic City. Home of Dante Hall, where I coach teens on cardistry; Formica Bakery, where I buy the cannoli for Making Mr. Right; White House Subs; St. Michael's Church; and Tal's gym.

When I enter, Tal is stretching. He cut his hair since the last time I saw him. Military-short, it emphasises the hard lines of his face and piercing eyes. He watches me take off my jacket and hang it next to his black leather one. Wiry and graceful, he owns the gym the way Da owns the stage. He's taut, tight, secretive – the original Mysterious Loner Dude, according to Stormie. Israeli-born and fifteen years older than me, he has trained me since I was sixteen in Krav Maga – an Israeli form of self-defence and street fighting – as well as situational awareness. Da's idea. A way to keep me safe if trouble finds me. Tal knows my story, but after years, I still don't know his. My first massive crush, and yet he remains a mystery.

'Ready?' he asks, shifting on his bare feet.

I kick off one sneaker. 'Fight hard.' The other sneaker.

We circle each other. I don't give him time to think. With a snarl, I'm on him. A tangle of rage, grief, helplessness, I use every weapon he taught me – wrestling, striking, grappling. He fights back, and I'm glad. We stop short of actually hitting each other, but it's savage because of me. He blocks my every move, but he can't lock me in place. I'm fighting for... Van. For me. For life.

When we stop, every bone in my body cries out in pain. Sweat drips in my eyes. I've been through a war. Tal throws me a small towel. I rub it over my head and face. I'm a walking, breathing swamp, but deep down I'm elated. I can fight. Like Tal, I'm a warrior. I'm not helpless.

'I'm sorry about Van.' Tal scrubs his face and neck. 'But you should have gone to Vegas with Declan and Maze.'

'I can't go. Stormie and I have a show tonight.' I push my feet inside the sneakers. Tug on my jacket.

'You have no idea what's going on, and you can't handle this alone.'

The exact wrong thing to say. 'Out of my way.'

'Is she pushing you to take risks?'

'Stormie? No, why?'

He frowns. 'You surround yourself with dangerous women.'

'I don't know what that means.'

'Don't be stupid. Women who don't play it safe.'

'I've played it safe my whole life. Maybe it's time to break free.'

His eyes flash. 'Even if it kills you?'

Tal taught me to fight by developing my animal essence. He's the tiger – strong and wise, who knows when to fight and when to refrain. I'm the crane who makes up for her lesser strength with misdirection. My aim is to be light and evasive, never where you think I am.

'I'm the crane, remember? I can flit around the tiger and peck him to death.'

Tal studies me for a long moment, so long it chills me. 'What if he's not a tiger?' he asks quietly. 'What if he's a snake, creeping along the ground, patiently waiting for his one perfect killer shot? You won't see him until it's too late.'

17

As I head north on the boardwalk, the wand for Van's ceremony pokes out from my magic bag. It's the magic hour, my favourite time of day, when sun and moon share the sky like two magicians on stage. Halloween is in two weeks, but a group of leering Scary Clowns are heading my way. Shops are decorated with orange and black balloons, ghosts and witches, dried corn bundles and chocolate pumpkins. The boardwalk Halloween parade is coming up. There will be competitions for best costumes, live music, and fireworks. Across the wooden rafters, Central Pier blasts disco and boasts Go-Karts and an arcade.

Enormous spider webs shroud posters on the grey stone façade that advertise Midnight's five entertainment venues: the Crypt, where Dead Men Rising is performing; the Vamp Lounge, where Misty and the Boardwalk Babes dance; Fang's, near the casino, where a comedian 'will shock the pants off you!' Hell, the newly renovated black box theatre in the basement, where Elvis Jones performs. And Black Widow Theatre.

My gaze goes unwillingly to our poster. All dazzle and colour: the three rebels. Van in the centre, forever frozen in the act of hurling a knife. It hurts, but I'd rather remember her this way than in the box. I agonized over the Broken Wand and came up with a twist I'm not sure my father would approve of.

I cross the boardwalk, grip the railing, and look down at the beach. About twenty-five to thirty people have gathered. I recognise most of them. It's a great turnout for a woman who wasn't in town very long. In the glow of the setting sun, Central Pier, with its concrete pillars rising from the sand, resembles an ancient, crumbling palace. The small band of grey-bearded homeless men who sleep beneath the pier's weathered boards advance on the sand toward us. From where I stand, they are foreshortened like gnomes.

When I told Stormie they reminded me of elves, she said, 'You see elves. I see homeless dudes sleeping and pissing on the sand.'

She is already on the beach. We're both wearing dresses from Red Light Vintage, the resale shop run by her mom and Nana. Stormie's turban and gown are fiery orange – Van's favourite colour. According to Van, the crushed velvet dress I'm wearing turns my grey eyes ice-blue.

Ruby's voice splinters the sky with an old blues song, 'Atlantic City, you'll be the death of me,' a song that chills me each time I hear it.

I first heard Ruby's powerful voice last fall. Like a siren she lured me to the corner of Boardwalk and New York Avenue, where a small group huddled. I looked around for the singer. When I realised it was the radiant Black woman in a wheelchair, shock whooshed through me, an ocean wind, as if I were suddenly hollow.

She sings from a wooden deck on the sand, leaning forward to play the battery-operated keyboard on her lap. Finger, lips, teeth, tongue – today, she brings out all her artillery. She's quadriplegic with limited use of her right arm and hand. The arm is rigid but there's enough mobility to move the hand across her battery-operated keyboard and to play with the index finger, the only part of her body beneath the neck that she can move with dexterity.

One night, she told me about the accident: she dove into a pool and hit concrete – and the end of her dream of becoming an Olympic swimmer. Her boyfriend broke up with her, and her family sent her away. She was nineteen. 'I don't blame them,' she said. 'I'm not easy to take care of. I had years to get over it.'

A man in a black hoodie and faded jeans hunkers down at Ruby's side on the deck. Elvis Jones.

Detectives Torres and Wax survey the crowd from the steps that lead to the beach.

Off to one side Gus holds his vape pen to his mouth and inhales. He glances up over his red-framed glasses and gives me a hello nod.

Midnight's cocktail waitresses and dealers have gathered: the women in long black wigs, skin-tight orange dresses, thigh-high stiletto-heeled boots, and the men's faces dead-white under widow's-peak wigs, bodies draped in black capes.

Four dancers in tight satin dresses sway, flowered wreaths in their hair – Misty and the Boardwalk Babes. She moves away from the Babes toward Charlie. He looks elegant in a tailored black jacket and black jeans, his dark-blond hair blowing. His profile is stern – glasses, thin nose and lips – but there is a softness in his cheek, a sweet smile when Misty whispers in his ear, and he presses his hand to the small of her back, beneath her waterfall of pale hair.

It might have been me.

When Ruby's song ends, Elvis Jones wheels her down the ramp to a low wooden platform facing the stage, where Jinx Faust sits front and centre, her crimson-painted lips a sign of defiance against old age, disability, and death.

Ruby joins her. Arms crossed, Jones stands behind her. With a mocking smile, he watches me descend to the sand.

Stormie beckons to me. 'You look pale.'

I press my fist to my forehead. 'Wilens' hangover. How come you look so good?'

She shrugs. 'Nana swears by gefilte fish for a cure.'

'I don't trust any food encased in a gel.'

She snorts. 'You don't trust anything or anyone. Listen, after tonight's show, we're meeting Charlie and Gus at the Speakeasy. Charlie needs an act to play the Widow. If it's not us, it's gonna be someone else.'

Charlie moves to the deck. He thanks Ruby for her song and says a few words about what a wonderful performer and human being Van was, and how she'll be missed by the Atlantic City community. 'Lucy Moon is going to do something for Van.' He gestures to me.

I grab the wand and leave my bag with Stormie. Alone onstage, I look out at the people gathered to honour Van. 'Seeing all of you here would have meant so much to Van. When a magician dies, our community mourns their passing in a traditional ceremony we call the Broken Wand. We break the magician's wand to mark the end of their magic as well as their life. Now, I confess I've never done this before, and I've never seen it done by a woman.'

'You should have asked Declan to do it!' says Gus.

Thank you, Gus. 'He's not here, but I'll do my best.'

I hold up the wand – slim and black with a silver tip at each end. 'I chose this wand for Van because it's sleek and strong yet deceptively light. Like Van.'

I throw it in the air and catch it.

'Vanessa Kim was five foot two, weighed a hundred pounds, and hurled knives with more strength, ferocity, and grace than any man or woman I've ever seen. Depending on her mood, she billed herself as either Kick-Ass Asian Babe or Lady Miss Van. Truth: she's both kick-ass and a lady, the definition of a dame.'

'Amen!' cries Ruby.

'Van's magic tested limits and broke rules. She created an aura of danger and tension that left us on the edge of our seats. At the same time, she was having so much fun we couldn't help but share her enjoyment. She'd been burned many times in life and love, but all you had to do was look at her and hear her laugh to know she'd never stop believing in... in us. In love. More than the knives, that was her true magic. And it lives on. She was all promise and potential. I'm furious she was torn from her life before she had a chance to become whatever she wanted to...'

My voice catches. 'It's time to break the wand, but because this is Van, I'm giving tradition a twist that I think she'd appreciate.'

I hold out the wand again and break it in half. Orange flowers burst from the halves. Fiery petals rain around me.

Jinx's husky voice rises. 'There's something called a dame. Every one of you knows what it is, because our town is a dame. Beat up, knocked out, left for dead too many times to count. A lot of dirty hands stirring her pot. But what does she do? Tell us, Lucy Moon.'

I clear my throat. 'A dame picks herself up, puts on Carmine Red lipstick, and gets back in the ring.'

The night Van came up with the idea of rebel magicians, she said, 'We'll be just like those tough dames of the forties. After all, magic is no game for pussies. You need blood and fists, and you can't ever get old.'

My heart squeezes. *You won't ever have the chance to get old, Van.* 'Van's murderer thinks he won. But the fight's not over. Van's down, but not out. Her friends are here, and we'll find him.'

A woman wearing a three-tier hat that belongs at Buckingham Palace moves closer to the stage, revealing a man I hadn't noticed before. He's wearing a red, black, and white knit New Jersey Devils cap and a black leather jacket. The hard gaze, the thin-lipped scowl. It's him! The man in the third row. He's frowning at me.

Gripping the flower-stuffed wand, I run down the stage ramp, but Detective Torres holds up her hand and blocks me. 'Lucy! We need to talk.'

'Wait!' I move around her in search of the guy in the New Jersey Devils cap. Where did he go? I see him running up the ramp toward the boardwalk. Shit!

I take a few steps after him, but Torres catches up to me and cries, 'Lucy! Stop now.'

'It's the suspicious guy I saw opening night. The man in the third row.'

'Where?'

'The boardwalk.'

She rushes with me up the ramp. We scan the area, right and left, but he's gone. Disappeared, as if I'd conjured him.

18

'He's gone now,' says Detective Torres. 'We'll find him. But first, you and I need to talk. I need your help. You know everyone here, the Midnight crew, and all these people who interacted with Van. Did you notice anyone acting strange? Doing something unusual?'

'No.'

'Keep your eyes open.'

'I will.'

She lowers her dark glasses. 'Tell me again what you saw when you looked inside the sawing box.'

My heart jumps. 'I saw Van. The orange scarf.'

She moves closer, blocking the light until all I see is her. 'What else?'

I must tell her. It doesn't incriminate me. 'A black flutter. At first, I thought it was a small blackbird.'

'But it wasn't a bird. What was it?'

A cough sticks in my throat. 'A black flower. I think.'

'A black polyester rose.' Her eyes are bright and dark. 'I've been told you use flowers in your act.'

'Yes. In the Cone of Flowers and my *Bewitched* routine. But my flowers are made of crepe paper.'

'What does the black rose symbolise?'

I've looked it up enough times. 'Death and mourning. Rebirth. But I use white roses, yellow, pink. Not black.' *Never black.*

'Is there anything else you want to tell me?'

'No.'

'It's a criminal offense to withhold information that might help solve a crime, and it's a human offense when it involves your friend.' She pushes up her glasses. 'And don't try to track down the man you saw. That's our job. If you see him again, tell us.'

I can't tell her about the rose. Not yet. It will open a Pandora's Box that leads her down the wrong trail and that will put Da, Auntie Maze, and me in danger.

A handful of people linger on the beach. The greybeards have returned to their palace beneath Central Pier. Stormie perches on the edge of the deck, swinging her legs as she talks to Jinx. On my way to join her, a soft voice calls my name. Misty. 'Oh, Lucy. I didn't know Van well, but she seemed strong and brave. I wish I could be that brave.'

'Me too.'

'Something she said to me bothered me. I couldn't sleep last night, and I kept thinking about it. She said, "When you don't have family, your boyfriend becomes your father, mother, best friend – he becomes everything."'

'Did she tell you who he was?'

'No. I wanted to warn her: honey, you can't trust anyone that much.'

'That's the truth.'

She fists her small hand. 'We need to fight back. You volunteer at the youth centre at Dante Hall, right? Teaching magic?'

'Cardistry. The art of card flourishes.'

'I'm going to teach a course next week. Belly dancing for teen girls.'

'That's great.'

She blushes. 'I hope it helps build their self-esteem.'

'How's everything going with you and Charlie?'

'Good. We're taking a couple days off to go to New York. In a week or two.'

'What are you gonna do?'

'Go to a show, walk, explore. He used to live there, and it's a chance to get away. Oh, and I've always wanted to take the ferry to Staten Island.'

'Or the A train, if it's cold.' Charlie arrives, looking moody and windblown. 'I wish you hadn't said that about the murderer, Lucy.'

'Why not?' asks Misty.

He takes off his glasses and rubs them against his jacket. 'What if he's here and takes it as a dare?'

'Lucy was letting him know that he can't win. We'll get him in the end.' Eyes glowing, cheeks flushed, the most passionate I've seen her. She touches Charlie's arm. 'You just don't believe in happy endings.'

'You call that a happy ending? Maybe I don't know what a happy ending is.'

'Maybe I don't either,' she says, still in that breathy voice. 'For a happy ending you have to trust each other, right?'

I wonder if that's a dig, but the corner of Charlie's mouth tips up in a secret smile. 'I don't know much about happy endings, but I'd say we're a happy beginning.'

She looks at him. 'It's a start.'

He fights a smile, but his dimples show. Are they teasing each other?

Misty turns to me, her eyes shining wet. 'The wrong man can happen to any of us, even strong, brave women like Van. Scary-dangerous men. My ex is one. I was lucky enough to get away from him. Poor Van didn't have the chance.'

I retreat from these two gorgeous creatures – Charlie's arm around Misty, her face upturned to his – and bump into someone. Before I can turn, a man's hands grip my shoulders. A voice murmurs in my ear, 'Lucy Moon, anyone tell you it's not a good idea to taunt a killer?'

I whirl around. Elvis Jones – so close I see the bitter coffee eyes, the stubbled cheeks and chin, the curl of his upper lip. So close I step back, and water sloshes into my shoes. I didn't realise I was so near to the water's edge. Beneath my feet, shells crunch. Wind bites into my skin, a salt-burn that will itch in the night, like the prickle moving up my throat.

'The witch in *Bewitched*, Miss Scarlett, *The Sorcerer's Apprentice…*' At my look, he shrugs. 'I saw you on TV. You and the Moon dynasty on *Sesame Street*. Declan taught Cookie Monster to do the Linking Rings with chocolate chip cookies.' Behind the bland smile lurks an evil grin. 'You're the masters of playing it safe.'

'You just said I'm taunting a killer.'

'You're the odd one out.'

'And you're a Moon-hater.' I can't help the disappointment in my voice. Moon-haters are as bad as Moon wannabes. Neither group sees us as human.

'I don't hate you. I just think of what I'd do if I had that – that power.'

'Yeah? What?'

'I'd push the boundaries, blur the edges. Make people wonder what's real and what's magic. Make them wonder if reality is magic. Give them the unexpected. At the end of the show, I want them to walk outside and see life a little differently.'

'I try to do that too.'

'Huh.' He tilts his head to the side. 'You play a lot of characters, but which one is Lucy Moon?'

'They're all me. But bigger and better.'

'If you didn't know Van was in the sawing box, then what was going on?'

'What was going on with *you*? Why did you come onstage?'

His eyes are slits. 'I wanted to know what happened to Van. You, Stormie, and Becker were acting as if nothing was wrong. That's my story. What's yours?'

I don't trust this man, and I don't owe him an explanation. 'Nice talking to you, Jones.'

'You're a puzzle with pieces that don't fit. I'd like to see what you're hiding behind...' He smiles again, a bland, wicked smile that bristles the hair on my arms, '...those bangs.'

I touch them. Despite ocean wind, the bangs stand firm, a sticky fortress. 'Nothing. Aqua Net Super-Hold hairspray. The purple can.' Damn, I sound as breathless as Misty. 'I'd like to see what *you* hide under that hood.'

He pushes back his hood, revealing a long white feather pinned to his hair. A thrill quivers through me. Without thinking, I tell him about the crane who makes up for her lack of strength by being quick and elusive.

He listens intently. His hair, swirling over his face, is the same black as his eyes. They remind me of Ruby's voice: bold, dark, and bitter. He's not handsome, exactly. But on a day of death, he burns with life.

I add – still breathless, damn it – 'She can't get caught.'

His smile starts in his eyes. So warm I wonder how a moment ago I could have found them cold and bitter. 'I know the crane,' he says. 'She's like a leaf blowing in the wind, but a large animal can catch her. She needs to be very careful.'

Is that a warning or a threat?

He extends his hand. An intricate blue tattoo edges from the wrist and disappears under the sleeve of his hoodie. He shakes my hand, his grip hard and warm.

'How well did you know Van?' I ask.

'Hardly at all.' He releases his grip on my hand. 'But what I knew, I liked.'

In my palm is the white feather that had been in his hair. Nicely done.

'I'm way out on the fringes,' he says. 'Nowhere near the Mooniverse. But if you feel like slumming, the feather will get you in.'

I squint at the tiny writing on the spine of the feather: *GO TO HELL. MIDNIGHTS AT MIDNIGHT. ELVIS JONES.*

When I look up, he's walking backwards, away from me. A couple of seagulls hover over his head as if they're watching over him.

19

The sun is setting when I join Stormie, Jinx, and a middle-aged woman, squat and strong, her grey hair styled in a mullet bowl cut – sadly even more unflattering than it sounds. Jinx is perched on the deck. She bobs her cane at me. 'Sit with us, Lucy. Meet Dasha Sills.'

Dasha seems to be standing guard. Arms crossed, she squints into the distance though I'm right in front of her. Like Jinx, her lips are smeared with Carmine Red.

'That was an interesting ceremony,' says Jinx. 'I've only seen the Broken Wand once before when your father did it. He said a few words and then broke the wand.'

Stormie pats the place next to her on the deck. 'That's the way it's done traditionally. But I like what you did with the flowers. I didn't like what you said about finding him.'

I sit at her side. 'I didn't plan to say it.'

Dasha says, 'You were giving him a heads up that you're not gonna let it rest.'

'Exactly.' Stormie nudges me. 'Anyway, Jinx was telling me about being a girl reporter in the early days.'

'I was the first girl *The Atlantic City News* hired.' Jinx holds out a frail, freckled hand weighed down by an enormous ring that glitters like the ruby on her cane. 'I learned there are always two stories: the official version they print and the hidden version, what really happened.'

'Jinx was out in the field and on the front.' Dasha's voice is low and amused. 'She got stories none of the boys could. People trusted her. She covered murders, the Death Row Dames.'

'Dames who kill,' says Jinx. 'That's why the boys called me Jinx. They said I sniffed out death.'

'They were jealous,' mutters Dasha. 'You worked harder than they did, and you got there first.'

'Elvis!' cries Jinx. 'Sit with us, you sexy devil.'

Elvis Jones sits at my side, squeezing me against him.

When I stir, his thigh presses against mine. The pressure of his arm, the heat of his leg. This man disturbs me. He doesn't have to say a word. It's his presence.

'Go ahead, tell 'em about the first Death Row Dame.' Dasha squints at us. 'Bertie Wilcox poisoned her four husbands and two fiancés. Six men dead.'

'Bertie drove me to a cabin that belonged to one of the husbands. The next morning the coppers found us.' Jinx pauses, looks beyond us. 'So did the reporters. One says to me, "Hey Jinx, I got your headline: 'My Night with the Monster.'" But see, I spent the night with Bertie. We drank whiskey from the same bottle, shared a can of spaghetti. She told me her story, and I looked in her eyes and saw the human trapped inside the monster. Or the monster trapped in the human.'

Jinx's growl lowers to a raspy whisper. 'Under certain conditions it can happen to any of us.'

'What did they do to Bertie?' I ask.

'They zapped her. Old Sparky did the job.' Jinx rubs her eyes, smearing mascara down one cheek.

'Which story did you write?' asks Stormie.

'That time I wrote the truth.'

'She got the Pulitzer for it,' says Dasha. 'But other times she had to write the official version.'

'Sometimes the Mob, the Family, whatever you call them, tell you what to write.' Jinx sighs. 'You can't escape them. They're under the boardwalk, in the air, in the shadows. Even when you think they're gone, they're here.'

I shiver. The sun spreads red puddles in the water and the

moon glows, a pale sphere against the darkening sky.

'Even during Camp Boardwalk?' asks Stormie.

'Especially during Camp Boardwalk. You're all too young. You can't even imagine what it was like.'

'Tell us,' murmurs Jones.

'Ha!' Jinx lifts the cane. The red jewel glows. 'We used to stay up all night because we didn't believe the sun would rise. The summer of '44, the word "love" was shoved like sandbags against doors, painted on windows to keep enemy planes from sighting us, sneezed and coughed until the whole city was infected.' A sharp laugh. 'Not Cleo West, of course. She thought she was immune.'

I breathe salt, sand, the usual beach smells, and something else – familiar, but wisping away in the breeze.

Stormie asks, 'How well did you know Cleo?'

Jinx is silent. Then, as if the words are being dragged from her, she says, 'She was my closest friend.'

'What was she like?' I ask.

'Tender. Too tender. Sparkling... from the inside.'

'Who did she fall in love with?' asks Jones.

'Morelli the magician,' says Stormie. 'There were engaged, right?'

'Yes,' says Jinx, 'but the man she fell in love with was Frank, a wounded war hero.'

'Wasn't he the one who killed her?' I ask.

Jinx sighs heavily.

'How can you see the monster in the human?' asks Jones in the rich voice that reminds me of Da reading Yeats by firelight.

'You can't,' says Dasha. 'They could be walking among us. Someone we think we know.'

Jones goes rigid at my side.

A sense of disquiet. The night falling so swiftly. Waves pound the shore. Another story trembles like an earthquake beneath the one Jinx told. Cleo and her brutal lover, Van and her murderer, Misty and her scary ex, and even Amazing André. His sudden fury when I turned down his marriage proposal. 'You're nothing without the Moons,' he snarled and clenched his fist. He wanted to hit me. I should have kneed him in the groin and pushed my fist up his nose. I had the training, I had the power, yet what did I do? I ran.

'Lucy's thinking of Amazing Asshole,' says Stormie.

The problem with being sisters.

A choked laugh from Jones. 'Are you talking about André? You went out with him, Lucy?'

'Thanks for bringing him up, Storm.'

She grins. 'So Amazing asks Declan – Declan Moon! – if he wants to see a card trick.'

'Ah,' says Jinx. 'I believe I see where this is going.'

Stormie snickers. 'Maybe not. Amazing proceeds to do a card trick and...'

'It was one of Lucy's tricks,' says Jones.

My jaw drops. 'How did you know?'

'I didn't. But I know André.'

'He tried to pass one of Lucy's tricks as his own. To her dad, who just happens to be one of the greatest magicians on the planet.' Stormie shakes her head. 'Sheer chutzpah. And now Lucy's off men.'

Dasha suggests slyly, 'Maybe you need a woman, not a man?'

'What for?' I ask. 'To open myself to rejection from the other half of the world?' Over their laughter, I say, 'Anyway it's not men I'm off, it's magicians.'

Jones says, low, 'Not every male magician is so weak he needs to steal effects from his girlfriend.'

A hush, broken by Jinx. 'Time for this old dame to go home.'

Dasha helps her up, and I can't resist asking how they met.

'Dasha is Bertie Wilcox's daughter.'

Over our gasps, Jinx adds, 'After her mother died, she found me.'

'I appreciated how she wrote about my ma.'

'She became my assistant though I didn't need one in those days.'

At Dasha's humph, Jinx grins. 'Dasha insisted on sticking around.'

Dasha mutters, 'Jinx insisted I stick around.'

Jinx sniffs. 'Long story short, Dasha and I have been driving each other crazy longer than you've been alive.'

After they leave, Jones, Stormie, and I head to the boardwalk. Stormie and I are going to Midnight for our show, and Jones is meeting someone at the Speakeasy, but the three of us stand quiet under the boardwalk light. I'm still prickly and uneasy. A mix of sensations. Voices under voices, a story under a story.

Stormie says, 'When I grow up, I wanna be twisty and yeasty like Jinx.'

'You're already there,' says Jones.

I look at him in surprise. He's right. Stormie has been an old soul since she was a kid. 'Elvis Jones, you said you barely knew Van. Were you friends?'

Jones's face is all mockery and angles. 'Friends,' he echoes. 'What do you mean?'

'It's not that difficult.'

He raises an eyebrow. 'Define friends.'

Every word he says tingles my nerve endings. 'You're impossible.'

'Not for you, Lucy Moon. For you, I'm very possible.'

Stormie groans. 'Jones, you're ridiculous.'

His eyes glint. He's laughing behind his eyes and mouth. 'On second thought, maybe Hell is too far from the Mooniverse. Stay away, Lucy. Stay far away.'

We watch him leave. 'That is one sweet honey of a butt. Firm yet cheeky.' Stormie cups her hands around imaginary peaches. 'Totally *geshmak*.'

'If by *geshmak*, you mean arrogant...'

'It means delicious. A pinchable tush.' She nudges me. 'Go to his show. Call it research if it makes you feel better. But bring your knife.'

20

After our show, Stormie and I change and head to the Speakeasy. Sadie's smoky croon welcomes us inside. The manager Dom looks up from the counter and waves us in. Like the Speakeasy, Dom's style is forties noir – fedora, striped barbershop quartet shirt and suspenders, baggy cuffed pants, and spats. Rolled-up sleeves reveal muscular arms covered with tattoos, including a red heart that says, 'MOM'.

Van loved this place. So do I. It has the warmth and coziness of a true Irish pub, the soft lights of a place where you can go to hide from others and yourself. The walls are covered with posters of noir films and glamour shots of Bogart, Bacall, Mitchum, and Stanwyck. A man and woman are entwined on a bench in the corner booth. A woman wearing a pointed witch hat and long black gown pulls a man from the bar stool and dances with him.

Stormie and I settle in a wooden booth across from Gus. Charlie's running late. We nurse shots of Jameson (me) and Espolòn (Stormie) while Gus licks the salt rim of a margarita. Tonight he's gone Willie Nelson, with two fraying braids, one over each shoulder.

He raises his glass and toasts us. 'Good show tonight, girls.'

'Thanks.' Stormie and I drink, but I know we're both thinking that Van's absence leaves a gaping hole. We'll never have the show we envisioned. We'll never move in together. One week ago, in this booth, Stormie and I told Van we'd decided to move to an apartment together, and we wanted her to join us. We'd found a three-bedroom apartment on Fairmount Avenue in Ducktown, vacant on the first of January. If the show worked out, maybe we'd get a long-standing gig at the Widow and send out feelers for work in the Philly-New York area.

Van smiled and held up her drink. 'Hell yeah!'

I remember my surprise when I saw Van's studio off the Vegas Strip. Tiny kitchen and bath, mattress on the floor, a chair and small table, and two open suitcases against the wall. A place to land, and then, to fly off again. 'Don't look so sad,' she said. 'This isn't my home.'

'Where is your home?'

'You. My friends.'

Great friend I turned out to be.

'Well, the results of Van's autopsy are in,' says Gus.

Dread presses against my chest.

'Homicide by ligature strangulation.'

'How do you know?' asks Stormie.

'I know things you can't imagine.' He licks his fingertip. 'I can show you.'

I scowl at him. 'Do you really know what happened?'

'The perp fractured her hyoid bone. In case you don't know, it's a small, delicate bone, high up, near the chin. This is not like shooting a person or even knifing them. This is murder at its most intimate. He pulled a cord around her throat and tightened it.' Gus touches his neck with long pale fingers. 'Most likely a paracord. See, fingers don't leave as deep an impression. The cord leaves raw red brush burns.'

He peers over his red-framed glasses. 'You didn't see the marks because he hid them with the scarf.'

I draw in my breath. 'We've all been saying "he". What if it was a woman?'

Stormie shakes her head. 'I don't think a woman would be strong enough to carry her.'

'It could be a woman,' says Gus. 'First, Van was tiny, and a woman could have wheeled Van in a cabinet or cart. No one would have seen her.' An odd smile fleets across his face. 'But the staging points to a man.'

'The staging,' I repeat. 'You mean the sawing box?'

He dips his finger in the glass and swirls it. 'He posed her to make it look like a lust crime. Naked body, scarf, a dead woman inside a box where women are sawed in half. But there's no evidence of rape.'

Stormie and I sigh in relief. At least that. But I remember Stormie telling me she heard that Gus likes it rough.

'What about the rose?' she asks.

I kick her under the table. Really? No need to mention the rose, especially not to Gus.

He sits up, eager. 'The perp wants to distinguish himself. The rose is his signature, an artist signing his work.'

She grimaces. 'Wouldn't he want to stay anonymous?'

'You'd think so, wouldn't you? It's a tightrope. He doesn't want to get caught, but he wants to be appreciated so he leaves a sign of ownership: this girl is mine. But the rose is personal. It means something to him.'

Stormie nudges me, but I keep my focus on Gus. 'Maybe it's part of setting the scene,' I say quickly. 'Maybe it's misdirection. He wants us to look at the rose so we don't see who he really is.' *Maybe it has nothing to do with me.*

Gus nods. 'On another note, what do you ladies say to a magic show *à trois* later tonight? *Á trois* means the three of us.' He pronounces it 'a trix'.

'I heard you have a girlfriend,' says Stormie with admirable restraint.

'She broke up with me. I'm available. She called me Gus the Great, just saying.'

Stormie clicks her tongue. 'Why did she break up with you?'

He grimaces, and for a moment he looks genuinely pained. 'She was mad that I used her as an alibi for Tuesday night.'

I choke on my drink. 'The night Van was... Where the hell were you?'

21

Gus glances in every direction, then leans toward us. 'I'll tell you, but this has to stay between us. You both have to swear not to tell anyone.'

Stormie raises her eyebrows. After a moment, she nods. 'Okay.'

I add a grudging, 'Okay.'

'I work undercover for the cops.'

'No way.'

He rubs his finger around the salt rim again and lifts it to his mouth.

'What do you do for them?' asks Stormie.

He mimes zipping his lips. 'I can't talk about it.'

'Did you tell Van?' I ask.

'No. You're the first civilians I'm telling. Remember I told you I saw–'

'Sorry I'm late.' Charlie slides in next to Gus, who clamps his lips shut. What was he about to say? Was it about Charlie arguing with Van?

Charlie throws back his head and downs his drink in a single gulp. 'Double shot of Gentleman Jack,' he mutters. 'I need it.'

Charlie is rarely frazzled, but I know him well enough to sense he's bothered. A sudden fear: is he going to cancel our show? The management may have pushed him, and he doesn't want to tell us.

'Go ahead.' I nod at him. 'Tell us.'

He blinks. 'Tell you what?'

'What's bothering you.'

He looks at me, his grey eyes thoughtful, until heat rises up my throat. The damned blush I can't control.

After a moment, he says, 'This will sound terrible, but what happened to Van sparked interest in the Widow. They're getting calls, media requests…'

Gus nods wisely. 'People love blood. They want to get next to it.'

'Not all people,' mutters Stormie.

'Gus is right.' Words I never thought I'd hear myself say. 'You saw the audience tonight.'

'Rubberneckers,' says Charlie. 'Chasing the crime. Anyway, the management wants the show to go on. The question is: Do you?'

Stormie clutches her Star of David necklace as if she'll never let go. We haven't talked about this, but we worked so hard on this show, put our souls into it, and to stop it now is silencing not just Van, but us too. I release a shuddering breath. 'We want to go on.'

'I hoped you'd say that. Second question: Should we add another magician to replace Van?'

Stormie and I turn to each other. We have names of other magicians on the tips of our tongues, but she shakes her head.

'Make it two rebels instead of three,' I suggest. 'Just Storm and me.'

Gus says slyly, 'And the ghost.'

I slant my eyes at him. Another surprise. 'You feel Cleo?'

'Hell, yeah. The ghost with a bad case of PMS.'

Charlie grins and brings out his calendar. He's the only person I know besides Da who marks his appointments in a pocket-size leatherbound diary. 'Tomorrow night we'll carry on with the same show. Sunday and Monday are dark.' His lifts his head. 'Monday morning, let's meet in the Widow to revamp the show. We need a couple days to spread the word – online, radio, TV, new posters… I'll take care of it. You'll do a few interviews. We'll open Wednesday night, the twenty-fourth. Sound good?'

Storm gives him a thumbs up, and I say, 'Perfect.'

'Gus?'

Gus nods. 'Always ready. A shame to let this show die.' He checks his phone. Swipes left. Right. Left. Right. He looks up with a smirk. 'Hate to leave the sparkling company but I have another engagement.'

Charlie lets him out, then sits with us again.

Dom brings another round of drinks to our table. 'Gentleman Jack for the gentleman, Espolòn and Jameson for the ladies.'

Charlie lifts his glass. 'Rebel Magic, back in business.' We drink, and he smiles at us. 'I want you both to plan an effect you can perform together in honour of Van. How does that sound?'

My eyes brim with tears. 'Like something you'd do. Thanks, Charlie.'

'I should have kept a closer eye on her.'

'No, I should have. Did you see her here?'

'Sure. Almost every night, while I waited for Misty to get off work.'

'This will sound strange, but did you argue with Van the night she was murdered?'

He jerks back. 'Me? Why would I?'

'I don't know.'

'No. I didn't.' He frowns. 'But I saw her with Jones that night. In front of the Speakeasy.'

I startle, and he gives me a curious look. 'He and Van were... I don't know if they were fighting, but he was talking, and she didn't look happy. I should have asked if she was okay, but I went inside. I don't want to say anything against him.' He hesitates. 'I'll just say he's not all that he seems to be.'

'What happened after that?' asks Stormie.

'That's the last time I saw her. When I went back out, they were gone. And I got caught up in phone negotiations with Dead Men Rising.'

'What's the problem with them anyway?'

'They want cases of Diet Coke, crates of Bacardi rum, cartons of Marlboros. Oh yeah, and a monkey.'

Stormie laughs, and he gives a rueful grin. 'I'm serious. I was on the phone with their manager so long I missed dinner with Misty. She was mad at me, too.'

His phone vibrates on the table. He glances down. 'Oh shit, Dead Men Rising again.'

As he slides out of the booth, I cry, 'But Charlie, we haven't told you our demands yet.'

He smiles at me, and my blush goes full-flower.

When he leaves, Stormie says, 'The hell's going on with you two?'

'I wish I knew. I wish I understood men. I wish I knew which ones can be trusted.'

'It's hard to tell the difference between good danger and bad danger.' She nudges me. 'Did you notice? Tonight, Gus seemed more... human.'

'Yeah, but I'm still reeling over him working with the cops.'

'Undercover though. It suits him. There's something secretive about him.'

'Yeah. Like how he lives in the shadows.'

'It does explain how he knows so much about crime.'

'Doesn't explain why he's so excited about it.' I let out a sigh. 'What did happen that night? Gus saw Charlie arguing with Van, and Charlie saw Jones fighting with her. Unless she argued with both of them, someone is lying.'

'It's hard to trust any man right now.'

22

Stormie and I are about to leave when Dom sets down another round of shots and sits across from us. He raises his beer. 'To Lady Miss Van.'

I down my third Jameson of the night in a single burning gulp, then tell him we're carrying on with the show and ask him to spread the word.

'Wiz pleasure.' He tips the fedora back on his head.

Van would have been in good hands with him. He supervises everyone who enters and leaves, making sure the 'ladies who visit my establishment' are safe.

'Dom, do you remember Van meeting guys here?'

'How about Gus?' asks Stormie.

'Yo, Dom!' A man seated at the end of the bar raises his glass. 'One more.'

Dom lifts his hand. 'Gimme a minute. I'm talkin' to two ladies.' He turns to us. 'Gus? He's here almost every night.'

'Did you ever see him with Van?' I ask.

'Sure, a few times.' He cocks his head as though thinking about it for a moment. 'Our latest forties trivia night? He and Van teamed up and won.'

Stormie rolls her eyes. 'How about Charlie?'

'He's a regular too. Lately, Misty joins him.'

'What about Elvis Jones?' I ask.

'Wild card.' A brief laugh. 'Comes every night for a week, disappears for another week, then shows up again.'

'Alone?' I ask. 'With Van?'

'He makes the rounds.' Dom scrunches his face in thought. 'Usually he's with his drummer. But there's another dude. Quiet, talks to nobody. Stands by the bar and cases the joint. Always in black leather like a tough guy. Orders two, three shots of Wild Turkey, tips big, leaves alone. A few nights ago him and Van walk out together.'

'Was that Tuesday night?'

'Monday or Tuesday.'

I curve my hand around my throat. Here it is. I feel it. The man Charlie saw her with. 'What's his name?'

'Dunno.' He brings out the whisper that means listen up. 'I told Van to watch her ass.'

'Why?' asks Stormie.

'She's a sweet thing. Him, I don't like.'

I lean toward him. 'Why not? Is there something strange about him?'

'Damn right.' He points to his eyes. 'He's a hunter. Saw Van, aimed, shot.'

I wonder if it was the man in the third row. His face was ruddy, even-featured. But I remember the force of his gaze and the small twist of his mouth as if he knew something no one else did.

'Hungry eyes.' I rub my palm over my throat. 'What did Van say when you warned her?'

'She said, "Dom, sometimes you don't know what you're looking for till you find it."'

23

Saturday October 20

Earlier this afternoon, I moved my magic gear and a suitcase filled with clothing and cosmetics to a room on the sixth floor of Midnight, a few doors from Stormie.

Tonight's show was another sold-out performance, the crowd hyper and raucous. I'm so wired I can't sleep. I put on my power outfit: a fitted man's black suit, black string tie dangling over a white shirt, and flat black shoes. I leave my purse in the room and fill my jacket pockets with my phone, credit card, several bills, Swiss Army knife, and the white feather that serves as the passport to Hell. No purse, hands free.

Before I leave my room, I google Elvis Jones. He has a steady gig at Midnight, where he's been for the past seven months. For a performer, his social-media presence is surprisingly limited. He's not on Twitter or Instagram but I find eighteen Elvis Jones listed on Facebook. Finding much beyond that would be an all-day affair.

There are two interesting links. One mentions that he is 'a fraction Lenni Lenape,' another name for the Delaware Indians based mostly in New Jersey, and that Crazy Wind, who accompanies him on hand-drums, is a full-fledged member of the Lenape tribe. The second link leads to *Genii, The Conjurors' Magazine*, where I click on an article – not about him – *by* him. Only the first paragraph is provided before a pay wall intrudes:

He's in the front row, giving you that straight-ahead unblinking stare, while his thumb taps the phone. He's looking up your trick on YouTube or Wiki, convinced that when he finds the secret, he'll win. Win what?

you might ask. Win the ancient battle between the magician and the audience. The secret is literally at his fingertips. In a second he'll have you beat, and your magic won't have any power over him. Magic will be reduced to a trickster performing a puzzle he can solve, a trick he can buy online. Order will be restored, and he'll sleep well tonight. We can't stop him. So what can we do?

That's Elvis Jones?

What can we do? The primary challenge confronting twenty-first century magicians. The old guard struggles to keep their secrets hidden, passing them down from master to apprentice in books that contain the esoteric wisdom of the world. But if magic's survival depends on secrets, then has the internet killed it? I believe we have to find new ways to create wonder.

I find a few mentions about Jones's show at Midnight. His reviews are the most cryptic I've ever read. Most begin with: 'I don't want to give away his show,' and end with: 'You need to see it for yourself.' One person writes, 'I'll call it magic because I don't know how else to describe it.' Someone on Reddit says bluntly, 'Elvis Jones is the devil.'

I square my shoulders. Time to go to Hell and see the devil.

*

It is Saturday night in the off-season in a city rumoured to be dead, but Midnight casino is jumping. Midnight's motto is, 'It's always Halloween at Midnight,' which makes it Atlantic City's meeting place for Goths, vamps, and zombies. Bats swoop from the high ceilings of the glittering red, black, and gold casino and spider webs lace the walls. Whenever a player hits a winning number at the slots, a woman shrieks through the loudspeakers, mimicking the knife-stabbing shower scene from *Psycho*.

Midnight's ear-splitting craziness intensifies during the Halloween season. Dogs bay, wolves howl at the moon, masked figures brush your cheeks, and skeletons dance around as if it's the Day of the Dead. A gory crew of zombies and ghouls play roulette. Dealers wearing Dracula wigs with white-streaked widow's peaks, their shoulders draped in black satin capes, lean over gaming tables. When they smile, they reveal fangs. Cocktail waitresses, hair dyed white-blonde or coal-black, serve drinks. They are visions to inspire a bloodsucker's lust: breasts squeezed into red and black bustiers, tiny frou-frou skirts, fishnet stockings, and thigh-high shiny black boots. The gamblers themselves are dressed in silver, black, and red, their skin studded, pierced, tattooed.

'Monster Mash' blasts in the lobby, where a costumed group is gathered. Skeletal fingers point to Bloodthirsty Bar, Fang's Deli, Coffin Café, and the Loch Ness Pool that bursts into a blood-soaked fountain every half hour. I pass the entrance to the Vamp Lounge, the gentleman's club where Misty and the Boardwalk Babes dance. A large poster shows her smiling playfully as she bends over in a tasselled bikini, miraculously managing to look innocent. A moment later I slow down in front of Coffin Café. Misty is at a corner table with Charlie. She's gesturing, he's listening. It looks intense, I won't interrupt.

I leave the glittering lobby and crowded casino area to follow a bloody amputated finger down a winding staircase to Hell. During World War Two, when the hotel was converted into a hospital, the basement theatre was a workshop where they made artificial limbs for wounded soldiers.

The door to Hell is draped with black satin. An usher, his face pierced in so many places I can't look at him without wincing, leads me through the small cobweb-draped black box theatre. Except for the stage, every inch is crammed with tables and chairs, and to my amazement, every seat is occupied. Punks and

Goths in sequins and spikes scowl at the stage. Mammoth bikers – tattooed, studded, black-booted – hold up sloshing skull-shaped goblets and yell for refills. I smell weed, perfumes, sweat, booze. Nearly everyone wears black leather. The Hunter could be almost any male in this room.

This is a rough crowd, and I do not envy Jones. I do not envy the people seated in the front row, either. Volunteer hell for a magic show.

At one end of the room, below the stage, a young, heavily tattooed guy with a sweep of long black hair slams his palms against hand-drums as if in a trance. He must be Crazy Wind.

The usher leads me to a table for two directly in front of centre stage. One seat is taken.

'Oh, no.' I step back. 'I can't–'

He sticks his punctured face in mine, and I shudder. 'It's the only empty seat in the house.'

As I sink into the chair, a hand pinches my thigh. With a snarl I turn to my companion at the table, a grizzled cowboy who looks like he wandered in from *Gunsmoke*. He hisses between his teeth. 'Sss, hot mama! Now we're cooking!'

The lights go out. The screech of chalk on a blackboard is followed by a man's voice: 'Testing, testing, testing, testing, testing, testing, testing...' and a sudden barking order to turn off cell phones.

'The fuck I will,' mutters Cowboy.

Okaay. It's going to be that kind of crowd. Poor Jones.

'And here we go,' says the loudspeaker voice with forced enthusiasm. 'Man, oh man, are you in for a treat. He's here! Back from his world tour to places far and wide.' He pauses. 'Genoa and Lackawanna County and the great Jake's Bar & Grill. By the way, a shout out to Jake and the gang for letting me – I mean, Elvis – sleep behind the bar... Anyway, he's here, back from his triumphant tour where he shattered records!'

'What kind of records?' A roar of laughter from the table to my left, where half a dozen bikers form a wall of black leather.

'Let's give a hearty Atlantic City welcome to the elegant, the elegiac and effervescent, the Electrifying Elvis Jones!'

About five people applaud. I'm one of them, simply out of habit, already pitying the guy who can't tape a decent intro for himself.

From the ink-black stage a voice calls, 'Turn on the lights.'

The room stays dark.

Jones growls, 'I'm here, dammit!'

I choke back a laugh. Electrifying Elvis, Amazing André, Magnificent Morelli. Gus the Great! Men and their oversized egos.

Blinding lights go on to curses and drunken cries from the bikers' table. I can't see their faces, only bandannas and the gleam of studs piercing their jackets.

Dressed in black, Electrifying Elvis slouches toward centre stage. He clutches a lopsided assortment of props, including a top hat, book, and oversized deck of cards. A woven bag with a beaded strap swings from his shoulder. Arms close to his chest, he gestures awkwardly. They forgot to give the poor sucker a table to set down his props. I scrunch in my chair. I can't believe this is Jones of the evil grin and mocking eyes. I wouldn't have recognised him.

He lifts the hand holding the deck of cards and waves. 'Hi.'

I'm in front, and I barely hear him.

Someone yells, 'Sing "Feelings."'

A man shouts, 'He's a magician, dickhead!'

'Then do some fucking magic!'

'I am the Electrifying Elvis Jones.' His voice breaks. I've seen it before: arrogant on the street, terrified on stage. This is going to be painful. If I weren't front and centre, I'd sneak out.

'I am now going to attempt to–' He clears his throat and says firmly. 'I am now going to read your minds.'

Shifting his props, he steps to the edge of the stage and peers into the audience. 'You, sir.'

He chose one of the bikers. Red bandanna on his head, he straddles his chair and kicks out his pointy cowboy boots. Jeez Louise, doesn't Elvis Jones know the first thing about selecting volunteers? Magic 101.

'Think of a number from one to ten. Okay? Now focus on that number. Okay? Now tell us the number.'

Red Bandanna growls, 'Three.'

'That's the number I was thinking of too.'

A beat passes. 'Huh?'

A woman cries, 'For fuck's sake, Jones, that's the stupidest trick I ever saw!'

I squint. Iridescent pink dots shimmer in her bright hair. Is that Dr. Lose, the Bone Whisperer I saw on TV?

'You, Madame. Think of a colour.'

'Dream on,' she says, gruff. 'You tell me first.'

It *is* Dr. Lose. The polka-dot ribbon, the orange mullet, the gruff voice. I remember that voice saying, 'Too many dead girls...'

Why is she here? Is she a magic lover? Is there a connection between the murders in the Pine Barrens and Elvis Jones?

'Yellow,' says Jones.

Dr. Lose snickers. 'Red.'

There is no air in this theatre.

'You drove here in a black Mercedes,' he informs a man with a bushy black beard.

'I took the bus.'

'You are worried about your mother,' he tells another man with a shaved head, wearing a long white butcher's coat.

'I would be, dawg, if she was still alive.'

Someone yells, 'Where'd you buy your magic license?'

Dr. Lose cries, 'Ebay!'

The woman is harsh but Jones deserves it. His incompetence is an insult to all magicians. Doesn't anyone love him enough to tell him?

Be kind, Moon. Maybe he's having a bad night.

I let that thought sink in, but no one's night is this bad. What the hell were Stormie and Van thinking? And what about all those online reviewers?

Choose me, idiot. I can help you through this. And set down the damned props. You look like you're on a shopping trip.

As if he hears me, he sets the props on the floor and holds up the cards. Half the deck spills out and falls to the stage. He scrambles to pick up the cards and slouches toward me with no sign of recognition. 'You, Miss. Shuffle this deck.'

I grab the cards before he drops them again. While I shuffle, I quickly scan the backs. Very subtle markings. A clever six-year-old could work with these. I shuffle, cut the deck, and hand it to him. *Keep it simple,* I tell him silently, then watch him perform a trick so convoluted I lose track after the seventh step, and I know card tricks. To make matters worse, he mumbles to himself.

What's wrong with the man? Behind me, everyone talks and jokes as if he isn't even onstage. If I could figure out the trick, I'd give him the answer he wants. But he lost me. And if he lost me, he sure as hell lost everyone else in the room. Conversations grow louder, the jeering obscene.

'... and the card you chose, Miss, is... ta dah!'

Ta dah?

As if once isn't pathetic enough, he repeats, 'Ta dah! Queen of Hearts. Turn it over, please.'

I turn the card. King of Spades.

If anyone wants to know why I hate bad magic and mediocre magicians, the answer is right here, in this card.

Elvis Jones stares, his eyes dark and intense. Now what? Should I lie and help him out? Instead of getting a good night's sleep, I'm wasting hours watching fourth-rate magic, hours I'll never get back.

'Miss! Tell everyone what your card is.' His voice shakes.

'Queen of Hearts.' I sound pretty shaky myself.

He actually spasms. I startled him. I startled myself. After a moment, he steps closer to me.

I'm helping you. Don't screw it up.

Sweat drips down his cheeks and throat. A terrible actor as well as magician.

At the next table, Red Bandanna demands, 'Lem-me see that card!'

'It's a scam,' says Dr. Lose.

Cowboy shouts, 'Show me the damn card!'

'Show us the card, dickhead,' someone snarls.

Shit. I got him in deeper. God, I wish I could get out of here. Over shouts from the crowd, Jones says, 'Show him the card, miss.'

Sorry, I tried.

I hold it up, and Cowboy gasps.

24

I turn it over and find myself face to face with the Queen of Hearts herself. *The Queen of Hearts!* I stare at Jones in shock. How did he change the card?

Cowboy grabs it from me. 'It is the fucking Queen!'

Elvis Jones leans closer. 'Give me the card, sir.'

Cowboy hands it to Jones, who holds it up.

'What is this card, sir?' he asks Red Bandanna. I notice his voice doesn't quaver.

Red Bandanna says, slow, 'Queen. Of. Fucking. Hearts.'

I release my breath. The card was in my hand the entire time. I did not look away from it, not for a second. It was the King of Spades. No way in hell Jones could have switched it. He can fool the humans but not someone who's been doing card tricks since she was six and who was trained by Declan Moon.

Jones walks from one end of the stage to the other, displaying the card. Clearly visible: the Queen of Hearts.

'Can I tell you a story?' Jones's golden voice is back.

With that voice you can tell us anything.

'It's a story about a boy...' He rolls up the sleeves of his shirt.

'Take it all off!' shrieks a woman, and someone titters.

'The boy caught a fever that paralysed his legs. After a year of treatments and surgery the doctors said he'd never walk again.'

He pushes the sleeves above his elbows. A vivid blue bird twists around his right arm from his wrist. The tattoo disappears under the sleeve. How far up does it go? To his bicep and shoulder? Does it curve around his chest and down his back?

'The boy lay in bed, stared out the window of his cabin and dreamed of being a bird. His mother's father worked with animals, especially birds and snakes. Some people called him a whisperer. The boy believed his grandfather was magic. A devil or a god, he was never sure.'

He rubs the tattoo absently. 'The grandfather opened the window of their cabin. Then he sat on a chair next to the boy's bed. "You have wings," said the old man. "You can fly." The boy touched his useless legs. "I can't walk," he said. "How can I fly?" "First, you must believe you have wings. Second, you can't be afraid to fall. You can't fly if you're afraid to fall..."'

Jones's long fingers stroke the bird from elbow to wrist, slow and sensuous strokes, over and over.

'The boy imagined himself flying over wild waves surrounded by sky, sea, and sand. Wind whipped his feathers, salt air burned....'

That voice, golden and warm, hypnotises me. The accompanist's hand drumming, soft and relentless, follows the voice. 'White birds surrounded the grandfather and lifted him in his chair until he rose to the ceiling.'

All I hear is his voice, hushed and tender.

All I see are his fingers stroking his arm faster and harder.

'Birds clung to the boy's arms as if they were his wings. They lifted his legs and carried him up... up... up until he faced his grandfather. "You see," said the old man. "You can fly."'

The head emerges first. It sprouts from his arm.

Then the feathered wings.

Impossible. Of course, it's impossible for a seagull to emerge from a man's arm. The idea of it, let alone the reality, is primal, mythic, terrifying. But there it is, in front of us: a real live seagull. Small white head, steel grey back and wings, an unwieldy enormous bird that Jones holds onto with great difficulty.

A woman in the audience lets out a cry as raucous and haunting as the cry of a seagull. It isn't me, though I feel the cry deep inside.

The bird squawks, a baby's first cry. A great tide of air sweeps through the room as if we all released our breath at the same instant.

'He's not a pet,' Jones says apologetically. 'I call him Bird because every name is a form of prison.'

Oh, I understand that.

'Imagine being named Elvis. It sets up all sorts of expectations. It's only when you leave all that behind that you can soar. You can fly.'

He turns slowly in a circle, then faster. And faster. The seagull flies with him, his head and chest gleaming in the dark theatre, his wings beating in the air. With a shrill laugh, 'Ai-ai-ai!' the bird flies free. The drums grow frenzied, the dance ferocious, the mix of man and bird and drums enthralling and unsettling. It reminds me of the eerie nights when Auntie Maze communes onstage with Nellie Moon and delivers messages that are uncannily accurate and impossible to explain. Though Da does his best.

Cold wind blows from the stage. My neck tingles.

The drumming stops.

The room is silent.

Gradually, he stops turning and faces us, hand pressed to his chest, bird perched on his shoulder. '*This* is why I love magic,' he says, breathless. 'It's not about tricks or fooling you. It's about pushing the limits of who we are and what we can do. Think of Houdini. He broke out of jail cells, locked trunks, straitjackets, and ropes to show us no lock can hold us, no chains keep us down, no jail imprison us.'

A crystal goblet appears in his hand. We watch it fill with dark red liquid. 'Shiraz. Sorry I don't have enough to share but it's the only way I can calm Bird.'

I've performed the same Liquid Magic illusion. I need to ground myself. I am not a human watching magic for the first time. I've breathed, swallowed and practiced magic since I was a child. It can all be rationalised.

'He's afraid I'll... lock him inside again.' Jones sips from the glass. 'He's right to be afraid.'

He extends his arm. The tattoo has disappeared. His flesh is the colour of raw honey.

The seagull lowers his bill – yellow, with a black ring around the end. Jones tilts the glass and pours wine down the bird's throat – does a seagull even have a throat? – until the goblet is empty. The bird rests his small head against the magician's shoulder. Two fierce animals, trusting each other.

He sets the empty glass on an invisible shelf. It remains suspended as he turns around slowly, his back to the audience for several seconds. The seagull's head is visible over Jones's shoulder. He turns and faces us again. The bird is gone.

I hear gasps.

He holds out his arms and says ruefully, 'Bird hates when I do that.' The tattoo glows vivid glorious blue.

My heart beats fast. It's more than the magical production and vanish of the seagull. The tattoo turning from visible to invisible to visible again. It's the magician himself. Elvis Jones's shirt is blue when I distinctly noticed he was dressed all in black. He stands taller than I remembered. Unshaven, hair tousled. *Here* is Jinx's sexy devil. Was the awkward magician also a tattoo branded into the flesh? This guy holds himself differently and surveys us with a lazy, sardonic smile. His gaze stops at me. I suck in my breath. There is a trace of sadness in his self-mocking smile. The smile of a boy who dreamed of being a bird.

In a swift, graceful move, he crouches and picks up his shoulder bag and props. He asks us to please not share what we saw tonight so others get the full experience. And then, with a bow, he drawls just like Elvis Presley, 'Thank you, thank you very much.

And a heap of gratitude to Crazy Wind, who does magic with drums.'

Da often says that the highest tribute a magician can receive is silence when the audience is too stunned to applaud. When the applause for Elvis Jones comes, it is sporadic, stunned, like claps of thunder.

He walks off stage. I wouldn't be surprised if he flew, but he walks, like any other human.

No one moves. We stare at the crystal goblet hovering in the air. After a moment it shivers and falls, shattering in the exact spot where the magician stood. The crash sounds like a small fireworks explosion. Overhead, the loudspeaker crackles, screeches, and moans. A desultory man's voice: 'You can turn on your cell phones.'

Lights go on, and we look at each other sheepishly. What just happened? Is the show over? Will he return?

'What the fuck!' explodes Cowboy.

Nervous laughter sweeps through Hell.

25

As people file out of Hell, I approach the forensic anthropologist. 'Dr. Lose, I saw you on the news. The Bone Whisperer. You were in the Pine Barrens.'

She grunts and wriggles into a camouflage Army jacket. Her red hair is cropped in a spiky mullet like Jinx's assistant, Dasha.

'I'm Lucy Moon, a magician.'

Dr. Lose takes that in. 'What's going on? A murder of magicians sweeping in like a murder of crows.'

'Are you here because of Jane Doe?' I ask.

'I'm here to see a magic show, that's all. But is this magic?'

She's shaken. So am I. By the magic, and by the magician.

She says slowly, 'His show makes me think of tales in the Pine Barrens.'

'What kind of tales?'

'The kind that make you believe in magic that spills beyond the stage.'

I follow her gaze to the stage where half a dozen people take selfies.

'Do you think the story about his grandfather is true?' she asks.

'I don't know. Why?'

She stares at the selfie-takers. 'Magic passed from a grandfather to his grandson, like a gene.'

I invite her to Stormie's and my opening night next Wednesday in the Widow. 'I'll leave you a ticket at the Box Office.'

She picks up her purse, a shiny rectangle disguised as a lockbox. 'I'll try to come to your show. Goodnight, Lucy.'

She clumps toward the door, a strangely vulnerable figure with a red mullet and combat boots. I picture her hacking through weeds and thorns in the Pine Barrens.

'Can I call you if I have any questions?'

She turns. 'About what?'

'About crime and... I found Van Kim's body. She was my friend.'

'I'm sorry.' She frowns. 'I don't know what you want from me, but I'm not at liberty to discuss details of an ongoing case.'

Without another word, she strides out of Hell.

Jones's accompanist glides toward the stage, silky hair swaying.

I intercept him. 'Crazy Wind, I'd like to talk to Jones.'

'You're not the only one.' He gestures to the selfie-takers at the other end of the stage. 'Members of El's fan club.'

'He has a fan club?' I say faintly.

'They come at least twice a week. They used to talk along with El, like Rocky Horror. We had to stop them.'

'Is he that scripted?'

'That's part of his gift.'

'Do you mean the boy who couldn't walk but learnt to fly?'

'I'm not giving away his secrets.' After a moment he says, 'You tried to cover for him.'

Heat creeps up my throat. 'He's a fellow magician.'

His mocking grin reminds me of Jones's. 'Yeah, right.'

I hold out my hand. 'I'm Lucy Moon.'

We shake. 'Wait a minute. Lucy Moon? As in *the* Moons?' His grin deepens. 'Ha! Does El know? He tried to fool a Moon. That's classic. And he got you, didn't he?'

I force a smile. 'Yeah, he got me.'

'Ouch,' he says with mock sympathy. 'And you wanna get back at him.'

'Oh, yeah.'

'After the show he takes Bird for a run on the beach. He likes to be alone.'

'Where?'

'Head north past Midnight.' His eyes shine with mischief. 'Tell him Crazy sent you.'

26

Hands in my pockets, one clutching the Swiss Army knife, I walk on the boardwalk along the railing. Shrubs and sand-brush poke through like nosy neighbours. The sky, a heavy, starless curtain, merges with rolling waves. A few stragglers, heads lowered against the wind, move in the opposite direction, returning to lights and action. I pass Showboat and Ocean Resort Casino – the resurrected Revel, that silver monolith. Condos in various stages of construction appear abandoned.

If I keep heading north, I'll reach the half-moon where the boardwalk curves and continues along Absecon Inlet. And if I keep going, I'll see the Absecon Lighthouse, where Van and I stood on the last morning of her life. I know this stretch of beach intimately. I grew up here, went to lifeguarding camp, raced my bike, flew kites with Stormie. Tonight, it feels new, as if I've never been here before. Great magic does that: it turns the familiar strange.

A seagull flies toward me, shrieking, 'Ai-ai-ai-ai!' Swoops low, claws first, and smacks its hard head against mine. Sparks, tiny stars, explode before my eyes.

The seagull flies to Elvis Jones, in his eternal black hoodie, who waits below on the sand. Aha, it's Bird. I recognise jealousy, whether it's a bird or a human. I lean against the railing to watch. Jones dips low, pretends to fall, and leaps in the air. The seagull cackles in delight. As if the beach is a stage, Jones and Bird swoop, duck and butt heads until the bird envelops the man with his wings and shriek-laughs again. They frolic – the only word that fits.

When they tumble to the sand in a mass of wings and limbs and laughter, my heart clutches. It is wondrous and tender and strange like a fairy tale... though I remind myself these tales are much darker than we remember. The prince is not the prize he seems to be, the woods are deep, and there's always a wicked witch lurking.

I go down a few wooden steps that lead from boardwalk to beach and sit on the bottom step. This man and his bird are true magic, the kind Auntie Maze talks about.

When Jones turns around, he's laughing. The instant he sees me, the laugh dies. Bird squawks in a fury and flies around my head. I'm an intruder in their private moment.

Jones scowls and turns away.

You can't do magic like his without going somewhere deep and dark. He needs time to become Elvis Jones again. I also need time after a show to decompress. Perversely, the fact that he wants me to leave makes me want to stay.

After a few minutes he moves closer and sits next to me. Large, male, hot, and sweaty, emanating his dark energy, but he doesn't scare me. At least not at this moment. He opens a bag of fast food and scatters burgers and French fries on the sand that Bird immediately devours.

His shoulder brushes mine as he bends over to feed Bird from a big paper cup.

'What's in that cup?'

'Strawberry milkshake. His favourite.'

'Why?'

'Good question. I prefer vanilla. How about you?'

I give him a look, and he smiles, the bland smile that ruffles every hair on my body. The words force themselves out: 'You are awesome.'

'Thank you.' A side glance, almost shy. The boy who dreamed of being a bird because he wanted to be free. My heart quivers, a crazy little leap.

'Onstage,' I add, to bring myself down to earth.

'You nearly threw me off, you know.' That golden voice burns through my veins.

'I was trying to help.'

'Mmm.' Another side glance. 'No one ever lied for me before.'

He brings out another bag of fries and feeds Bird, one fry at a time.

'How did you do it?'

A low laugh. 'Aw, Moon, ask me something easy. Give me your hand.'

'Why?' My voice so sharp Bird stops eating to move closer.

'So he knows you're my friend,' he says, mild. 'You're not out to hurt me.'

I let out a jarring giggle. What is wrong with me? 'Is his name really Bird?'

'He has another name. Just between him and me.'

'What kind of bird is he?'

'A ring-billed gull.'

'Is it legal to own a seagull?'

He winces. 'Legal is a word I try not to use. You could say I grandfathered my way to having a wild bird.'

'Do you really have a grandfather?'

'Yes, Lucy Moon, I really do.' He slants me a look. 'Do you?'

'Of course I do.' Why did he ask me that? Is he probing for information or am I being paranoid? I clear my throat. 'His name was Artagan Moon. He and my grandmother, Isobel, founded Moon Magick in Ireland...' While I'm talking, Bird pecks at my feet. 'What does he want?'

'He senses your hostility.'

'I think he's jealous.' Bird head-butts my calf, pokes his beak against my legs. I squeeze them together.

'Talk to him. He needs to know you're not an enemy.'

Feeling like an idiot, I smile. 'Hi, Mr. Bird. I come as a friend.'

He pushes harder, as if searching. I set my hands on my knees and say brightly, 'You were great onstage, Mr. Bird. A real natural.'

He caws, sudden and strident. Thanking me? He jumps and laughs.

'He's showing off for you.'

'You're a great actor, Mr. Bird, but I don't like you that way. It's me, not you. I hope we can still be friends.'

A muffled sound next to me. Not quite a laugh. 'Unlucky in love, Bird and me.'

'How did you tame a seagull?'

'He's not tame. He's trained. That's very different. I found him when he was a baby. Wounded on the beach. I took him in and hand-fed him. I had to work to gain his trust. As he got stronger, he started to fly in the cage. After a while when I opened the cage, he flew right to me.'

I like the tenderness in his voice when he talks about Bird. 'One of my cousins, Mick Moon, has an act with doves. I worked with him a few times. The doves hated me.'

'I worked with doves too. I prefer my birds big and wild.'

That voice talking about big wild birds and a seagull trying to get between my legs. Would any other woman find this combination erotic? And why are the three of us suddenly melded together, Jones pressed so tightly to my side that if I turn we'll bump noses?

He holds out his palm. His large, warm hand covers mine like a turtle shell. I close my eyes and let him guide my palm over the seagull's feathers and nape, from soft to coarse. 'Bird, meet Lucy. I think we can trust her.'

'Does that mean you'll tell me how you did the Queen of Hearts?'

Another side-glance. 'Come on, you know I suck at cards.'

I snort. 'You pretend to suck at cards. You lead us down one path and then hit us with the unexpected.'

'Huh. I used to do card tricks at kids' birthday parties. I was so bad the kids threw things at me... You think that's funny.'

'I can't help it. What did they throw?'

'Whatever they had. Once the birthday boy threw a piece of cake.'

'Poor Jones.'

'Yeah, I hear the pity. People never laughed at you?'

I give him a look. 'I was an angel – my father's idea, the Christmas show. I'm in feathery wings and a harness, attached to wires and swinging across the stage, tossing white confetti. You're not saying anything.'

'I'm picturing it.' He tightens his hold over my fingers. We stroke the bird the way he stroked the tattoo on his arm.

'I smashed into the backdrop...' I cringe, remembering the tangle of feathers and wires as I tumbled to the stage.

'Yeah? Then what?'

'The reviewer from *Magic Magazine* said, "Some Moons are not meant to rise."'

'Poor Moon.' His eyes gleam. There it is again, the smile lurking behind his mouth. 'But you don't need a harness and feathers. You can fly.'

I wriggle my fingers under his, and he releases my hand. 'I cannot fly.'

He touches my shoulder, digs his fingertips into the flesh. 'Feel that knob? That's where your wings sprout.'

He says it so matter-of-factly that at first I don't react. The pressure of his fingers massaging the tight knob of flesh. I don't want him to stop.

'I can show you how to fly...' His voice merges with the waves and wind. We lean against each other in silence until Bird shrieks. With a whir of wings, he soars around us.

Jones and I jerk our heads up. At the same moment we stumble to our feet and fall into each other.

Okay, I fall into him, and he catches me. His arms enfold me like warm, strong wings. For one crazy, beautiful instant I feel safe, standing heart to heart with Elvis Jones. His throat pulses against my cheek, his heart races against mine, and he whispers my name in that Jameson voice. Too golden, like the sun burning in the night.

I push him away. I'm letting myself get distracted. My friend was murdered. I need to find out who did it. 'I have to go.'

'Give me a minute to get Bird in his cage.'

I crouch and pick up food wrappers while he croons to Bird. He's a bird-whisperer. I almost let him become a Lucy-whisperer. I throw the scraps in the trashcan.

Bird shrieks through the bars, the sound of his betrayal heart-rending. He reminds me of Auntie Maze's cat Aidell each time my aunt dares leave the house without her. 'Must you lock him in?'

He covers the cage with a cloth, and we climb the steps to the boardwalk. 'Too many people here. I have a place a little farther away, more private, where I can set him free.'

I forgot how dark and deserted this stretch of boardwalk is. I need to return to lights and people. He keeps up with my quick pace as we return to Midnight.

'I'm sorry,' he says, quiet. 'I scared you.'

'I'm not...' I begin, then swallow the lie. He did scare me on the beach. He didn't grab or kiss me, didn't even hold me with force. I felt safe until he whispered my name, and every part of me burst into shivers. I want to ask him if he argued with Van the night of her murder, but I'll wait until we return to lights and civilisation.

He shifts the large cage to his other hand. 'It's almost two. When we get to Midnight, I'll leave Bird in my room. Where do you want me to take you?'

I should go to my room in Midnight and sleep, but I thrum under the skin, where his golden voice sparked my nerve endings. I feel like Van, burning to take a risk and go somewhere I've never been.

As we walk, I hear myself say, 'Let's go for a drink.'

'Now? Well, the Speakeasy is open till four.'

I draw in a sharp breath. The matchbox in Van's cosmetic bag. 'Do you know the Lollipop Club?'

He hesitates. 'I've heard of it.'

'I want to see it, but I don't want to go alone.'

A long pause. 'Let's go.'

27

Elvis leads me through the Midnight parking garage and proudly introduces me to a beat-up jeep. 'Lucy, meet Lenny. He's the real thing, a 1987 Jeep Wrangler.'

Tufts of stuffing poke out from Lenny's seats. A canvas folding roof sags in the middle. When Elvis slams his door, the entire jeep rattles.

'Magic not paying off?' I click my tongue with sympathy.

He tightens his lips, jiggles the gearshift and steps on the gas. One, two, three times before the car sputters, and we jolt. The engine heaves, and a thin pillar of smoke rises from the edge of the hood.

We turn on Pacific Avenue. Lenny coughs like a chain smoker, reminding me of Uncle Conor Moon, an old grump never without a cigarette or complaint. As we chug loudly down the road, I keep one hand in my pocket, gripping the Swiss Army knife, but at the pace we're moving I'll jump out if he tries anything. 'I think you need a new car,' I yell over Lenny's coughing.

'Hey! Don't let him hear you.' The outrage in Elvis's voice is palpable. 'A few parts, and he'll be good as new. You don't get rid of a classic because he's lost his shine.'

A man who heals wounded birds and ancient cars; who fixes things. I hope he doesn't break them first. Before we left, I messaged Stormie and told her I was going to the Lollipop with Elvis Jones.

Her response: three flame emojis and one knife.

I'm on guard, knife in one pocket and phone in the other.

He turns to me. 'I guess you drive a shiny new Moon-mobile.'

I picture my old Festiva. 'No way. You can't break into a new car.'

He raises an eyebrow. Really. 'Is that what you do for fun?'

'I'm always losing my keys so my cousin taught me to break in with a wire hanger.'

'You could say, "unlock the car."'

'Breaking in sounds more exciting.'

He smiles – the real thing – but by the time we chug into the parking lot of the Lollipop Club, I'm exhausted and cold and wishing I'd just gone to sleep. We're in Egg Harbor City, the edge of the Pine Barrens, where Jane Doe was found. I've driven down Black Horse Pike many times, but I've never stopped at any of the seedy bars and clubs.

I step onto the gravel lot. I feel I'm getting closer to the mystery of what happened to Van. The Lollipop is sandwiched between a sleazy motel and a gas station that looks abandoned. Across the street, a fight is going on in front of a bar.

'Don't stare,' says Elvis. He steers me toward a red neon sign, *The Lo__lip__p Cl__b*. The club's crumbling black-painted façade is decorated with an enormous painted red lollipop and faded posters of nearly naked women.

The bouncer wears fingerless leather gloves and bumps fists with Elvis. When I hold up my fist, he grunts and turns away.

Elvis insists on paying the cover charge. I tell him I'll pay for drinks. The bouncer opens the door, and a pounding beat crashes into us like a tidal wave.

For a moment I can't move. Drums stomp like boots in my chest. The ban on smoking hasn't reached the Lollipop. I smell cigarettes and weed, spilled beer, sweaty perfume, and something else thick enough to slice with a knife.

Through red and blue strobe lights I glimpse three dancers – one onstage, another at the bar, and a third gyrating around a pole that Elvis tells me is called the Lollipop Stick. As far as I can tell, I'm the fourth woman in the club. A dozen men sit in front of the stage and at the bar, watching the dancers. Two men in suits, their backs to the women, gesture with cigarettes.

Elvis takes my hand and leads me towards the bar past empty cups and bottles and peanut shells strewn on the floor. 'Safest thing to order here is beer,' he whispers in my ear.

I'm too nervous to ask how he knows. He orders while I place a twenty on the bar. A small bowl holds matchboxes marked with the red lollipop. I'm in the right place. Van was here. Maybe I'm sitting where she did. My heart does a crazy dance. I'm going to find something. I wish Stormie was here too.

The bartender sets down two foaming beers. I'm about to ask him if he remembers Van when he says, 'Slap down a Hamilton.'

'Fifteen bucks a beer in a dive,' I mutter to Elvis.

'You're not paying for the beer. You're paying for this.' He twirls my stool so I face the stage.

The dancer onstage leans over, her back to us, her large muscular ass vibrating – one cheek, then the other. She twists around slowly, still shaking her booty. Tall, white, and big-boned, she wears pasties that barely cover her nipples and a G-string. The control she has over her booty awes me. So does her bright smile, as confident as Stormie's. She winds strands of hip-length blonde hair around her floppy breasts and wiggles into the audience. Men tuck bills in her thong.

The song changes to sultry neo-soul, a woman's breathy voice confiding that she can't wait for it, not a minute longer, not a second, not a fraction of a second. The lights shine on the pole dancer. Pale, with a long dark ponytail, she wriggles up the Lollipop Stick, turns herself upside down, spreads her legs and shimmies down, ponytail swinging. For an agonising moment I worry she'll lose control and fly down and land on her head. In the nick of time, she catches herself, grips the pole with her thighs and wriggles to the floor.

As I sip my beer and watch the dancers, I notice the clear divide between men and women. The women seem to hold the power. The men are a sea of Hunters – hungry eyes and hands – yelling, touching, stuffing bills wherever they can. Are the women working here by choice? Do they get paid more than female magicians?

The third stripper, a beautiful Black woman in a low-cut rhinestone bra and thong, sways toward Elvis and me. Slender with a platinum Afro and curvy golden body, she smiles. I set down my beer. My hands are clammy. I feel strange – a woman watching another woman dance to arouse desire in men.

She stops in front of me, not Elvis. 'I'm Nya.'

'Hi. I'm Lucy.'

She leans forward and pushes up the cups of her bra, squeezing her breasts together. I'm more than clammy, I'm sweating. Shaking her hips, she smiles – at Elvis? At me?

I don't want to see the avid hunger in his eyes. Then it strikes me, of course, she wants money. Without looking away from her, I fumble in my pocket. She pushes closer and presses her thighs against my legs, reminding me of Bird earlier tonight. I blink sweat from my eyes.

She pushes up her breasts again, inviting me to... touch?

I meet her laughing eyes. She nods.

As I reach toward her cleavage, she wiggles and leans closer. I touch the flesh between her breasts and pull out a card. Oh God. A playing card. Sweaty and damp, musk-scented. She grins at my shock, and the men around the bar cheer.

Fooled twice tonight. First, Elvis. Now, her. This time, it's the context. I didn't expect magic in a strip club. And this is excellent magic. I turn over the card. Queen of Hearts. Inevitable. This Queen is naked, but she still rules over Hearts, and mine quivers again. I'm following breadcrumbs that lead to the Hunter. Maybe the Lollipop is his playground, and he's watching me? Did he send this dancer as a warning?

I dig into my pocket, pull out a bill, and turn to give it to the dancer. She is pressed against Elvis, his arm around her.

A shaft of – it can't be jealousy – pierces through me. But what the hell is going on? Do they know each other? The card trick. Of course. Elvis Jones gets around. Time to ask him where he was Tuesday night and why he argued with Van.

I lean closer. Nya murmurs, 'El, baby, I'm sorry about Van...'

He says a few words I can't hear. Damn. I tilt my head toward them.

Nya says, '... and she danced with him that night.'

Is she talking about Gus? *He's a great dancer.* Did Van meet Gus here? Is he her connection to the Lollipop? If so, why didn't he mention it? Instead, he was quick to point out that he saw her argue with Charlie.

Nya whispers. I lean toward them, and suddenly she's in my face. Beaming. 'Got you good, didn't I?' She sticks out her hip.

I push the bill into her thong, and she looks me up and down. 'You scared of your body? You got titties in that man's suit, don't you?'

'I got 'em,' I retort. 'Doesn't mean I have to show 'em.'

'Doesn't mean you have to hide 'em, either.' She lifts her girls again, squeezing them together. 'Own your titties, girlfriend.'

'Thanks for the tip, Nya.'

'You're welcome, Lucy.' She winks and struts toward the other men at the bar.

When I trust myself, I twist on my barstool. Elvis watches her laugh as she accepts the bills raining on her.

'El, baby.'

He stiffens, then turns to face me. 'Yeah?'

'You taught her the magic, didn't you?'

He lifts one shoulder.

'You come here a lot?'

'Now and then.' He coughs. 'Nya's a quick learner.'

'Fifteen minutes to closing,' says the bartender. 'Time for your second round.'

'I'll take care of it.' Elvis sets a bill on the counter.

The lights dim, and a new song begins – a man's husky whisper against a hard, relentless beat: 'There's no one but you you you...'

The three performers mill through the crowd, dancing up close and personal for the men, thrusting breasts, hips, and asses in the men's faces. I'm scared for them, and a little envious.

The man sings, 'I want you.'

Words I've never said to anyone, ever. Pitiful, but I always believed desire was based on trust, and I never trusted any man enough, not even Amazing André. We had sex, but I guarded my inner heart to the explosive end – thankfully! With André I never felt this ache in my belly, the need to... to...

I squirm on the bar stool. My skin pulses, a trapped animal struggling to escape. *You scared of your body?*

No! But the man's suit suffocates me. I tug at the collar to loosen the tie. In my tight-shouldered jacket and shirt, high-waisted trousers, and blocky men's shoes, I'm the anti-stripper. The only flesh visible besides my face is a triangle of throat and my hands. I extend my arms and wiggle my fingers. My hands are small, a challenge for lifts and vanishes, but they are strong and graceful, my favourite part of my body. I appreciate the strength in my arms, abs, and thighs, but I worked too hard to get them. The hands are mine, and the truth is they wanted to claw the beautiful Nya, or Elvis himself.

With a shudder I lower myself from the stool. I want to dance. Not for him. Not for anyone else. For me. I close my eyes and shift my hips to the beat, the hypnotic beat. Raise my arms above my head, stretching the jacket seams, and sway them like heavy palm leaves in a tropical breeze. My hips move sultry and slow to a beat that tastes like rum. I'm dancing barefoot on a sunny beach… *I want you, I want you, I want you…*

I open my eyes, lazy and full. Elvis leans forward on the bar stool, watching me with a heavy dark gaze. I move slow and easy until I press against his knees. I'm not drunk. I just want to forget Lucy Moon and all her defences for five minutes and let this shameless creature I've become have her way.

I look into his eyes and sway in front of him.

He slides from the stool. Eyes glittering, nostrils flaring, he grips my hips and presses against me. *Sexy devil.* Burning mouth to my ear: 'What do you want?'

Nothing. This. I don't know.

He breathes in my ear. A shiver zigzags through me – from my ear all the way down to my toes. A long winding journey. I clutch his shoulders and lower my face to the hollow of his throat – the prickle point that warns me of danger. His throat is open, vulnerable. His skin, smooth and hot. The smell of him – salt, bird, sand, ocean, sweat – brings me back to the beach where he, Bird, and I pressed against each other. I rub my nose and mouth against the sloping curve of his neck and burrow like a cat into his heat. He moans. My lips move against his throat. Between a kiss and a nuzzle, animal to animal, crane to seagull.

He lowers his face and kisses the curve of my throat. Desire spreads like wildfire and scorches my flesh. Nothing to do with trust. *I want you, I want you, I want you…*

Eyes sparkling like black diamonds, he touches my cheek. 'Lucy–'

The music stops. Lights shine bright. He releases me and steps away. I almost forgot we were in the Lollipop.

The dancers join the men around the bar and greet many by

name, teasing and joking with them, same as the Moons mingling with the audience after a show. I wouldn't have expected such friendly intimacy in a strip club. In the light Nya glows, a golden angel with a mischievous smile.

The stage dancer's blonde hair is a wig and her belly flops over her thong, but she has a kind word for every man in the place, and they clearly adore her.

From the neck down, the pole dancer resembles a gymnast – short and compact with thick muscled thighs – but her expression is vacant, her face clammy-pale, her heavily made-up eyes bloodshot, her ponytail greasy. She looks stoned out of her mind. Both she and the stage dancer greet Elvis as El and hug him.

While he talks to Nya, he watches me. My cheeks burn from the heat of his gaze. The absolute worst time for desire to kick in. Still reeling from the shock of Van's murder, the Hunter and the Queen of Hearts tracking me through the night, as if they know where I'm going before I do. I'll ask about the Hunter and then clear out. I'll start with the stage dancer. As I walk toward her, a door against the back wall opens, and a man steps out. Short dark hair, ruddy face, black leather jacket.

The man in the third row!

28

The man lifts his hand in a signal and disappears behind the door again.

I head toward the door.

Elvis sets his hand on my shoulder. 'Where are you going? They're closing.'

'The man who went in the back room. Who is he?'

'Rex Saylor, the owner of the club.'

'I need to talk to him.'

'Why didn't you tell me you wanted Rex?' He sounds exasperated.

I give him a full look. 'Why didn't you tell me you were a regular, El baby?'

He leads me across the club to a black-painted door. 'He's scolding Trudy.' At my blank look, he says, 'The Lollipop Stick dancer. She's having problems.'

The door bursts open. The drugged pole dancer staggers out, bloodshot eyes, sickly pale. She gives Jones a dazed look. 'Hey, El.'

'Be good to yourself, Trudy. You're worth it.'

'Trying.'

I enter an office cold as an icebox that reeks of cigarette smoke and stale air. Rex stands behind the desk, phone pressed to his ear. Ruddy cheeks, non-existent lips. Mid-forties, greying hair, a deep indentation between his eyebrows. Cigarette in the corner of his mouth, he lowers the phone. 'Lucy Moon. What can I do for you?'

I hug myself. Jeez, it's cold in here. 'You came to our opening night. You were at Van's memorial. Why?'

He fixes that hungry, hard gaze on me. 'What's this about?'

'Van was my friend. I'm trying to figure out–'

'Hey.' He holds up a large hand with thick, stubby fingers.

'Don't try to pin nothing on me.'

'How did Van know you?'

I hear a sharp yelp from behind his desk. Rex looks down and mutters a few words.

'What's that?'

'I need to close up. We done here?'

I ignore his question and move towards the desk. What is he hiding? A dog? A prisoner? I lock eyes with a boy hunched over his phone. Headphones, mouth open. A kid, about ten or eleven, playing games on his phone. After a moment, he lowers his head and returns to the game.

'Your son?'

'Yeah. The ex-wife dropped him off.'

Close-up, Rex is freckled, like his boy. And the ring on his pinkie finger is made of chewing gum wrappers. 'Van did magic for him.'

Of course she did. 'She gave you a ticket to our show. But you came alone.'

'The ex-wife took the kid.' He shrugs. 'She brought him back today. He's still mad he missed the show.'

'I'll give you tickets.'

His son gives me a thumbs up.

'Van was a sweet girl.' Rex's gravelly voice.

'Do you know anything about what happened to her?'

'My guess is she pissed off the wrong person or trusted the wrong guy. It ain't hard in this town. Now, I gotta go.'

'One more question, please. How did you meet Van?'

'She came to the club.'

'By herself? Did someone bring her?'

'People show up all the time. They don't need an escort to come here.' But he's not looking at me – he's glaring over my shoulder. I turn in time to see Elvis Jones walking away.

29

I'm on his heels. Back in the club, only a handful of people remain. Heart pounding, I grab his arm. 'Talk to me, Jones.'

He stops but keeps his head lowered. 'Not here,' he mutters. 'Not now.'

'You said you barely knew Van, but you brought her to the Lollipop. Will you tell me the truth?'

He grits the words, 'I told you this isn't the time or place.'

I can't look at him, can't listen to him. I feel sick. Shades of André. What an idiot I am.

I rush outside. In the past hour winter blew in. While I check my Uber app, the front door of the club opens. Elvis Jones steps out. 'Lucy! I'll drive you back.'

'I'm not going anywhere with you.'

'Come on, let's get out of here. I'll explain later.'

'You lied to me. "I barely knew Van." Yeah, the way you barely knew the Lollipop.' I swing out my fist. 'Who the hell are you?'

'You want it to be me, don't you? That way you can pretend nothing's happening between us.'

What an asshole. 'Nothing is happening between us.'

'Okay, I lied to you. I'm sorry. But what about you?'

I stiffen, feel the blow coming.

'I have a theory, Lucy.'

He doesn't move toward me, but the threat is clear in his voice.

'I don't want to hear it. Get away from me.'

He aims his shot like a bullet: 'See, I don't think you're a Moon.'

I rear back. 'You're crazy!'

'Am I? Tell me who you really are.'

This man is dangerous. I need to get away from him. This second. I run around the club to call an Uber. Or Storm. Or both. I must get out of here. Why doesn't Rex put up lights behind the club? The air stinks of rotting garbage, marshy swamps.

I hear footsteps. I smell him in the dark, wild and untamed, like his seagull. What if he killed Van? I press against the shadowy wall and pull out my knife. Click it open.

The only light comes from moon rays clawing the ground like bony fingers. I step out blindly, knife in hand.

'Lucy, don't go out there!'

'Don't come near me! I have a knife!'

'I'm not going to hurt you!'

His voice is getting closer. Twisting away from him, I trip over a rock and fall smack on my knees and elbows.

Pain surges up my legs.

The phone flies out of my hand, but I killer-grip the knife and aim it high. With my other hand I scrabble at a wall of dirt. I've fallen into a shallow ditch. Dry, not marshy. But it reeks of rot and decay. A dead animal? We're at the edge of the Barrens, where anything can happen.

My palm hits the dirt and touches a cold object. Slick and hard. It feels wrong. Terrifyingly wrong. I try to crawl back but thorny vines tangle around my knee and hold me fast.

I reach out again with trembling fingers and touch... the same cold, slippery object.

Footsteps approach. Jones's voice just above me. 'Lucy, for fuck's sake, let's get out of here. We'll talk. Just come with me.'

His phone light darts until it finds me. It flashes on the ground, illuminating my fingers clutching... oh shit. Oh, God, no! A woman's hand. Chipped red fingernails. A woman. Black insects crawling from her mouth.

Jones crouches low, near me, and shines the light on her face.

Not insects.

Black petals.

30

'Stop screaming!' The bouncer with the fingerless gloves. He shakes a fist in my face. 'Shut the fuck up.'

I close my mouth and stare at him in shock. He holds out his hand and pulls me up. I stagger to my feet. I ache everywhere. My throat is cracked.

I hear someone running toward us. Rex Saylor. 'What the fuck happened to the light?'

'Smashed,' says the bouncer.

'What's going on?' Rex squints at me. 'Lucy Moon. Why are you yelling?'

He aims his phone light at me, on Jones, and the body. 'Fucking hell, no.'

A figure fleets past and crouches at the ditch. A shriek shatters the sky. 'It's Gina!' cries Nya. 'Oh, Rex. It's Gina.'

Rex's phone light exposes the bloated face and body, skin puffed out and stretched. I wince at small gouges, where insects fed. Her lips are full, slightly parted. Black petals peek out. Just like Van. A choker of red brush burns circles her neck.

Before anyone can tell Nya not to touch the body, she bends over and lifts the woman's hand. The hand I had grasped.

I move closer. Jones's light illuminates blue letters tattooed on her wrist. A name: LAURA.

Nya lowers Gina's hand. 'Her daughter's name is Laura. Rex used to–' She glances at Rex, then at Elvis Jones.

Rex used to work with her? Hook up with her?

'Gina was a sweet girl,' says Rex. 'Till the drugs got to her.'

Within minutes the police and forensic team arrive. So do members of the media, the local paper, and Channel 10. Not Pam Woodson, but a male reporter I've seen on TV. And my old friends,

Detectives Torres and Wax, who immediately shoot me dark, suspicious looks. The first thing Wax says to me: 'I can't think of a single good reason for you to be here, Lucy Moon.'

The next hour goes past in a blur of loud voices, horrifying sights, gruesome smells that knot my chest and belly. *Putrefaction*, says a police technician.

'Who found her?' asks Detective Torres.

Nya points at me. 'She did.' Her voice suddenly high-pitched and childlike.

Detective Wax sticks his huge jaw in my face. 'Making a habit of finding bodies?'

'She wouldn't find them if someone wasn't making a habit of killing them.'

My surprise defender: Rex Saylor.

Rex identifies the victim as Gina Nardo, a former dancer at his club. She turned tricks to pay for drugs. Nya says that Gina was a single mother with a seven-year-old daughter, Laura.

The detectives question us, one at a time, in Rex's office. While I wait, I manage to gather a few bits of information. Like Van, Gina was strangled to death. Also like Van, after she was killed, the murderer transported her body to another place. The murder took place within the past couple days, probably soon after Van. Cold weather preserved her body, but her skin has begun to slip. The light over the rear exit to the club was smashed, probably by the killer. When they view CCTV footage, they may be able to identify him.

Frigid early morning air chills me to the bone. My teeth click against each other. My trousers are torn, my knees scraped. So much for my power suit. The starless skies seem to part, exposing secrets and horrors. The season of Samhain when the doors between the dead and the living are open.

By the time Torres and Wax confront me, I'm falling asleep on my feet – despite the fact that my heart is thundering.

We sit in Rex's office, still freezing-cold. His son is mercifully gone.

Same setup as in the casino manager's office: Torres behind the desk, Wax to one side, and me in a low chair that makes me feel like a kid being scolded by her parents. The way they're looking at me – impatient and exasperated – doesn't help. The tape recorder is between us.

Torres nods. 'Let's start with what you're doing at the Lollipop.'

'I came with Elvis Jones for a drink.' My throat is still cracked and dry. And I need to pee. I wish I'd worn a heavier jacket.

'You often come to the Lollipop?'

'No. My first time.'

'Why tonight?'

'Because I… I found a matchbox for this club in Van's cosmetic bag.'

'Where was the cosmetic bag?' asks Torres.

'In her room at Midnight.'

I can feel her effort to control her anger. 'When were you in her room?'

'The night I found her.'

After a moment, she asks, taut, 'Why didn't you report it as evidence?'

'I found it after we spoke.'

'Why didn't you contact me and tell me?'

'I don't know.'

'Where is the matchbox now?'

'In my room at Midnight.'

'You took evidence from a crime scene and brought it to your room,' says Wax. 'Then you planned to come here with Jones.'

Torres looks at me, long and hard. 'You've never been to the Lollipop before, yet you feel comfortable enough to go to the rear of the club where the lights don't work.'

'Walk us through that,' says Wax.

'I wanted to leave and call an Uber. But Elvis Jones followed me around the club.'

'Why didn't you leave with him?'

I'm chilled and sweating at the same time. 'We argued.'

'About what?'

You're not a Moon.

'What are you not telling us?' Torres runs her index finger along her scar – a purple-white vein that curves down her cheek.

If I tell them, the whole story will come out. If I'm in danger, so are Da and Auntie Maze. How can I throw them in the path of this killer? But if he killed Van and Gina, and I have information – even bits and fragments – that help point a finger at him, then how can I keep it inside? A lifetime of secrets, all my defences crumbling. And how does Elvis Jones know?

Torres leans toward me. 'I stumble over bodies, Lucy. But I'm a cop. In less than a week, you've stumbled over two bodies. Want to clear that up for me?'

Dimly, I hear Wax's voice, 'Put it this way. Three things connect Vanessa Kim and Gina Nardo: the cord, the flower, and you.'

They turn off the tape recorder. I jump to my feet, but they don't move. They study me.

Wax rubs his hands together. 'You're not being open with us. Are you trying to protect someone?'

Yes.

Lucy Moon.

Whoever she is.

31

October, 24 years ago

Atlantic City

Everywhere was magic. A canvas jacket hung upside down from a hanger, its long sleeves brushing the floor. Spooky masks and posters hung on the wall. A suit of armour leered by the draped window. A large rectangular box, its lid decorated with the painting of a woman. Books on shelves that rose to the ceiling, stacked on every surface – enormous, ancient books about to topple over like falling trees and crush us. One gold-lettered book leaning against the wall was taller than me.

But nothing was more magical than the man behind the desk. My nose barely reached the gleaming surface. I stood on tiptoe to see him better. He was huge, with coppery hair that glowed like new pennies. His large hands riffled through a deck of cards.

'Who are you?' he asked.

I could curl up and sleep inside the song of his voice.

'What... is... your... name?'

I don't know. How had I arrived? Had someone driven me? Had I walked? Who'd brought me? I was weightless, as if I could float to the ceiling. As if I'd left the heaviest part of me behind on the doorstep.

'Do you know how old you are?'

That I knew. I held up one hand with my thumb curled in. Someone had taught me to do that. A grown-up, left behind on the doorstep, too. 'Four and a half.'

'Four and a half,' he repeated. 'A very important age.'

If he asked me another question, I would refuse to answer. Words were a sign of weakness. Someone had taught me that as well.

'What do you remember?'

I stared at him, but I didn't say a word.

After a while, he stood and came to me. A giant with wild hair, he crouched until we were eye to eye. His eyes were as bright and hot as grass under the sun.

'You are afraid.'

Afeared.

Yes. At the edge of my vision, a memory flickered, a flaming finger that beckoned me to turn the corner. But I would not turn the corner.

'What do you see with those moonstone eyes?'

I was silent.

'May I see what's pinned to your coat?'

I nodded.

'A black rose. Some say there is no such thing as a true black rose because she doesn't exist in nature. But you and I, we know better. The black rose is both real and not real, made of petals and dreams... like magic.'

As he spoke, he gently unpinned the rose, and a torn scrap of paper fluttered to the floor. It was covered with scribbly black writing. After he examined it, he set down the rose and the note. His eyes were even brighter.

He held out his hands and turned them over to show me that they were empty.

He indicated that I should press my palms together. I did. He pressed his palms around mine, enclosing my hands. The heat of his hands surrounded me. He was a great fiery sun.

He murmured words that were music.

He lifted his hands away.

For a moment I was cold.

He stared at my hands, waiting.

I parted them gently. Between my hands was a small gemstone. Bright blue. Solid, real. I cried out and watched it drop to the floor.

'You found the love stone! I wondered where it went.' He picked it up and tucked it back into my hand. 'It's yours now. It will keep you safe.'

There were so many questions I wanted to ask. I bit my tongue to keep from talking. I would not weaken.

That was the first time I experienced Declan Moon's famous one-eyed squint. Close-up, it was terrifying, as if he saw through me, and even around the corner where the scary things lurked. He held out his hands again and nodded. I explored his hands, between his fingers, and looked up at him.

After a moment he sighed. 'Ah lass, you drive a hard bargain. A magician never reveals his secrets. But I can show you. Would you like that?'

With the love stone in my hand, I nodded.

We remained in the room I would forever after call the Temple of Magic. He allowed me to practice on him with red M&M's that melted between our hands. As we worked, we nibbled M&M's, and he talked about magic. He didn't ask questions about where I'd been or who I was, which made me happy because I had no answers. When I passed the red M&M into his palm – quite a feat considering the disparity in the size of our hands – he threw back his head and laughed in sheer joy.

To my shock, I flung my arms around him.

He stayed still, utterly still, until I pulled back.

When I left the room, holding chocolate-sticky hands with the giant, I had a name, a father, and a magic stone to remind me of the power of love.

*

Da shut down the house in Atlantic City, cancelled his engagements, and took me to Ireland, where we stayed for a year. Fiery-haired, mischievous cousins led me through the forest, fields, and the famous deserted village of the island. When we returned to Atlantic City, Da's sister Maze accompanied us. An Irish witch with a cloud of auburn hair and eyes as pale and ethereal as sea mist, Auntie Maze was almost as magical as Da. She told tales in which gods and humans roamed the earth, watching over little girls in particular. Now, I had a father, an aunt, cousins, a home, newly dyed red hair, and a backstory as rich as anyone's: A frail child, little Lucy Moon was sent from America back to the homeland for the bracing sea air of the island, where Da, Auntie Maze, and the extended Moon clan cared for her.

Da had explained, 'Magic is a story we tell ourselves. Without the story it's just tricks. With the story it's a lie that reveals the truth. The story will be your coat of many colours to disguise and protect you.'

Lucy Adelaide Moon was born in Dublin on October 31st, a fitting birthday for a budding magician.

Lucy. Da informed me that the name, 'Lucy,' means 'light'. It's also the name of a saint whose eyes were gouged out.

Adelaide, after Adelaide Herrmann, a female magician from the early twentieth century.

Moon. The youngest member of a clan of Irish magicians from Achill Island off the western coast of Ireland, where memories of Nellie Moon – the first Moon witch – remained vivid.

Back in Atlantic City, I moved into the brick and frame house in Lower Chelsea, a block from the boardwalk and beach. At twilight I often leant out the window of my third-story room to peer at the sky and breathe in the salt air. I was convinced the Moon house was magic. Da's study, of course. Auntie Maze's 'parlour,' where she gave private readings using a mix of Tarot cards, her crystal ball, and messages from Nellie Moon.

And the ghosts.

Da's first family – wife, son, and daughter – all three had gone down in a plane that crashed at sea, no survivors. I heard and felt the spirits of the little red-haired brother and sister who remained forever frozen at four and five years old, and Theodora, their delicate fairy-like mother who'd been known as the Queen of Box Jumpers. Da called her Teddie. A flame-haired family, radiating mischief and sorrow both. I often passed them on the stairs – not seeing them exactly, but breathing in a secret, hearing a child's giggle, glimpsing a light – and then continuing on my way.

At the age of six, I joined Da and Auntie Maze on the stage of Black Widow Theatre on the 13th floor of Midnight Casino to perform in public for the first time. Dressed in ruffled pink, I burst from the roof of a large dollhouse in The Living Doll, and cried out, 'I'm here, Da!' The instant I saw my father's proud smile I knew that whatever mysterious circumstances had led me to this moment, I was born to be a magician.

New publicity photos of the flamboyant, theatrical Moons were distributed. Declan, a modern-day Henry VIII – moustached and bearded, in full velvet regalia – transplanted to Atlantic City. Auntie Maze, wild-haired, with eyes that reflected misty Irish mornings, draped in layers of brocade and lace. And the child, red-haired like her father and aunt.

Similar, yet different. The key to hiding in plain sight.

At eleven, when I complained about the restrictions placed on my freedom, Da led me to the Temple of Magic. He held out a small white scroll, a scrap jaggedly ripped from an envelope, a few lines scrawled in black ink:

Mr. Moon, if you're reading this you know I was murdered and my daughter is an orphan. Please keep her safe. Tell no one about her or he will

He will... what? Find her? Kill her? Who was *he*?

'Where's the rest of the note?' I demanded.

'There was nothing else, *a cushla*.' He looked at me with so much pain my eyes stung. *A cushla*, the beat of his heart.

But my mother had written these words. The mysterious, elusive mother who flitted in and out of my dreams like a butterfly. This note and the rose were the only things I owned that she had touched with her own hands. But who was she? Even in my dreams, she was faceless, like the masked man. How had my mother known she would be killed? Who was after her? Why had she chosen the Moons? They weren't the most likely choice for benefactors unless... unless she herself was a magician or magician's assistant.

Da explained that this note was the reason why I had to be vanished and transformed into a Moon. I must remember that I was Lucy Moon, daughter of Declan, niece of Maze.

After all, Da reasoned, if Houdini could vanish an elephant at the Hippodrome and David Copperfield could vanish the Statue of Liberty, then Declan Moon could certainly vanish a tiny girl child. And make her reappear, transformed.

It was an amazing illusion, perhaps the most amazing ever created and developed by the Moons, on or off-stage. Ironically, it was a secret. No one knew but us.

And it was a matter of life or death to keep it that way.

32

early Sunday October 21

Here's what I know. It was late October, same as now.

A woman and a small girl appeared on the corner of Pacific and Dover. Hand in hand, the woman and girl walked down Dover toward the boardwalk and beach. They stopped at the second-last house on the left side of the street. The pink house and banana moon doorknocker must have reassured the woman that she was doing the right thing. If you were looking to vanish a small girl, could you find anyone better than a man who vanished rabbits, doves, and even his assistant-wife onstage?

Mrs. Giardelli had watched from the window of her boarding house across the street on Dover. She died fifteen years ago. I have a fuzzy memory of a woman with a blue-white perm knitting at her window, always looking out. Her curious gaze made me uneasy. Mrs. Giardelli told Da that she'd seen a woman draped in a long purple scarf lead a little girl to the Moon house.

I climb the steps to the porch where Mrs. Giardelli saw the woman crouch and kiss the girl, then rise and knock on the door. The woman returned to the corner. Although many unusual people visited the Moons, Mrs. Giardelli was sufficiently intrigued by the veiled woman and child to keep watching. The woman waited on the corner until the Moon door opened, and the girl disappeared inside.

When Mrs. Giardelli turned back, the woman was gone.

If it weren't for Mrs. Giardelli, I'd believe I dropped from the sky.

*

It's five in the morning when I enter the Moon house. Dark and dim without Da and Auntie Maze here. I hurry upstairs to my room, rummage in my closet and bring out my Treasure Box, the small wooden chest Da gave me years ago to hold 'moments of wonder.' I sit on the bed, and bring out the objects, one by one.

The turquoise and gold-threaded love stone Da gave me the first day I entered this house.

A photo: Da, Auntie Maze, and me holding hands on stage.

A playing card from David Copperfield inscribed with my name, a twisted silver spoon from Uri Geller, magic flyers from some of my favourite Moon Magick shows.

A pair of Tal's dark glasses. I'd stolen them in the hope he'd let me see his eyes – his only point of vulnerability.

My mother's note. A few lines scrawled in black ink on a jagged scrap ripped from an envelope.

Finally, I lift out the black rose. *My* rose. A polyester faux-silk black rose with a short green wire stem, identical to the ones found in Van and Gina's mouths.

No, there's one difference: theirs were new, and mine is crumpled, petals folded in on themselves, tear-stained. My rose still emanates a faint sharp-sweetness, cinnamon, and cloves. After nightmares, I tucked it beneath my pillow or clutched it in my hand.

I place the rose and the note in a small plastic bag, and for the first time, carry them outside.

33

Monday October 22

The key to understanding this killer is through his relations with women.

After a troubled night, I wake up with that thought. I don't know where it came from, but it makes sense. The Hunter strangled two women to death: Van Kim and Gina Nardo. What connects them in his mind? If he murdered two women in one week, he must have killed more. Maybe he left a trail of victims. Who is he in daylight? A nondescript little guy who goes unnoticed by most women? A swaggering bully who insists on being seen and obeyed? Is he capable of more than a one-night stand? Does his public persona crumble under the pressure of too much intimacy? Does he alternate between setting women on a pedestal and knocking them down when they inevitably disappoint him: angel or whore, nothing in between?

I have an hour before I need to shower and meet Charlie, Stormie, and Gus at the Widow. Yesterday, after I packed my mother's rose and note, I drove to Midnight. I couldn't spend the night alone in the Moon house. While I make coffee in the small carafe the hotel provides, I decide to dig deeper into all the men involved in some way with Van or Gina: Rex, Elvis, Gus, and Charlie. They had dealings with Van, worked with her or went out with her. And Elvis lied about it. That makes him my top suspect. Rex wouldn't talk, but he was involved with both Van and Gina.

And there's Gus. Apparently, he works undercover for the cops, but cops can be crooked, and his misogyny and macabre interest in murder make him suspicious. Tal told me that a woman's greatest defence is to trust her gut instinct about a man. The physical repulsion I feel when I'm near Gus – could it be my spider-sense warning me about him? Besides, he has access to the entire casino and hotel.

So does Charlie. Kind and sweet, but is he hiding something? Where was he the night Van was murdered? Misty expected him for dinner, but he didn't show up. How late did he stay out working on his problems with the band playing the Crypt?

I grab my coffee, laptop, and notebook, and back in bed, plunge into the black hole of the web. I begin with Elvis Jones. Last night's cursory search already revealed a man in hiding. I don't have time to uncover his secrets, but I use explore every link and connection on social media – Google, Facebook, Twitter, Instagram, LinkedIn, Reddit, magicians' chatrooms. I'm dying to plunge into the dark web. For years I've been wanting to search for my mother in the depths of the web, where mirror versions of surface websites, news outlets and sites provide hidden answers to questions, but my father and Tal kept warning me not to go there. It's difficult to stay anonymous, and if my mother's murderer is watching, it might bring me to his attention.

I find a thread on a magicians' chat board, in which a handful of magicians respond to Jones's show with comments as cryptic as the ones I found yesterday:

I saw him at the Magic Lounge in Chicago. Unexpected. Unforgettable. Inexplicable.

The thread ends there, but it makes me wonder: Where is Elvis Jones from? Did he live in the Midwest? Where was he before his Midnight gig? How is it possible for a performer to have such a limited social media presence? Unless he's trying to hide. A master of transformation, he may have changed his name. *A name is a prison,* he said at his show. Jones – you can't get more anonymous than that. Elvis – not so much, but it must have meaning for him.

I can't forget how he leaped to the stage for the sawing box finale. A normal magician would not do that to another magician, but a murderer would get as close as he could to savour the reaction. He saw me discover both Van and Gina. He knows I'm not a Moon. Is the black rose a symbol to taunt me? Is this really about me?

I turn to Rex Saylor. I can't find a single photo of him online. No mention of his ex-wife or son. He exists on the internet only as the owner and manager of the Lollipop Club. It takes way too long to unearth a single article from five years ago that quotes him during the investigation of the Rope Strangler. This killer was notorious for two things: the complicated knots he tied around his victims' throats and the vicious bites on their bodies. He raped and murdered three prostitutes and left them in a pit behind a cheap motel on Black Horse Pike. The Rope Strangler was never caught. After the three murders, he disappeared or changed his MO.

But here's an article from *The Atlantic City News* that makes me sit up: Mona Andrews, the Rope Strangler's third victim, worked for Rex at the Lollipop. A photo of her shows a pudgy face with overplucked eyebrows and tightly scraped-back hair that reminds me of Detective Torres. The only colour in Mona's face comes from her exaggeratedly puffy red lips.

'Mona danced in my club,' said Saylor. 'She was a sweet responsible girl until she got hooked on heroin. She showed up late and missed shifts. Next thing she's found in a ditch with a rope around her neck.'

Isn't that what Rex said last night about Gina? He also called Van a sweet girl. He was not considered a suspect in Mona's murder. I google the motel where Mona was found. It's a two-minute drive from the Lollipop Club. Maybe Rex had an affair with Mona and murdered her. But why would he kill Van? He seems to care about her. He sounded bitter about his ex-wife. Bitter enough to hate women and murder them?

I glance at my watch again. In about twenty minutes I need to shower and meet Stormie. I return to the web, this time looking up the two men who'd worked with Van at the Widow.

Charlie Becker. Unlike Rex and Jones, Charlie has an actual presence on the web. His gorgeous face smiles in photos with Midnight executives. He appears with Jinx as she receives plaques and honours for her work with the Atlantic City Historical Society. There's even a photo of him with Da and Auntie Maze at Moon Magick's opening night last July. He is quoted as a spokesman for the historic boardwalk, the renovation of Black Widow Theatre, and the future of Atlantic City. No social media, blogs, or updates. He's not a performer so it makes sense that he lives his private life off the web. During last summer's Moon Magick run, women always waited for him after the show, trying to get his attention. Before Misty, he went out with a few, but he's discreet. I can't find a single photo of him with Misty – or any other woman.

I look up Misty. No Facebook or Twitter presence. How can she and Charlie stay so invisible? I search for her on Instagram, where selfie-production is a daily, even hourly, mission for 'beautiful people.' No sign of her. That's odd. The only place I find her is in publicity shots for the Boardwalk Babes.

My fingers freeze on the keys. Oh jeez. I get it. Her scary, dangerous ex. He's probably looking for any excuse to screw up her life. Kudos to her for laying low.

Gus Wigman. Chief lighting designer and technician at Midnight Casino. Another surprise: for someone who works undercover, he appears in numerous articles about casino organisations and city boards dedicated to preserving Atlantic City history. One photo shows him, Charlie, and the casino manager in front of Midnight. In another, he receives a prestigious industry award for his lighting designs. He worked at the Tropicana, Harrah's, and Trump Taj Mahal before it became Hard Rock, and on Moon Magick productions for the past few years. Da has praised him for understanding the special requirements of staging magic shows.

I have no idea where Gus comes from either. I remember him mentioning the Kansas City Chiefs, the football team. Why mention them unless he's from Kansas City? Even if he is, how does that help me discover Van's murderer?

Frustrated, I shut my laptop. What have I learned? Gus is everywhere, Elvis Jones is nowhere, Charlie is in the middle, and Rex is a suspicious character. What connects these men to Van? And what connects Gina to Van?

A pigeon pecks at the window. When I open it, he flies away with a raucous cry. Same view as Stormie's room. The outdoor parking lot, where I spot the roof of my midnight-blue Festiva. The boardwalk. And as I lean to the right, I glimpse a sliver of beach and water. Seagulls soar, pale sun glimmers.

You're out there, I know you are. Who are you? Why are you killing women? Is this about me? Are you working your way to me?

34

After morning rehearsal, Stormie and I walk toward DiBruni's Pizzeria for lunch. She punches my arm. 'The rose your mother left you. The rose on Van. The rose on Gina. One plus one plus one equals you. This is about you.'

Yesterday I gave her a bare-bones account of Saturday night, including the rose in Gina's mouth. 'There's something else,' I tell her now. 'Elvis Jones knows about me. Maybe he knows something about the rose too.'

She whistles, low. 'Speak of the devil.'

Elvis Jones is crouching next to Ruby's wheelchair. Hoodie lowered, black hair blowing back.

'I don't want to see him. Let's go to DiBruni's.'

She sniffs. 'First, give me something good. You went to the Lollipop with him. You danced with him. And now you're hot and bothered.'

'No, I'm not!'

'He's man-sexy.' She pokes her elbow in my side. 'Walks down the street, flashes his killer smile, and mm-hmm. Just like Michael B or young Denzel.'

'Storm. You're not listening to me. He introduced Rex Saylor to Van! And he somehow figured out I'm not a Moon.'

'He does have that dark edge. But he makes your girl parts tingle.'

I flush. 'What? No! Plus he's a regular at the Lollipop.'

'Like I said, he makes your girl parts tingle.'

'Will you shut up about my girl parts? They'll tingle when I damned well tell them to tingle.'

She hums one of her favourite songs, Anita Baker's 'Sweet Love,' and its sensual groove brings me back to last night when I danced with Elvis Jones.

At that moment he turns his head. His dark gaze locks on us.

Stormie nudges me. 'He did not look at Van the way he's looking at you. Aw Luce, I hope he's a good one.'

'I can tell you right now he's not.'

Ruby clings to the final words of the song, leaving behind traces of melancholy, like falling leaves. Two women are dead, the boardwalk is nearly deserted, winter's coming, and there's no going back. I shiver, wishing I'd worn my jacket.

Jones murmurs in Ruby's ear, and she laughs. 'You're terrible.'

As soon as he straightens and steps away, Stormie and I walk to Ruby. 'It's getting slow, isn't it?' asks Stormie.

'Yeah. And cold. I'll move inside soon.'

'Come to the show Wednesday night,' I tell her. 'Our new opening night. We're doing something special for Van.'

'Charlie said.'

As I back away, a warm weight settles over my shoulders. I don't have to turn to know it's Jones's black hoodie.

'Lucy.' Just that. My name in his golden, Jameson voice. I slide my arms into the sleeves.

'How are you today?' he asks.

'Good.' After a long pause, I face him. 'You?'

The smile begins in his eyes. 'Much better now.'

That smile does funny things to me.

'Hey, Elvis.' Stormie stops in front of him. 'Come share a pizza with us.'

I gape at her. What's wrong with the girl?

Ten minutes later we're installed in a booth at DiBruni's. Squirming on the wooden bench, I face Stormie and Jones over pizza and Cokes. While they talk about Van and Gina, I chew on my pizza and brood over my upcoming meeting with the cops. In my bag is my mother's rose and note. The first time I've taken them out of the house.

Jones sets down his slice of pizza and stares at me as if he just saw a ghost.

I set down my pizza too. 'What?'

'The Lollipop Club matchbox you found.'

I shoot Stormie a look, and she shrugs.

'A Goth casino on the boardwalk, a strip club on the Pike. He chooses his places. Makes me think of the Karma.'

'The Karma Club?'

'You know the Karma?' he asks.

'I know enough not to drive by in case I get stuck at a red light.' The cops shut it down every few months.

'Huh. A friend of mine worked there a couple years ago. She's a… um… singer.'

Of course she is. I picture another gorgeous Nya crooning, 'El baby.'

'She was on her break and went out back for a smoke. It's a trouble spot, and the alley behind is shady.'

Shady is not the word.

'A guy grabbed her from behind in a choke hold. Her head jerked back, and he teased a knife across her throat.' He hesitates. 'She said he breathed down her neck.'

I listen with every cell. He's gloating over the description the way Gus did when he described what the killer did to Van.

'He laughed. She said it was high-pitched, like a girl.'

'What happened to her?' asks Stormie.

'She got lucky. A bartender came out and yelled. The man ran away.'

Stormie frowns. 'A coward. He bullies women, but he's scared of men.'

'Did he hurt her?'

He blinks and focuses on me. 'He made a small cut on her

throat, but she's okay. It could have been much worse.'

Stormie asks, 'Did she call the cops?'

He lifts one shoulder. 'They said it was a random attack. Attempted rape. Could have been any woman. But she told me this guy didn't want to rape her. He wanted to slash her until she bled to death.'

'Wait. Are you comparing the Widow to the Karma Club?'

He chews his lower lip. 'If this is the same guy, he's going to places where he feels comfortable. Think about it. The Boardwalk. Black Horse Pike, the bars and clubs leading to the Pine Barrens. Downtown. He's not going south to Chelsea or Avalon.'

Chelsea? Is that a dig at me? Does he know where I live?

Stormie says, 'That makes sense. He's not going upscale. He wants places on the edge where there aren't too many people.'

'But the boardwalk?' I hold out my hands. 'Come on. It's the only place most tourists go.'

'The boardwalk after dark,' he says. 'Especially when you get away from the lights.'

The curve of my neck itches. The beginning of the prickle. Happens every time I'm with him. A warning? Trust your gut, says Tal. It's a woman's best defence. My gut says, stay away from this man.

Jones glances down at his phone. 'Sorry, I have to take this.'

As soon as he leaves the booth, I scowl at Stormie. 'Don't you think it's weird he told us that story? And why did you ask him to join us?'

She pushes aside her pizza. 'It's the best way to find out what he's hiding.'

A minute later he slides into the booth next to Stormie. 'That was Nya at the Lollipop.'

I tighten in dread. 'Did something happen?'

'The cops want to interview Rex. He called his lawyer and

went to the police station.'

'Do they suspect him of killing Gina Nardo?' I ask.

'Nya says he's a person of interest.' He stares at his hands. The bird tattoo whirls around his wrist. I imagine it taking flight. 'Gina Nardo worked at the Lollipop, and apparently, she went out with Rex for a couple months.'

'Did he go out with Van too?' I ask.

He hesitates. 'I'm not sure.'

Did you go out with Van?

Stormie says, 'Do you think Rex is the guy Dom saw her with at the Speakeasy? The one with the hungry eyes?'

'Yeah. A few years ago a woman named Mona danced at the Lollipop, turned to drugs, and was found strangled to death in a ditch.' My gaze is on Stormie, but Jones leans forward, listening. I feel him absorbing my words. 'I don't know if Rex and Mona hooked up, but what happened to Mona sounds very much like what happened to Gina.' Except for the black rose.

As soon as I think it, Jones says, 'You didn't mention the black rose.'

'What black rose?' I sound shrill.

'Was a rose found in Mona's mouth?'

'I don't know.'

Jones gives me a measuring look. I give it back. I remember how he played the bumbling fool onstage and then, before our eyes, transformed himself.

Outside DiBruni's he punches his number into our phones and tells us to call him if we need anything. The temperature has dropped at least ten degrees. I'm chilled inside and out, but there's no way I'm hanging onto Jones's hoodie. Before I return it, I search his pockets. A small weight sags in the left one. My fingers close around it, the usual for a magician: a deck of cards. A pack of gum. The other pocket, a few coins. Nothing else.

I shrug off the hoodie, and he gives me the bland smile that prickles not only my neck but every part of my body. 'You missed the inside pocket,' he murmurs.

He slips it on and backs away, head tilted to the side, watching me.

Stormie nudges me. 'That man is giving you the fuck-me squint. The one that says: "You. Me. Together. Now."'

'That's not what I see,' I mutter. 'He's not young Denzel, but he could be Hannibal in disguise.'

'Fair enough, but I know my girl, and she has a jones for Jones.' She calls after him, 'Jones! You a good guy or a bad guy?'

'Trying to be a good guy.'

'Then wear a grey hoodie. You're confusing us.'

He smiles and waves at us.

I scowl at him. 'Until I find out different, black hoodie suits that man just fine.'

35

A camera light blinks from the corner of a windowless interrogation room that smells of vomit. Detectives Torres and Wax switched places, probably to unnerve me. I face Wax, slit-eyed with deep pouches beneath his eyes, while Torres sits to the side. The tape recorder sits on the table between us. I've run through discovering Van and stumbling over Gina. Again. They ask questions while I build up the courage to tell them my secret.

'You never saw Gina Nardo before?' asks Wax.

'Not until last night.'

'Did Van have any connection with Gina?'

'As far as I know, the Lollipop is the connection. And Rex Saylor. I heard you took him in for questioning.' I pause, hoping they'll give me information, but they stare back stonily. With a sigh, I set the Lollipop Club matchbox on the table.

'Tell us what that is,' says Torres.

'The matchbox for the Lollipop Club that I found in Van's cosmetic bag.'

'Did you ever see Van with a black rose?'

'No.'

'What about you?' asks Wax. 'Do you use a black rose in your act?'

I shake my head, then say, 'No.'

'What do you think the black rose means?'

'I don't know.' *Death. Rebirth. He's back.*

Wax is in my face again. 'Tell us about your relationship with Elvis Jones.'

Shit, here we go. My hand goes up to my throat. I can't help it.

A small smile. He knows. 'Go ahead, Lucy.'

'We don't have a relationship.'

Torres slips in. 'On Saturday night you went to his show. Then you went to the Lollipop Club with him. Today you had lunch with him.'

My fingers clutch my throat. They *are* watching me. 'I have to show you something.' I lower my hand. 'It's in my magic bag.'

I zip open the large inner pocket and search the bag with my fingers. Rummage through cards, tools, notebook, pens. Oh, God, where is it? My face burns. 'Do you mind?'

This bag contains multitudes. I sift through three decks of Moon Magick cards, an assortment of magic gems, stones, and coins, business cards (mine and others), Sharpies, scissors, tape, glue stick... and pull out the plastic bag. Cheeks on fire, I set the crumpled black polyester rose and the torn envelope on the table.

'Describe these items,' says Torres.

'This is my mother's rose. Twenty-four years ago, she left me on the doorstep of the Moon house with the rose and this note.' I clear my throat and read it aloud:

Mr. Moon, if you're reading this you know I was murdered and my daughter is an orphan. Please keep her safe. Tell no one about her or he will

I wait for a bolt of lightning to stab me. No lightning. But Wax leans closer. His heavy-lidded stare goes on so long I'm ready to confess to something... anything. I swallow. The air tastes like puke. I need fresh air. 'The truth is I'm not Lucy Moon. I mean–' a harsh breath, 'I don't know who I was before. I don't know who my mother was. I believe she was murdered.'

Wax says, cold, 'You obstructed justice by withholding information. Why did you wait so long to tell the truth?'

'Does it matter so much that I'm not a Moon by birth?'

Wax mutters, 'What matters is the black rose and your connection with the murders.'

Torres adds, 'What matters is keeping secrets from the people who are trying to discover the truth and keep you safe.'

The disappointment in their eyes makes me wince. 'I'm sorry. We've kept this secret since I was a kid. Very few people know. My father and aunt were afraid that if my mother's murderer found out I existed, he'd come after me. It truly was life or death. Not just for me, but for them too. They protected me from whoever killed my mother.'

I catch my breath. 'At first, I didn't think Van's murder was about me. The black rose could have been a coincidence. But now, with the second black rose... it seems connected to my mother.'

Torres nods. 'We'll talk more about your mother another time. We have resources that may help track her down. What else are you holding back?'

'Nothing.' I extend my hands, palms up. 'That's it.'

Wax studies me. 'You will immediately contact us with any developments.'

'Yes, of course.'

They shut off the tape recorder.

'You can keep the note, but please can I have the rose? It's the only thing I have that my mother touched.'

'No,' says Wax. 'We're keeping the rose and the note to process for DNA.'

I look at the rose I've guarded for so long. 'After all these years, the DNA must be all confused.'

'Only a lab can determine whether there's usable DNA on the items.'

I get up slowly, wondering if I'll ever get it back.

Torres says, 'It may help us track down your mother.'

The kindness in her voice encourages me. 'One more thing,

Detectives. Last year Stormie, Van, and I did a magic cruise, where we previewed the Rebel Magic show. A man brought his late wife's ashes onboard, and we held a ceremony for her on the deck. Van told me, "This is the way I want to go. Please throw my ashes into the sea."'

'We can't release the body yet,' says Torres. 'This is an active investigation.'

'When it's done, can you–?'

'When it's over, yes.' She sighs. 'But it's not over yet. Don't leave town.'

36

Monday night

It's ten at night, and I'm exhausted, but too wired and frustrated to sleep. Missing Van. Telling the cops the truth. Brooding over what I know, what I don't know, and what I don't know that I know. I'm tingling, head to toe. I need to walk or run. I pull on my jean jacket and shove the knife, phone, and Midnight room key in my pockets.

The sharp tang of salt air stings my nostrils. A handful of people are outside. I'll just go to the Speakeasy and back, the most lit-up area of the boardwalk. I walk next to the railing, letting the night sky, caw of gulls, and steady beat of waves soothe me. This is what I needed.

I hear footsteps behind me.

When I spin around, I see no one. The centre of the boardwalk is empty but shadows flicker under awnings and in doorways.

I take a few steps.

Stealthy footsteps follow me.

I stop, hard.

So do the steps.

I open the knife and hold it low, against my side. I'm approaching the Speakeasy. Central Pier, ahead to my left. I race-walk toward the lights.

Footsteps pound after me.

Over my shoulder, I see him. A man in a black hoodie running after me. Elvis Jones? But he'd call my name, wouldn't he?

Not if he's the Hunter, and I'm next.

With a cry, I leap down the steps to the beach.

Glance back. He's a few yards behind me.

I run under the pier. Black water rushes between the concrete pillars. No sign of the homeless men. I flatten myself behind a pillar. Stormie and I used to play hide-and-seek here. I peek out. He darts a flashlight at the pillars. I immediately duck back. Who is he? Jones? Rex Saylor? The man who knifed Jones's friend at the Karma Club?

A shadowy figure hooded in black, he advances purposefully beneath the pier. The instant his light shines on my pillar, I dash to another one. The light dances madly around the pillars. I rush and hide behind another one, the way I used to with Stormie.

He's playing. He wants me to scurry like a mouse. I press my face to the cold concrete. Should I run to the boardwalk and scream at the top of my lungs? Stay motionless till he comes after me, then kick? No. I'm not fool enough to confront him in the dark, alone. Tal's first rule of survival: *The best fight is no fight. But if you must fight, make sure you win.*

He shines the flashlight in erratic circles.

A shrill, high-pitched laugh. My heart freezes. The inhuman laugh of my nightmare. The laugh Jones's friend heard at the Karma.

Then... silence.

Heart thudding against the pillar, I press my nose and mouth to the cold stone. Is he hiding in the shadows?

After a long minute, I detach myself from the pillar. I don't see him, but I hear voices from above – not on the boardwalk, beneath it. Several years ago, homeless people created tent cities under the boardwalk known as the Underwood Motel. Three-foot high crawl spaces filled with crumpled cardboard boxes, needles and syringes, knives, empty bottles, and cigarette butts. There were so many rapes and stabbings the cops finally cleared them out. I remember hearing you could only enter from the beach. Is someone still there, hiding between worlds?

As I move silently between the pillars, I smell whiskey and ancient mosses with a trace of vanilla. I know that smell. Auntie Maze burns peat when she converses with Nellie Moon. Who is burning peat on the boardwalk?

Music fills my ears, familiar strains... not the usual disco blaring from Central Pier, but a man singing, 'I'll Be Seeing You,' a World War Two song I recognise because Charlie and I danced to it the night we kissed in the Orange Room.

The gap between the rafters widens. A blue light glows. A pinprick hole opens, like an ancient camera.

Am I dreaming? Is this real?

I reach up toward the light and music.

37

A hand grabs mine and yanks me up to the boardwalk. I twist around to see who pulled me up, but I'm alone. And it's no longer night. The sky is blinding blue, the sun so large and close its rays seep into me. The ocean sparkles, a thousand diamond-bright pinpoints of light.

'I'll Be Seeing You' blasts from Steel Pier – not the tawdry amusement park I know, but a brilliant, bustling mass of people and attractions. Women drenched in jewels and shifty-eyed men puffing on cigars. Faces loom close, drawn with harsh strokes, splashed with dizzying colours.

Maybe I fell asleep under Central Pier and the smell of burning peat wafted me into a trance state.

A regiment of uniformed soldiers marches toward me.

I touch a GI's arm. My finger slides away.

One soldier's hand swings toward me. In horror, I jump back, but his hand goes through me.

In this world I'm the ghost, a trespasser. Auntie Maze would say I'm having a vision. But I've had visions before, and none has ever felt this vivid and rich.

A piercing whistle. A GI slows down and yells, 'Cleo! Over here!'

A woman in a red dress and high heels turns with a toss of her wavy strawberry blonde hair.

Cleo West!

'Love you, Cleo!' cries the GI. 'Marry me!'

With an impish smile, she leans over and adjusts the seam of her stocking.

The GIs whistle and move on.

When they pass, Cleo straightens and stares directly at me,

the way she did in the vanity mirror backstage at the Widow. She sees me!

With a quick nod, she sashays toward Steel Pier. She carries a large black handbag.

I follow her – I'm gliding rather than walking – past men wearing fedoras and women in broad-shouldered dresses, past bustling stores and hotels.

Cleo stops in front of Midnight – not the hotel-casino, but Haddon Hall, transformed into Thomas England Hospital.

Without warning, I'm jolted from the boardwalk. A dizzying leap, and I land so hard my head spins.

Woozy, I look around. I'm in a hospital corridor crowded with doctors, nurses, and patients. I breathe in ether, sickness, and Cleo's faint lavender scent. I follow her into a ward where wounded soldiers smile from their cots and call out to her. While she opens her bag and prepares her tricks, the head nurse, white cap over frothy brown curls, looks her over. 'How are you today?'

I recognise her from the Camp Boardwalk reunion – a sparrow with a froth of white hair. But now, she's young, bright-eyed and rosy-cheeked.

'Don't worry about me,' says Cleo. 'How's Roberto?'

The nurse sighs. 'He passed in the night. And Little Mac's girl sent him a Dear John letter.' She points to a dark-haired soldier sitting up on a cot.

Cleo wiggles to Little Mac's cot. He clamps his right arm ending in a shiny hook around her wrist. 'My girl found someone else. Will you marry me, Cleo?'

'I sure will, Little Mac. I promise. When the war's over.'

'I might not be alive then.' His eyes are wide and frightened. He's so young. They're all so young.

'You'll be alive. I promise! Hey, look at that!'

A small red velvet heart appears on the tip of his hook. 'Keep that heart with you always. It will bring you good luck.'

The nurse accompanies Cleo through the ward. 'That rascal Billy the Kid sneaked a bottle in his prosthetic limb again.'

I remember him too – wearing a grey fedora and seated in a wheelchair! He can't be more than eighteen. Freckled and grinning, he passes a bottle of whiskey to the soldier in the next cot. Cleo pulls a rainbow scarf out of Billy's ear and winds it around his throat, looping it into a colourful bow tie.

She does simple tricks, the kind I do at the Children's Hospital in Philly. The magic is *her* – the warmth and humour she conveys, the way she looks each man in the eye.

'Take a gander at the dreamboat,' says the nurse.

The man seated in the cot against the window watches Cleo as if he just received the shock of his life. Bandaged chest and arm. Rumpled golden-brown hair, lean face, and eyes as hot as a summer sky at noon.

'His name's Frank.'

Frank. The man who killed her.

'He survived the Battle of Salerno,' says the nurse. 'He waded through a sea of dead bodies to find his buddies blown to pieces. Shrapnel pierced his chest, touched his lungs, and damaged his left arm and hand. An honest-to-God hero. And will you look at those peepers? As blue as Gary Cooper's.'

I follow Cleo as she zigzags her way through the ward, the sun's rays guiding her to him. Her breath quickens as she stops at the side of his cot. 'Hi Frank, I'm Cleo. Welcome to the best ward in Thomas England.' She performs a graceful one-hand shuffle and holds out the deck. 'Pick a card.'

He taps a card with his right index finger.

'King of Hearts. Good choice. I bet there's a pretty girl waiting for you back home.' She presses a tiny red velvet heart into his right hand. 'Keep it, Frank. It'll bring you luck.'

His hand closes around hers, and she sinks to the edge of his bed. He lifts her hand, still curled inside his large, warm grip, and kisses the red heart, then presses it into her palm. 'Keep it, Cleo. It'll bring you luck.'

He smiles, and it's warm and beautiful, and I wish I could pull her away before it's too late.

'Watch your back, Cleo,' mutters the nurse. 'Jimmy the Crab is spying on you. Morelli is getting closer.'

At the entrance to the ward, Jimmy the Crab, a short guy in a black hat and a suit that swims on him, watches Cleo.

When I turn back, we're no longer in the hospital ward, but on the boardwalk. Cleo walks on Heinz Pier past the seventy-foot tall sign, '57 Varieties,' and the large glass-walled pavilion. I've only seen Heinz Pier in photos. It was destroyed in the Great Atlantic Hurricane.

At the edge of the pier, Cleo sits, takes off her high heels, and dangles her legs over the rafters.

I crouch at her side. Below, on the sand, GIs in wheelchairs tilt their heads to the sun. Others do manoeuvres and shoot machine guns into the ocean.

Cleo opens her palm and looks at the red heart Frank gave her. She kisses the red heart and puts it inside her bra.

She puts on her heels, gets up and rushes back over the pier.

She moves so fast I lose her. I trip on the rafters.

Time – past, present, future – whirls around me. Faster and faster.

38

I slam to the boardwalk on all fours.

It's night, and I'm back in front of Central Pier.

My knife, phone, room key are a few feet away. Panting, I grab them and scramble to my feet.

Was I really in Camp Boardwalk?

The smells, sounds, people – they were too real to be a dream. This must be what Auntie Maze calls a thin place, where borders between worlds are porous. Achill Island, where I saw Nellie Moon. Da would not believe me if I told him the Atlantic City boardwalk is a thin place. Neither would Stormie. I can hear her: 'There's a realistic explanation for you seeing Cleo in Camp Boardwalk. Maybe you were dreaming awake.'

I'd think so, yes. If I hadn't smelled the peat burning. If Cleo hadn't looked at me. If I hadn't followed her through the ward and seen the way she and Frank looked at each other. The Purple Heart hero. The man who murdered her.

*

As I return to Midnight, I navigate the dizzy journey from the past to the present. No smell of burning peat. No soldiers or men in fedoras. No women in broad-shouldered suits. To my right, Steel Pier extends over the water. Quiet and dark, the Ferris Wheel is still. To my left, Midnight Casino looms with its gargoyle-encrusted doors and Dracula's Castle façade. But if I squint, traces of the old hotel and hospital and soldiers in their wheelchairs linger. We don't erase the old stories – we merely draw over them.

39

Tuesday October 23

Charlie, Stormie, and I spend the morning doing publicity for our opening night tomorrow. A local TV reporter interviews us in the Widow. Stormie and I also visit a local talk radio show and discuss Van, the Widow, and our new show.

Afterwards, Stormie heads to Angel's Beauty Salon and I return to my room at Midnight.

Cup of coffee in hand, I turn on the TV and watch the local news. A drug bust on Rosemont Place, a Ventnor woman pleads not guilty in the killings of her mother and grandmother, and a second dead woman has been found in Atlantic City in the last few days. Gina Nardo. I turn up the volume. The newscaster names both Van and Gina but does not mention the black rose or that the murders are connected.

The next story moves to the Pine Barrens and the burial pit where Jane Doe was found. The area is marked off with police tape, and a few officers peer into the pit. One officer turns his head. I choke on my coffee, spilling burning liquid on my T-shirt. Detective Wax. And sure enough, at his side, Detective Torres. What the hell are those two doing there?

I set down my coffee, move to the edge of the bed, and hunch in front of the TV.

Pam Woodson, the blonde reporter, turns to the grizzled grey policeman I remember from the last newscast in the Barrens. 'Lieutenant Martini of the New Jersey State Police. Your forensic team has compiled a description of Jane Doe. Can you share it with us?'

In a slow, deep voice, he reads the description of a woman who may have been reported as a missing person about twenty years ago. 'A female, European ancestry, thirty to forty years old, 5'4' to 5'7. Hyoid bone broken, which could signify homicide by ligature strangulation. The body has been in the ground approximately twenty years. If anyone has any information, please contact...'

A phone number flashes on the bottom of the screen.

Homicide by ligature strangulation. A phrase with which I'm unfortunately growing familiar.

Pam Woodson thanks him. 'Detectives Torres and Wax from the Atlantic City Police Department are also here. Detective Torres, your beat is Atlantic City. Does your presence at Clarks Landing mean that you see a connection between Jane Doe and the recent murders you're investigating?'

Torres looks pained, her face stark and pale. 'I can't talk about that, Pam. But at this point there's nothing to report.'

When the news segment ends, I search online for Dr. Lose, forensic anthropologist. I find a few links, all leading to Jane Doe. This must be her first high-profile case. Dr. Lose works at the forensic lab in Galloway. She made it clear she won't help me. But Galloway is a gateway to the Barrens, and according to Pam Woodson, the crime site is in Clarks Landing.

Dr. Lose said she fuses bones to form a human being. I'm trying to fuse wisps of information: the connection between the Pine Barrens and the murders of Van and Gina. Van's curiosity about the Barrens. Gina's body found on the outskirts of Egg Harbor City. The presence of Detectives Torres and Wax at the burial pit. Dr. Lose's presence at Elvis Jones's show.

I call the number for the forensic lab and ask for Dr. Lose. To my surprise, they connect me.

'Lose.'

The gruff voice almost makes me lose my nerve.

'Dr. Lose, this is Lucy Moon. Can you please show me the pit where Jane Doe was found?'

'No.'

'Why not?'

'You're a civilian as well as a potential suspect and witness. And it's the site of an active police investigation. Are we through here? I'm working.'

'Please, Dr. Lose. I believe I have a connection to that site.'

'What?'

'The black rose!' The words come out before my mind catches up.

Silence. Then: 'What are you talking about?'

'My mother.' I swallow hard. 'She left me a black rose before she disappeared.'

I hear a sharp hiss through the phone. 'What kind of rose?'

'The same kind found on Van.' I catch my breath. 'And on Gina Nardo. Please, can I see where Jane Doe was buried?' Again, I hear the words as if someone else said them.

'I told you, it's a fresh crime scene. You need to talk to the police.'

'You're working with them, aren't you?'

'I'm not with the police. I'm a forensic scientist. Go to the police. Tell them what you told me.' She disconnects.

I stare at the phone. If I call Torres and Wax, they'll tell me to stay here and do nothing. I already gave them the rose and the note. This is on me now.

40

I shove my flashlight, knife, and map of New Jersey with an enlarged view of the Pine Barrens into my magic bag. I tap the address to Dr. Lose's lab into the GPS. It takes less than half an hour via Absecon Boulevard and White Horse Pike to get to Galloway. I pass the police station and forensic lab, both located on East Jimmie Leeds Road. With a wistful look at Dr. Lose's building, I continue on my way. I can do this. I'm not entering an absolute wilderness. I'll stay on the roads, such as they are, until I arrive at the burial pit.

I stop near the entrance of the Forsythe Bird Sanctuary, clearly marked on the map. Salt marshes, feeding ground for migratory birds. Blue herons, egrets up in the trees, sandpipers. I wonder if Elvis Jones brings Bird here. This is his kind of place – only the slightest veneer of civilisation.

I spread the map on the dashboard. At the top is a statement:

The Pine Barrens is part of 1.1 million acres of the Pinelands National Reserve, which ranges from northern Ocean County south and west, and occupies 22% of New Jersey's land area.

It's intimidating, no question, but I tap in Clarks Landing as the destination, and a route appears on my GPS. The map itself warns that phone and GPS signals can waver the deeper and more off-road you go, but I plan to stay on-road.

At first, I pass houses and signs advertising tours and a ghost town, but after ten or fifteen minutes, the GPS instructs me to turn right where there is no road. It becomes clear the GPS and I are on two different roads. The car jolts over pits on a winding dirt road. The nature is grand: enormous trees and webs of bushes and plants. But I don't see any signs. How do people find their way around?

The GPS's brisk woman's voice sputters to life again, instructing me to turn left, then right, and left again. The otherworldly aura of the mists, broken pines leaning toward the ground, shadows of branches dappling the windshield, fiery leaves, birds shrieking, and the isolation...

I haven't passed a single car or seen a single human being. A thrill rushes through me, a sense that anything is possible here. I can fly or dance or sing. I can lose myself in these vast woods.

The Jersey Devil doesn't want you to find the pit. He takes care of his own.

Where did that creepy thought come from?

The Devil's Tree. I'm nowhere near it, I hope. The most haunted place in New Jersey. On my eighteenth birthday Stormie and I went there with two guys. The other three were excited. I was cowering as usual, trying to dig up courage where there was none.

Dark, when we got there. A full blue moon shone over a single oak tree. We climbed out of the car and circled the tree. It had been hacked with axes and chain saws. According to legend, the tree curses anyone who dares disfigure it. Later, at home, I looked up the Devil's Tree. In the 1920s, the area was a centre for the Ku Klux Klan, where they burned crosses and held rallies, and possibly lynched African Americans. Reason enough for the tree to carry evil weight, its branches to swing low and menacing. That night the guys told Stormie and me Halloween horror stories, scaring themselves as well as us, until a truck with monster wheels appeared out of nowhere, its headlights blinding us. We leaped into the car and raced out of there.

Why am I thinking of that now? It's daylight, I'm safe in my car, and there's no such thing as a Devil. Only evil humans. Did I pass this road before? I remember a field of tall grasses swaying in the breeze. Am I going in circles? I should have told Stormie where I was going. The GPS voice has stopped speaking to me. My phone has lost its signal.

A stark blue tent rises from a field of grass stalks. A sign of civilisation. Maybe someone has set up camp. I park on the side of the road. Phone in hand, I cross the gravel road to the field and trudge through the waving stalks. The air rustles, or is it the grass? I feel movement near my feet. Snakes... Please, no.

'Hello!' My voice sounds small against a vast, pale sky. I hear a sound and whip around. When I turn back, I'm facing a rifle aimed at me. I can't even scream.

A man with long, tangled white hair and beard glares over the gun. He's dressed in camouflage, and he's not much taller than the grass, but he's spitting curses and crackling with fury.

'I... I... I... just...'

'Get the fuck outta here or I'll shoot.'

I back away, keeping my eyes on him. 'I... just...'

'Three. Two...'

I turn and run to the car, throw myself inside, and step on the gas. Heart racing, I hurtle down the road. I come to a turn. A hard left, a few yards. I stop and lock the doors.

Who is he? The way he sprang in front of me, dressed like a soldier, rifle in hand, ready for war. He may have a car parked behind the tent, and he's coming after me now. I need to get out of here.

But I have no idea where I am.

I lean over and scratch under my socks. I tug up my jeans. Tiny red marks on my ankles and up my calves. I knew something was scurrying in the grass. I dig my nails into the flesh, wanting to draw blood. This was a fool's mission, and I'm a fool, and now I have a crazed man with a gun on the hunt for me and I'm lost in the devil's playground.

A faint smell stings my nostrils and throat. Not tears though I'm on the verge of crying. The scent is familiar – pungent and peppery. Van. Gutsy, fearless Van. If I want to find out what happened to you, I need to absorb some of your courage.

I unlock the door and step out. Phone in one hand, keys in the other. No sign of the white-bearded warrior. He may have been guarding his territory.

I breathe in fresh water and follow the scent to a wide beautiful river. The Mullica. Used for boating, kayaking, fishing, but at the moment it's still and serene. Another thing I read: the river is dotted with tiny islands, many with historic graves. Birds skim low over the water, their cries as mournful as this place.

A faint breeze blows from the river. I glimpse a figure. A woman moving inland. I can't see her face, but for an instant she reminds me of Cleo beckoning to me. I follow the woman toward a small stretch of sand strewn with trash, beer cans, bottles. The sand stops at the edge of a large pit bordered by yellow police tape. A sign warns people to stay out of the crime scene.

I whirl around, but the woman who led me here is gone.

The air crackles with blue motes, the ground hisses sharp and snake-tongued. I breathe in wormy overripe fruits, yet nothing grows here. Only death. I swallow the bitter blue taste of evil.

PART TWO
LITTLE NICK

41

Tuesday October 23

He parks on Old Port Republic Road, where Lucy drove into the Barrens. No way he'll follow her. Even barricaded in his car, the vines from the past wind around him and suffocate him. Winters blur into summers and back to winters huddling in front of the wood stove. He has never returned here, not once. Besides, he knows exactly where she's going and what she will find.

He sees himself the long-ago night his grandfather, Big Nick, swore to make him a man, the night they docked the sneak boat at Clarks Landing and dug open an ancient grave for the sad lady. Little Nick shovelled dirt with his eyes closed. He didn't want to see the sad lady's glassy stare as she lay on the ground, and he didn't want to look up and see the moon.

'Open your eyes, boy!'

His eyes shot open.

'It's deep enough.' Big Nick handed him the saw. 'Hold it steady.'

He gripped the handle with both hands, raised it to his chest and blinked at the lady, so pretty and sad. He lowered the saw and kept his eyes down.

'Whaddya waiting for? You wanna be a man or not?'

He had to remember this lady wasn't his ma, even if she had the same sweet voice. She'd never know it was him who was going to sever her head from her body.

Big Nick growled, and Little Nick clenched the saw again, his fingers sliding down the slippery handle.

The sad lady stirred on the ground.

Little Nick dropped the saw and jumped back a foot.

With a heavy sigh Big Nick took a small bottle from his pocket. The apple jack moonshine he brewed himself. He threw back his head and drank, then passed it to Little Nick. 'Boy, you need liquid guts.'

The moonshine blazed to his feet and shot back up to his head.

'Ima ask you again. What kind of man you gonna be? A sissy-man or a real man?'

'A real man.' He wasn't no goddamn sissy but knowing the Jersey Devil was buried in one of those old tombs made him shivery to his toes.

'Women take advantage of a man's weakness. You gotta toughen up. Drink like a man.'

He tasted apple jack and the rotten egg taste of fear.

'Now tell me why we saw off the head.'

'So she can't tell no more lies.'

Big Nick threw back his head and drank. 'That's right. What else?'

'So no one will know who she is.'

'Without a head she could be anyone. We don't want nobody looking for her. Now do the deed.'

A howl rose from the pit they'd dug.

'The Devil!' cried Little Nick. 'He's in there.'

'Lemme tell you about the Jersey Devil, seeing as we're in his resting ground. The Devil started out human, same as you and me. Couple hundred years ago Mother Leeds was birthing her thirteenth not far from here. It was a hard delivery, and she screamed, "May this child be a devil!" The thirteenth child was born normal, but he turned into a monster. They say he killed the midwife, then the other twelve kids. The only one he left alive was his mother. That's their version of the story. Let me tell you how I see it.'

Not again. He'd heard this story at least a hundred times. All he wanted was to get out of here and leave the sad lady be, but once Big Nick started, you couldn't stop him.

Big Nick drank again. 'First off, that bitch Mother Leeds got pregnant by cheatin' on her husband. Then she cursed that baby while he was still in her belly. If he turned into a monster it was her own damned fault. When she come out of that labour and saw him, he looked like an angel for about a minute, then he started yowlin' like the other twelve. Well, guess what? She's the one who turned into a monster and killed them all. She was the true devil but she blamed it on her own kid. That's been the way of broads, ever since Eve cheated on Adam with a snake. Ever'last one of 'em is dark and sneaky as a blackbird that pokes at you and pecks out your eyes. You gotta get her before she gets you.'

He handed Little Nick the saw. 'Do it, boy. The first one's the hardest.'

The sad lady's hair was matted and blood-soaked. Her throat, purple-bruised from the old man's hands. Little Nick's heart pounded so hard it was about to burst from his chest. The sad lady had told him he reminded her of someone. Well, she reminded him of his ma. The sadness in her voice, the softness of her hand ruffling his hair, her pale eyes sparkling with blue tears. Same as his ma before she'd disappeared.

He jerked up his head. 'I can't do it, Big Nick.'

Big Nick stared, eyes cold and mean as one of his snakes. He grabbed the saw out of Little Nick's hands and swung at the sad lady, nearly slashing the boy who ducked and fell back on his butt.

With a growl like a maddened bear, Big Nick sliced the air. 'Blackbird, die!' he roared, and the boy could have sworn the roar came from the Devil's tomb. Truth be told he wouldn't have been surprised if the old man laughed and said, 'Meet the Jersey Devil, boy. Right here in the flesh.'

After all, he'd said himself the Devil started out human, and if any man was half-Devil, it was Big Nick.

The blade whistled, and Little Nick covered his head with his hands. After a few seconds he peered between his fingers. Big Nick toppled side to side, a tree on the verge of crashing to the ground. He swung again so wildly the saw went spinning through the air and slithered to the ground like a silver snake. Little Nick crawled there and sat in front of it.

'You make my blood boil! This is your fault, you took so damned long.'

'Let's just bury her.' The sound of his voice, small but firm, shocked him.

The old man spat on the ground. 'Boy, you been a trial to me since day one. There ain't but one reason I saved your life. Something I need you to do.'

'Wha-at?' His voice cracked.

'You ain't ready yet. You ain't even ready to become a man. Now make yourself useful.'

Little Nick helped roll her into the pit they'd dug. When the old man turned his head, he reached in his pocket and dropped the thing the sad lady had given him into the pit. At school he'd seen pictures of ancient Egyptians buried in crypts with the things they loved most, even their pets. He hoped it would make her feel less alone to have something of her own down there. Then he shovelled dirt over her to hide her from the moon and his grandpa, hoping they'd forget about her. He knew he never would.

*

One thing I asked you to do, rages Big Nick. *Set fire to the fucking theatre and get rid of that slut once and for all. Did you do it? No!*

Little Nick looks up from his fingers clutching the steering wheel. What the hell is he doing here, minutes from the horrors of his past? He never should have come back to Atlantic City. He should ignore his grandfather's dying wish. Setting the fire won't help Big Nick rotting underground with the Jersey Devil, but it sure as hell will hurt Little Nick. He's trying to follow the light. But why is the dark always on his heels, a dog baring his teeth and snapping at him?

42

October 16,
one week ago

He and Van stumbled up the dark stairs of his apartment building. They clung to each other, blind-drunk and laughing while trying to be quiet. He fumbled in his pocket for the key and dug it out.

Van carried on, 'That bar was so sleazy...'

'Hey, you wanted to see the real Atlantic City. I obliged.' When he tried to bow, the key dropped, and he crouched dizzily to pick it up. He held out his hand, and she helped tug him up.

He pressed one hand against the wall to steady himself. 'Come for the casinos, stay because your car is gone.'

She giggled. 'Now I see why they call it the armpit of New Jersey.'

'Nah, that's the Pine Barrens.' He stabbed the key at the door again.

'I don't know about the Barrens but in this town the whores are so skanky they wear sweatpants.'

That one did it. He laughed till it came out his nose. He never laughed like that. This girl got past his defences. He enjoyed her toughness. A tiny force of nature, she was all silver edges and gleam like her knives whistling through the air. She excited him and moved him at the same time. He'd heard her being called a ballbuster, but in a world of creeps, a woman needed to protect herself. The question was how to protect himself from her.

The door opened and they nearly fell inside. Pressed against each other, they stared.

'*This* is where you live?' she asked in a voice he'd never heard from her, and in one second flat, he was stone sober. Like a fool he'd driven her to his secret place. The only place he could rip off the mask and let Little Nick breathe freely. He brought women to his other apartment in the city, the one he called his showplace. Until tonight, he and Van had gotten together in her room at Midnight. But now, here she was, a vivid blot in his private space.

Get rid of her! Big Nick roared in his ear.

But Little Nick couldn't move.

She went into the tiny kitchen and opened cupboards, bringing to light jars of crunchy peanut butter and bitter orange marmalade, packages of Cap'n Crunch and ramen, lined up like soldiers. He watched her mess up the magazines and decks of cards he'd arranged on the counter. She ignored the S&M porn and leafed through women's magazines, *Cosmopolitan* and *Glamour*. After a brooding, 'You're more complicated than I thought,' she moved toward the bed. Finally. Sex, and out. That was the plan.

But he should have known that, with Van, nothing ever went according to plan.

He led her to bed and wrapped his arms around her, but after a minute she slid away and studied the bedside table. His three sacred texts, a deck of cards, a small basket of black roses. He couldn't let her open the drawer. He leaned over her and picked up the cards, shuffled them one-handed while she picked up *Tarbell's Course of Magic (Volume One)* and paged through it.

'Everyone's first magic book,' she said. 'I had to hide mine from my sister.'

The only book Big Nick owned; it had been Little Nick's entry not only into magic, but also into showmanship: the secret ingredient that determines the success and failure of a magician. Tarbell taught him that personality is a tool to be used both on and off stage. It took Little Nick years to create a 'personality,' as natural as the cards in his hands.

Van examined the other two books: *Pinocchio* and *The Tales of Edgar Allan Poe*. When he was a boy, he'd salvaged those two from a garbage heap in Egg Harbor City and brought them home. Crumbling, dog-eared, underlined, corners turned down.

'I love Poe.' She wiggled her fingers. '"The Purloined Letter" could have been written by a magician. It shows how easy it is to hide something in plain sight, just like misdirection.'

'Exactly,' he said.

Here was a happy memory: a winter night, wind howling outside, and him alone in the cabin, sitting in the wooden box, reading Poe and *Pinocchio* by the light of the kerosene lamp and drinking apple jack to stay warm. He loved Poe's wild imagination, his humour and despair, the telltale heart – there it was! The human heart beating inside and betraying you. Little Nick got it – oh, God, did he get it, a punch in the gut. Poe knew what it meant to be alone, to know from the beginning that you were different. What you saw no one else saw, and what they saw you didn't see at all.

At his side, Van breathed in the pages of *Pinocchio* and wrinkled her nose. 'Spiders and moths live in these books!' But she kept thumbing through. 'Isn't *Pinocchio* a Disney movie?'

'Yeah, but the real story is much darker. Old Geppetto, the puppeteer, formed a wooden puppet. Geppetto was kind and good, but he couldn't stop Pinocchio from going bad.' Strange to hear himself talk about the book that was his guide to life every bit as much as Tarbell.

She tilted her head encouragingly, and he went on. 'Right off the bat, Pinocchio got in with a bad crowd, smoked and drank. Each time Pinocchio did wrong and lied, his nose grew.'

Each time Little Nick had wicked, dirty thoughts, his dick grew.

'He tried to be a real boy but failed miserably.'

Same with Little Nick. Whenever he tried to be a real boy and act nor-

mal, people looked at him weird and made rude comments.

'See, it's a lesson.'

'About lying and cheating, right?' she asked.

'No, it's about transformation.'

'Like in magic?'

'Yeah. More than anything, Pinocchio wanted to be a real boy.' How to put this in words? He should just shut up. But she watched him with tenderness, as if she got it. 'You're not born a boy. You start out wooden and clumsy, and you have to learn to become human.'

Step by painful step.

After an excruciating pause, she threw her arms around him. 'You blow my heart wide open.'

He shivered to the core. In a way, this tiny fireball blew him wide open too. Yeah, he was drunk, but he'd never brought anyone to Little Nick's refuge, and the fact that he'd brought Van here meant she'd gotten under his skin. He leaned over and kissed her. Within minutes they were in bed, naked and curved around each other.

After they had sex, he went to shower. When he came out, he found her in the kitchen, wearing his T-shirt. She'd clipped one of the black roses to her hair.

He kept his voice low. 'What are you doing?'

She turned. 'I'm starving. Aren't you? How do you like your eggs?'

'You don't have to–'

'I want to.'

She refused to let him help. How was he going to get her out of here? He sat in bed and cringed at the clatter and banging, the muffled curses as she dropped utensils and slammed drawers. This girl, the essence of grace with her knives, was a klutz in the kitchen. Flushed and sweating as if she'd just been through a marathon, she carried the dishes to the bed and served him.

They sat side by side and ate in silence. The eggs were overcooked with bits of shell embedded, the toast burned. Careful not to look at her, he forced down a few bites.

'I'm hopeless.' She raised tragic eyes to him. 'I wanted to impress you.'

'You did. You do. Every minute.'

The Van-smile lit her face. 'C'mere, you. Let me show you something I am good at.'

After a while, they cleared up the kitchen together, teasing each other and laughing. When they returned to bed, she said, 'It's weird, you and me, happening so fast, but you feel it too, don't you?'

He nodded.

'So what happens next?'

'Aren't you going back to Vegas?'

'I don't have to.' She traced a finger down his chest. 'I think we should try living together. Look, I'm as scared of commitment as you are. I know you see other women. We'll be a great pair. Free and independent but taking care of each other. We're good together.'

'We are,' he said, thoughtful. The years with Ellie in St. Louis were the best he'd ever had – until Big Nick roared to life just like the Jersey Devil and shattered his peace. But for years now, since he'd moved to Atlantic City, he'd stayed quiet and under the radar. He was older, wiser, and desperate for another chance to live a normal life with a normal woman. Another woman had recently asked him to marry her, but Van would be better. She craved her freedom nearly as much as he did. They'd move into the showplace apartment. Maybe he could even get rid of this place. It was time to bury Big Nick so deep underground he'd never rise again. Time to become the man he truly was, most of the time. The man he could be all the time if he could just peel Big Nick off his skin and out of his mind.

Van cuddled against him and his arm went around her. He felt a strange lightness, as if he were flying over the bed, and could see the two of them as he looked down. Hope. He'd almost forgotten what it felt like. A warm woman in his arms. What it looked like. A rose blooming in concrete. What it smelled like. Van's black-pepper.

He was ready to fall in love, settle down, and once and for all, become human. Why not?

Big Nick rose from the depths. *You don't get to have dreams like that, boy.*

43

early Wednesday morning October 17

Van pressed against him in bed. Hope fluttered its wings around them. What if...? Two misfits: a little warrior who hurled knives like some kind of samurai and a wooden man without a heart or soul. Maybe together, they could learn to be normal.

Not ready to go to sleep, Little Nick switched on the TV and searched for his favourite Discovery Channel show when a familiar sight caught his eye. The camera panned over the Pine Barrens – a wilderness vibrating with autumn colours reflected in swamps and winding rivers.

Memories slammed into him. Still, he didn't connect it. Not until he saw the haunted graveyard overrun with uniforms. Without warning he lurched back to the long-ago night when Big Nick had sworn to make him a man. The sad lady disappearing under the dirt, the moon's eyes watching and judging...

On TV, a woman's voice, harsh as a gunshot: 'My team and I are testing the bones and charred fragments.'

He blinked at the screen. A nasty looking woman with clown-orange hair. Spittle dotted her lips. 'We will determine how long they've been underground and to whom they belonged.' She kept talking, but the only thing that stuck was, 'We're lucky with Jane Doe. Her head is still attached.'

Big Nick growled in his ear, *You fucking fool, I warned you about the heads!*

'The entire Pine Barrens is a graveyard.'

Little Nick blinked again.

On TV, the lead cop, with the mournful gaze and jowls of a bulldog, said, 'You've seen *The Sopranos.* That's not just TV. It's reality. The killer believes he's safe.'

He couldn't help glancing at Van sitting at his side, staring at the screen.

Bulldog Cop pushed closer. 'Like these bones and bodies, the past always rises. We will find him.' He looked right at Little Nick as if he saw him in bed with Van. 'I will find you,' he promised.

Time to get the fuck out of Dodge! Big Nick shouted. *Pack up and move on! But first do what you swore you'd do. Set that fire!*

I told you I'd do it, but it has to be the right time.

They're digging up the bodies, said Big Nick. *How much time you think you got?*

Not yet, he protested.

You always been a sissy.

Fuck the old man. Every year around Halloween, he sneaked through a crack in the door. Sometimes Little Nick managed to slam the door shut on him. Not this year.

Van nudged him. 'Hey babe, this is the Pine Barrens, right?'

He didn't look at her. 'Yeah, I guess so.'

'You mentioned the Pine Barrens before.'

He did? When? Why?

'Remember? When we were on the beach, you pointed out the Pine Barrens and said you used to live there.'

Was he that stupid? What happened to him around this woman? He let go of all his controls. He needed to say something. 'I must have been joking. Or drunk.' He closed his mouth. Don't make it worse. Don't smile. It doesn't fit.

'Who's Nick Cray?'

He turned slowly. His head weighed a ton. Van's mouth was a fiery furnace. Somehow her orange lipstick had remained flame-bright through the night. He opened his mouth to speak, but words stuck to his tongue.

What did I tell you? growled Big Nick. *They're all blackbirds, every last one. Cheatin', lyin' sluts that wanna peck out your eyes. You peck theirs out first.*

No, no, no. *I'm not you, old man. I'll fix this. My way, not yours.*

She breathed into him with her sharp black-pepper smell. He fought the urge to sneeze.

'I saw his name written inside the cover of your old books: Nick Cray from Egg Harbor City. Is your real name Nick Cray? It doesn't matter if it is.'

The eggs he'd eaten rose to his throat. He tasted shell slivers in a rubbery mess.

'You transformed yourself, babe. We both did. Like Pinocchio, right? We were meant to be one thing, but we became another, right?' She spoke as if she needed reassurance. Her mouth said one thing, but her eyes said another. She gave him the look he dreaded, the sign his mask was crumbling.

Beyond Van, the white wall turned blood-red, the clock's hands froze, the voices on TV stopped talking. He breathed in sweat and the stink of evil that rose from the haunted graveyard. Her black pepper scent choked his nostrils. An orange mouth gaping open, a fiery cave.

She edged to the side of the bed. 'I think it's time to go. I need sleep, and tomorrow is opening night.'

Rage flamed through his belly. What kind of idiot did she think he was? She'd never let it rest.

'You don't have to drive me back. I'll call an Uber.'

He reached into the bedside table drawer for his trusty friend. He hadn't touched it in years, but it was there, waiting. The instant before she climbed out of bed, he hunched toward her as if to kiss her. When she jerked, he pulled the cord around her neck, tightened it and drew her toward him. She screamed and arched back, a wild cat hissing and scratching. A black moment of confusion – where was he? Who was she? Her hair wasn't butter-yellow, it was coarse and black with orange tips. She smelled bitter – not sunny vanilla, but sharp pepper. When did she pierce a diamond in her nose?

Get her outta here! raged Big Nick.

*

A few hours later he peered down at the puffy face, clammy and pale, and the body he'd lowered into the sawing box in the theatre. She couldn't leave well enough alone, she had to push and probe. Why did she have to ruin everything? They could have had something special.

The clean-up, the transport, the grunt work – he'd forgotten how much he hated it.

He decided to transform it into pure theatre. He took the rose she'd clipped to her hair and set it between her lips. Spin the wheel and point the arrow of suspicion. Spin the wheel again and point the arrow of discovery. You just had to know where to look.

44

Thursday October 18

He stared out the window at a sky and ocean the turbulent grey of his mood. For the past week, his mind had veered madly from present to past, crashing into corners, reversing, and shooting forward, a bumper car out of control. A few times lately, he'd been in action in the outside world when Little Nick seeped through the mask, squinted at the light, and said or did something stupid, forcing him to do rapid-fire repair.

It reminded him of the final days in St. Louis when everything came crashing down. Big Nick was back in full force, yelling in his ear night and day. And the world was locking him in a sawing box as narrow and airless as the one Big Nick used as a punishment. Until a few days ago, he'd been flying high, almost touching the sun. Then came Van. And last night, the whore with rotting teeth. He was free-falling. Two fuckups in one week.

Big Nick growled, *I always told you to leave the sluts alone or they'll be the end of you.*

How did last night go so wrong? He'd gone to his favourite bar on the Pike, the one that reminded him of the old Green Bank Tavern in the Barrens. All he wanted was a couple of drinks, a release from the Van fuckup. Rowdy men's men crammed at the bar, holding up their beers and shouting at a screen where other men's men in helmets and outsized shoulders played football.

He drank his beer alongside them, as if he was one of them, the so-called normal men. They didn't know what it meant to be a man any more than he did. They played a role, same as he did. It was all showmanship. Each time he fucked up it was because of the yearning to be what he was not, the thing that might not even exist on this earth: a real human man with a heart.

He was ready to head out when the blonde at the other end of the bar caught his eye. Even under weak light she was no prize, but he recognised her. One of his tribe. Pretty or ugly, they radiated fear. The same fear he felt, only he'd learned to hide it.

She swayed toward him. Close-up, her bleached blonde hair was coarse, her mascara and lipstick smeared, her greying bra strap safety-pinned. Worse, she had the dead gaze of an addict. She could be anywhere between thirty and fifty. Her smile exposed a missing front tooth. 'Dance?'

He avoided slow dancing. He didn't need a shrink to tell him what it symbolised but fuck it. He was drunk enough to give it a try. After all these years, what did it matter? He'd travelled far beyond that long-ago night.

They hadn't taken two steps when the jukebox blasted, 'Saving All My Love for You.'

He stiffened. He hadn't heard that song since the night his life was sliced in two.

Before the dance.

After the dance.

Don't go there, he ordered himself. *Do not fucking go there.*

But the woman wrapped her arms around him, and his arms went around her, and they moved, peanut shells cracking beneath the soles of his boots. She said something he couldn't hear because he was back in the high-school gym in Egg Harbor City, dancing with the most beautiful girl he'd ever seen. The girl's butter-yellow hair shone as if she carried the sun with her, as if the sun loved her so much it couldn't bear to let her go in the dark. Her sweet vanilla scent tickled his nostrils. So *this* is life. For the first time he understood: This is what everyone else feels, why they talk to each other and smile and touch – for *this*. To feel like maybe you weren't alone in the world. Like maybe there's someone else, not a devil-man threatening you with savage threats and beatings, but a soft someone who smells of cookies. He, Little Nick, the Reject, was in the circle of knowing with the others. In the blazing centre of the sun. The light so bright it blinded him. The joy so intense he thought he'd explode. *Here* was where he belonged. Not in the dark with Big Nick, but in the burning brightness with the normal ones.

He floated with her, lost in the song, when all of a sudden, she pushed away from him and twisted her face, that beautiful heart-shaped face, and pointed down at him, 'Get away from me, you pervert!' He looked down at his boner poking through his trousers, and he erupted into flames right there in the dance hall in front of her and everyone.

'Ouch!' shrieked the woman in his arms. Her hair wasn't butter-yellow. She didn't smell of cookies. She smelled of rot like Mordecai Swamp.

She scrunched her face, then spat, 'A man with two left feet shouldn't wear boots! You crushed my fucking foot!'

Rage exploded, a volcano burning lava that seethed and bubbled down the flesh.

One look at him, and she quickly tried to fix it: 'I'm sure you're better in bed.' She laughed, loud and drunk, trying to make it better.

He saw her through a red veil. 'Let's find out.'

'Hey, it ain't free, honey.'

'I got money. Let's go outside.'

Heart thumping in his ears, he danced her across the sea of peanut shells past the men too busy punching the air with fists and screaming like maniacs to notice him. He opened the door and stepped into a cold blast of wind. The door to the bar slammed shut behind them. The parking lot was all shadowy cars, no lights. He grabbed her hand.

'Hey!' she said. 'Where we going?'

'My car. We can talk in there.'

The moon watched him always, always. He couldn't look at that broad flat face, the eyes that burned through his masks, one after another.

The instant he got her inside and closed the passenger door, a pick-up truck screeched to a halt next to him. A guitar twanged, a woman whined about her man. The driver shut off the radio and climbed out. Baseball cap worn backwards, flannel shirt open over a faded T-shirt. He grinned and winked. 'Got her where you want her, doncha?'

Little Nick nodded.

The guy stuck up his thumb and swaggered across the parking lot toward the bar.

Three days later, squinting through the window of his room, he knows exactly what he should have done. He should have opened the door, told her to get the fuck out, and gone home alone. He was ready to do it when up burst Big Nick, the Jersey Devil himself. *That fucking blackbird laughed at you. Do it, do it, do it!*

That was all it took. He sat behind the wheel and leaned toward her. Bashed his forehead against hers.

She blinked, dazed. Mewled, pitiful as a stunned cat. Flung out her fists and punched his chest, but she was too drunk and bleary to make a dent.

His hand slipped into his pocket and pulled out the trusty paracord. He stretched the cord around her neck and yanked the ends tight. He didn't release his grip until her body slumped forward and her head hit his chest.

From soaring high to immediate crash.

He looked at this swollen, drunk, stupid, dead addict and smacked his forehead against the steering wheel. *Why?* Why risk everything he'd been fighting for?

He scanned the lot. The door to the bar opened, letting out screams and music. The door shut again. He didn't see anyone emerge, but it was time to get out of here.

He started the car and drove down the Pike, searching for inspiration, when he remembered the Rope Strangler who'd terrorised Atlantic City several years ago. He used to bite his female victims, tie fancy knots around their throat, and leave them in ditches behind strip clubs and bars, right here on Black Horse Pike. Little Nick knew the exact spot to leave her. Make them think the Strangler is back in action. He drove around the back of a strip club he knew too well and pulled into the deserted lot.

A single light shone over the back door. He pushed the hoodie low over his forehead and climbed out. In the shadows, he picked up a rock and smashed the light. He heaved her in his arms and arranged her body in the shallow pit. Lifted her top to bite her and confuse the cops when in the nick of time he remembered Bundy got caught when they analysed the marks his teeth left in a woman's skin.

He burned rubber back to his refuge. Even before the blazing shower to scrub her off, he crossed the street to the sand and ran against the salt wind, letting it crack against his skin like the waves. Panting, thighs burning, he returned to his favourite spot, leaned against a sand dune, and gulped the salt-bitter air. He'd worked so hard for this life. Inching his way to normal.

He headed back to his refuge for the Black Night and to begin the painstaking process of becoming a man again. As he crossed the street, he decided this was it. Yeah, he'd fucked up with Van, and even worse with the other one, but this was it, he was done. No more. Time to go clean and throw away his trusty friend. He had no intention of hurting a woman, any woman, ever again.

45

Friday October 19

Morning sun slanted through the blinds. He'd survived another Black Night. He never knew how much was real, how much he inflicted on himself, how much he imagined. The Black Nights lasted from six hours to forty-eight. Considering how ugly, unplanned, and unfinished the Van fiasco was, followed by the whore at the bar, he'd gotten off easy.

Now came the process of rebuilding himself from the inside, layer by layer.

He shuddered to his feet, his bones as brittle as Big Nick's on his deathbed. Reached for a half gallon of water, gulped, and swallowed, wiped his mouth. He pulled on sweatpants and went outside for a run. Nothing cleared his mind like salt wind, seagulls cawing and swooping, waves cracking. He pushed himself, heart thumping, hard sand beneath his sneakers.

Back in his room, he showered. Time for strong black coffee and his favourite breakfast. He spread Jif Creamy Peanut Butter on a toasted sesame bagel and topped it with a spoonful of bitter orange marmalade. The mingling of textures and tastes revived him. The run, followed by a shower and breakfast, was part of the ritual of showmanship. Humans enjoy routine and repetition. If you perform an act often enough, it becomes part of your daily life.

He picked up a deck of cards. The smooth surfaces sliding between his fingers quieted the savage beast. The one thing he had in common with Big Nick. Pacing the room, he practiced the Elmsley Count, Oil and Water, The Diving Rod. The magician Ricky Jay called his deck of cards his fifty-two assistants. Little Nick called them his fifty-two friends. For years he'd practiced lifts, passes, and shuffles at least two hours a day until the cards were an extension of his hands. Cards and magic made it possible for him to survive among people.

He'd noticed that his grandfather handled cards with the same tenderness with which he handled animals. Despite Big Nick's desire to lay low, he couldn't resist performing now and then at the Green Bank Tavern. He'd brought out brilliant card magic for the roughest group of bikers and Pineys you could imagine. He performed his transparent card routine, in which cards symbolised people and connected with each other in mysterious ways. Little Nick had watched in awe as his grandfather gentled the wild crowd. As Little Nick got older, his grandfather let him do a few rounds of magic at the Tavern. Little Nick loved the moments when a jaw dropped in astonishment, someone cried out in wonder or backed away in a mix of awe and fear, 'How'd you do that, boy?'

Magic hours were stolen hours. They melted the bitterness. He stopped being Little Nick and became a Magician. What a relief, like shedding a heavy coat in summer.

Shortly after Big Nick's death, Little Nick went to Atlantic City. The instant he stepped onto the boardwalk, ocean wind clawed him with pincers. Pinched his chest and constricted his breath. The boardwalk – the stretch of wooden rafters that had once welcomed Presidents, celebrities, and streams of tourists – was lined by fossilised casinos grounded like dying sharks. Hunched men pushed rolling chairs past souvenir shops, T-shirt emporiums, and booths offering psychic readings, massages, or both.

Sea gulls screamed, and waves curved – an invitation, a promise – and a knot inside him loosened. He'd never been in Atlantic City before. On the other side of the bay, it had loomed mythic and forbidden. Big Nick had never told him about the beauty and sadness of the boardwalk. Thousands of things Big Nick hadn't told him. That was the curse of being raised by a man whose entire life was a broken record that jammed in a single groove. Big Nick was a one-note song inside his mind, on endless replay: *Women are all blackbirds, cheatin', lyin' sluts that wanna peck out your eyes. You peck out theirs first.*

It was while standing on the edge of a pier overlooking the ocean that he decided not to keep his deathbed promise to his grandfather. Why should he set a fire that could potentially kill many people? He was *not* Big Nick, and he would *not* become Big Nick. He would not let his mind sink into that broken song. He was young and free. It was time to live his own life.

He took the next bus west.

That was many years ago.

And he still hasn't managed to shed Little Nick. Or Big Nick. But now, it's time to get back to the human show.

PART THREE
RISE

46

Tuesday October 23

When the signal returns to my phone, I call Dr. Lose and tell her where I am.

After a long pause, she asks, 'Are the police there?'

'No.'

'You need to leave right now.'

'I would, but I have no idea how to get out of here. A man with a rifle threatened me.'

'Where?'

'Out there somewhere... he had a blue tent. I just wanted to ask him for directions.'

'Ben Briggs on Hay Road. You're lucky he didn't shoot you.' She tells me not to touch anything.

Twenty minutes later, she pulls up in a forest-green SUV, accompanied by a magnificent grey and white Australian Shepherd who circles me, sniffing. A polka-dot ribbon pushes back Dr. Lose's hair as bright orange as the leaves. She wears an Army jacket, olive-green fatigues, and hiking boots.

'Thanks to Salt we found Jane Doe.' She gestures to her dog. 'He discovered this pit when we were hiking.'

I crouch. His mismatched eyes – one blue, one brown – shine with unnerving intelligence. 'Hi, Salt. I'm Lucy.'

He wags his stubby tail in acknowledgement.

As we walk, Dr. Lose grumbles about illegal trash dumped on the riverbank.

We stand behind the tape barricade. The pit is larger than I imagined. So many secrets buried that will never surface.

She gestures. 'Used to be a town. What happened, nobody

knows. Whole towns dropped into holes. Smallpox epidemic? Massacre? There are rumours about murderers and the Jersey Devil. Every fifty years or so, entire families were butchered. They blame the Devil. Easier than blaming human beings.'

'Are the police still investigating the pit?'

'Yes. I told you, this is an active site. An officer from the State Police is usually standing guard.'

'But you're not a cop.'

'No, but I often work with them, especially when I see a link to one of their cases or when they need access to the Piney Nation. Pineys don't talk to cops.'

'But they talk to you.'

She shrugs. 'I'm a Piney, born and bred. You know the Barrens were originally settled by the Lenni Lenape tribe?'

Lenni Lenape. Where did I just hear about them? I half-listen as she tells me about Revolutionary War battles in this area when my memory sparks: Elvis Jones. I read online that he is a fraction Lenni Lenape. Did he come from this region? Is he the reason Van asked me about the Barrens the day we climbed to the top of the lighthouse? Is that why Dr. Lose went to his show?

'Tried living in New York City but missed the crazy sauce of the Pines. I grew up with stories of pirates smuggling between the Caribbean and Brigantine. And the Devil.' Her freckled face gleams. She looks alive, in her element. 'Rumour has it that the Jersey Devil was Old Man J.D. Leeds himself. You heard of the Leeds?'

I shake my head.

'They're one of the historic founding families of the Barrens. Mother Leeds was rumoured to have given birth to the Jersey Devil.'

'Do you think there's a real Jersey Devil, Dr. Lose?' I can't believe I'm asking. It's the harsh bite of the air. The blue that shadows everything, even her face and Salt's fur.

She glances at me through pale lashes. 'The weird thing about the Devil is how he appears every fifty years or so. What if it's an ecosystem in the Pines? Every fifty years a certain mushroom sprouts a spore that blooms and makes people go mad. It sounds like a crackpot theory, but it makes as much sense as anything else. Okay. Now you've seen it. Let's go. You can follow me out.'

'Wait! Dr. Lose, please. Can we go in, just for a minute? I swear I won't touch anything.'

She grunts, then says, 'Five minutes.'

I follow her and Salt inside the marked-off area.

Reeds and grasses surround the pit and blow in the wind.

'Tell me about your mother's rose,' she says abruptly.

'Black polyester. Faux-silk. Exactly the same as the ones found in Van's mouth, and Gina's.' My eyes burn. 'Mine is crumpled and tear-stained. I slept with it for years.'

'Where is it now?'

'I brought it to Detectives Torres and Wax. They're sending it to the lab to check for DNA.'

Staring into the pit, she says, 'We found two bobby pins and fragments of black polyester. Funny thing about polyester. It never dies. Damned thing will outlive us all.'

My breath catches. 'Is it possible... the fragments were part of a black rose?'

Dr. Lose doesn't answer.

Salt moves from the pit, looks back at me. Herding me like a shepherd with his flock, guiding me away from danger. I'd moved too close to the edge. I follow him.

'Salt is my best friend.' Ida's voice comes from a distance. 'He doesn't usually take to strangers.'

She looks from Salt to me and says briskly, 'I shouldn't be telling you this, but Jane Doe wasn't the only victim buried in the pit.

We're analysing samples from the soil, bugs, and body remains that span decades. The ground has high silica content, which means it's highly acidic. No flesh remains on the bones. Just teeth. We're still looking to match dental records.'

She lowers her gaze to Salt, still guarding me. 'When it comes to the Pines, I can't hold back. No one gets us right. They watch *The Sopranos* and believe we're all madmen or murderers.'

But the horror of what happened here through the years thrusts up from the ground. 'Jane Doe was murdered, wasn't she?'

'It's time to go.'

Salt pushes against my side and lets me lean against him. 'Do you have any idea who killed her?'

'I can't talk to you about this. I've already said too much. Let's go, Salt.'

'Thank you for showing me this place.'

She says nothing as we walk back to the clearing where the cars are parked. At the side of my car, Salt nuzzles my leg. I hunker down on the sandy ground, throw my arms around him and bury my face in his fur. My eyes sting, my nose and throat.

I hear Dr. Lose's gruff voice behind me. 'Two men's names come up. Both from that era, both known for violent tempers. Ben Briggs, a Vietnam vet and ex-con. The guy who nearly shot you. They've locked him up more times than I can count. And Big Nick, a snake catcher who lived on Joe Mulliner Road with his grandson, known as Little Nick. They both disappeared about twenty years ago, but the old man did magic now and then.'

I twist around. 'Magic?'

'Not Elvis Jones kind of magic. Card tricks at a local tavern.'

'Do you remember anything about the tricks?'

'Regular card tricks. Oh, there was one in which a card turns into another card. Mysterious something.' She grunts. 'This stays between us. I could get in trouble for talking to you.'

I follow her back through the Barrens. Minutes later, we emerge onto the main street. She drives away, and I pull over to the side. I need a minute before returning home.

Detective Wax said the only things connecting Van's and Gina's murders are the killer's cord, the rose, and me. But I see another connection. Magic. That must be the reason my mother brought me to Declan Moon.

Big Nick, the snake catcher who did card tricks.

Mysterious something. A memory flashes, a lacy black shadow at the corner of my eyes. My father might remember. He's an encyclopaedia of magic. I need to talk to him.

I meet my reflection in the rearview mirror and imagine my mother's rose in my hair, above my ear, the way I press a white rose to my hair in the *Bewitched* illusion. As I stare at my own eyes, glowing feral with the blue light of the Barrens, the idea comes to me. A way to bring the Hunter out in the open.

I pull out onto the main road and pass a parked car. The driver lowers his head. But not before I glimpse a black hoodie.

47

Little Nick

He drums his knuckles on the steering wheel, waiting for Lucy to come out of the Barrens. The instant he sees her face, he'll know how much she knows, and then he'll figure out what he needs to do. No matter what the carrot-haired bitch tells Lucy, she can't come close to the truth of his life with that old psycho.

He spent his last month in the Barrens caring for him. Big Nick had the worst kind of tobacco heart. At the end, he stormed through his past, screaming about the Slut-whose-name-can't-be-spoken, sobbing he'd loved her, roaring that the Timber Rattlesnake was sucking his blood. 'She claims I stole something from her, and she won't leave me alone. You need to set fire to that hell-hole and get rid of her once and for all,' he insisted. 'Swear you'll do it.'

'I swear, I swear.' Little Nick washed him. Fed him with a spoon.

With a final rattle of the throat, as if one of his own snakes had entered him, life disappeared from Big Nick's eyes.

While Little Nick dug a hole and buried his grandfather, blackbirds circled the cabin. The snakes were there too, coiled in secret places. He didn't see them, but that didn't mean they weren't there. The old man had scared him half to death, but he'd also fed and watched over him. What was a Little Nick without a Big Nick? An appendage, a rib wrenched from Big Nick's chest.

He went back inside their cabin on Joe Mulliner Road. It smelled of sickness and death. He took the money Big Nick had hidden under his mattress. Found a dog tag in his stuff. Didn't belong to Nicodemus Cray. Stolen. It figured. A handful of clothes tossed into a canvas bag. A few decks of cards. His three guides to life: Tarbell, Poe, and Pinocchio.

He poured gasoline over the wood floor and threw a lit match.

Halfway down Joe Mulliner Road he heard wood crackling and turned back to watch the cabin burn. Goodbye, Big Nick. Goodbye, Little Nick. He'd already decided on a name. 'Peter,' because it sounded like the Three Musketeers: Poe, Pinocchio, and Peter. 'Wilson,' because of Poe's story, 'William Wilson.'

Peter Wilson walked out of the Dark Ages and into the future. He didn't know where to go or what to do, but he knew one thing: He'd go to the ends of the earth to rip the strings that tied him to the Barrens, the cabin, and especially Big Nick. Peter Wilson was going to transform himself into a real human.

That was years ago, many transformations ago. He sees Peter Wilson, the young man sailing into the future like the Fool in the Tarot, blindly optimistic and certain he was free of Big Nick. He shuts his eyes. Burning wind crackles in his ears, ashes disintegrate on his tongue. Peter Wilson died a long time ago.

Big Nick roars, *What the fuck are you waiting for? Do what you promised and get the hell outta Dodge!*

He presses his palms over his eyes. His head is exploding. Set the fire or leave town? Big Nick is right. Too late to fight it. Burn the Widow, burn his past, set fire to the whole mess, and then clear out and start over somewhere else. A new life, a new name.

A car horn startles him. Carrot Hair is at the wheel of a green SUV. She drives off.

Lucy's Festiva appears. Lucy stops the car and lowers the sun visor. It's not sunny so she must be looking at herself in the mirror. His chest twists. He knows that feeling, when you have to check your reflection to recall which face you're wearing that day.

Sometimes, just to make sure you have a face.

What the hell is she doing? Pressing her hand against the side of her head. He squints. Fuck. She knows something. The bitch knows. That fucking Carrot Hair was stupid enough to show her the pit. He overheard the cops talking about her: *A damn Piney who can't keep a lid on it. Keep her in the Barrens.*

That prejudice against Pineys. He fought long and hard to break out of that box. He almost feels sorry for Carrot Hair. But it's her fault. Her and her dog. They brought up what should have stayed buried.

He smashes his fist against the steering wheel. He thought Lucy was different, but she wants to bring him down like the others. Carrot Hair, Van, the whore – all the same, fucking blackbirds screeching in the dead of night. Peck peck peck at a man till nothing is left.

Suddenly, Lucy is driving toward him. She stares through the windshield at him. He ducks instantly, hoping the hoodie pushed low shields his face. He waits a minute and cautiously lifts his head.

When she pulls away, he's behind her.

48

When I emerge from the art supply store in Philly, river wind blows from Penn's Landing down South Street and coils around my chest. Trembling with excitement I set the packages of black crepe paper on the back seat. I can already see them blooming onstage. I'll stop at home to pick up the glue and tape measure.

As I slide onto the driver's seat, my phone vibrates. No Caller ID.

Fear chokes me. The timing of it. The dark magic of the Pine Barrens permeates my car. The back of my neck tingles. I feel someone watching. Maybe the driver who was parked outside the Barrens, a black hoodie lowered over his face. Is Elvis Jones the Hunter? Did he follow me? If he did, he knows I went to the Pine Barrens. And he must know what I found.

I lock the doors and sag against the wheel.

Elvis Jones is not the only person in the world to wear a black hoodie. It could be Gus or Charlie. It could be Rex. The police let him go, and he tracked me.

Feeling like an idiot, I start the car. A prank call, must be.

I hear the alert tone. Foot on the brake, I grab the phone. Click for the message and press the phone to my ear.

Someone breathes.

I wait.

The breathing quickens. As if he's running or excited.

I throw the phone down and slam on the gas.

The breathing rises from the floor until the message runs out.

Scarier than if he spoke. Words are not his true language. His shrill laugh, panting on the phone, hands tightening around a woman's throat as he watches life leave her eyes. That's the way he talks.

With a shudder, I get on the Expressway to Atlantic City. He scented me. Tracked me. Found me. He wants to know what I found in the Barrens.

I *feel* his eagerness, a Great White wanting you to come out and play.

Game on.

My move. Tomorrow night, I'm going to lure him into the open with black flowers.

49

Back in Atlantic City, I turn on Mississippi, and my phone vibrates again. I'm scared it's the Hunter again, but my father's warm smile lights up the screen.

Auntie Maze says, 'Hello, darlin'.'

Then, Da: 'We're back, love. In time for your opening night.'

My throat catches at the sound of their voices. 'I'm on my way. I need to talk to you both.'

Back home, the three of us settle in Da's Temple of Magic, the room where Lucy Moon was born. Auntie Maze and I face Da, who sits behind his desk, and I see myself as a child approaching the edge and rising on tiptoe to see this curious giant. His magic eyes and voice, the heat he emanated, the love he gave so freely to a little stranger.

'Remember Jane Doe, the woman found in the Pine Barrens? I was there this afternoon. I saw the burial pit.' I draw in a sharp breath. 'Scraps of black polyester were buried with her.'

My aunt's eyes widen. 'Like the rose?'

I nod.

'Many things are made of polyester,' says Da.

I lean toward him. 'Back then, when you searched for my mother, did you find any clues?'

'If we had, you'd be the first to know.'

'I was too young to understand. Maybe it will make more sense now.'

'Declan called in a private investigator,' says Auntie Maze. 'About five years had passed.'

'Why did you wait so long?'

Da says, slow, 'We wanted to be sure that if he didn't already know you existed, he'd never find out. The investigator went through murder reports in Cape May County and Philadelphia. Around that time many women were attacked, battered, murdered. None coincided with our dates and situation.'

'Then we thought she might have gone missing,' says Auntie Maze. 'When women disappear, no one notices, as if they're invisible. It's a two-edged sword. A woman can hide and resurface as someone else. More often, the sad truth is she simply vanishes.'

Da takes over. 'We learned that during the season you came to us, half a dozen women in the Atlantic City area were reported missing. We had to be very discreet because we didn't want to get in the way of police investigations. And of course, we didn't want to alert the man who took her.'

'What did you find out?'

'Two of the missing women were African American. A third woman, over seventy, suffered from dementia and wandered off.' I can hear him remembering. 'Another was severely disabled, and those who knew her assumed she'd committed suicide. Of the six women, only two seemed possible, but when I checked, neither one had children. One woman was from South Philly. An addict who either died on the street or fell into the Delaware River. The other woman fought with her boyfriend, ran out the door, and disappeared. The boyfriend had a strong alibi.'

'Did you keep checking?'

'We did, lass. As far as I know, none of the women were ever found.'

We sit quietly for a moment. 'I gave the police my mother's rose and note. I think she came to you, Da, because you're a magician. One of the suspects in Jane Doe's murder is a violent snake catcher who lived in the Pine Barrens and who did magic. There's a link here. I see it at the edge of my mind, but I can't grasp it.'

Da steeples his hands. 'G'wan, g'wan then, tell me what you know.'

'He did card tricks, and he was known for one in particular. Mysterious something.'

'What kind of trick was it?'

'He changed one card into another.'

'One card into another,' he repeats. 'That's not so unusual, but to call it Mysterious… mysterious…' He squints one eye. 'Well, that brings an old trick to mind. I'm thinking Hofzinser's Transparent Card.'

'Can you tell me about it?'

'I'll show you.'

While Da prepares the illusion, he explains its history. 'Hofzinser was a nineteenth century magician who used to call card tricks "the poetry of magic." Lovely, eh? He created an effect about transformation using the Hofzinser Card, a mysterious and wonderful artifact, a card that has been called transparent. The effect is overly complicated with heavy-handed sleights that wouldn't fool anyone today. But a World War Two magician learnt the effect from one of Hofzinser's students and updated it. He called it "Mysterious Connections."'

Da opens an old wooden box I've never seen before and brings out a candle, a candle holder, and a deck of cards. He shuffles the deck, then holds it out and tells Auntie Maze and me to each pick a card. She chooses the Six of Spades, and I choose the Four of Hearts.

He lifts Auntie Maze's card. 'What do you see?'

Auntie Maze and I both say, 'The Six of Spades.'

He holds up my card. 'And this one?'

'The Four of Hearts.'

'Two different cards, like two different human beings. But let's imagine one person's card magically transforming into the second person's card, as if these two people are somehow connected. Tell us again, Maze, what was your card?'

'Six of Spades.'

He lights the candle, then holds her card in front of the flickering flame and flips the card around. 'Now, what do you see?'

Auntie Maze and I peer at the card. I draw in my breath. 'My card, the Four of Hearts.'

'Ah. Two cards, two human beings, and yet the power of a single flame, a single light, reveals the truth. Under the surface, these two are perhaps not so different, not so separate. They can become one. *We* can become one. Do you see? Like the cards, we share a mysterious connection.'

Da blows out the candle and gathers the materials back into the box. 'Sometimes we don't have the ability to see what is before our eyes. Magic is the special light that allows us to see what is not ordinarily visible, the connection that draws us together.' He smiles at me. 'The way I was knowing your face from the first time I saw you.'

My heart catches. 'Do you ever regret taking me in?'

He looks at me full-on with those bright green eyes. 'If I had the doing of it again, I'd do exactly the same.'

The memory flashes before me. 'Magnificent Morelli was the World War Two magician.'

When he nods, I sigh. 'The night I found Van, Jinx was in the audience, and she mentioned Mysterious Connections, the trick Morelli performed. But how did a snake catcher in the Pine Barrens get the trick?'

'Magic tricks pass from hand to hand.'

Cleo felt a mysterious connection with Frank, the man who later murdered her. Maybe my mother felt a mysterious connection to Big Nick and followed him into the Barrens, where he murdered her. Is it possible that Jane Doe was my mother? 'How could a violent man like Big Nick perform such a delicate trick?'

'Magic soothes the savage beast. I've seen it happen with wild practitioners of the art. The learning of magic disciplines that force. As you well know, we Moons have a touch of that wildness.'

Auntie Maze sniffs. 'More than a touch.'

He continues, 'Not that magic tames you, but it...'

'Trains you?'

'Exactly, lass.'

A fist seizes my heart as I recall Elvis Jones talking about his seagull. *He's not tame. He's trained. That's very different.*

50

That evening, back at Midnight, Stormie plumps up the pillows and sits on my bed, laptop on her knees. As soon as I told her about the Pine Barrens and Jane Doe, she decided we needed to do research online. 'We'll search for flowers and dead women. Dead flowers. Not just black roses. There must be a link we're missing.'

I bring my laptop and notebook to the chair by the window and set my feet on the sill. Stormie puts on a Marvin Gaye song, and his sweet voice fills the room.

It's oddly comforting to search for connections together.

After nearly an hour, I move to the bed. Side by side, Stormie and I stare from my notes to our screens, chilled by this gathering of hothouse blooms. I never imagined there would be so many unsolved murders of lone women in the 1940s, named after flowers: Gardenia, Orchid, Red Rose, Black Dahlia. Women who were stabbed, strangled, mutilated, and dumped like rubbish in an abandoned coal yard, a clump of bushes, a golf course, a field.

I added Cleo West to the list because a returning soldier killed her.

My mother hovers, a shadowy figure in back.

Van and Gina complete the bouquet.

Stormie presses against my shoulder. 'This is totally *ferkokt*.'

'If by *ferkokt*, you mean–' I strain to find a word that encompasses the pain and grief and loss of these women.

'That's exactly what I mean.' She rubs her Star of David necklace. 'What the hell was going on in the forties?'

'I think there were two wars. One in Europe and the other one back home in the U.S.'

She sets down the laptop and sits, cross-legged. 'The guys

come back from overseas where they were heroes. They killed for their country, and they come home to find–'

'Another war: the battle of the sexes.' I set my laptop aside, hunch over my knees and face her. 'Women left the kitchen and took over the men's jobs. Worse, the women were going out alone at night. They didn't need men anymore, not the way they did before the war.'

'That's no excuse for killing women.'

Through the window, the sky is deep, lush evening-blue. I should turn on the light, but I don't want to move yet.

'Here's what I don't get.' She hesitates. 'The connection between the 1940s and now. These poor girls back then, and Jane Doe, and Van, Gina, and–' She breaks off, but I hear the word, 'You,' as clearly as if she said it.

She sighs and gets to her feet. 'I need an early night. Hot bath, the works, and then tomorrow, pu pu pu, we're gonna have an opening night.'

'I told you not to pu pu pu around me. Weirds me out.'

'It's to fight the evil eye.'

I get up and turn on the light, blinking at the sudden brightness.

'Wet tech rehearsal in the morning,' she reminds me. On her way out, she does an exaggerated doubletake and gestures to the riot of black paper flowers in the midst of preparation. 'Wait a minute. The hell is this?'

I stiffen, instantly. I know that voice. 'Okay, so... you know how I use white flowers in *Bewitched*?'

She fixes me with a look that pins me in the hot seat. 'You are not, tell me right now, you are not that idiotic.'

Worse than getting scolded by Da and Auntie Maze. Stormie knows too much about me. 'It will bring him out in the open.'

'Really? You have access to his mind?'

'Is this a cross-examination?'

'Girl, you call *this* a cross-examination?'

'I don't need to answer to you.' Hurt flickers in her eyes. 'Storm, I'm going to find out who he is and who I am. The truth, once and for all. I can't go on not knowing.'

'What do you think he's going to do when he sees you on stage with black flowers? Do you think he's going to stand up and confess? Come on, girl. Be real.'

'He's going to betray himself, somehow. I know it.'

'You've really lost it.' She stalks toward me, hands on hips. 'You know the idiot in the movies who stays in the house with the killer?'

I'm blazing inside. 'What kind of friend are you?'

'The kind who says, "Don't go back in the house where the killer is waiting."' She strides to the door and turns back. 'Did you ask Charlie about this?'

'I'll ask him tomorrow morning. He'll probably say it's good theatre.' *I hope.* 'If he okays it, will you play the blind date?'

'You're fucking kidding me.' She opens the door and throws her parting shot. 'You want to become a dead flower too, go ahead. I won't be part of it.'

I stomp around the room for a few minutes and grab my notebook. The list of dead women confronts me. I see a new one.

The Black Rose: Lucy Moon. Atlantic City. Cause of death: homicide by ligature strangulation.

When I blink, it's gone. But the shadow remains on the page.

*

I rehearse in front of the mirror, incorporating the black flowers, hoping they'll look enough like roses to pass. I jot notes, revising the script, and check the timing. After two hours, I've got it: the transformation of *Bewitched* into Mask and Shadow. The darkness was always there, hidden under the script and magic. The wacky witch in *Bewitched* fought her powers because she was married to a human. She used up tons of energy trying to pass as a normal housewife, but the magic kept happening. The more she fought it, the more it erupted around her. The same thing happens in Mask and Shadow, but this time her magic is darker, and it spills out of her because she can't hold it in anymore, it breaks free, and all she can do is watch it erupt around her. Van told me once that I'm a film noir trapped inside a rom-com. Wait till she sees this! She'll be so proud–

Grief pierces my chest, a pain so sharp I sink to my knees on the floor. For a moment I forgot. It's real. Van is gone. She'll never see the act. I'll never smell her spicy perfume again and make her laugh. Oh, Van, I need to know what you were thinking the last week of your life. Why you danced with Gus at the Lollipop, argued with Charlie, and fought with Elvis Jones. What were you looking for? Why didn't you share your thoughts with me? You said I was your closest friend...

I squeeze my eyes shut and see the two of us on the morning of the last day of your life. We stood on top of the lighthouse, wind blowing back our hair. You asked me about the Pine Barrens.

Big Nick, Little Nick. Magic Connections. But why would the murderer go after you, Van? Are you still close by? Can you hear me through the door that's ajar? Help me find him.

51

Tuesday night, October 23

As always, Ruby's corner – the corner of New York Avenue and Boardwalk – pulses with energy. The psychic's parlour, DiBruni's pizzeria and Ruby's spots are empty, but I sense my mother watching over me. I know she's dead, but I've always felt her presence on the boardwalk, especially on this corner at this time of year. I search women's faces for a spark of recognition, a gaze that lingers. Blue shadows and copper glints lend their faces an air of mystery.

I peer into the psychic's dusty window. A mirror dangles between a crystal ball and a suspended Tarot deck, revealing my pale reflection. Dark roots add a sinister look to my tangled sunset hair.

I cross the boardwalk toward Central Pier. The arcade is bright and loud. 'He's the Greatest Dancer' blasts through the loudspeaker. I climb down the steps to the sand.

Beneath the pier, peat burns. The blue light glows between rafters. On tiptoe I reach up as far as I can. *Please, Cleo!*

This time, I'm instantly swooped up through the opening. *Yes, thank you.*

Camp Boardwalk – late afternoon sky, salt air so sharp it cuts. A pretty girl holds open the door to a restaurant, and two soldiers on crutches enter. A laughing couple poses on the corner: he's in uniform, she's in a suit cinched at the waist. A few GIs toss confetti. A photographer shoots the bride and groom while a slim young woman with a short bob scribbles notes. She lifts her head, revealing a mischievous grin that says, 'Don't mess with me.'

Seventy-five years later, Jinx has the same grin.

I have barely a minute on the boardwalk when I'm whisked to a corridor in Thomas England Hospital. I lurch through the doorway of a ward, but the transition from place to place is smoother than last time. Purple-grey light shines through the windows. The soldiers are resting or reading. I recognise the ward where Cleo met Frank.

I advance toward Frank's cot by the window. He's not there, but Cleo is curled up, her face smashed into his pillow, her shoulders shaking.

I sit on the edge of the bed, wishing I could comfort her. The rosy-cheeked head nurse presses her hand on Cleo's back. 'Take a deep breath. Coop's in surgery. The doctor is removing the shrapnel in his chest. He didn't get it all the first time, and Coop woke up with his lungs blocked.'

A moment later, the ward is dark, moonlight glinting through the windows. Some of the soldiers moan in their sleep. Cleo must have fallen asleep too. She stretches suddenly, scrambles off the cot and smooths her dress.

She rushes to the head nurse's desk. 'How is Frank?'

'He's in recovery,' says the nurse.

A look of unearthly joy fleets across Cleo's face. She kisses the nurse on both cheeks.

With a suddenness that twists my stomach I'm back on the boardwalk under full moon and lush black sky. Cleo and I slam to a halt back at the entrance of the hotel-hospital. Jimmy the Crab, fedora shading his eyes, cigarette in the corner of his mouth, taps his watch. 'The clock's ticking, and you was with the boys again. Dirty Hand ain't happy.'

'You told him!' Cleo hits his arm. 'I hate you, Jimmy!'

'I didn't tell him nothin'. Swear to God, Cleo.'

She looks at him, doubtful.

'He's got a finger in every scam in town. People talk. He seen you with the hero.'

With another jarring leap, we land in the Scarlet Room. Light blazes through the glass, setting the red seats on fire. As I follow Cleo up the steps to the stage, I see the Cleo of the Nile box sitting centre-stage. A wave of nausea sweeps through me. Fist pressed to my stomach, I trail her backstage.

Magnificent Morelli waits in the dressing room. The posters make him look taller. His eyes are dark slits between heavy lids and eye pouches. He smiles and holds out his hand as if inviting her to dance. I don't like his eyes. Or his smile. Or the thin black moustache that looks painted. After a long moment, she gives him her hand. Still smiling, he rips off her dress and punches her in the chest with his fist. She falls to her knees, lowers her head to the ground. I cringe at the black and blue marks staining her back.

'I got eyes all over the boardwalk!' he roars. 'Next time I'll smash your face. See if he still wants you!'

While he yells and curses her, she twists her head toward me. Her silvery eyes are mascara-smeared, her cheeks wet with tears. She holds out her hand. Trembling, I press my palm to hers. A bolt of electricity. Heat blazes up my hand to my arm.

The shock jolts me.

I fall hard and fast.

And land on my butt. Back on the boardwalk.

It's still night.

'Miss, you okay?' A uniformed cop bends toward me.

A cop from here and now. I'm back in my world, my time, but I brought back something this time. I press the palm of my right hand to my cheek. It still burns.

Don't think on it too much, said Auntie Maze. *Trust the sudden knowing*. Cleo touched me. I touched her. Through the doors that separate the dead and the living. She wanted me to see that she loved Frank, to know that Morelli beat her, to understand that things are not what they seem.

'Miss?'

'I'm fine,' I tell the cop. As I get to my feet, I remember Jinx's words: there's the official story and then, there's the one behind the headline. The true story. The one Cleo wants me to see.

52

Wednesday morning, October 24

The door to Charlie's office is ajar. I take a deep breath and knock. I'll run Mask and Shadow by him. If he says no, I'll back out. Truth is I'm starting to get scared already.

I peek inside. The office is empty and dark, the single window shaded by blinds. He must have already gone down to the Widow for our final rehearsal for tonight's show. I'll talk to him there, but... according to Gus, Charlie argued with Van the night she was murdered. Charlie denied it, and I don't know how much I trust Gus's word, but this is my chance to search Charlie's office and find anything that totally clears him.

I turn on the light. The walls are covered with posters of productions at Midnight's five venues, including black and white images of the Scarlet Room that don't capture the glamour or fiery light I saw last night. I sit in Charlie's chair behind an antique wooden desk. A hulking desktop computer, a vintage pencil sharpener, a cup filled with pencils, and a small bowl of erasers. Who still uses pencils and erasers? Charlie Becker, that's who. Elegant and world-weary, with a gentle charm that comes from another era. The half-empty bottle of Johnnie Walker in the bottom drawer cements the impression of him as Philip Marlowe, shoes on the desk, sitting back, drinking as he interviews a femme fatale, and taking notes... with a sharpened pencil.

I open the other desk drawers. Office supplies – pens, stamps, envelopes, official stationery with *Midnight Casino and Hotel* in flowing black letters. Scissors, measuring tape, pliers, screwdrivers, a hammer, a container of light bulbs, a cup filled with thumbtacks and nails.

At the corner of the desk, Charlie and Misty smile from a framed photo. If there is a more beautiful couple outside of Hollywood, I haven't seen them. After our kiss last summer in the Orange Room, he asked me to go out with him. I said, 'No.' The pain of André was too fresh, my self-confidence at an all-time low. What if I'd said yes, and he and I had hooked up? Would we be a couple today?

With a sigh, I get up and examine the file cabinet. The drawers squeak open and release dust. I scan the folders: Black Widow Theatre, The Star Inn, and many names I don't recognise – crammed with yellowed invoices, playbills, and issues of *The Atlantic City News.* No one has looked at these files and papers in years. On top of the file cabinet sits a coffee-table book, *Images of Atlantic City*. I flip past photos of Atlantic City through the decades – grassy stretches of beach, the first boardwalk, the mobster years, Camp Boardwalk, nightclubs and glamour, Club Harlem and Babette's, Miss America, families sunning themselves, casinos.

Wait, what's this? I flip back to a double page spread that shows the history of one woman... and her city. Hotels sink and casinos rise, jitneys roll past, families invade and take over the beach, mayors come, and presidents go. But through every era, here's Jinx, witness to it all: cigarette in the corner of her mouth, pen in hand, wearing a man's jacket and trousers, one booted foot on a car fender or leaning on her cane. The gaze gradually hardens into the weary glitter of someone who's seen it all, but the mischievous grin has never changed.

I set down the book. What will I do if Charlie catches me snooping inside his office? His jacket – a grey blazer – hangs from a hook on the back of the door. Oh God, Moon, are you really going to...

I search his pockets – Tic Tacs, a white handkerchief, several keys on a Midnight keychain, a handful of coins. My hands tremble as I reach inside his jacket. Men's jackets usually have inner pockets, so useful – especially for a magician. I inserted them in my man's suit.

Here! I pull out a small leather-bound calendar with a pen in a holder. One page per day. This volume holds two months: October and November. My fingers fumble with the pages until I arrive at today: Wednesday, October 24. Charlie's notes are written in black ink, narrow letters slanting to the right:

10:00: *Rebel Rehearsal*

12:00: *Lunch JE, Caesar's. Call Forte*

Forte is one of Midnight's Marketing Directors, but I don't know who JE is. A series of afternoon meetings follows with names I don't recognise.

4:00: *Conference call*

A list of names and phone numbers crammed into a few lines.

He scrawled a large *Widow* across the entire evening. Our opening night.

I go back a few pages, skim the past week. More production meetings for the shows and events at Midnight's venues.

Wednesday, October 17: one week ago, the night Rebel Magic was set to premiere. The same *Widow* scrawled across the bottom third of the page.

I turn back a page to Tuesday, October 16, the night Van was murdered.

Meetings, meetings... Dead Men Rising, the heavy metal group that played the Crypt last weekend, underlined, boxed, and surrounded by question marks. I remember Charlie telling us about their demands. He drew a large *M* over the bottom half of the page.

I scan the rest of October. *M* takes over most of his evenings. Unless *M* stands for 'murder,' or he and Misty kill as a team, he spends most nights with her. I shove the calendar back in his inside pocket.

A last glance over my shoulder. On the wall, a lurid red-and-black poster I've never seen before:

Magnificent Morelli
Death-defying Stunt!!!
The Bullet Catch!!!

Suave, moustached Morelli aims a pistol at Cleo, her long hair rippling in fiery-gold waves. Her mouth opens in an O, and she holds up her hands to stop him. The Bullet Catch is notorious in magic, probably the most dangerous trick of all. So many things can go wrong. At least six magicians died while performing it, assistants wounded, real bullets substituted for gimmicked ones. The poster is crudely drawn and painted, but now that I've seen Cleo and Morelli, I know the artist drew them from life. His dark-eyed scowl, her terror.

'Lucy!' A man's sharp voice.

I jump.

'What are you doing here?'

I turn slowly. Charlie's dark-blonde hair is neatly parted, his pale blue shirt tucked into black trousers, but his face is violently flushed. Thank God he didn't find me with my hand in his jacket pocket.

'I… I was looking for you… and the door was open… and I came in… about to leave…'

He stares at me.

I swallow, my tongue feels enormous. 'I have an idea for the show. But–'

'But what?'

For a moment he scares me. Utterly still and cold. Angry, but not wanting to show it. He doesn't exhibit the usual Charlie charm to ease the awkwardness. After an endless moment he takes off his glasses, rubs them against his shirt and puts them back on. He grabs his jacket from the hook.

I lick my lips, dry and cracked. 'That poster... the Bullet Catch. I... never saw it before.'

He glances at the wall.

'Did they ever perform it?'

'No,' he says, tight.

'She looks terrified.'

'She didn't trust him. He didn't trust her.' He flicks his hand, impatient. 'Turns out they were both right.'

My cheeks burn. 'Maybe she was scared he'd rig the gun and shoot her for real.'

'If Dirty Hand was mad enough, he'd shoot anyone.' After a moment, he adds, 'That was Magnificent Morelli's nickname.' He gestures for me to leave first and locks the door behind me.

'What's your idea for the show?'

As we climb down a flight of stairs to the thirteenth floor, I describe Mask and Shadow: 'The face we show the world and the darkness we hide inside. Based on my *Bewitched* effect, but I changed the script, and instead of white flowers, black ones.'

'Are you thinking of Van's black rose?' When I nod, he asks, 'Why?'

'I need to do it.'

Halfway down the stairs, he stops. 'Are you giving it a happy ending?'

'Do you mean the Prince showing up at the end of Making Mr. Right?'

'Hey, as the guy who played Prince Charming, I can tell you I didn't think it was a happy ending. You chose a dog over the prince, didn't you?' The corner of his mouth tips. He's teasing me. The relief is overwhelming. This is Charlie, my friend, and I don't want to lose him.

He continues down the stairs. At the thirteenth floor, he holds open the door to the hallway. 'What if Van's murderer sees the black roses and takes it as a dare?'

My chest tightens. If Charlie is the Hunter, then he followed me to the Barrens, and he already knows about the black roses. So does Elvis Jones, who has disappeared since our lunch at DiBruni's. Unless he's been on my trail.

I'm ready to go into the Widow, when Charlie says my name, low and soft.

There's a question in his voice. I know what he's asking. The same question I ask myself when I'm near him.

We're alone in the hallway, across the door marked 13 ½ that leads to Gus's booth, but instantly I'm back in the Orange Room, the night we danced and kissed. Even though we've never talked about it, the secret memory lurks behind our voices and eyes each time we see each other.

'Yes?' I whisper.

'I'm curious about us.'

I've been staring at his throat, pulsing and vulnerable, but I force my gaze to go higher, and I see the inevitable flush rise and darken his cheeks. I don't have to touch my cheeks to know they are flaming.

'I'm curious about us too. But you're with Misty now.'

'And you're with Elvis Jones.'

I recoil. 'Oh my God, no way!'

'Oh, sorry. He said–' Charlie tightens his lips.

'He said what?'

'Nothing. It's okay.'

'It's not okay. Just tell me what he said.'

'He said you went dancing together, and after, uh, you and he...'

I glare at Charlie, who flinches as if I slapped him.

'Hey, I'm sorry. I shouldn't have said anything. Let's go.'

I follow him into the theatre. Men. At this moment I'd like to be free of all of them. There isn't a single one I trust. Not even Charlie. Definitely not Gus, who says hello to my breasts as I pass him. Least of all, Elvis Jones, that lying creep.

53

Stormie is still mad at me, and I'm mad at everyone. Despite that, rehearsal goes smoothly. We're in a groove until we get to the finale and I describe Mask and Shadow.

'Sure you can prepare it by tonight?' asks Charlie.

'Yes. It's just a few switches and substitutions. I edited the script, and I have the props. I've been making black flowers like mad. And I can work on the light cues with Gus.'

'I know one person who will hate it.' Gus aims his heat gun at me: 'Bang bang! Another chick bites the dust.'

As if Gus's presence and words aren't jarring enough, today his hair is in pigtails.

'I'm with you, Gus,' says Stormie, a phrase I never thought I'd hear her say. 'Some people have a death wish.'

Charlie says mildly, 'It's good theatre.'

'Is good theatre worth risking your life?' She shakes her head. 'You insist on doing it, go ahead. But I won't play the blind date.'

She crosses her arms and stares us down.

'Tommy's back. I'll ask him.'

Charlie shakes his head. 'He's already gonna do the prince in Making Mr. Right. We need him on sound and set up. I'll do it.'

'It's too much,' I protest.

He shrugs. 'It only takes a minute, and all I have to do is put on a baseball cap.'

When I thank him, he says, 'I just want to get this show on the road. You all with me?'

Everyone mumbles agreement, and he says, 'Get some rest, everyone. I'll see you back here at six.' His gaze lingers on me. He blinks behind his glasses, and for an agonising moment we stare at each other. It strikes me that just as we were finally going to talk about the weird whatever-it-is between us, we got sidetracked by the great disrupter, Elvis Jones.

After an eternity, Charlie's mouth quirks.

So does mine.

His walkie-talkie crackles, and he walks away.

Stormie leaves the theatre without looking back.

As I'm walking to the door, Gus looks me up and down, the vape pen in the corner of his mouth. I give him the same top to bottom look.

'The dark side of the Moon. I like it.' He doesn't seem worried or anxious. He smiles, and without thinking, I ask, 'Gus, where are you from?'

'You mean where I was born? Raised?'

'Yeah. Where did you live most of your life?'

'I'm an Army brat. Lived in nineteen states. Born in New Jersey.'

I let out a startled gasp. 'Where?'

He smirks. 'You mean what exit?'

'I mean what town?'

'Newark.' He moves closer. 'But Atlantic City is my town now. Just like you.' He moves closer. 'What else do you want to know about me?'

Newark is not the Pine Barrens. But there's something off about this man. As if he learned seduction techniques through a manual. 'Did you sleep with Van?'

I can't believe I just blurted that. But now that I did, I wait for an answer.

He flicks the vape pen as if he's flicking ashes from a cigarette. 'Why do you want to know?'

'First tell me. The truth.'

He blinks. Through the red-framed glasses his eyes are enormous. 'We came close,' he admits. He rubs his thumb and index finger together. 'That close. We kissed, and she loved it.'

Oh, Van. Really? Or is this his wish-fulfilment? He and Elvis Jones aren't that far apart.

'Why do you want to know?' He wiggles his eyebrows. 'Admit it. You're interested.'

'Not in that way.'

'I noticed you picked Diablo for your Prince Charming.'

'Your dog, not you.'

'Look harder. I have surprises for you.'

54

Little Nick

After he showers and gets dressed, he carries supplies to his car and shoves them in the trunk. He looks across the road at the site of his daily runs, a deserted stretch of beach near his secret refuge, between Brigantine and the salt flats of the Barrens. Minutes from Midnight and the Atlantic City boardwalk, but it's a world away. This cursed place won't set him free.

Look at the history of Atlantic City. Whenever this doomed mutt of a town tries to lift itself from the swamp, there's always someone at the edge to shove it back down. No hope. No chance for a new life. Like the sugar sand that sucks you into the cold depths of the Blue Hole. Fight all you want, you'll never break free.

When the car is loaded, he slams the trunk shut. He may get lucky. He may not. But he's ready to go at a moment's notice. The first lesson Big Nick taught him. The snake eats smaller snakes to survive. The treefrog and two-headed Timber Rattlesnake change colour to carry on. The corn snake sheds one skin to reveal another.

Just like him.

It's called survival.

Here's what he wants to tell all those people who would judge him. You think a devil and a man are so different? Look harder. A devil is nothing more than a man turned inside out.

55

An hour before the show, I enter the dressing room to find Stormie staring at the vanity mirror. Taped to the glass: a photo of me, jaggedly sliced in half.

I grip my throat. That photo was taken during one of my rare performances of Sawing a Woman in Half. The photographer took me from above. The lid of the sawing box is open, and I'm curled inside. Naked fear in my eyes, not even an attempt at a smile.

Someone ripped the photo in two. Midway across my body, exactly where the saw would later slice me in half. Exactly where the Black Dahlia's murderer cut her body in half.

'Hey, gals, break a leg!'

I wheel around.

Misty. Serene blue eyes, pink sweater soft as a cloud. 'I have two shows tonight so I'm sorry I won't make your new opening.' She glances from Stormie to me to the mirror, and her smile fades. 'What's this?'

I sink to the bench in front of the mirror. 'This is what he wants to do to me.'

'Oh, no!' Misty presses her hand to her chest. 'The same guy who killed Van and Gina?'

'A fucking psycho,' mutters Stormie. 'It wasn't here this morning.'

Stormie's gaze is fixed on me. 'Gus?'

I feel a panic attack coming on. It starts deep in my belly and surges up through my chest. Not before the show. Oh God, please no. I swallow, remembering the eerie feeling I had talking to Gus this afternoon. *I have surprises for you.* 'He works for the cops.'

Misty's eyes widen. 'Gus, a cop? Really?'

'He's still a suspect.' Stormie flicks her wrist. 'There are plenty of crooked cops. What about the Lollipop guy? Rex?'

'I don't know if the cops released him or if they arrested him.' I turn to Misty. 'Where was Charlie the night Van was murdered?'

'You don't think–?'

My heart thunders in my chest, my ears. How will I perform tonight?

'Was he with you?' Stormie asks, gently.

'We were supposed to have dinner together, but he had work. Problems with Dead Men Rising. He came later.' Misty lets out a loud sigh. 'It's complicated. Charlie and I are staying on the down-low till my divorce comes through. I'm counting the days. See, my ex is a–'

'A deadshit?' supplies Stormie. 'A douchebaguette?'

I choke on my tongue.

'Douchebaguette is too nice. Deadshit is closer. He's dangerous. He enjoys hurting me.'

The three of us stare at the slashed photo.

Misty slants her eyes at me. 'Are you seeing Elvis?'

Not this again. 'No!' I cry.

She murmurs, 'Okay, sorry,' and turns to go.

'Wait. Why?'

'He's... you know the secret staircase to the Widow?'

'Yeah.' Charlie must have shown it to her.

'A couple hours ago I came up the back stairs. I wanted to surprise Charlie. Elvis was ahead of me, and normally, I'd have said hi, but the way he looked around and opened the backstage door... it felt wrong.'

'Did he see you?' I ask.

'I don't think so. I pressed against the wall. I got the feeling he didn't want anyone to see him. And I didn't want him to know I saw him.'

Stormie looks sick. 'Elvis Jones was here, backstage. Oh shit, he could have done this.'

With a groan Misty rips the pieces of the photo from the mirror and throws them in the trash.

'Why'd you do that?' asks Stormie.

Misty rubs her hands together. 'Don't look at it anymore. Don't think about it.'

'But isn't that evidence?' My voice is so faint it doesn't sound like me.

'I'm sure he wiped away any fingerprints. Have a great show.' She blows a kiss and disappears.

'That was strange,' mutters Stormie. 'We need to find out who her ex is.'

'Her ex wouldn't do this to me. But Elvis Jones would.'

'Girl, you better be careful tonight. The man who did this won't stop at ripping up a picture of you.'

56

Detectives Torres and Wax block the theatre doors and grimly watch the crowd. By the time the final illusion, Mask and Shadow, comes around, everyone involved in the show is tightly wound. Tension has spread, infecting not only the performers and crew, but the audience.

At the last minute, Stormie told a relieved Charlie that she'd take over as my blind date. I hugged her, and she sighed. 'I can't let you do this alone.'

Carrying a wand, I cross the stage – black and scuffed, used and abused, its history squeaking through every strip of glow tape and white paint. Between each window stands a sconce light that sheds diffused rays of yellow light. This little theatre reaches inside my heart and yanks a chord. Truth: I don't play the Widow, she plays me.

My first time performing this illusion in public. The Hunter's goal in slashing the photo was to unnerve me. He succeeded. But I'll make sure no one else senses my fear.

Jinx sits in the front row with her partner Dasha at her side. Tonight, they're dressed in black – Jinx in a long gown, and Dasha in a tux.

Da and Auntie Maze sit in the third-last row. Da's preference, so he can survey the audience as well as the show. I feel their anxiety. I didn't tell them what I'm doing, but they know me well enough to sense my nerves.

Charlie stands in front of the doors, next to Torres and Wax.

Gus controls the lighting from his booth.

Jones is not in the audience. Damn, I wanted to see his response.

Dr. Lose didn't come.

Neither did Ruby.

After a quick scan of the props on my table: purse, perfume, hairbrush, hairspray, gold tube of lipstick, I smile at the audience. 'Halloween is my favourite holiday because transformation happens not only onstage but on the street. Women know a lot about transformation. We do it daily with our hair, makeup, clothing...'

While I speak, I dab perfume on my wrists and throat, put on lipstick and blot my lips, squinting at the audience as if they are my mirror.

I didn't see Jones arrive, but suddenly there he is – tailored black jacket and jeans, arms crossed, leaning against the back wall same as he was the night I found Van.

I brush my hair and spray it with a fine mist of Aqua Net. His eyes glint, a smile tugs at his mouth, and I know he's thinking, 'Jersey Girl magic.'

'Transformation is the fundamental law of magic: out of lies and deceit comes... truth. Maybe not the truth we expect, but as my Granny Moon used to say, "Truth, like love, comes at you zigzag, never how or when you expect." Magic comes at us zigzag too. It reveals the crack in the Mask, the eyeholes through which the secret Shadow peeks. Sometimes a girl just can't suppress her magic. Sam on *Bewitched* was a good witch who performed white magic. She disguised herself as a housewife in an apron, but her magic kept bursting through. Like a...' I twitch my nose à la Sam. 'Like a...' Twitch again. 'Like a...'

I sneeze, and a white flower appears in my hand.

'But the Shadow can be darker, a compulsion that makes us do things we shouldn't do. Dexter, TV's favourite serial killer, called his shadow the "dark passenger," as if it rode behind him in the back seat of his car. Ted Bundy, a real-life serial killer, called his shadow, "the entity," and claimed it told him whom to attack.'

I blow on the white flower, and it turns yellow.

'Maybe you think your secret is safely hidden behind the Mask you show the world. But there's always a clue, a tell, a reveal that links the Shadow to the Mask.'

I examine the yellow flower, turn it in my hand, and blow gently.

'The mask cracks, and through the cracks...'

Petal by petal, the yellow flower turns black. I gasp and drop it.

'... the shadow breaks through.'

I hold out my hand. A black flower sprouts between my fingers.

I push it away.

Another one replaces it.

Then, another.

'But which is the true self? The smiling mask we show the world, or the dark shadow we hide? Maybe they're both true, and we need both to live. The danger comes when our deepest shadow, the dark passenger, moves from the backseat to the front, takes over the wheel and becomes the dark driver. Then we're in trouble. And so are the other cars on the road.'

Black flowers appear behind my ears, on my hair, from my dress.

'My shadow appears in the form of black roses. They don't exist in nature. They have to be manmade – for example, a white rose dyed black – which makes them all the more frightening when they bloom. Legends and rumours surround their existence. People who claim to have seen them are accused of lying, but we know better, don't we? A black rose is both real and not real, made of petals and dreams... like magic.'

Wearing a baseball cap and carrying a red rose, Stormie appears onstage. She stops a few feet from me and knocks on an invisible door.

'My date!' I cry. 'Time to put the mask back on.'

Thankfully, the rest of the effect is in pantomime. Black roses blossom around me. With frantic motions, I push them away, stuff them into my purse and under the table, but all the while I am deeply aware of the audience.

I don't look at my father and Auntie Maze. I don't look at the cops either, but I know Torres's eyes are locked on me and Wax's huge jaw juts in disapproval.

Gus hides behind his board, manipulating lights. He's moving step by step with me.

Charlie scans the room, his gaze moving from the audience to the stage. He glows from within, so intense and focused on me that I know he gets it.

So does Jones, who lifts and lowers his hand instinctively at my every move as if he's become part of the story.

I tease out the suspense of whether or not I'll be able to hide the roses in time to pass as normal until it's almost painful, for me as well as the audience. Fear and excitement surge through me. This is my illusion, my creation, my story, but tonight, my own dark passenger is taking over the wheel.

Stormie glances at her enormous wristwatch and knocks again.

I pat my hair and dress. Squint again at the imaginary mirror. Jones squints back at me. He's echoing my moves. Pain shoots through me. *I'm going to find out what you're hiding and who you are.*

Mask in place, my shadow hidden. *I can pass as normal.*

I open the imaginary door and accept the red rose that Stormie hands me. As soon as I touch the rose, it turns black. I shove it down my bra and walk offstage, arm in arm, with Stormie, 'unknowingly' leaving a ribbon-trail of black roses.

While the audience applauds, Stormie and I return centre-stage and bow. When I raise my head, Jones is gone.

And Rex Saylor stands in front of the doors and glowers at me.

57

Charlie has arranged an opening night celebration in the East Room, at the other end of the thirteenth-floor hallway from the Widow. During World War Two, when fatalities were particularly high, this room was used as a temporary morgue. As soon as Charlie, Stormie, and I enter, a blast of cold air hits us – the spirits of dead soldiers transforming the room into an icebox. But a bartender prepares drinks, waiters circulate with trays, and about a hundred guests mingle.

Stormie and I are wilting, but we survived opening night without another body surfacing or the cops breaking up the show. I keep my gaze on the doorway to see if Rex enters.

Charlie grabs champagne flutes from a passing waiter, hands one to Stormie and me, and takes one for himself. 'That was one helluva show.' He holds up his glass. 'Moon and Weather. So proud of you both.'

I down mine in a single gulp. It fizzes inside me, making me feel light and buoyant, as if I can float through the rest of the night.

'Stormie.' A smile flickers behind Charlie's mouth. 'Nana's Phone Call is always good, but tonight it was fantastic. We needed to laugh, and you had the audience in the palm of your hand. And as for you, Ms. Moon, I think we just witnessed the birth of Lucy Noir.'

'I didn't want to love it,' admits Stormie. 'But it's so you.'

'So Mask and Shadow stays in the show?'

'As long as you want to do it.' Charlie gestures to the black flower I pinned to my hair. 'The black roses brought out the heart of the piece. And what you both did with Mother Nature was amazing. Van would have–' He stops. 'Enjoy the rest of the night. You deserve it. We're going to have a good run with this show.'

He leaves us to circulate among the guests.

'Misty's a lucky girl,' says Stormie. 'So, did it help you figure out who the Hunter is?'

I study the empty glass. 'Rex came in at the end, looking furious. Gus, Charlie, and Elvis were watching, but... none of them pulled a black rose from his pocket.'

'They wouldn't do it in front of the audience. They'll wait till they're alone with you. Be careful.'

She shimmies toward the bar, and I head toward my father and aunt, but Rex strides toward me. Black leather jacket, thin lips taut. 'Taunting a killer with your little tricks. The flower in your hair like Gina and Van. You think you're smart, don't you?'

He's a mad bull charging at me. I step back.

He moves closer, breathes in my face. I smell whiskey. He must have been at the bar till now. 'I should rip that flower from your head.'

'Wait a minute!' Finally, my voice.

'She said you were smart. You ain't smart.'

'I'm not–' I breathe hard. 'She?'

'Van said you were the smartest girl she knew. Her best friend.'

I falter on my feet. He grips my arm and steadies me. 'I worried about her. Like one of my girls.'

A huge sadness fills me. I wrap my arms around myself to keep it from spilling out. 'How well did you know her? Really?'

'She came to the club a few times, and we talked.' The rough gravelly voice pauses. 'Same one who got her got Gina.'

'Did he kill Mona too?'

He doesn't seem surprised that I know. 'These girls got in the way.'

'In whose way?'

He shrugs. 'You live here. You know the score. They've been running this city since it began.'

'You think the Mob is involved in their murders?'

'Wherever there's drugs, they're involved.'

'Van wasn't into drugs.'

'She might've got in their way. It ain't hard.'

'Then why are you mad at me? Why aren't you mad at them?'

'I'm mad as hell, but there's not much you can do against the Mob. Not if you want to stay alive. Look at the flowers they stuff in the girls' mouths. Someone wants to shut them up. That someone knows you found them.' He glances around the room, then back at me. 'Don't play with a killer. Van said you were smart. Prove it. Stay safe for her.'

He's halfway across the room when I call his name. He turns back.

'Bring your son to the show, please.'

He nods, and I watch him leave the East Room. Is the Mob behind their murders? Jinx said the same thing: they've been in Atlantic City since the beginning, and it's impossible to escape them. How did Van get on the wrong side of a Mob killer? Is that what happened to my mother too? Maybe that's the connection.

As I turn toward Da and Auntie Maze, Gus appears in my path and holds out an arm to stop me. Tonight, a single grey braid coils like a fat, unsteady snail on his head.

A heavily tattooed Midnight waitress stops in front of us. Gus and I each take a glass of champagne. He raises his. 'To you, Dark Side of the Moon.' While I drink, he adds, 'To us.'

This time the champagne doesn't fizz but sinks flat and cold to my chest.

When I don't respond, he says, 'Saw you talking to Rex Saylor.'

'I know you danced with Van at the Lollipop Club.'

'Just once, but it was memorable.' He rubs his chin. 'In retrospect, Van said something curious that night...' He swirls his tongue in his champagne flute.

'Well? What did she say?'

He looks beyond me. 'There are things I can't share with a civilian.'

'If I find out you're holding back information about Van...'

He lifts his empty glass in mock-surrender. 'Hold on. Didn't say I wouldn't tell you. But information doesn't come free.' He rubs the fingers of his right hand together.

'You want me to pay you?'

He smiles. The green vampirish tinge of his skin turns my stomach. 'I saw the way you were watching me tonight, Lucy.'

'I was watching everyone.'

'You can tell yourself that, but you and me, we know better. How about tonight?'

'No.'

'You think you know me, but you don't.' He licks his lips and walks away.

There is something... off about this man. I shake off the unease and hurry toward my father and aunt. Radiant in green and black velvet, they glow – a fairy king and queen bringing tidings from another world.

After we hug, Da says, 'Why the black roses, Lucy?' The pain in his voice. 'What if Van's murderer was watching?'

'He *was* watching.' Auntie Maze's sea-mist eyes darken. 'He's here.'

For the first time I absolutely believe in my aunt's *seeing* powers. 'Where?'

'In this room.'

My heart beats fast. 'Who is he? Do you see him?'

'He's like the *aos sí*.' Every Samhain she brings up these restless spirits, descendants of pagan gods, roaming between worlds. She blinks and focuses on me. 'He passes as one of the living, but he hides with the dead. That's why it's so hard to find him. But he can't disguise the smell of death.'

The weird smell Gus emanates, as if he crawled out from a pit. His green skin, the way he forms words as if testing them to see what works. I don't think I've ever heard Gus laugh. Is his laugh shrill like the man who followed me to Central Pier? His excited breathing on the phone. The rage that led him to slash the photo of me.

Auntie Maze stares through me. 'You've been there and back, haven't you, darlin'? And you're learning to trust the sudden knowing.'

'But I don't know who to trust.'

'Move back home,' says Da. 'I'd feel better knowing you're safe with us.'

My eyes brim with tears. I see them through the mist, but they can't protect me. Not anymore. I hug them again and swear I'll be careful.

As soon as I turn away, my phone pings with a message from Dr. Lose: I'm heading to Midnight later. I have a question for you. I text her back: What?

I'll show you.

Let me know when you get here. I'll meet you.

When I look up, Detectives Torres and Wax are standing in front of me. Wax shakes his head as if he's disappointed in me. 'Lucy Moon, do you understand the meaning of danger?'

'Talk to us,' says Torres.

I tell them about the torn photo of me in the sawing box. 'Someone taped it to the dressing-room mirror between 6:30 and 8:00.'

'Is it still there?' asks Torres.

'Misty threw it away.'

Wax growls, 'Of all the fool things to do!'

Heat flashes from my throat to my forehead. 'She was thinking of me. So I wouldn't have to look at it through the show.'

'Corrupting evidence,' says Wax. 'And why did you go to the Pine Barrens yesterday?'

How many people were on my trail? I need to see what Dr. Lose wants to show me before I tell them about Jane Doe.

Wax looms in my face. 'You have no idea what's going on, and you're going to get hurt.'

The same thing Tal told me. Is Wax warning me about the Mob too?

I let out a hoarse breath. 'Why don't you talk to Gus? He knows more than I do.'

Wax slits his eyes. Torres scowls, bringing the scar into relief. 'What are you talking about?' she asks.

'He's working undercover for you.'

Torres says carefully, 'Who told you that?'

'He's not?'

'No, he's not. Did he tell you?'

'Yes, he did.'

Torres tightens her lips. 'He has offered his services to the police, but no, he does not work for us.'

Gus has been trying to insert himself in police investigations. The way criminals notoriously do. I paste on a smile and back away. 'I'd love to stay and chat, Detectives, but I need to mingle with the crowd and do *my* job.'

I turn and laser-eye Gus, who is still at the bar. A heavily jewelled woman shakes her finger in his face. He throws back his head and laughs, and the snail-coil of hair wobbles. He lied about working for the cops. On the night of Van's murder, he danced with her at the Lollipop. He knows more about Van than he let on. Gus Wigman, I'm going to get into your lighting booth and find out what game you're playing.

58

Someone unlocked the doors to the balcony, and a few shadowy figures smoke against the black velvet sky. It's not till I step outside beneath a fiery moon so large and hot it singes my eyelids that I remember the other name for the October full moon: Hunter's Moon. A hungry moon. A hungry killer moon. I smell death. A rotting skeleton behind a smiling face.

Dasha sucks on a cigarette, her gaze on Jinx. In the moonlight Jinx is a fierce queen leaning on her cane. Ancient and compelling – a woman who has seen it all.

I join them at the railing and watch the illuminated Ferris Wheel on Steel Pier revolve.

Without turning, Jinx says, 'You had to do it your way, didn't you?' Her throaty voice is deeper than usual, tinged with sadness.

I breathe in Jinx's scent mixed with Dasha's tobacco. 'Are you talking about the black roses?'

'She used to say, "Shuffle all you want, you can't beat the cards."'

'Who said that?'

Dasha says quietly, 'She's sad tonight. Your act brought back memories.'

'Jinx, what do you know about Mysterious Connections?'

'It was a card trick. She tried it on me first. In the Scarlet Room.'

'Ah, you're talking about Cleo.'

'Am I?'

Jinx's scent rises and evaporates at the edges of my mind. Familiar, elusive. 'What is this smell?'

'Patchouli.' Her face creases in a smile. 'I've loved it since the sixties.'

'Jinx, were you a hippie?'

'An older one. All you need is love, flower power, dancing in the street, getting high. The sixties softened the edges of the forties and fifties.' Her fingers rub the jewelled cane.

I feel strange, almost drunk. The patchouli, and Jinx herself veering between past and present, revealing a hidden knowledge.

'You know something about me, don't you? Tell me!'

'Dasha,' she says imperiously, but Dasha's back is to us.

Jinx's black wig is awry, the smear of Carmine Red twice as thick as her lips, her eyes shockingly young. I lean closer to her. 'I went back to Camp Boardwalk, and I saw you, young.'

'Are you channelling Maze?'

'I saw Morelli beat Cleo.'

Jinx cringes.

'Cleo and I touched hands. Palm to palm.' I hold out my hand. 'I still feel the heat.'

A tear trickles down the wrinkled map of Jinx's face. Impulsively I lean over and kiss her cheek. Delicate skin, rice-paper thin. Strands of white hair peek out from the wig. The smell of patchouli rises again, nearly suffocating me. I've smelled it recently. When? Where? I strain to capture the scent.

She squeezes my hand in hers, and a shudder jolts through me. I've felt this before: her hand squeezing mine with unexpected force. In another time and place. I see a purple-veiled woman holding my hand as we walk down a street. We stop at a pink frame house, the second one from the ramp that leads to the boardwalk and beach. When she stoops to kiss my cheek, the pungent scent of patchouli wafts over me again. A chill rises up my legs.

'You took me to the Moons! It was you!'

Her face seems to collapse. She looks even older, truly ancient, a primal being. Tears catch in her wrinkles.

'Why, Jinx? Who are you?'

'The question is, and always has been, who are *you*?'

Leaning on her cane and holding Dasha's hand, she advances

into the East Room. I watch them move slowly toward the door. It wasn't my mother, but Jinx Faust who took me to the Moons. Why? Before they left, Dasha whispered, 'I'll talk to her in the morning.'

I'm about to look for Gus when I catch a surprising glimpse of Elvis Jones, half-shielded by a few Dracula-caped dealers and high rollers. Face lowered over my phone I sidle toward them. Charlie is part of the group too, his back to me. I move close enough to see his hands. Dumbfounded, I watch Charlie twist the cards in a sinuous twirl. The Ascari! That takes serious chops. What the hell?

'Your turn.' Charlie holds out the deck to Elvis.

I inch closer. This, I have to see. The man who insists he sucks at cards. His face is hidden by one of the dealer's capes, but I have a clear view of his hands. He separates the deck in two and slides the cards into each other, smooth as a zipper. From the Faro Shuffle, he curves the cards as they fall through his fingers in a lovely Cascade. My breath catches in my throat. So... Gus is a liar, Charlie is a snake-charmer, and Elvis Jones transforms cards into liquid paper. I've been had by all three.

'I'm banning you two jokers from my table,' says a dealer.

'You oughta be banned from casinos,' says one of the men.

'Maybe we already are,' says Elvis.

'In some states,' adds Charlie. 'Not Jersey.'

Elvis turns, and we're suddenly face to face.

It's not just my neck that prickles, it's the roots of my hair, the shadow between my breasts, the heat between my legs. Is this going to happen each time I see him? He may be a card god and a sexy devil, but he's also a liar, and I do not trust him for one second, and my girl parts can go to hell.

A wicked smile lights his eyes. 'Hello, Lucy.'

'Where are you from, Jones?'

His smile fades at my harsh tone. 'Ah, so I'm not Elvis anymore? Now I'm Jones?'

When I don't respond, he says, cool and mocking, 'Where I was born doesn't matter, but I was raised in Bridgeton. You don't need to look at a map. It's kind of... part of the Pine Barrens.' His upper lip curls in the way I hate. 'Does that answer your question, Moon?'

Yes and no. He's from the Pine Barrens, but how does he know what I'm really asking? He'd only know if he'd tracked me like a hunter, waiting to find out if I'd discovered the truth about him. And then breathing on the phone. Damn him. 'Were you at the Barrens yesterday?'

Before he answers, Charlie says my name. I turn, facing the group of men, and he gestures to me. 'Have you guys seen Lucy Moon work a deck of cards?'

One of the high rollers gives me a dismissive glance. 'Nah, girls use special decks for little hands.'

Another one mutters, 'Her hands are small, but she's a Moon. Declan's kid.'

The first high roller says, 'I bet a grand she can't beat these jokers.'

'I bet she can,' says another man.

'I'll match you.'

All the men turn to me. Eyes glittering, eager to see what I'll do. They want a pissing contest. I've faced the good ole boys' club many times through the years. And the way I feel tonight, I'm itching for a fight.

Elvis chews his lower lip. After a moment he hands me the deck he used. I lower my gaze to the cards. 'Ooh, such a manly deck.' I run my hands over the cards and giggle. 'So big and hard. So warm.'

Elvis makes a sound in his throat. Charlie mutters, 'Wish I could bet.'

I flutter my lashes. 'I'll try to get my itty-bitty hands around them.'

Fuming inside, I prepare the cards. Elvis did the Cascade. I'll do another Cascade: the Waterbend. I start with a Faro Shuffle too, then pivot the cards and guide them to ripple down a slippery staircase to my pinkie. Damn, why aren't people as easy to read and control as cards?

With a smile, I straighten the deck and hand it back to Elvis. Charlie applauds.

'Thanks, guys.' I smile sweetly. 'Gosh, maybe size doesn't matter, after all.'

One of the high rollers whistles. 'Hey, you do adult birthday parties?'

I turn my back on them. I need a minute to gather myself. Gus, Elvis, Charlie – each one misrepresented himself to me.

I glance over my shoulder and crook my finger to Charlie. When he stops in front of me, I say, 'You've been keeping a secret.'

His jaw drops. The flush tints his cheeks. Oh shit. I feel the blush work its way up my throat. Here we go again. 'What?'

'Charlie! You know cards!'

His eyes are wide through his glasses. 'Oh, that? I just mess around now and then.'

'Don't bullshit me.'

His flush deepens. 'I do it mostly when I'm alone or bored. When I watch TV. Helps me think.'

'Me too,' I say, grudging. 'But why keep it a secret?'

'I don't!' He sounds genuinely shocked. 'Ask Misty. I'm always playing with a deck of cards. But it's totally amateur. Can't compare to you.'

'But you could help me when I give teen workshops at Dante Hall.'

'I will.' He checks his watch. 'I have to go. I promised Misty I'd catch the end of her act.'

'Wait a minute. Where are you from?'

'New York.'

'Where?'

'Staten Island. After that I lived in upstate New York for years. Then I moved here. What's going on?'

'I'm just... finding out about people.'

'Oh, Lucy.' He leans over and hugs me. Suddenly, I'm near tears. He pulls back. 'Don't let all this get you down. We'll get past it. Think about this: we had a great opening night, and we're going to have a good long run. Get some sleep.'

He walks to the door, where Gus catches up with him, and they leave the East Room together. My fingers dig into the curve of my neck and scratch. The Hunter is getting closer. He didn't pull a rose from his pocket, but Auntie Maze said he's here, in this room. His dark, half-dead energy is mingling with the ghosts of the restless World War Two soldiers. No one wants to stay buried. The past is taking over Jinx's mind, the men's shadows are rising. Maybe my Mask and Shadow did have an effect, and he's trying to show me who he is. I spoke to all of them tonight: Rex, Charlie, Gus, Elvis. One of them gave me a clue – it's gnawing at the curve of my neck – but what the hell is it?

A hazy plan forms in my mind. Stormie is at the far wall, chatting with Da and Auntie Maze. I don't have time to get to her. I hurry out of the room in time to see Charlie and Gus turn midway down the hall toward the elevators. They enter an elevator with a handful of guests.

I check my phone. No word from Dr. Lose yet.

It's 10:45. All evening, people have milled between the Widow and the East Room, one of the rare occasions that both rooms are open to the public. Charlie will return after Misty's set to lock up. Gus will return – when? Who knows? In ten minutes or not till tomorrow.

I hurry to the door marked 13 ½. Curve both hands around the doorknob and pray the door is unlocked.

It opens.

For an endless moment I stand in shock.

Then I slide inside and let the door shut behind me.

59

I climb the short, dark staircase to the thirteenth and a half floor. At the top of the stairs is the door to Gus's booth. I turn the knob. Locked. No!

I twist the knob again. Still locked.

I set down my purse and turn on my phone flashlight. If this door has a simple spring latch, I may be able to jimmy it open. I pull a credit card from my wallet and slide it into the vertical crack between door and frame, tilt the card toward the knob and away, wiggling it back and forth a few times.

The door at the foot of the stairs opens. My chest roars like a train.

Footsteps climb the shadowy steps. My neck didn't prickle in warning, but it's him, I know it. The dark driver, the killer. I lose my grip on the credit card.

The footsteps draw closer.

My back is to the person on the stairs, my knife in my purse on the landing next to me. When the roaring in my chest stops, I hear nothing.

The footsteps stop halfway up.

'Lucy.'

That voice. I whip around so fast I kick my purse down the steps.

He leans over and picks it up.

I aim the phone flashlight at him. In the dim stairway, his face is shadowy, his eyes pinpricks of light.

'What are you doing here?' My voice is clotted with fear. How am I going to get past him and down the stairs?

'I came to tell you the truth.'

I don't move. Not because I don't want to. I can't. My body goes cold with dread.

'I slept with Van.'

Oh, Van. My sweet Van.

'The night she came to my show.' He moves up a step.

I hold up my hand. 'Stay where you are.'

'Okay, okay. I liked her. A lot. She was a restless heart looking for something.' He hesitates. 'Not me.'

'Why not you?'

'I'm not a good bet.' He lifts a shoulder. 'I'd gotten out of a heavy relationship and didn't want to commit.'

'Why didn't you tell me the truth?'

He's quiet. 'I don't know. I didn't want you to look at me the way you're looking at me now.'

'Why did you take her to the Lollipop?'

'She wanted to see the real Atlantic City.' He lifts his shoulder again. 'I introduced her to Rex.'

'Did you see Gus there?'

'Yeah, sure.'

'The night she was–'

'I wasn't there that night.'

Should I believe him? 'Where were you that night?'

'In my room.'

'Where?'

'Sixth floor of Midnight.'

'After that?'

'In Hell, for my show. Afterwards, on the beach running with Bird. Then back to Midnight.'

'You argued with Van that night.'

'What?'

'Outside the Speakeasy.'

He thinks for a moment. 'We were talking. She said she was seeing a guy.'

'Who?'

'I wish I knew. She was excited, but secretive. Something didn't feel right. I warned her to be careful.'

'Did you know Gina Nardo?'

'No.'

The problem is that I want to believe him so badly it scares me. Makes me doubt my judgment, and even my memory. The lies he tells, the secrets he hides, the way he shifts mood so quickly. Misty sensed a dark energy in him. Maybe that's when the driver overpowers him. Maybe it's stronger than he is. When it takes over, it inhabits his body. It *possesses* him. He looks like Elvis, talks and moves like him, but inside is a creature who kills. With a trembling hand, I touch the flower pinned to my hair and wait to see if he responds. He doesn't say a word.

I lower the flashlight, and he climbs the remaining steps till he stands one below me, bringing us eye to eye. 'Your turn. What did you think you'd see in the sawing box?'

I'm cornered at the top of the stairs on a floor that shouldn't exist: 13½. This man disturbs me. *He makes your girl parts tingle.* Oh, God, Stormie. Hell with it. 'I'm scared of the sawing box, okay?'

'Ahh.' He considers that. 'The box, the trick, or the man performing it?'

'The whole thing. I hate it.'

'But you know it's never about the box. It's how the magician approaches it. It's the story you tell.'

'That's what my father says, but for me it *is* about the box. It cuts at me. I've tried every story, it doesn't matter. I don't want to talk about it. And we're running out of time.'

'You want to search Gus's booth because you don't want to believe it's me. Come on, I'll help you. Hold up the light.'

He pushes next to me on the narrow landing. I aim my phone light at the doorknob while he plays with the card, jimmying the catch that springs and squeaks.

'What happened with the heavy relationship?'

'She broke up with me. She said I fly away whenever there's trouble.'

I test the waters. 'You must have been very angry.'

He grows still. 'Very.'

'What happened to her?'

'It was... unfortunate.'

Tension seizes my chest. 'Jones! What happened?'

'She married a human. A banker, I believe.' He clears his throat. 'A sad story. Last I heard they reside in the wilds of Idaho.'

I shoot him one of my darkest looks.

'Ta dah!' He flashes a triumphant smile. 'Stay behind me.' He opens the creaking door.

Is it possible for an adult male who says, 'Ta dah,' three times in a week to hide a murderous secret identity?

He finds the switch and turns on the lights. 'Time to find out what Gus is hiding.'

Time to find out what you're hiding too.

The narrow room is as old and crammed with memorabilia as the rest of the theatre. It's cold too. Icy air mingled with dust. My arms tingle with goose bumps. Gus's canvas work apron hangs on a hook, tools poking from its pockets. Shelves burst with lenses, par cans, gels, cables, and cutting boards. Charts, light plots, and stacks of paperwork are spread across the counter. Autographed black and white headshots of performers decorate the wall over the top shelf as well as playbills from former shows at the Widow and the Scarlet Room. Framed posters, hazy with dust, lean against the back wall. A modern lighting control panel and computer screen sit on a table beneath the carved black square window.

Elvis moans.

I spin around, hand to heart.

Crouched before the stack of posters, he holds one up, sneezes and waves away the motes to show me a picture of a smiling Black man:

Fetaque Sanders
Ghost Alive on Stage
The Great Fetaque
Say Fe-Take
Dramatic Magician
(in person—not a moving picture)

'I heard of Fetaque,' he says. 'He toured with the USO during World War Two.'

'He might have worked here, when it was the Scarlet Room, and Cleo and Morelli performed for the troops. Many performers and magicians passed through.'

He returns to the posters and moans again. 'I love him.'

I peer over his shoulder at the magician wearing a top hat, monocle, tux, and white gloves. Da showed me the only existing footage of Cardini: a tipsy gentleman trying in vain to control cigarettes that light themselves and decks of cards that multiply around him.

'I love Cardini too. My father calls him the Fred Astaire of magic.'

'His act is a dance,' he says. 'Look at that bemused smile. As if he's more surprised than anyone.'

'As if he hasn't caused the magic. It's the world around him that's magic, not him.'

'Huh.' Elvis slants me a look. 'I'm working on something new, inspired by Cardini and a short story by Julio Cortázar.'

'With Bird?'

He tugs off his jacket and sits on the floor, ignoring the dust. 'It won't be possible to work with Bird much longer. The new show will be a guy who lives in a magic world surrounded by objects that have their own will.'

I crouch on my heels, one hand on the floor, the other clenched at my side. This is not a truce – we're playing a waiting game. 'Like Cardini's cigarettes and cards.'

'A day in the life. He tries to put on a sweater, but it tangles him inside, a kind of straitjacket. It's not just the sweater. Everything he touches rebels and wants to do its own thing.'

While he speaks, I stare at his sweater – grey and worn. A thread dangles, where his right nipple would be if he tore off the sweater... or if I yank the thread. Why, why, why am I thinking of his nipple and his bare chest?

'Hey!'

My guilty gaze shoots to his. Heat flares up my throat.

'I haven't told this to anyone. Why am I telling you?'

'Too late. My hidden wire has captured every word.'

The smile starts in his eyes and slowly heats them. The creases around his eyes, the sunburst of laugh lines – paler than his golden skin – make him look older. Make him look real. By the time the smile reaches his mouth, and yes, I'm waiting, I know I'm in trouble.

'Let's search. We don't have much time.' I move away and kneel to examine the books piled on the floor. *The Psychopathic Killer, Crimes in Atlantic City, The Mind of the Violent Killer, The Stranger in Our Midst.* Bedtime reading for Gus, wannabe cop or Mob killer? The corner of a manila envelope pokes out beneath the books. I bring it to the counter and turn it upside down. Photos spill onto the surface.

Elvis hears my gasp and moves to my side. Draws in a sharp breath.

Gruesome crime scene photos of homicide victims, all females. Bodies in pools of blood. Sawed-off arms and legs. Feet without bodies. Decapitated heads. Women's breasts, their nipples hacked off. Close-ups of bullet holes and bite marks.

'How did Gus get access to these photos? He doesn't work for the cops.'

'He could have bought them on the dark web,' he says. 'You can get anything if you pay for it.'

My eyes itch, sand-dry. Here is true noir, as dark as it gets: undisguised hatred of women. Photos of naked women in ditches. One woman's face is turned to the side, a thick rope knotted around her neck. A victim of the Rope Strangler. Another woman's lips are clamped shut, her throat slashed and bruised.

Elvis pushes the photos into the envelope. I shove it back under the books, but the images burn behind my eyes. 'Why does he have them?'

'Maybe the answer is here.' He holds out a cardboard box of printer paper so stuffed with sheets the lid doesn't close. He sets it on the counter and lifts the top. The first sheet is neatly typed:

The Dead Don't Die:
Atlantic City's Murderous History
by Augustus Wigman

'Gus writes about true crime!'

Elvis pages through and reads phrases aloud: 'Famous murders in America's Playground... The Mob was running its scams... Body bags and sandbags, World War Two in Atlantic City.' He lifts his head. 'Listen to this: "In this city the dead have a hard time staying underground. There's too much action happening above the rafters for them to stay peacefully beneath."'

He turns to the last page. 'Seven hundred fifty pages and he's only at the 1980s. Good luck getting that published.'

'I don't understand why he keeps it secret.'

Elvis shrugs. 'He gets more information that way. And people don't ask when it will be finished or published.'

Gus is living undercover, though not as a cop. He's living a lie, pretending to be something he's not and hiding the fact that he's a writer.

'You said tonight that everyone has their shadow.' Jones returns the pages to the box and sets it back beneath the shelves.

Including you. Suddenly I can't bear to be alone with him in this claustrophobic room. No one knows I'm here. 'Let's get out before someone comes.'

'Just a minute.' He turns off the light. 'I want to see how the theatre looks from up here.'

He leans over the large screen and peers through the carved square opening. I move next to him. We're the only two people in the world on a mountain peak. Does Gus believe he's a king up here, controlling light and dark? *You were watching me tonight.*

The Hunter's Moon, full and hungry, shoots rays that trace patterns on the carpet, stage, and chairs. Norse gods carved into the lintel watch over the theatre. Curtains frame the stage, a black hollow illuminated only by the ghost light, a slender brass pole topped with a screwed-in light bulb that gives off a diffused yellow glow.

His voice breaks the silence. 'I've never seen one of these before. It doesn't provide much light.'

'It's supposed to light the way for spirits.'

'Ah.'

I can hear the smile.

After a moment, he says, 'I can fly.'

'I believe you. I've seen you with Bird.'

'I mean, I know how to fly.' He doesn't look at me. 'I can show you how. The secret to flying is that you can't be afraid to fall.'

I turn my gaze back to the theatre. In the moonlight it seems to wait breathlessly for something to happen. I imagine myself crawling to the edge of this opening, spreading my arms, and leaping out.

'You have to fall before you can fly,' he says, low, as if talking to himself. Or as if he hears my thoughts. 'It's like swimming. When you fight the water, you sink. You have to let the water move through you until you become part of it. Same with flying. Instead of struggling when you're in the sawing box, surrender. Don't forget to breathe, let yourself fall and let yourself rise...'

'You're trying to whisper me.'

'Tonight, what you did on stage? You shook the soul out of me.'

It takes a moment to absorb the words. What does he mean? Because I touched his soul? Or because I got close to the truth about him? 'I... why didn't you say anything before?'

'Don't you get silent when something moves you?'

You move me. You stop my breath. You terrify me.

He turns to face me. 'It doesn't help that you don't trust me. Deep down, you suspect me.'

'Not so deep down. I can't find you on the internet. What are you hiding?'

'I'm protecting someone I love from someone I hate. I also believe in privacy. Crazy for a performer, right?'

'You're slippery with truth.'

'We're liars by trade. Lies are our truth.'

'Onstage. But we're not onstage.'

'You mean you take off the mask when you get offstage?' He shakes his head. 'I don't believe it. You and me, we use our masks to keep from... letting others see us. And from getting hurt.'

He sounds so rational, so much the way I want him to sound. Am I deluding myself? 'How did you know about me?'

He chews his lower lip and studies me while I study the way his teeth bite into the soft flesh of his lower lip. 'This is going to sound stalkerish.' He chews again. His tell? 'I look at you a lot. Way more than I look at anyone else.'

'That's not enough. Tell me the truth.'

'I looked you up. You don't appear in Moon photos till you're about eight, and when you do, you stand apart. Even with the red hair. Your magic is different and–'

He grabs my hand. A cry sticks in my throat.

'Get down. Someone's here.'

60

'Anyone here?' calls a voice from below.

Charlie. Here to lock up. He walks towards the stage. I hope he doesn't come up here. What reason can I give for hiding in Gus's lighting booth with Elvis Jones?

Elvis checks his watch. I glance at mine. 11:23. His midnight show! He needs to go downstairs to Hell, to change and prepare Bird and himself. Our eyes meet, and he reaches for my hand.

Below, in the theatre, cold air rustles and whirls. The scent of lavender rises all the way up to the booth. It should be sweet, but it's rotting-ripe, like a… dead flower. Cleo is here, and she's angry again. I wonder if Elvis senses her presence. He releases my hand and peers through the opening.

Gripping the wall, I lift myself and stare in disbelief.

Smack in the centre of the stage, the ghost light's yellow bulb is suddenly flickering madly. As we watch, it transforms into a flame. An honest-to-God purple flame, as if Cleo's lavender breeze infiltrated it. I'm not dreaming. Elvis glances at me, his expression stunned.

Charlie's pale hair gleams. He stands motionless at the foot of the stage, staring at the newly alive ghost light. The purple flame whirls above the brass pole as if an invisible man is spinning it around, faster, faster. Spinning, dizzying. Wind gusts through the theatre. A cold lavender wind.

'Leave me alone!' cries a faint, high-pitched voice.

Is that Charlie? Or Cleo crying out through the flame?

The flame sputters and disappears. Once again, the ghost light is a yellow bulb on a spindly brass stick – a pale defense against the darkness.

Charlie wheels around and stares at the back wall.

Elvis and I freeze in the shadows.

I don't breathe until Charlie strides back through the theatre and closes the doors.

We wait ten minutes before leaving Gus's booth. Elvis opens the door. On my way out, I absently touch Gus's work apron hanging on a hook. I didn't check the pockets. I dig my hand inside. Tape measure, flashlight, screwdriver, wrench, circuit tester, and something soft and feathery. I pull out a black paper rose. One of mine. Horror sweeps through me.

'You coming?' Elvis calls to me.

I move towards him, holding the rose. Elvis's gaze goes to my hand, then to my face. 'Where'd that come from?'

'Gus's apron pocket.'

'He must have picked it up after your show.'

'Yes, but why?' A rose to set between the lips of his next victim?

'He could be a fan, that's all.'

Charlie locked the door to the thirteenth and a half floor, but luckily it opens from inside. We hurry to the elevator. Elvis's show begins in twenty minutes. When did I start thinking of him as Elvis again, rather than Jones?

On the Casino level, Elvis stands between the open doors, blocking them. His eyes shine with tiny lights. He pulses with energy. I wish I knew what he's thinking. He holds out his hand to shake mine and squeezes. When he releases my hand, I find a skull-shaped Midnight room key in my palm.

He smiles, the shy smile of the gawky magician. 'My room. 618.'

'Why?'

'Because I want you to trust me. Go to my room. Relax, take a bath, watch TV. Search the damned place. I'll be back after I take Bird for a run, around 1:30.' When I don't say anything, he adds, 'If you don't want to, how about breakfast on the beach tomorrow with Bird and me?'

'What?' I'm so tightly wound it comes out like a shriek.

'That meal in the morning. I've heard some people enjoy it.' The bland smile is back, the glint in his eyes.

'You're leaving it up to me?'

He blows me a kiss and dashes out.

I get off on the sixth floor. In my room I set Elvis's room key and Gus's black flower on the dresser. I remove the flower from my hair and set it next to the one I found in Gus's pocket. Of course they're identical.

I check my phone. No word from Dr. Lose. I decide to take a chance and message her: Did you leave for Midnight yet?

While I wait for a response, I message Stormie: You up?

No answer.

I hear the ping of a message. Dr. Lose: Sorry, need to take care of work. Will you be up late?

Yes!

Ok, let you know if I'll make it tonight. If not, tomorrow morning.

Trembling, I set down my phone. What did Dr. Lose discover? Think, Lucy. Twenty to thirty years ago, Jane Doe was buried with a black rose in her mouth. One of the suspects in her murder is an old snake catcher who did magic on the side. Twenty-four years ago, my mother took me to Declan Moon, a magician, and left me with a black rose. She was worried she'd be killed.

The magic trick, Mysterious Connections, reveals links that are hidden until you look at them in the right light. I see the roots of an immense tree spreading underground and branching into tunnels. What if my mother trespassed into the Barrens and uncovered a secret so dangerous she had to be vanished? The earth swallowed her, but the black rose refused to stay down. It found its way to me and surfaced on Van and Gina. Maybe Rex knows its secret. He's in his late forties. He could have known my mother.

A shudder racks through me. *Trust the sudden knowing.* I don't have a name or proof, but it's her, I know it. My mother is Jane Doe. Oh, God, how am I going to wait for Dr. Lose?

The skull key to Elvis Jones's room glows on my dresser. It opens the door to revelation or to danger. More likely, revelation that leads to danger.

I kick off my heels, tug off my dress and pad to the bathroom. I strip off my makeup and wash my face. Remove the mask from my face and body. Naked in the mirror, body tingling. The truth is that if Elvis had led me from the elevator to his room, I'd have gone. The hour and half gap until the end of his show gives me too much time to think. I've already changed my mind half a dozen times. Besides, what's the point of going to his room? What do I think will happen?

Even in the dark, even alone, heat pools between my breasts and down my neck.

Nothing can happen between us. The terrifying leap of faith to cross from me to him. I don't have the guts. Besides, he's an admitted liar, a man with secrets. The truth is we never know what hides behind the mask. *Never.* The fear is intensified when it's a woman wondering if she can trust a man. I can't make that mistake again. It hurts too much. And this time the stakes are much higher. If I trust the wrong man, I won't have a second chance.

Idiot! He's not in his room. Get the hell over there and find out what the man is hiding. I tug on a T-shirt and sweatpants. Pull on my sneakers, grab my phone and knife.

61

I glide into Elvis Jones's room like the Apprentice stealing into the Sorcerer's Workshop. For a moment, the thrill of being in his room paralyses me. Slivers of gold moon slash through the blinds. His room is larger than mine, a king-size bed in the centre, a blue sweater tossed on his pillow. Snacks on the dresser for Bird. Laptop on the desk.

I turn on the light. At the foot of the bed, two pairs of shoes and one pair of sneakers line up, toes pointing toward the door. Next to them lies a battered backpack.

His black hoodie hangs on the chair. I reach inside the pockets. An unopened pack of gum. A handful of coins. I frown at the bed. Did he sleep with Van in this room? What happened the morning after? She tried to pin him down. His former girlfriend said he flies away at the first sign of trouble. He grew angry, he reached for her–

I turn from the bed and face the mirrored sliding doors of the closet. Inside, a black leather jacket, a few shirts – all black. The man has a theme. Two folded pairs of jeans – one black, one faded denim. Two sweaters, neatly folded on a shelf.

The bathroom is spotless. The only personal item: a zebra-striped cosmetic bag filled with hotel-size bottles – aftershave, a lemony shampoo, toothpaste, and a folding toothbrush. I sniff the aftershave, but don't recognise Elvis's dark woodsy scent. In spite of myself, my gaze lingers on the tub. *Take a bath,* he said.

As if I'd leave myself so vulnerable.

But I picture myself naked in the tub – head back, eyes closed, satiny warm water coursing over my body. When I open my eyes, he's in the doorway to the bathroom and then he's moving toward me, kneeling next to the tub, and reaching for me.

Oh, God. I meet my reflection in the mirror. Eyes glowing, lips parted. One hand touching my breast. Alone in his room, I can admit it. This man sparks me. A prickly shiver, combined with fear. When I'm with him, I'm as electric as he is. The only man who touches me... without touching me. How can I be attracted to a man who might be a murderer?

Stop this. You're here to find out who he is and what he's hiding.

I return to the bedroom and open the top drawer of the dresser: T-shirts, underwear, socks. The other drawers: empty. The man travels light. Him and his seagull, ready to leave at a moment's notice.

With a sigh, I sit on the edge of the bed. The room is bare, but it is a hotel room. Elvis said he has another place, a private place where he lets Bird fly free. A house in the country? A stretch of land?

I examine the bedside table. A few white feathers – the tickets to his show. A small bowl filled with coins. Three decks of cards, still wrapped in plastic. I open the drawer. Empty.

It's 12:40. He and Bird are whirling in their dance onstage.

The laptop beckons, a silver box hiding his secrets. The screensaver glitters, a sea under brilliant sun. Locked, waiting for his password. Bird? His birthday? Birthplace? I wild-guess three variations. All three fail. I know nothing about this man.

I shut the laptop and jump to my feet. Glance over my shoulder. He gave me his key, but he removed every personal or revealing item. A conman, he manipulated me into believing he'd show me his true self.

One last try before I leave. I sit on the bed again, careful not to disturb the shoes. The backpack! I turn on the bedside lamp and search the compartments. Sunglasses, a black knit cap, rolled-up socks, two vintage paperbacks, page corners turned down. A small black notebook, the same kind in which I jot ideas for illusions. The inside cover: his name and phone number. No address. Below, he has copied quotes by magicians, including some of my heroes: Eugene Burger, Bob Neale, Jeff McBride, Tommy Wonder.

He filled half the notebook with sketches – many of Bird, others with set-ups for tricks. I study the sketch and plan for The Sweater, the effect that he described in Gus's lighting booth. It reminds me of Teller's illusion about a mischievous Red Ball that refuses to obey its owner. My gaze moves from the sketch in his notebook to the sky-blue sweater in a heap on the pillow. I press it against my chest. Soft and hand-woven. I breathe in Elvis. *Here* is his unmistakable salt-fresh scent. Nothing magic about this sweater, except that it belongs to him.

Girl, you've got it bad. Hurry up and get out of here. But I slip the sweater over my head and feel its soft warmth as if his arms are wrapped around me. I push up the sleeves. Maybe it will guide me to his secrets.

He scribbled phone numbers on the last page of the notebook, including Nya's, Charlie's, and a phone number for 'G'. Gina Nardo? Gus? I memorise the number. I'll call it as soon as I get back to my room.

I shove the notebook in the backpack and zip open an inner pocket. An army knife. A length of paracord. No. No!

Fingers shaking almost uncontrollably, I uncoil it. The perfect length to strangle a woman. Why do you have this, Elvis Jones? Did you use it to strangle Van and Gina?

The air stirs. My head jolts back.

He stands at the entrance to the room. I didn't hear the door open. I freeze, the cord stretched between my hands.

The hush deepens, a hush so vast it's an ocean between us. He's breathing hard. So am I. As we face each other, the hush becomes tangible, a black wall rising between us.

Taut with tension, I don't notice the enormous silk-covered cage he holds until Bird squawks.

I release my breath and drop the cord.

He carries the cage to the window, sets it on the floor and pulls off the silk. Bird screeches a cry of joy. Elvis hunkers down and whispers to Bird, giving me the chance to escape with dignity. Putting the choice in my hands, again.

I get to my feet and back away silently toward the door.

Without turning, he says, 'I use the paracord to leash Bird in dangerous situations.'

I stand motionless, a few feet from the door. *What else do you use it for?*

He rises and faces me. Hands at his sides. 'What do you want, Lucy?'

The choice is mine. The power back in my hands, where I like it, but he's a master of deception and transformation, I don't trust him.

'This is the wrong time.' I retreat another step toward the door. 'You're the wrong man, I'm the wrong woman.'

'We're in the business of turning wrong into right, lies into truth.'

One more step away from him. 'You really believe that?'

He gives me the kind of look I don't remember getting from any man, ever. I should run, as fast and far away from him as I can.

'A black rose,' he murmurs. 'Real and not real, made out of petals and dreams...'

Hearing my words coming from his mouth, in that Jameson voice... If there's ever been a wrong man at the wrong time, here he is. But I trusted the 'right' man before, the one who appeared solid and rooted as a tree. This man flies with a seagull. *Everything he touches becomes magic.* He is dangerous. But so am I. This night began with exposing shadows to light. It's time to admit the truth to myself: I'm almost as scared of myself as I am of him.

'Once,' I breathe.

'Then we'll make it a very special once.'

My heart quivers, wings fluttering against my chest.

He holds out his hand, and I leap across the gulf and fall into him.

*

Once is so furious and intense and rushed you'd think an eternity had passed since either of us made love. Even the first kiss is electric. He grips my cheeks, I dig my hands in his hair, and burning wires zigzag, hip to hip, belly to belly, chest to chest, up our throats to our lips. I haven't been kissed like this since I was eighteen. When we both come up for air, he says, 'Oh, God,' and we try to laugh but end up kissing again. And again.

He builds a shelter beneath the window out of a sheet, blanket, and our clothes. He insists on carrying me, awkwardly toppling out of his arms. Is this Lucy, gripping his shoulders, on the verge of bursting into laughter (*don't, don't shatter the spell*) or giving him one of those dreamy female smiles I hate on principle?

Go ahead, drop me, come on I dare you.

But he lowers me gently, him on top of me, and somehow we're all coiled up, arms and legs wrapped around each other.

'I know I won't come,' I mumble, as our fingers explore flesh, muscle, bone. 'I never do the first time with a man, not even the second time. And it's the first time I've been with someone in ages–' *Stop babbling, Moon. Shut up.*

Maybe I'm just too tired and scared, this man could be – *oh! that's nice, mmm yes, I like it* – I don't want to go through any more wannabe Moons, no more – *sweet, you taste like chocolate here, don't laugh, it's true, dark chocolate... no, that tickles!*

I suck on his shoulder to keep from looking at those laughing black eyes, to keep from letting some of my venom escape. I could so easily be nasty here, the situation *calls* for nastiness. I fasten my teeth on the slick shoulder and clamp. He trembles slightly, eyes startled, then crinkling, smiles down at me again. 'Ah, Lucy.' A sigh ripples through him. 'Brave Lucy.'

Brave Lucy?

I stare, speechless for once. He swallows. I swallow. The dark smile turns intimate, brooding. 'My Lucy,' he whispers.

I'm nobody's Lucy.

Then he lowers his face, and I can't see anymore.

The floor moves beneath us, tilting us back and forth as if we are rocking in a boat. Water sprays on us, spirits breathe down our faces and drench us with sweat, shake us upside down. 'I want to be an Elvis-whisperer,' I croon, tasting lime in the curve of his throat, salt on the wings of his bird tattoo, the blue woods on his belly and thighs.

To keep from seeing us from the outside, I squeeze my eyes shut.

To keep from crying, I kiss him back.

62

Little Nick

early Thursday morning October 25

He crosses the boardwalk toward the beach in front of Midnight. Thick fog swirls in from the ocean, drops of rain hang heavy, hiding the full moon. He zips up his black hoodie, pushes the hood over his head and tightens the drawstrings. One hand touches the paracord in his pocket.

Tonight things changed in a way he hadn't anticipated. The car is packed, down to a driver's license and passport in the name of Roderick Usher. He's ready to go, but he loves this doomed town. Big Nick says dreams aren't for the likes of him, but this town lets him pretend. He left a woman asleep in his bed, and he plans to return to that warm woman and stay with her till the last minute.

He hears his name and squints in the fog. That cropped mess of carrot hair. The gruff voice. The bone whisperer who can't keep her big mouth shut.

She approaches, and they stand under the boardwalk light. His radar pulses under the skin. It has steered him clear of danger too many times to count.

'We haven't formally met. I'm Dr. Ida Lose, a forensic anthropologist.' Close-up, her face is sun-freckled, large-featured. He shakes her hand. As rough and callused as her voice.

For an instant she reminds him of someone from another life.

'I sent you a message to see if we could meet tomorrow.'

'Did you?' His hand clenches and unclenches in his pocket. 'I haven't checked my phone tonight. What are you doing out here so late?'

'I was on my way to Midnight to–' She hesitates. 'To meet

someone.'

He smiles. 'I won't stop you. I'm going for a run.'

'Wait! I want to ask you a question.'

Her hand disappears in the pocket of her Army jacket and pulls out a glossy sheet of paper, creased and torn from a magazine. 'Look at this picture.' When he doesn't move, she adds, 'It was taken in the Pine Barrens.'

'Is this why you wanted to meet me?'

'Yes. It's you or your double.'

'I doubt that.' He mock-shudders. 'Swamps and bugs. Not my kind of place.'

'Look at it,' she insists.

'And you just happen to have it with you?'

She shrugs, and he steps closer to the light, spreads it out against his palm and studies the photo of a ragged-haired boy and a bearded man with mad eyes on a wooden porch. The bitch knows. It's a trap. She was on her way to meet someone and show them this picture. Every time he tastes freedom, a door slams in his face. Why won't they leave him alone?

She leans toward him, uncomfortably close. 'Didn't I hear you were raised by your grandfather? Read the caption: "Snake trader Nicodemus Cray and his grandson Nick Cray at the Green Bank Tavern."'

He opens his mouth to speak but his tongue is dry, caked with salt. He'd forgotten the *National Geographic* photographer who came to capture the notorious Pineys in their habitat. Big Nick had aimed his flintlock at the photographer, but the man not only got the shot, he got their names too. The sack of live snakes Big Nick had caught vibrated on the porch between them. Little Nick smelled the green air and felt his heart beating in anticipation of his first dance. When they went into town for supplies, he suffered. Painfully shy. Looking at girls with a hunger he couldn't disguise. Yearning toward them. Not mad at them. Not yet. Not until the blonde girl shamed him at the dance that night and awakened the rage.

Stop looking at the damned picture. Tear it up.

But slingshots snap behind his eyes. The boy on the porch has one more hour of innocence before the sun disappears behind Green Bank Tavern and Big Nick takes the money from selling the snakes and gets drunk. And Little Nick enters the dance hall and the blonde girl saws his life in two.

The carrot-haired bitch rubs her chin as if she's stroking a beard. 'The old man did magic now and then in the Green Bank Tavern, didn't he? Big Nick and Little Nick.'

He shudders inside, the shock of hearing the names spoken aloud. Like glass shattering around him.

'I'm not trying to bring back unpleasant memories. Little Nick was a kid but he might remember something that can help us identify Jane Doe.'

'You're not suggesting it's me?' A trace of impatience followed by a rueful smile. 'I've never even been to the Pine Barrens. Wish I could help but...'

She grabs the photo right out of his hand. 'Once a Piney, always a Piney. Isn't that what they say?' Her voice has razor-teeth, same as Big Nick. 'You clean up good, I'll give you that, but you can't wash off the Pines. The smell stays, the bones remember. And you got those Piney eyes.'

He doesn't want to ask. But he has to. 'What eyes?'

'Piney eyes are like sunglasses. No matter what colour they are, they keep out the light.'

'How do you know?'

She sneers. 'Can't you tell? I'm a Piney too.'

Oh yeah, she's a Piney, a wild card. Jagged edges. He pictures her marching through the Barrens with the Australian Shepherd he saw on TV and the polka dot headband that doesn't fit with an Army jacket and hiking boots. Some guy must have given it to her, told her it made her pretty. She'll never be pretty.

'Look, I just want to ask you about Jane Doe.'

What kind of fool does she think he is? As if his answers won't land him in a cell, where he'll die of suffocation. He was born free in the wilds, and he'll die free.

'I swear I don't want to ruin your life. You were a kid. Whatever happened, you had nothing to do with it. You're innocent. But can you tell me anything about Little Nick and Big Nick and the woman in the pit?'

Panic firecrackers inside him. It takes every bit of strength he has to keep from crying out. Why? When is this going to end? Will they ever leave him alone? This fucking world that won't let him breathe.

Here we go, mutters Big Nick. *Your time's runnin' out, boy. Do the deed and get out.*

'I may be able to help you,' he says. 'Let me see that picture again.' After a moment he remembers to smile.

She thrusts the picture at him, and he pretends to study it again. How the fuck is he going to get out of this?

'You can't keep running,' she says.

Is that pity in her voice? His head is crashing, the bumper cars smashing against each other again.

He looks at her, and she must see something in his gaze because she suddenly gasps, 'I told the cops who you are.'

He doesn't waste his energy on words. She's lying.

He shoves the picture in his pocket and leans toward her, backing her against the railing.

She kicks him in the shin. Hiking boots with spiked soles. Then she headbutts his chest. With a growl, he whips his arm around her neck and wrenches her head back and neck-locks her.

Kill her kill her kill her! roars Big Nick.

She curses him, wriggles her arm free and shoves her elbow into his groin.

He twists her around so she's facing the ocean. Grabs her hands in both of his. Kicks the toe of his sneaker into the back of her knee. Knocks her off balance.

She screams, and he yanks her arms, forcing her into a backbend, and rams her, belly-first, into the railing. He shoves his chest and hips against her back. She squirms wildly but her hands are locked. He presses harder, a mountain wearing her down, doubling her over the railing.

She screams again, a hoarse cry, and he risks lifting his right hand to yank the cord from his pocket. Loops it around her neck. Crushes her hands between her back and his chest.

She digs the spiked heel of her hiking boot against his leg, scrapes it down his shin and slams into his foot.

Pain shoots up. So blinding for a second he forgets where he is.

She takes off running toward Central Pier.

He races after her, grabs her from behind, tackles her to the boardwalk. She fights, a street cat, punching, kicking and screeching, until he sits on her.

Panting, he glances around, a quick scan. The fog is thick, a cloying cloud, no lights nearby. He doesn't see anyone. Prays no one sees them.

'Killing me won't... won't solve anything.' She's panting.

He finger-grips each end of the cord and tugs until it's taut – a wire tightrope across her throat.

She kicks out behind her, but she can't lift the heavy boots.

He forces the cord harder, tighter, and yanks back. Crosses his hands at the rear of her neck and applies more pressure.

His hands.

Her neck.

Nothing else exists.

Only his rage. It soars, pure and true, a gold arrow piercing the dense grey fog.

Here you are, says Big Nick approvingly.

Here I am.

It's about fucking time. Don't know why you fight it so much, boy.

He doesn't believe a word she said about telling others. She's a lone wolf too. She counted on scaring him into confessing.

He unwinds the paracord from her throat and stuffs it back in his pocket. Gets to his feet. Heart drumming in his ears, he squints in every direction. No one. At least no one he sees. The fog is thicker than ever, a murky soup that hides monstrous things. Like him.

He crouches and picks her up. The solid mass of her, those combat boots alone weigh ten pounds each. His shins will be black and blue, and his foot still throbs. He carries her down the steps to the beach through mist that stinks of sulphur and dead fish.

Another stroke of luck. The fog and cold must have sent the Central Pier bums to a downtown shelter. Defying the old man growling in his ear, this Piney bitch who couldn't leave him alone, and the moon's hundred black eyes, he hums Ruby's song, 'Atlantic City Blues,' while he does damage control. As he works, it strikes him who she reminds him of. Not puffy and dead, but before – solid, freckled, large-boned. Ellie. His Ellie.

He'd been working his way north along the Mississippi the night he met Ellie at a bar in St. Louis. He asked her to dance. When she said yes, he couldn't believe his idiocy. He hadn't danced since the terrible night in Egg Harbor City. A flame seared through him. Sweat dripped down his forehead. Within five seconds he stumbled over her feet. He lowered his arms and stepped back. Wet with nerves and rage, he needed to get away, *now*. If she laughed or made a snide comment, he wouldn't be able to control himself.

She held onto him. She wouldn't let him go. Instead, she leaned her head on his shoulder and said, 'Let's try this together.'

His heart pounded, sweat poured down his throat to his chest. After a moment, he wrapped his arms around her, and with baby steps, inched closer. They danced until the bar closed.

'Thanks for being so patient with me,' she said. 'I'm Ellie. What's your name?'

He looked at her closely for the first time. A farm girl, freckled and sweating, bright brown eyes, a wide smile. Not fat, but solid and large, and when he held onto her, he felt anchored for the first time since he'd left the Barrens. He hesitated an endless moment. 'Peter Wilson.'

One last sweeping look. He's alone in the world, same as Poe, cloaked in an impenetrable foul-smelling blanket. Only one thing glows: her headband, polka dots crawling like ladybugs over her hair.

He's too drained to do anything but stagger back to his room and the woman waiting for him. And collapse. He'll figure out the rest tomorrow. Improvise the way he always does.

63

I'm falling, falling, falling...

'Lucy. Lucy.'

... to my death...

A man's arms cushion and catch me the instant before I hit the ground.

'You had a bad dream. I'm moving you to the bed.' He sets me down gently.

Between dream and waking, still dizzy from the fall. A masked man pushed me off a roof, but I'm still here. Alive.

In the distance, something stirs. He covers me with the sheet and blanket, curves behind me, his warm hand on my belly. The blue woods I tasted on his body, the darkness he inhabits. He smells of salt and wind and sea. 'Were you out?'

He murmurs blurry words and kisses the back of my neck. 'Go back to sleep.'

*

Light on my closed eyelids, heat from his body next to mine. Be careful, Lucy. Watch your heart. This man is dangerous on so many levels. He's not a killer, he can't be. But after one night, he's more of a threat to my heart than André was after a year.

It's the dreaded morning after. If he doesn't say or do something to ruin it, I will. Best thing: sneak out of bed before he wakes and return to my room and safety. I wriggle an inch toward the edge of the bed.

Another inch.

Another.

A rustle of wings. I open my eyes. Blue light stripes down

the walls and over the large cage. This man and his bird. And his hands and his voice. I turn my head just to see–

He's watching me.

For a long moment we stare at each other. The inked bird on his arm glows in the light as if waiting for a signal to break free and fly. In the night I stroked the bird's wings, and the man cried out, almost in pain. The way he touched me, the words he whispered, tasting them on his tongue.

With a sigh, I turn on my side and face him. 'You were watching,' I accuse him.

'I had to see how it would end.'

'It hasn't ended yet.'

'But that sigh. Was it a coffee sigh? A tea sigh? Or a–'

'It's an Elvis Jones sigh.'

He smiles. 'Come here, beautiful.'

I wriggle toward him and nuzzle his throat. His warm arms fold around me. Heavy-eyed and lazy, we make love as if we have all the time in the world. As if there is no world outside this room.

After a while Bird squawks. 'My alarm clock,' says Elvis.

We dress slowly, finding excuses to touch. The plan is to have breakfast on the beach with Bird. While I finger-comb my hair, my phone buzzes. I follow the sound to my phone on the bedside table, next to my knife.

Stormie. 'Oh, girl. Oh, girl.'

I stiffen. 'What's wrong?'

'Are you sitting?' she asks.

When I disconnect, Elvis asks, 'What happened?'

'A woman has been found under Central Pier.'

'You mean dead? Drowned?'

'Murdered.'

He flinches. 'Oh, God, not again.'

PART FOUR
REVEAL

64

Thursday October 25

Before we leave the room, Elvis sends Crazy Wind a message to feed Bird. Stormie waits for us at the sixth-floor elevator. She's in pink sweats, her long ropes of hair coiled in a large bun. When she sees Elvis and me together, her eyebrows rise so high they nearly touch her hair. She's dying to comment but we go down to the lobby in silence.

As we walk toward Central Pier, wind smacks our faces and snakes beneath the flesh. We pass a few people, their faces hidden. Elvis holds my hand. I close my other hand around Stormie's.

Pale sun glimmers on the pier, but still my bones tremble with cold. Police cars and a white news van are parked on the boardwalk. The area of beach adjoining the pier is marked off by yellow police tape.

We join other locals and the press at the boardwalk railing next to the pier. It's a sombre group, mostly men, including the two DiBruni brothers, boardwalk shop owners, casino dealers and employees, and a handful of greybeards who probably lugged their stuff from beneath the pier. I've seen more of the locals in the past week than in the past year.

Elvis's phone rings. He steps away to take the call.

The early morning light spares no one, emphasises crags and veins, turns everyone into a sallow, weary version of themselves. Even the most gorgeous couple I know appears stark, dishevelled, and weirdly put together. Charlie, hair spiked and tousled, dark stubble poking through his cheeks and chin, flannel shirt hastily buttoned so it hangs unevenly over torn jeans. Misty, in a white hoodie and sweatpants that balloon over her slender frame.

They move toward Stormie and me. The four of us huddle for a minute. When we pull apart, Charlie takes off his glasses. I squint one eye like Da and try to see through the beautiful face, the soft cheeks and sensitive mouth. His grey eyes are bloodshot, deeply shadowed and pained.

'Are you okay?' I ask him.

He rubs his forehead. 'I didn't sleep well last night.'

Misty winces. 'My phone again?' When he shrugs, she says, 'My ex.'

I push closer. 'Who is he?'

She purses her lips. A natural beauty, but even she is wrung out, a rag doll who lost her stuffing. 'A dealer at Harrah's. Works nights. That's his alibi. But every night he calls to check on me. I don't answer, but it usually wakes me–' She glances at Charlie. 'Or us. But last night I was so beat I slept through it.'

'Shut off your phone,' advises Stormie.

'I can't. My dad is in the hospital. I need to be on call.'

'Change your number,' I suggest. 'Only share it with the people you trust.'

'That's what I told her.' Charlie looks at his glasses and without wiping, puts them back on.

'I will.' Misty looks from Charlie to Stormie and me. 'But he's the kind who won't give up.'

'You can make it harder for him,' says Charlie.

Misty hugs herself. 'How are we supposed to do shows tonight? We have to, but doesn't it seem like we should stop and... and let this settle?'

'You cancelled the show after... after Van,' I tell Charlie. 'Stormie and I appreciated that.'

'It used to scare me when I was a kid,' says Stormie. 'How when a person dies, everything goes on as if nothing happened. People walk right over the hole they left. After a while, we stop noticing the hollow space.'

'Aw, Storm.' I wrap my arm around her. She's thinking of her father, a charming, handsome man who taught American history at a local high school. He was struck down ten years ago by a drunk driver. 'You don't forget. You keep them alive by remembering them. Like your dad. Like Van.'

I feel as if we're all talking about different things, conversing with ourselves, not really listening to each other. Anything to keep from talking about the latest victim.

The DiBruni brothers distribute cups of coffee. 'Another chick bites the dust,' says the silver-moustached brother. He shakes his finger at Misty, Stormie, and me. 'Youze girls better watch yourselves.'

The coffee burns my tongue and chest, hurtling me from dreams into reality. I need clarity, but my mind feels as thick and clotted as the fog. Stormie and I move toward Pam Woodson, the blonde newswoman. She confers with her cameraman at the steps leading down to the beach. She's in full makeup mode, but behind the thick coating of mascara and blush, her eyes and cheeks sag.

'What happened, Pam?' I ask.

'A jogger found a woman's body snagged against the rocks beneath the pier.'

'Are they sure she was murdered?'

'I'm going to find out.'

She turns back to her cameraman, and I press my hips against the railing and look down.

Detectives Torres and Wax are talking to their team of officers and white-garbed technicians. A tent has been set up on the sand. A photographer shoots the underside of the pier.

Stormie's long fingernails rap a nervous rat-tat against the railing. 'I suspect every man I see. Jones. Him.' She gestures toward Charlie. 'You know, I like him scruffy. And this sleazeball.'

Gus sidles over, his hair hanging loose in coarse grey stalks.

'Morning, ladies.'

I narrow my eyes. 'Well, if it isn't Gus Wigman, Undercover Cop.' And collector of crime scene photos of women.

'At your service.' A mock-bow.

'We need to talk,' I begin, but there's activity below. They're moving the body into the tent.

'Late October, water's pretty warm.' Gus pushes next to me. 'Barnacles, they'll cut you up sharp as a knife.'

'Shut up, Gus,' mutters Stormie at my other side.

'Sand crabs too.' He adjusts his large, red-framed glasses. 'Small bait fish. She won't be bloated yet, but they'll have been feasting on her.'

With a shudder, I ask, 'Do you know who she is?'

He smiles as if he can't help himself. I never noticed how many teeth he has, how small and tightly packed they are. 'Well, now that you ask, I...' He breaks off and stares beyond me at the beach.

I turn back to the beach. A glimpse, an instant only, as they move her. A woman's head, a tangle of hair. Darkened, matted with seaweed. A shredded band wrapped around her skull. Polka dots. Pink and black.

My knees fold. My head sinks over my chest.

Gus grabs my coffee cup before it drops.

A long moment before I can lift my head.

Stormie says, quiet, 'Feeling sick?'

I shake my head, but the movement nauseates me. I grip the railing to pull myself up.

Gus asks, 'Do you know who she is?'

'Ida Lose.' The words seem to come from outside my body.

'Ida Lose,' he repeats. 'The Bone Whisperer.'

'Do you know her?' I swallow and taste raw, sour fog.

'I've seen her around.'

Ida Lose, the woman who talks to the dead and understands their language. Who tramps the Pine Barrens with her best friend, Salt. Who shared the place she loves with me and who discovered something she wanted to show me. Had she been on her way to Midnight? And why didn't she take Salt with her? He'd have torn apart anyone who attacked her.

Ruby wheels toward us. Her eyes are wide with terror. 'I just heard.'

'Don't look, Ruby,' says Gus. His face has a yellow-green cast, like the fog. As if he's about to be sick too.

She draws in her breath. 'Do you know who did it?'

'Him.' I swallow again. 'The man who killed Van and Gina.'

There is no stranger-Hunter. The murderer knows magic. He knows us. We know him. He's one of us, hiding in plain sight. We just can't see him yet.

65

The police set up a temporary command post in an RV parked on the boardwalk. Patrolmen take our names and contact information and tell us to wait until we're called in to be questioned.

Inside, Detectives Torres and Wax are seated at a small table. I sit across from them, a tape recorder between us. Torres's ponytail is coming undone, tendrils of dark hair over her cheeks. Both she and Wax look frazzled, exhausted, and irritated.

'We meet again, Lucy Moon.' Detective Wax releases an exaggerated sigh. 'At the scene of a crime.'

Torres holds up three fingers. 'Three homicides. And oddly enough, one of the first people on the scene is you.'

'I'm staying at Midnight. It's natural for me to be here.' I throw back my shoulders. 'I know the victim, Ida Lose, and I believe I know why she was killed.'

Torres frowns. 'Let's back up. How do you know her?'

'We met at Elvis Jones's show.'

'Did you see her in the Barrens?' asks Wax.

I flush. 'Yes. The same place you were. Clarks Landing.'

'Talk,' says Torres. 'This time don't hold anything back.'

'Dr. Lose said fragments of black polyester were found in the burial pit with Jane Doe. The same kind of black polyester as the roses found on Van and Gina. Same as my mother's rose.'

My gut clenches so hard it hurts to breathe, especially in this small, crammed van. I still feel on the verge of throwing up or passing out. 'Dr. Lose believed Jane Doe may have been murdered. She wasn't investigating, she said that's not her job, but she's from the Pine Barrens, she knows it inside out...' I clear my throat. 'She hears – heard – things outsiders wouldn't.'

'Like what?'

'She mentioned two suspicious characters, both from the Barrens. Ben Briggs, a Vietnam vet who's been in and out of jail, and Big Nick, a violent snake-catcher who lived with his grandson, Little Nick.'

'Keep talking,' says Torres.

'Briggs is still alive. When I stopped at his tent to ask for directions, he threatened to shoot me. Big Nick and Little Nick disappeared about twenty years ago.' I catch my breath. 'Last night Ida Lose messaged me that she'd found something and was heading to Midnight to show me.'

'Why the hell was she talking to you?'

I flush at Wax's tone. 'Because I told her about my mother's rose.'

Torres scowls. 'Ida had no right to share information with you.'

'Jesus.' Wax shakes his head. 'The woman had no limits.'

'Why didn't she take Salt with her?' I ask. 'He'd have fought the killer.'

'No animals allowed in The Star Inn,' says Torres. 'That's where she stays when she's in town. When did she contact you?'

'After last night's show.'

'Before you spoke to Detective Wax and me?'

'Yes. I told her to tell me when she arrived at Midnight. At quarter to twelve, I asked if she'd left yet.'

I scroll through my messages to find Ida's last one, when I see another message.

On my way. You need to see this.

'I just saw this!' I hold out my phone. 'She sent this one at 2:35. That's when it happened. She was on her way to see me. On the way to Midnight, she ran into him. It's my fault.'

'Slow down,' says Wax. 'Read us the message that came before this one.'

I read: Sorry, need to take care of work. Will you be up late? 'You received this message at quarter to twelve,' says Torres. 'Where were you from the time you left the party until then?'

'When you told me that Gus lied about working undercover, I... I decided to search his lighting booth.'

Wax's eyes are slits of disapproval. 'We told you not to interfere.'

'I'm sorry.'

'What did you find in Gus's booth?' he asks.

'A book he's writing about crime in Atlantic City. Crime scene photos of women. And a black paper rose in the pocket of his work apron.'

Wax strokes his chin.

'Not polyester. A paper rose like the ones I used in my act.' They watch, impassive, so I continue. 'He could have picked it up from the stage.'

'Where did you go after Gus's booth?' asks Torres.

'My room. Dr. Lose sent me another message: Ok, I'll let you know if I can make it tonight. If not, tomorrow morning.'

Wax turns his steady brown gaze on me. 'Did you leave your room again?'

Heat blazes up my throat and cheeks. 'I went to Elvis Jones's room.'

He asks, 'Did you stay with Jones all night?'

'Yes.'

'Did he leave the room at any time during the night?' Torres's voice is soft, but it grates.

'No.' A hazy vision niggles at my brain. In my dream a masked man pushed me from a rooftop. Was I still dreaming when Elvis carried me to bed? He smelled of the cold, as if he'd been out.

Torres leans toward me. 'Lucy?'

My stomach twists. 'He did go out.'

'Did he tell you where he went?'

'He said a few words. I was half-asleep. But he smelled like the ocean.'

'How long was he gone?'

'Not long.'

Torres asks, 'Did he take his seagull?'

Odd question. 'No.'

I want to cry out: It can't be him! We kneeled on the floor in moonlight, and he pressed my palm to his cheek, and in his eyes, I saw the reflection of the boy who flew with his grandfather.

Torres runs her index finger along her scar. 'What was Jones's relationship to Ida Lose?'

'When we met at his show, she said it was her first magic show. She didn't seem to know him.'

'What did you talk about with her that night?'

'His magic disturbed her.' I stare at the tape recorder, but I see Ida Lose frowning at the stage, saying his magic was a reminder of the unexplained legends of the Pine Barrens. 'In the show he talks about his grandfather. She asked me if the grandfather is real.'

'Is he?'

Do you really have a grandfather?

Yes, Lucy Moon, I really do.

'Yes.' Is his grandfather – the magician who taught him to fly – Big Nick Cray? Is it possible that Elvis is Little Nick?

They turn off the tape recorder and dismiss me, but I don't leave right away. My words remain like black smears in the air. Did I just sign Elvis's death warrant?

'Many people have grandfathers. That's not a crime!'

Torres glances up from scribbling in a notebook. 'We'll contact you, Lucy.'

'Did the killer leave a black rose this time?'

Wax says, slow and heavy, 'We know you want to help, but this is murder. Don't get in our way.'

Torres adds, 'Don't get in his way.'

66

I stumble onto the boardwalk. Fog is lifting, sun peeking through, but salt air clings to my skin, sticky like black tar you have to scrub furiously to wash off. Like the black smears of my words.

'How did your statement go?' Gus sticks out his thumb as if he's hitchhiking. 'I already gave mine. I can tell you there's a definite direction this investigation is going.'

My throat is dry. 'Gus, you–' It's hard to form words. I swallow and start again. 'You don't work for the police.'

He flushes – maroon blotches against his cheeks. Light glints through his glasses so I can't see his eyes. If I ask him about the crime scene photos or the rose in his apron pocket, he'll know I sneaked into his booth. First, I need to find out why he lied.

Before I can ask, he says, 'I wanted you to see me. And you did, for a while.' He doesn't sound like 'Gus the Great,' cocky and swaggering.

'I see you.'

'You think you do. You think you see Jones too. I'll do you a favour. He was seen at Central Pier last night. And a white feather, the invitation to his show, was found in the Bone Whisperer's vagina.'

A hand presses on my shoulder.

I shriek and whip around.

Elvis stands in front of me. The dark, dark eyes and hair blowing back. A cop stands at his side. They're arresting him.

No, not yet. Get a grip. They have to question him first.

Elvis presses harder on my shoulder. The heat of him. The taste of him. I don't want to believe it. I can't believe it.

'I'm next. Meet me after?' When I don't respond, he tilts

his head to the side, listening to everything I don't say. 'What's wrong?'

The cop gestures, 'Come on, Jones. Let's go.'

'Coming.' But he doesn't move.

'You went out last night. Where did you go?'

'For a run.'

'Why?'

He winces at the shrillness of my voice.

'It was... too much to hold inside, you and me, like a dream.' A faint smile crosses his face. 'I didn't want to wake you.'

'Did you see Dr. Lose?'

He searches my face the way I'm searching his. 'What are you asking?'

Don't get in his way. But words push themselves from the back of my throat. 'Are you Little Nick?'

A small light flickers in his eyes, then extinguishes. His eyes, dead-black, lock on me.

I don't want to meet that cold, flat gaze.

'Look at me, for fuck's sake.'

I raise my head.

'It's not me. But you want it to be me.'

'No!'

'Makes it easier not to trust me. To keep hiding. You've built your own sawing box and locked yourself inside.'

The cop takes his arm. Jones takes two steps, then twists around. Eyes bleak and bitter, upper lip curled. 'Goodbye, Lucy.'

When he enters the police van, I turn. Gus has disappeared.

But a few steps away, Dasha watches me, cigarette in hand. 'Keep your phone handy,' she says. 'You'll get a message.'

67

An hour later, after we've showered and changed, Stormie and I meet at the Coffin Café in the Midnight lobby. Over coffee and blueberry muffins I tell her that I believe Jane Doe is my mother. And that Jinx knows something about my past. 'And now, I'm finally going to find out who I am.'

She looks up from the muffin she's decapitating. She only eats the crumbly top. 'Hate to break it to you, girl, but you're already who you are.'

'An imposter Moon.'

She gives me one of her looks. 'It looks like a Moon, talks like a Moon, and makes magic like a Moon, what are the odds it is a Moon?'

'Very funny.'

'Now, you gonna tell me what happened last night with Elvis?'

'I slept with him.'

She chokes on her muffin. 'Jeez, warn me next time.' She swallows. 'How was it?'

'Amazing.' I stare at my coffee. 'But.'

She cocks her head. 'But?'

'His white feather was found in Ida Lose's vagina.'

'What?'

'The invitation to his show.'

'He's not that stupid.' She pauses. 'Wait, is he?'

'A man who shoves a flower in a woman's mouth wants to be recognised. Deep down.' I sound numb, as if I'm reciting a report. Inside, I'm a scrambled mess. The look he gave me before he went with the cop. Black, cold, dead. Is that the same look he gave Van, Gina, and Ida? The dark driver taking over the wheel.

'Did you hear that from the cops?'

'From Gus.' I tell her about searching the lighting booth and discovering that Gus does not work for the police.

'Such a liar. How can we believe him? Did you see how excited he was this morning? Being around blood and death turns him on.'

'Storm. I found a cord in Jones's room, the kind the killer used. And a phone number in his notebook. With the initial 'G'.'

'Gus? Gina?'

I tap in the number I memorised on my phone and put it on speaker. We listen to the ringing until a man's voice says, 'This number has been discontinued.'

Our eyes meet.

My phone pings. A message from Jinx. I set my phone on the table, and Stormie and I read it together:

2:00. Mary. Midnight Casino. River Gambler slot machine. Go alone.

Stormie lifts her head. 'I'm coming with you.'

'She says alone.'

'I'll follow you and hang around the casino. You'll never see me.'

'As if. You're impossible to miss. Stay away, please.'

'Mmm.'

'Storm, I mean it. I'll call you the second it's over. I promise.'

*

Despite all the time I spend at Midnight, I rarely enter the actual casino. Most Atlantic City natives don't gamble. A night out for fun, sure, but when you work here, you generally don't play here. Still, I can't help being awed by the perpetual heightened excitement, a world spinning at full-tilt, neon glittering with music blasting through loudspeakers, and glazed eyes staring at roulette wheels and slot-machine screens as if their lives depend on it.

For the first time, my life does depend on it.

When I ask one of the cocktail waitresses where the River Gambler slot machine is, she points me to an alcove beyond the regular slots. She grimaces. 'Some people like to get their hands dirty and feel actual money.'

As I approach the alcove, I hear the unfamiliar sound of coins spilling into metal trays at slot machines. I'm used to the new electronic slots that reward winners with credit vouchers and a canned howl. But in keeping with Midnight's adherence to history, they've brought back vintage slots.

The guardians of the slot machines are two automatons: Zoltar, the eerie fortune teller, and Laughing Sally, a seven-foot-tall redhaired woman with a raucous laugh that's the stuff of nightmares. Past the threshold, about twenty machines loudly spit out coins.

To my surprise, most seats are not occupied by old-timers, but by the usual Goths, bikers, and vampire wannabes.

An older woman hunches in front of the River Gambler slot machine. A flowered scarf covers her hair. A clumpy faux-fur jacket hangs over scrawny shoulders, black trousers and white sneakers. A contained figure – a small purse in her lap, coin cup in one hand – she pushes the lever to the slot machine with the other.

I sit next to her, in front of Double Diamond, and draw in a deep breath.

68

Sweeping black eyebrows and turquoise eyes so brilliant they glow like jewels. Her eyebrows furrow with a kind of pain. 'Never thought I'd see you again,' she says in a hoarse smoker's voice. 'Little Hope all grown up.'

I remember those eyes, that voice. My chest cracks. A name emerges from long ago and far away. 'Terry?'

A smile breaks out and the glittering eyes soften. 'I'm Mary now.' She rubs the two deep lines between her eyebrows. 'Jinx said you didn't remember.'

'I didn't. Till today.' Just as with Jinx's patchouli, another scent-memory rises. 'Cheese.' I wrinkle my nose. 'I didn't like it.'

'When your mother worked in a magic show, you helped me in my uncle's cheese store. I sewed a tiny apron for you.'

'Where was the store?'

'South Philly, the Italian Market.'

How many times I walked past outdoor stalls and stores in the Italian Market, vendors with Italian accents hawking fresh fruits and vegetables from awning-shaded food stalls. I breathed in coffee, fish, meats and cheeses, sizzling pasta sauce, and pizza. I may have shopped at the cheese store where Terry worked. Moon Magick performed at the Market during the annual street festival.

I touch my cheek. Wet. 'Who was she? What happened to her?'

The smile disappears. 'Give me your hand.'

She tilts the cup and drops silver dollars in my palm. 'Play the game.'

Through blurred eyes, I slide a coin down the slot and pull the handle. Double Diamond springs to life. While we shoot coins into the machine and tug the levers, she leans toward me.

'When the bodies came up in the Barrens, I heard my uncle was asking questions. They want to make sure nothing connects them to the killer and the bodies. Jane Doe – it's her, isn't it?'

'It's her.'

Her eyes glisten with tears. 'You, me, and Joy, we were a family.'

'*Joy?*'

'Might've been made up, but that's what she went by. Joy Wheyre. W-h-e-y-r-e. And she called you Hope. You were her hope for a new life.'

'Do you know who my father is?'

'She never told me, but she moved to Philly to get away from him. Look, Joy was no kid. She'd been through hell. Life didn't work out the way she'd hoped, but she was strong, she was gonna make it work, and when you looked at her you believed she could do anything she set her mind to. We made a life, you know? I worked in the cheese store. She worked in a daycare centre, the kids loved her. She did magic when jobs came up.'

'What happened?'

'The one thing she couldn't shake. The need for revenge.' Terry glances over her shoulder. 'Lately, I feel people watching me all the time. I don't feel safe. You shouldn't either.'

She shoots a coin into the machine. 'One day Joy calls me all excited. 'I found him! I've been looking for him my whole life. I can't let him get away. Watch Hope, and I'll be back tomorrow."

'Who was he?'

'The one she was looking for. The man who killed her mother.'

She looks over her shoulder again. She's so on edge I'm terrified she'll disappear.

'Keep playing,' she says.

I slide in a coin, blindly.

'She didn't come back the next day. Or the day after. Or the day after that. I didn't take you to the daycare. I didn't let you out of my sight. We slept in the same bed. Something was wrong or she'd have called me.'

She picks up the cup and drops a coin in the slot. I'm suddenly aware of the jingling and clanging of coins. She speaks so low I lean closer to hear her.

'I'm waiting. I know it's gonna be bad. You and me are in the kitchen in back of the cheese store when a crazy-looking guy shows up. Long grey beard, a killer's eyes. I've seen those kind of eyes before. He's talking to my uncle, but he's looking around. He's here because he found out where Joy lives, and he wants to get her stuff. And my uncle is listening. Put money in the slot.'

I sit up and drop another coin in Double Diamond's mouth.

'My uncle was a mobster. Don't look so surprised.'

'What was he into?'

'Drugs, gambling. He had contacts here in Atlantic City.'

She stares at the River Gambler screen. 'Him and the bearded man were talking like friends. That's when I knew Joy was gone for good. That man killed her. Now, he wants to get rid of the evidence, make it like she never existed. And my uncle is gonna help him.'

I try to slide a coin into the slot, but fumble, and it drops to the floor.

'You're hanging on my leg, asking, "Where's Mommy?" in that little voice.'

The casino with its jagged colours and shrieks surrounds me, but I'm in the kitchen of a cheese store in the Italian Market, clinging to Terry.

'What happened?'

'I knew Joy would never tell this bastard about you. She'd let him kill her first.' Her eyes look hunted. 'That means he doesn't know about you. It's up to me to make sure he never does.'

'What... what about your uncle?'

'I never told him nothing. Joy and me, we kept each other's secrets. I had mine too.' She blinks. 'You're so much like her. Asking the world for answers. But you're different. I see it in your eyes. You expect answers. She never did.'

'You loved her.'

'Not a day passes when I don't think of her. We had something special.' She digs in her cup and brings out a coin but doesn't put it in the machine. 'I grabbed you and my purse, and we ran out the back door to the alley. We didn't stop till we got to the train station. The only person Joy talked to from her old life was Jinx, and she was in Atlantic City, so that's where we went.'

I force my last coin down the slot and killer-grip the handle.

'We met at her house. I told her what happened and how you needed to disappear. You were wearing one of Joy's roses in your hair. You'd say, "It smells like Mommy."'

Her hand on the lever, she pauses. For a moment the jingling of coins and howling of dogs and wolves stops. In the hush I smell cheese, Terry's cigarettes, my mother's rose, and Jinx's patchouli. My voice comes from far away. 'Jinx took me to the Moons.'

Terry sets the cup next to the machine and looks at me, her turquoise eyes shimmering. 'It broke my heart. I had to let you go. For you and Joy.'

'You saved my life. Thank you, Terry.' I lean over and hug her.

After a moment she pulls back, her eyes wet. 'I left Philly too. Never went back. Never saw my uncle again.'

I hear sudden commotion behind us. A man curses. A woman yells, 'Hey, *cretino*! Where ya going?'

Terry releases my hand and grips her purse. 'They found us!'

'Who? Why are they still after us?'

The woman behind us shrieks, 'You knocked 'em over, you pick 'em up!'

I leap to my feet. A tiny white-haired woman in front of a slot machine curses in Italian at a man crouched over the carpet, gathering coins.

She snaps, 'Next time watch where you're going, *cretino*!'

He hands her the coins and hurries past with an embarrassed grin. I've never seen him before. But like Terry, I feel someone watching.

I turn back.

Terry is gone.

My first instinct is to go after her. I still have so many questions. But she doesn't want to be found. She came out of hiding for me. I grab the coin cup she left behind. A handful of coins jingle inside. A faded colour photo. I sink back on the chair.

A woman and a child. Refugees from the Dust Bowl or the Great Depression, they've been wandering a long time. A mysterious dust storm scatters over them, clings to their thin jackets, settles over their faces. Creases from the photo are so deeply ingrained that the woman and girl look wrinkled. Two pairs of startling pale eyes, two stubborn chins, and not a hint of a smile. But they clutch hands so tightly their knuckles are whiter than their faces. Their wavy hair is so dark I don't see the black flowers at first. One rose clipped to my mother's hair. Another rose clipped to mine. *It smells like Mommy.* Joy, who went after *her* mother's murderer for payback and ended up in a burial pit in the Pine Barrens.

Stormie plops next to me, where Terry sat, in front of River Gambler.

'You watched us?'

'Of course. She left with a good-looking guy. Black, tall, and built, like a football player. While you were talking, I walked by a few times. He was watching you both. Waiting for her. They left together. I followed them to the boardwalk.'

I hold my breath.

'They turned at the ramp on North Carolina. I went after them.' She pinches the Star of David necklace between her fingers. 'When I turned the corner, he was waiting for me.'

'I told you not to watch us!'

'As if I'd listen. He grabbed my shoulders and said, "I saw you in there. Who are you?" "Lucy's friend." He said, "Mary risked her life to come here."'

'Oh, God, Storm!'

'She's behind him, but I can't see her face. I ask him, "Who's after her?" She moves next to him and says, "Let her go." Then she says to me, "Be her friend. Don't try to find me. Tell her to move on." I watched them walk away toward the parking lot.'

'If something happened to you, I'd never forgive myself.'

'She looked really scared.' She sighs. 'Her eyes were like blue-green stones.'

'They were in love, my mom and her.' I wipe my eyes with my knuckles. 'They lived – *we* lived – near the Italian Market. I always loved that place.'

I show Stormie the photo of my mother and me. 'Her name was Joy. And she named me Hope.'

Stormie looks at it for a long time. When she lifts her head, her eyes shine wet. 'You found her. You always knew you would.' She hands back the photo.

'She did magic.'

'Of course she did. It was in you before the Moons. So... now what?'

A thought strikes me. I'm on my feet. 'I gotta go. I'll call you later.'

'Wait! I didn't tell you–'

'What?'

'I don't know if it will ease your mind or make you feel worse.'

'Storm!'

'Okay, okay. On my way back here, I ran into Gus. He said Jones is at the police station. They took him in for further questioning. Does not look good.'

My cheek stings as if she just slapped me. 'Do you think Gus was lying?'

'I can't tell with him, but this time he seemed to be telling the truth. I'm sorry, babe.'

I wish I could crawl back to my room and hide under the covers. Pretend none of this happened. Go back to yesterday before I leaped across the gulf and fell. No, farther back. Before Ida Lose, Gina Nardo, and Van Kim fell.

I'm sorry, Terry, but I can't move on. Not till I find him. I give Stormie the photo of my mother and me. Then I head to the only place that holds answers to my questions.

69

Little Nick

He half-runs, half-staggers down the boardwalk to Ruby's corner. His mind is splintering, bumper cars smashing into each other. The cops asked questions he hadn't expected while Big Nick roared in his ear. They took him to the station and probed his relationship with women. He stumbled over his answers. The way they looked at him, they're setting him up for the fall. He's got to get out of this town before they come after him.

Then what the fuck are you doing back here?

One thing I need to do before I go.

His good luck angel is singing while the Central Pier loudspeaker blasts, 'I Will Survive.' The first good sign all day. He *will* survive. And so will his angel. He hates the image of her out here in winter's bitter cold. He brought a wad of bills for her but he won't leave them in her tin cup where any punk can steal them. He'll tuck them under her blanket.

People stroll past. Not a single one stops. How can she keep singing and hoping? The muscle in his chest pumps. This angel. This town. Lucy Moon. He'll never see them again.

Move, you asshole! You waiting for the cops?

He hunkers down in front of her. 'Hey, beautiful, what's cookin'?'

'Nothing till you showed up, handsome. Now my heart is beating a mile a minute.'

She's talking too fast, averting her eyes. The muscle in his chest pumps again, a warning. *Ruby knows.* The cops must have questioned her. A fixture on the boardwalk, she knows everyone, and everyone knows her. It would be ironic if in the end it's Ruby who betrays him.

Ironic's not the word, you stupid fuck. Get moving!

'Hey, you trying to feel me up?'

'That's my bonus. I gave you a little something to keep you warm in winter.'

'You're leaving.'

'Goodbye, Ruby.'

'Do you have to go?'

He can see in her eyes she knows. He lifts himself up and lurches down the boardwalk. Ripley's globe tilts toward him, an enormous bowling ball about to break off and crush his skull.

Behind him, Ruby's voice trembles as she sings, 'Atlantic City, you'll be the death of me...'

She's trying to call him back. Too late.

Instead of heading to his car, he runs to the steps that descend to the sand.

You got a job to do for me! Set the fire and get out of town.

Why is he back on the beach? The same stretch, where he dropped the Piney bitch. Next to Central Pier. He sees shadows by the pillars. Some of the bums must be back. Watching him. Ruby knows, they know, the cops know...

Do it do it do it!

Do what, you old fucker? Get thrown in jail for you? There's no escape. They'll lock him up. The one thing he knows is that he cannot survive in a cage. If they lock him up, he'll die, simple as that. He can't let them catch him.

You ain't a real man.

He can't extract Big Nick. To extract him, he has to extract himself. There's no other way. The devil needs blood, demands a sacrifice for the lives he took.

He grips his head between his hands. Why won't the agony

stop? He shoves his fists against his forehead and squeezes. Here it comes again. The endless horror. Sinking into the groove of the broken record, him and Big Nick, whirling round and round. The same note, the same scream, the same hollow… sinking, sinking… A carousel gone out of whack, spinning forever, to the end of time, no beginning, no end…

Why? That's all he wants to know. He accepts the curse on him, but *why?* The wooden boy who slept in a fucking cabin with a madman and wild snakes and birds, and who'll never be real, no matter how long he lives.

He weaves at the edge of the ocean. Waves break against the shore. He used to believe the black line of the horizon promised something more, but there is nothing. Just blackness, and more blackness.

He kicks off his sneakers and wades in.

The cold stuns him. Drenches his jeans. He slogs deeper. Heaves up one foot at a time.

Go deeper. End it now. The only way. No more bodies. No more Big Nick growling and biting his ear like a mad dog. No more women. No jail. No cell. No cage. No more running.

The water slaps his chest. He's numb below. The current sucks him into the centre of a whirlpool. Blackness swirls around him. Why didn't he do this years ago?

Underwater vines wind around his legs to trap him. He hears rustling, creeping, grunts, footsteps, creaking branches, gusts, animal howls. But behind the symphony of sounds is a deep profound silence, as if he's gone back to the beginning, when the world was still raw and unformed. Water blurs into land, dark into light. Stars fall from the sky, secrets drown in swamps, and he steers a sneak boat around the bend. He wades in the swampy river, dredging the mud… sun beaming on his upturned face. He falls from the sneak boat into the water, and it's so cold… he swallows a mouthful, salt-slick, and spits it out, choking and laughing... What's so funny?

Big Nick calls to him from the riverbank. *Get back here, you little turd.*

Not this time, Big Nick.

70

Central Pier looms, a weathered arm that extends over the ocean. The pillars root, giant legs in the sand. A squat monster. The crime scene has been closed. No sign of Ida Lose, the yellow tape or tarpaulin. Was that only this morning? It feels like days since I left Elvis Jones's bed. Hours since I played the slots with Terry.

Two greybeards lean against the pillars with their mounds of belongings. One of the men straightens and points his finger at me. 'Hey lady, got a buck?'

I hold out my hands, empty except for my phone, and the greybeard shakes his head.

I stop under the rafters where I entered the portal to Camp Boardwalk. Above me, feet thump and the Bee Gees sing, 'I'm a woman's man, no time to talk.'

Cleo, was it you calling to me?

Smoke seeps under my eyelids, through my nostrils, coats my tongue, and scratches my throat. Earthy, musky bitter peat that has been burning a long time.

I reach up toward the smoke.

A harsh clap. A bass drum booms. No blue light this time, no warning. Wind thrusts me up between the rafters.

The sky is black.

Screams pierce the air.

Rays of light reveal shadowy figures hurrying down the boardwalk, battling ferocious winds. Lightning jags the sky and slashes through Heinz Pier like an enormous knife. The large Heinz sign wobbles. With a sharp crash, the entire pier breaks off and smashes into the ocean.

A wall of black water heaves and surges over the boardwalk.

The Great Atlantic Hurricane. The night nearly four hundred people were wounded and nine killed. The night Cleo was killed. I may be able to see with my own eyes how a tender lover turned into a crazed murderer.

Shivering in the cold, I pass police and soldiers, people in slickers, everyone with heads lowered to avoid flying pieces of wood and to keep from being swept away by tidal waves.

Screams rise and fade. The boardwalk rocks like a boat in a tempest.

The hospital lobby is knee-deep in water. No lights.

As I wade through churning waves toward the stairs, I picture Frank, the war hero with Gary Cooper eyes and uncontrollable rage, hurtling down the dark stairs and bursting onto the boardwalk into the thunderous eye of the storm. The frenzy must have echoed the turmoil in his heart and mind. He'd just killed the woman he loved. Why go on living? Did he advance to the ocean and throw himself in? Did he fight the storm and escape from the city?

Before I reach the staircase, a force lifts me.

I land hard on the thirteenth floor, facing the theatre's tall wooden doors – the same ones we use today.

I pull one open, not sure if I'll find myself in the past or present.

The windows are shaking, winds pounding the glass. I feel my way through the dark theatre to the stage.

A man's voice growls, 'You ain't taking what's mine and running with it.'

An arrow of light pierces the windows. I squint at the stage.

Morelli advances toward Cleo. Her pale hair gleams.

'It ain't yours!' she cries. 'Nothing of mine is yours!'

A gunshot blasts.

I scream and run to the stage. Race up the stairs. The sawing box is centre stage. The ghost light too, the spindly brass stick holding an unlit bulb.

Another jag of light reveals Morelli bent over Cleo's body.

At her side, a man lies face-down. His body is twisted unnaturally. It's Frank!

'Dirty Hand!' A short, stocky man advances from the wings. A fedora shades his face. Jimmy the Crab, Morelli's spy. 'We ain't alone.'

Is he talking about me? Can he see me?

'Lucy!' A cry from far away.

My entire body jolts.

'Lucy!'

My hands and knees smash into the boardwalk. I cry out.

Open my eyes and blink furiously.

Bitter peat smoke lingers in my nostrils and throat.

The sky is light. It's still day. I touch my sweater and jeans. Dry. No flood. No winds.

But I was in the theatre. I saw Morelli shoot Cleo. Frank was already dead. Someone else was watching. Who?

'Lucy!' Ruby rams her wheelchair against my knees. 'Help!'

I wince at the pain. 'Ruby! What's wrong?'

'Not me! Him! In the ocean! Hurry!'

I weave to my feet and, knees aching, run to the beach. A jogger in black and yellow fleets past like a bumblebee. Waves rise high and splinter into foam against the sky. I stop at the edge of the water.

A figure moves deeper into the ocean. A black hoodie – oh God, no!

I quickly scan the area. The bumblebee jogger is already yards ahead, nearly at Steel Pier. No time to call 911 or grab a flotation device. I know the dangers of going in alone, but I'm a good swimmer. Besides, Ruby is watching from the boardwalk. If there's trouble, she'll call for help.

I throw off my sneakers and splash into the ocean. I trudge deeper, shouting, 'Stop! Elvis, stop!'

My gaze focuses on the bobbing figure in the black hoodie as I wade farther and tighten my muscles for the upcoming fight. The heavy jeans drag my legs down.

The instant I penetrate deep enough to dive, I plunge in.

The shock of ice water freezes my brain.

I push up my head and gulp air. My arms cut through water. A hard wave cracks against my skull and roars in my ears and head.

When I can breathe again, I squint into the setting sun and survey the horizon.

I lost him.

Where are you?

Ahead, I glimpse a small black rounded shape above the water.

I'm coming! I won't let you drown.

I dive up and under the waves until I close the distance between us. I burst up behind him in a sparkle of foam and grab him in a chokehold.

He thrashes wildly, arms and legs kicking the water.

I expected a struggle, but this is vicious. Even though I have the advantage of surprise, he attacks me, so desperate to die he'll drown us both.

I hold on with strength I didn't know I had. Only one thought: I won't let go.

Finally, he stops flailing. I release his neck and breathe. I have no idea how I'm going to make it back out with him.

You're going to make it because you have to. He's not going to die, and neither are you.

I breathe from deep in my chest, push my arms under his armpits and grab his shoulders.

Together, we tread water. When we reach the shallows and my

feet touch bottom, I loosen my grip. Gulp mouthfuls of air.

He leans against me, shivering. No longer a dead weight.

When I recover from this, I'm going to burst into tears.

Amazingly, the hoodie still clings to his head.

I wrap my arm around him. 'Can you walk?'

He turns and looks at me.

My heart stops.

Time stops.

The roaring in my brain and ears stops.

'You should've let me go.'

His voice thrusts me back to the surface.

'We can fix it, whatever it is.' I sound as if I'm still underwater.

'No,' says Charlie. 'We can't.'

71

I'm whirling in the centre of the seashell, the grainy roar so loud I can't hear, see or understand anything else. For a moment all I can do is stare at the sparkle of water on his lashes. The cold inside me is so profound this is what death must feel like. No hope. Utter blindness, shock.

Muscle. Bone. Teeth. Hands. Eyes. Oh, God, his eyes. No glasses, nothing between him and me. The glasses were a veil. I'm backstage watching the illusion unravel, the smoke and mirrors clear.

Despite the fact that he's wet, hair dripping on his cheeks, he looks strangely steady. Serene Charlie. The Charlie effect. His voice is gentle. Charlie's voice. But his eyes glitter, naked and grey-gold. So bright it hurts to look at them. We talked and laughed. We danced and kissed. We had a bond. A mysterious connection! My bones knock against each other. I'm outside in the open, in my town, standing on the beach I know, facing a man I thought I knew.

But I've never been so cold in my life. Never felt so lost. I manage one word: 'Why?'

'Why what?'

'Why–' I hold out my trembling hands. 'Why this?'

'I can't be locked up.'

'But did you... are you...?'

His arms go around me. 'Don't be scared, Lucy,' he whispers in my ear. 'It's only me.'

Only *him*. But who is he?

He's dripping wet. So am I. Both of us shivering like mad. My teeth, fingers, chest – every part of me trembles.

He pulls back. And the shock hits me all over again.

I swallow. Salt water still stings my nostrils and throat. 'Who are you?'

He says nothing, but he watches me as if he's giving me the chance to see him for the first time.

72

Little Nick

The ocean shocked the life-force back into him. Ice-clarity – colours, sounds, his own mind. There is no more muddy vagueness, bumper cars crashing, voices ringing in his ears. No more voices. His mind is as free and fluid as quicksilver.

He squints at the horizon. The great Atlantic Ocean spit him back out, but it swallowed Big Nick. No more Big Nick! *Extracted.* After years of struggling to free himself, there's a hollow in Little Nick's chest, in his head – the old man is gone.

For the first time in fifteen years, Little Nick is alone. Back where he started. The years of trying on other names and faces swept away in the waves.

He shakes off the water and stretches. Foam-sparkles cling to him. He shines, clean and new and fresh, as if he's been reborn. His mother – whoever she was, wherever she is – watched over him. So did the sad lady. Lucy Moon fought to save him. They helped him drown the dead psycho who refused to leave him alone.

He's been granted a miracle. He has become a fucking human.

Alive. And free.

Now what?

Lucy struggles to slip on her sneakers while slanting him suspicious looks. He senses her dilemma: her gut tells her one thing while her mind rejects it. His chest rumbles, a growl rises up his throat, and a laugh bursts through his lips. She wobbles toward him, then catches herself. He startled her.

He slips on his own sneakers. One after the other. His phone and glasses are still on the sand. He ignores the glasses and lifts the phone, shoves it into his hoodie pocket.

A laugh gurgles in his throat again. The sheer joy of his mind working at full blast, the clarity so intense it's painful. His mother didn't up and run off to get away from him, like Big Nick said. He sees the truth now: the old man himself killed her, same as he killed the sad lady.

But Big Nick is gone.

He is free. For the first time in his life, he is free.

On the boardwalk Ripley's globe tilts toward him; that broken globe that used to terrorise him. In another life.

His good luck angel Ruby pushed her wheelchair next to the railing. His vision is so piercing he sees the shock in her eyes and gaping mouth. She is part of the past, receding from his rearview.

A couple of people watch from the boardwalk. A jogger stops, lowers his headphones and asks if he should call 911.

'No,' he says.

'Sure?' The jogger glances from him to Lucy. 'Are youze okay?'

Probably hard to tell which of them needs more help. He and Lucy are both drenched and shivering in the cold air, their hair snaky tendrils. If his face is as washed-out pale as hers, he must look terrible. She nods at the jogger, her teeth clicking against each other.

The jogger shifts from foot to foot, impatient to get back to his run. 'Okay. Well, change into dry clothes for Chrissake. Youze wanna catch pneumonia?'

Headphones back on, he runs toward the pier.

He's been given a second chance. He straightens, digs his hands into his pockets. Wallet gone. Paracord gone. Floating away in the depths of the ocean. He won't need it anymore. His fingers close around two keys – one for the Widow, the other for his car parked in the Midnight lot.

'Talk to me, Charlie.' Lucy's black and purple hair drips into her ice-eyes. *Lucy in the sky with diamonds.* She squints at him, straining to see through the mask to the shadow. 'Are you Little Nick?'

Time to say goodbye to Little Nick, and to Charlie. And to Lucy as well. Time to start over. 'You saved my life, Lucy.' He keeps his voice gentle. 'Thank you. Now, I need to go.'

73

My brain is thawing, teeth chattering. Wind cuts to the bone. We leave behind Central Pier, the greybeards retreating under the pier. As we walk, the sand beneath my feet hums and pulses the way it did on Achill Island.

Ahead, the Ferris Wheel at Steel Pier revolves. Last night I watched it with Jinx and Dasha. A lifetime ago.

Around us, sand blows. Picnickers surrender to the wind and gather their belongings. Lovers, clinging to each other, face the water.

I glance at him, walking by my side, and picture him windblown at Van's memorial when he told Misty that you take the A train to Staten Island. And last night he told me that he was from Staten Island. That's what was gnawing at me.

'You're not from New York.'

He tilts his head, waiting.

'You don't take the A train to Staten Island. If you lived there, you'd know.'

He shrugs. 'I fucked up.'

I want to cry, but the tears are frozen. Why am I walking with the man who killed Van, Gina, and Ida? We pass the wooden deck on the beach where Ruby sang for Van, and I did the Broken Wand.

We're nearing the steps to the boardwalk in front of Midnight. Charlie said he left his car in the Midnight parking lot. We'll say goodbye and he'll get in his car and drive away.

I'll call the cops – shit! I must have left my phone on the boardwalk.

'I dreamt of this. You and me walking out in the open.'

I glance at him in surprise.

'We always had something, you and me. We both know it. But

We get in the elevator together. He presses 13 and the doors slide shut.

74

Inevitable that we end up in the creaky, windowless Orange Room. The fiery bulb sputters over historic posters, playbills, and props, including an ancient spirit cabinet and levitating table. Back here, the Widow shows her age. Her eyes are dark with the memory of nights gone wrong, her mouth a bittersweet diagonal, and her perfume: mothballs, musk and... lavender. Sweet, floral, and herbal, it wafts past. Cleo is here, the way she was the night Charlie and I danced and kissed.

On a table in the corner is her sawing box, Cleo of the Nile, where I discovered Van. Where he set her body.

Charlie lowers his head and taps a message on his phone, shoves it in his pocket, and crouches in front of a stack of magic posters. He flicks through them and sets the Bullet Catch poster against the wall. Side by side, we stare at the garish, crude painting of Morelli aiming a pistol at Cleo.

'There are two copies of this poster?'

'I brought it here,' he says, still staring at the poster. 'I should have known when I saw your eyes. But I didn't catch on until you went to the Barrens. You found out about the sad lady.'

'The sad lady?'

'They found her body.'

'Jane Doe? Did you know she was my mother? Her name was Joy.'

'She had the saddest eyes.'

'You–' I stumble over my tongue, 'you killed her.'

'Not me! My grandfather, Big Nick. She found out who he was, and she came after him. To kill him. He killed her first.'

I clutch my stomach, trying to process this. My mother went to the Barrens to kill Big Nick. The wild man with killer eyes, the man who did magic, the man who killed her mother. 'Then... who was Joy's – the sad lady's – mother?'

He turns slowly. Charlie, but not Charlie. Salt has eaten away at his edges. How could I have found him handsome? He's a wax figure, already melting. The soft cheeks, the too-soft chin. A horror movie playing out inches in front of me.

A howl rises from deep inside me. I shove my fist to my mouth to keep it in.

'Look at the poster. Cleo's eyes. The sad lady's eyes.' His voice is faint, high-pitched, a boy's voice.

I lower my hand and open my mouth like Cleo's in the poster, letting in bitter lavender, dizzying smells and voices. *What do you see with those eyes? Your mother's calling to you... She called you Hope...*

'Oh God...' I bite my tongue. 'Cleo West is my grandmother. And the man who killed her is Morelli. After he killed Cleo, he hid in the Barrens...' My voice is dulled, slow.

Morelli, known for Mysterious Connections, the transparent card effect that transforms one card into another, in front of your eyes. Light a candle, and suave magician Morelli transforms into savage old coot, Big Nick.

'That's right. We're family.' When I cringe, he flicks his hand. 'He's your grandfather too. Think about it, we're descended from a slut and a psycho. No wonder we're fucked up.'

'Who... who was your mother?'

'I don't know.'

'Your father?'

'Big Nick's son.' He sounds fretful, agitated. 'He died when I was a baby.'

I need to get out of this room, now, this instant. I step back toward the door. 'Look, you did what I did. Lock the past away. Bury it deep so you wouldn't see it. Change your name. Transform yourself into a prince. But you were never real.'

Another step retreating towards the doorway.

'You got it wrong. Little Nick isn't me. Charlie is the real one. I made myself Charlie the way you made yourself into a Moon.'

Another step. 'But Little Nick must have been struggling inside to breathe.'

He jolts violently, flings his arms fighting off invisible insects.

Another step. Almost there. 'What's wrong?'

'Cleo! Creeping under my skin.' He slaps his chest. 'Biting me. From the first time I came here, she knew who I was. She hates me. Wants me dead!'

Cleo is creeping under my skin too, icing the wet flesh beneath my sweater and jeans. I taste the rage and bitterness. I'm all goosebumps, every inch of me prickling with dread.

'Let's get out of here, okay?'

He slaps the air again. 'She drove Big Nick crazy, and now she wants to do it to me.'

'Let's go, Charlie. We'll feel better outside.'

One more step, and I'm out of this room. I'll race down the back steps to the twelfth floor.

He squints as if I'm far away. 'You think you're better than me!'

'No! I don't!'

'We're the same. Two fakes pretending to be real.'

'No! Charlie, listen–'

Before I finish, he leaps at me and closes his hands around my throat.

A precious second ticks past.

His thumbs squeeze the carotid artery on each side of my throat. My eyes bulge.

Prevent brain damage: seven to fourteen seconds. Death: within two minutes. Tal's lessons. *Keep breathing, keep fighting. If you fight, you live.*

I tuck my chin to my chest and swivel to the side.

He squeezes harder but my arms shoot up. One hand grabs his

wrist. The other shoves up his chin and keeps shoving up his nose till I hear bone crack.

He growls. Loosens the pressure on my neck.

I lift my knee and slam it into his groin.

He groans and cradles his balls. Sways for an instant.

I back away again.

Eyes slitted, he socks me in one breast, then the other.

My body screams.

I've never felt pain this intense. Everything in my stomach surges to my throat. In a second I'm going to throw up.

Suddenly, he lifts me. I'm so weak I can only thrash and kick.

He strides to the table that holds Cleo's box.

The lid is open, waiting for me. He dumps me inside. My body is still screaming, my stomach heaving.

He disappears, but I hear him moving around the room. I need to escape before he lowers the lid and locks me in. Pain shooting up my chest, I sit. Before I scramble to my feet, he returns to the head of the box.

Breathing hard, he grabs both my hands and winds thick nylon zip ties around my wrists.

I kick wildly, but within seconds, he fastens them tightly behind my back. He must have hidden the zip ties in this room.

He moves to the foot of the box, grips my ankles, pulls off my soggy sneakers and tosses them.

With the little strength I have, I slam the soles of my feet against his chest.

He doesn't seem to feel it. He binds my ankles together, sharp nylon digging into the flesh, and shoves my feet back inside the box.

Sweat drips down his cheeks and throat. His eyes are black. A red welt bursts on his cheek and throbs like a heart. Here he is. Charlie's shadow, Little Nick: a twisted mass of wires, veins, muscle that pulses through the flesh. 'I gave you a chance. But you went to Jones.' He snarls, 'You threw me away.'

'I didn't!' My voice is a gasp.

He rams his fist up my nose.

I hear the crunch of bone. Pain stabs to the back of my eyes, burns my cheeks. I shriek at the top of my lungs.

He disappears again.

I press the soles of my feet against the end of the cabinet for traction and squirm onto my right side, pressing my hip against the wood. My wrists throb but I manage to pull myself up to a seated position. Shifting my weight to the side, I push against the wood. Of course, it doesn't budge. Maybe I can shove myself forward and topple head-first to the floor.

Rotting lavender permeates the room. And the smell of... burning leaves?

The ceiling sputters with smoke and sparks. What is he doing?

Then I see him in a crouch, pouring liquid along the floorboards and exposed wires. Gasoline or kerosene. He's setting fire to this old wooden theatre, starting backstage – a warren of nesting rooms crammed with old newspapers, posters, costumes, boxes. It's always been a fire waiting to erupt. He will slam the lid on me and leave me to die.

'Charlie! Don't do this!'

He returns. Orange light flares over his face and burnishes his eyes.

'Charlie, please!'

'Little Nick,' he corrects me.

'You're not Little Nick. *He* was Little Nick. You're Charlie.'

'That's not a real name. Just like Lucy Moon isn't real.'

'We're friends!' I cry. 'You said we're family!'

He stares with wide, unfocused eyes. All pupil, all black. The welt on his cheek glows, fiery and volcanic, on the verge of bursting. 'You're the devil, not me. This time you're gone for good.'

He slams the lid. I hear him fasten the lock and walk away.

75

I can't scream anymore. Losing the little breath I have. Suffocating.

Twisted in a painful backbend, I open my eyes.

Blackness surrounds me. So dark, deep, and deadly it burns red.

I bite my tongue. Smell my blood.

Squirm side to side.

Kick my feet against the end of the box.

No strength.

No air.

No breath.

I can't... can't!

Calm yourself, Moon. Close your eyes. Slow your breath. Stop squirming. Useless.

But I'm going to die!

Instead of struggling when you're in the box, surrender. Don't forget to breathe, let yourself fall and let yourself rise...

Elvis Jones. A man who heals wounded creatures – a seagull, a car, a woman. The raw hard sweetness of a human male – arrogant, shy, sensitive, and most important, real. The way he made me feel terrified me. It was easier to believe the worst about him.

I press my bound hands against the side of the box and search with my fingers until I find a slight protrusion. Scrape the hard plastic up and down, over and over. I hear the scratching against wood. The knocking of my heart against my chest. I rub my wrists frantically against the wood. The ridged nylon cuts into my flesh.

Smoke sifts through the cracks. The fire is spreading, leaves crackling and burning. A low hiss and sputter. Behind my back, I scrape my wrists back and forth, up and down.

My hands still.

Cleo designed this box with Eddie Garland. You had Eddie install a safeguard, didn't you, Cleo? You were scared of Morelli, and you needed a way to protect yourself. Like the secret lever Marcus Lincoln wanted to insert inside the sawing cabinet for me. You rigged it, and only you and Eddie Garland knew. Morelli never saw it. Neither did the cops. They'd never been locked inside a sawing box. When Morelli locked you in, you slipped out of the ropes that bound your ankles and folded your legs in the top half. Then you freed your hands from the ropes that circled your wrists.

Shit! I can't do it. Not the way Charlie bound me.

But if there is a hidden lever, it has to be in the upper half, where Cleo curled. My fingertips probe behind me, against the wood and descend inch by inch. When I finish this side of the box, I'll shift my weight to my left hip and begin on the other side.

Don't think about the flames spreading, the room blazing into darkness, and Charlie stepping on the gas and roaring onto the highway.

My finger trips over a bubble in the wood. The size of a small button. Not on the surface, but behind the wood. It's solid, sandwiched between the layer I'm touching and the outer layer.

I press my two index fingers against it.

Nothing happens.

The smell of acrid smoke rushes through my nostrils to my brain. A fire starts at the ceiling, then lowers to the floor. It spreads, licking the wood. In a minute or two, no more, it will burst into flame.

Cleo, help me!

I dig the pad of my index finger against the button as if I'm ringing a doorbell. Eyes squeezed shut, teeth gritted, I press hard, harder, with all my strength.

A faint click.

The lid springs open from the other side, like a seashell.

Light flickers. The air reeks of gasoline.

For a moment I can't move.

Thank you, Cleo. Thank you.

I wriggle and push against the sides until I sit, then stand. I wobble for an instant before tumbling out.

My head bangs on the wooden floor. I belly-flop, smack-down.

Pain shatters through my head and down my legs.

Move. Get out. *Now.*

Black smoke puffs out through seams and cracks as if the room is turning into an oven.

My eyes and throat scorch.

Flames splinter the spirit cabinet, engulf the posters. This room is going to explode. Why didn't the fire alarm sound?

Wrists and ankles tightly bound and aching, I writhe across the floor toward the smoke-filled doorway. The opening to a black void. The only way out. No air. I'm in a red-hot oven.

Eyes gritted and stinging, smoke so thick I can't breathe... keep going... the hallway... almost there...

A hand snags my ankle and yanks me back into the burning room.

I twist my neck and see the horror of Charlie on all fours.

'Stay!' he cries.

'Let go!'

'No. This is the end for us.'

76

Little Nick

It's over. The end of their cursed line. Him and Lucy, doomed. He thought he'd freed himself from Big Nick. He was wrong. The old man will never leave him. He's inside – he's taken over. The dark driver steering the car, hurtling right and left, crashing into corners. Big Nick was always stronger. Little Nick is fading, weakening. Ashes and grit burn his eyes and throat.

Run, says a little voice. But he's not fooled anymore. It's Big Nick disguising himself, pretending there's somewhere left to run.

He did what he'd sworn to on Big Nick's deathbed. He locked the slut in the box and set the theatre on fire. Now he's done. No more running. No more fighting.

Flames leap toward him. A coil of bright heat. The sad lady smooths his hair. That sad, drooping smile. 'Where is your mother?' she asks.

She left. Said I was too much trouble.

'I don't believe that.' Her silver eyes glow so bright he squints. The heat so bright he can't see. She takes the rose from her hair and presses it into his hand. 'For you.'

And then Big Nick lunges on them both.

77

A figure rises from the flames and looms over Charlie and me. A beast baring his teeth. Blood-red eyes and teeth. A man-beast, long beard. Ghost. Devil.

Horror chokes me. I must be hallucinating.

But Charlie howls, 'No, Big Nick!'

The monstrous figure leans closer. His face wavers in the fire-light.

Charlie releases his grip on my ankle. He cowers and covers his face with his hands.

Breathing smoke and soot, I wriggle away on my belly and hips. In the doorway I glance back.

No Big Nick. Only Charlie, crumpled on the floor.

The instant I slide into the corridor, a beam collapses to the floor and blocks the doorway to the Orange Room. Flames coil to the ceiling.

I crawl down the corridor. Blue-orange sparks sizzle and erupt through protruding wires. Pushing forward blindly through hot black smoke, I crash into a bucket.

Bite back my scream.

Coughing and gagging, I keep my head down and push, praying I won't pass out. But I'm blazing. A single spark, and I'll ignite.

A black mushroom cloud billows across the ceiling and walls.

Flames burst from the dressing room.

Suddenly I'm lifted in the air. Pressed against a chest. Hard arms wrap around me. 'I got you,' says Elvis.

If my eyes and throat weren't seared dry, I'd cry. He carries me down the hall past the sandbags to the stage. Down the steps. Heavy waves of smoke and soot lower and thicken, cling to the windows and chase us through the theatre.

Firefighters aim hoses at the domed ceiling and stage.

Elvis hurries past the seats. He doesn't stop till we arrive at the theatre doors.

Wide open.

I glance back over his shoulder. Through smoke and smouldering embers, a glowing purple light coils to the ceiling. With a sputter, it disappears. *Goodbye, Cleo.*

The hall is chaos. Firefighters push past. Gus yells, 'Here she is!' Stormie shrieks, 'Let me see her!'

Elvis sets me down on the floor. His face is streaked with soot and grime, one eye swollen. It's the most beautiful face I've ever seen.

'Your nose is bleeding,' he says. 'Tilt forward.'

I squint through sand-burning eyes. Words I need to say, on the tip of my tongue, but I'm still fighting to escape Charlie and Big Nick.

'Oh God, look at you.' Stormie kneels at my side. 'I never thought I'd see you again.'

A firefighter asks, 'Anyone backstage?'

'Charlie,' I croak. 'Last room down the hall.'

He shakes his head, and I know it's too late. Charlie is gone.

Gus squats next to me and shoves a handkerchief under my blood-dripping nose.

I look at him and Stormie, and again, tears sting behind my eyes. 'How did you know?'

Gus nods, brisk. 'I ran into one of the fire marshals in the lobby. He said Charlie sent him a message to turn off the smoke alarm because we were using the hazer in the Widow. But we weren't using the hazer. The marshal and I knew something was wrong, and we needed to check it out.'

Stormie's arm goes around me. 'I saw smoke through the windows and bumped into Elvis on the way up. I wanted to go after you, but he insisted.'

'Elvis,' I croak. 'Where did he go?'

Stormie looks around. 'He was here a minute ago.'

'Becker must have had everything ready,' said Gus. 'He wanted to burn down the Widow, and himself in it.'

Stormie frowns. 'And Lucy too.' She opens a bottle of water and holds it to my mouth. 'Drink, *zissele*.'

I swallow and taste blood. Another swallow. It hurts. My throat is swollen, nose aching, wrists and ankles burning. 'Anyone have clippers or a knife?'

Gus takes a knife from his pocket and slices the zip ties around my wrists and ankles. The flesh is raw-red.

'Thank you, Gus.'

'You just might be the luckiest girl in the world. And I just might be the smartest guy. You still think the cops shouldn't hire me?'

78

A medic from the fire department checks me out. Broken nose, but luckily not displaced. Smoke inhalation, neck pain, chest bruised, wrists and ankles blistered, searing headache, and shivers that won't quit. The medic wants to send me to the ER.

When I refuse, he gives me an ice pack for my nose, ibuprofen for pain, and advises me to see a doctor when the swelling goes down, probably in a couple of days.

In the meantime, Detectives Torres and Wax have shown up, my father and aunt on their heels. While the detectives question Gus about the fire, my father and Auntie Maze hold me up and lead me to my room on the sixth floor. Torres and Wax will meet us here, later.

I clean my face with a wet washcloth, wrap a blanket around myself, sit in bed – head elevated, ice pack to my nose – and let my father and aunt fuss over me.

Stormie arrives with the detectives.

Da and Auntie Maze leave, but they insist on taking me home after I finish with the police.

Detective Wax reports that the fire was contained on the thirteenth floor. Charlie Becker, the only casualty. There's no more Black Widow Theatre, not as we know it.

I tell the detectives everything I remember. Breathing through my mouth and tasting smoke, I relive this afternoon. When I describe the surreal walk to Midnight, Wax says nothing, but I feel his effort to restrain himself. I tell them that Morelli was Charlie's grandfather, and mine, and Cleo West was our grandmother.

Stormie cries out, 'Jeez! I can't believe you and Charlie are related!'

'Cleo was scared of Morelli. He was insanely jealous and beat her. I think he punished her by locking her inside the sawing box. He'd wait till she was dead-scared, and then he'd lift the lid and let her out. She needed a safeguard in case one day he didn't release her so she and the designer, Eddie Garland, installed a secret hinge. You can't see it, you have to be inside the box.'

'You managed to break free,' says Wax. 'Then what happened?'

'Charlie tugged me back into the burning room.'

'He wanted you both to die,' says Torres.

The horror in his eyes, the anguished scream as Big Nick loomed over us. I'll never tell anyone what I saw... or imagined. Was Big Nick really there?

Or for a moment, did I see him through Charlie's eyes?

'Yet you saved him from drowning,' says Wax. 'Was it a suicide attempt?'

'Yes. He knew you were closing in on him.' I shiver, seeing the black-hooded figure plunge deeper into the water. 'I thought it was Elvis. Stormie said you'd taken him in for questioning.'

Stormie breaks in. 'I heard it from Gus, but at the theatre he told me he heard it from Charlie.'

'Charlie tried to frame Elvis.' I catch my breath. 'He wore a black hoodie, and he inserted the white feather... in Ida Lose.'

Stormie turns to Torres. 'Did you suspect Elvis?'

'He was a person of interest. But when we questioned Charlie this morning, he acted strange. There were inconsistencies in his story that made us look at him more closely.'

I sit up, pressing the ice pack to my nose. 'Can you tell me one more thing? Who was the witness who saw Elvis on the beach last night?'

Torres gives me a dark, steady look, and my throat constricts. Charlie, of course. Sweet, helpful Charlie.

79

Wednesday October 31

Six days later

Halloween. My twenty-eighth birthday, and my first as Lucy Hope Moon. I yank open the blinds of my room and push up the window. Lean over the sill and gulp in fresh air.

Sun shines over the street. It's morning of a new day, and a couple of bike riders race toward the boardwalk. Seagulls caw, and my chest pinches as I remember Elvis and Bird frolicking on the sand like two wild animals.

What happened to Salt, Ida Lose's Australian Shepherd? If she'd been allowed to keep him in the Star Inn, I'm certain he would have lunged at Charlie, and she'd be alive today. Salt must feel lost without her.

I phone Detective Torres, who tells me that someone at the forensic lab took the dog.

I call the lab and listen to the phone ring. No one picks up. I call Stormie, and she drives us to Galloway.

Two cars are parked in the forensic lab's lot. I pound on the door until a man opens it. I ask him about Dr. Lose's dog, and he tells me to wait.

A few minutes later, a girl appears. Purple hair rising in spikes, a dozen studs piercing both ears, she says she's Ida's intern, a grad student in Stockton University's Criminal Justice program. 'Ida has no family and no one else at the Lab can take care of Salt so I took him.' She holds out her hands. 'I love Ida, but I can't do it. It's too much with classes and interning here. Yesterday I took him to a local animal shelter.'

'Which one?'

My desperation startles her, but she gives me the address. 'They have a good rep, and they'll find someone to adopt him.'

Storm drives while I clench my fists and pray no one has taken him yet. I need to find that wise, beautiful dog who comforted me at my mother's burial pit.

The instant Stormie pulls into the parking lot, I'm out of the car and running toward the entrance. A man sweeps outside.

'I'm looking for Salt, an Australian Shepherd. He was dropped off yesterday.'

'I know Salt.' Plump and white-haired with twinkling eyes and bright cheeks, he reminds me of Santa. 'He's pretty blue. He realises his owner is gone.'

We follow him inside the shelter and down a hallway lined on both sides with large cages. Even before I see Salt, I'm trembling. While he unlocks the cage, Salt barks. The instant the cage door opens, he leaps on me and almost knocks me down.

As soon as I fling my arms around him and bury my face in his fur, tears burn my eyes, nose, and throat. After a while I whisper a few words to him, and I know he understands.

When I lift my tear-stained face, Stormie and the manager of the shelter are watching us.

Afterwards, in the small office, he says, 'Sometimes it happens that way, love at first sight.'

I fill out a long preadoption form. The manager promises to get back to me in the next couple days but tells me not to worry. No one else has come for Salt, and he can't imagine anyone else forming such a strong connection with him.

As we return to Atlantic City, Stormie says, 'My girl's in love. Watching you and Salt, all I could think was *bashert*.'

'If by *bashert*, you mean...'

She slants me a look. 'You know exactly what I mean. Destiny.

Soulmate. And look at you, girl. You knew it all along.'

'What do you mean?'

'In Making Mr. Right, who was your Mr. Right? Not Prince Charming, but–'

'Gus's dog, Diablo!'

'We've been looking for love in all the wrong places.' She sighs. 'Who knew love was waiting for you in a dog pound? Do you think Salt has a brother?'

80

'My birthday gift to you, Lucy, is the truth.' Later that afternoon, Jinx sinks onto the couch, Dasha Sills at her side. 'I hope it won't be a bitter gift.'

A small group has gathered in Da's study, the Temple of Magic. This room. The masks, books, and artifacts of a life devoted to studying, sharing, and performing magic. The first sawing box I ever saw. Da uses it as a coffee table. This afternoon glasses of champagne and slices of birthday cake are strewn on its painted surface.

Auntie Maze and Stormie distribute the cake, my favourite: caramel-apple with a splash of Jameson. To one side, the Zigzag Girl stands, waiting for me to enter.

They've just finished drinking a birthday toast to me when I hear a knock on the front door.

'You get it,' says Stormie.

I open the door, and for a moment I can't say a word.

'Stormie invited me.' The voice that prickles the hairs on my arms. 'Is that okay?'

I haven't seen him since he carried me out of the Widow. His hair is tightly pulled back, revealing sharp cheekbones and the golden column of his throat. The new grey hoodie he's wearing tugs at my chest. *Trying to be a good guy.* I forgot what happens to me when he draws near. The air changes. I change. I get stupid and tongue-tied.

'Happy Birthday, Lucy,' he says, soft.

So much I want to say. Thank you for coming after me. Sorry I didn't trust you, especially after our night together. The thing is: You punch my heart, and I don't like it.

He tilts his head to the side, listening. After a minute he murmurs, 'You were right not to trust me.'

'You're not a murderer.' Even after a week, my voice is still hoarse from screaming in the Orange Room.

'No, but I have secrets.'

I draw in my breath. A light in his eyes promises I'll learn them eventually. If I want.

'Want to have breakfast on the beach tomorrow with Bird and me?'

'That meal some people enjoy?'

The smile begins in his eyes.

I lead him inside Da's Temple of Magic. He looks around in wonder. I know how he feels. I can't help enjoying his sudden shyness when he comes face to face with my father and the slight tremble when Auntie Maze grips his hand and stares through him with her seeing eyes.

'You went into the burning theatre after our girl.' She hugs him fiercely.

When she releases him, he turns, dazed.

Stormie grins. 'Aww, Elvis is under the Moon spell.'

'I've been under the Moon spell since I met Lucy.'

Stormie hands him a slice of cake and glass of champagne. He sits on the floor near Jinx and Dasha and leans back against the wall.

Jinx taps her cane against the sawing box. 'Can we start? I'm getting older by the minute.'

Da and Auntie Maze move to armchairs, and Stormie and I pull up folding chairs, so we're all gathered around the sawing box. It's only fitting – the box has always been the heart of my story.

As if she reads my mind, Jinx says, in that rough growl, 'I want to tell you about Cleo West and the sawing box. She saw it as her way to fight Morelli. See, magic was a front for him. The Mob owned him. They called him Dirty Hand, but he was just the little finger of a dirty hand that spread all over town. By the time Cleo found out, it was too late. He spied on her. His thugs, especially Jimmy the Crab, followed her and reported to him. There was no way out for her, except on stage. Magic set her free. She loved it. I can still see her on stage. A star. So bright she hurt your eyes. You couldn't look away.'

Jinx stares beyond us. 'But Morelli was filthy, a Dirty Hand through and through. Cleo thought she could handle him. You can't handle a viper. I used to rub Tiger Balm on her wounds. The marks and scars he left.' She shakes off the memory. 'Then she met Frank. He was the real thing. Like her. After he was released from the hospital, he stayed in town to be near her. He worked for the Army. They should have gone before the baby was born.'

Joy, my mother. 'What was Cleo waiting for? If she loved Frank, why stay with Morelli?'

'She was waiting to have the baby.'

Dasha leans forward. 'She was scared to go. Scared to stay. When you live with a crazy person, you don't know what they're going to do. You live in hiding, waiting for the right moment to escape.'

Like her mother, Bertie, the Black Widow.

'How did Cleo manage the sawing box when she was pregnant?' asks Stormie.

'She was getting bigger,' admits Jinx. 'It was harder for her to get in and out. That's when she started coming up with other tricks like the card changing in front of a candle.'

'Mysterious Connections,' says Da.

'Dirty Hand took credit for it,' mutters Jinx. 'For all her tricks.'

Da and I exchange looks.

Stormie nudges me. 'Another Amazing Asshole.'

'Joy was born in the hospital,' says Jinx. 'I helped deliver her.

Cleo and Frank planned to run away with the baby the night the storm hit town.'

'The Great Atlantic Hurricane,' I say. 'Where were they going?'

'Chicago, Frank's hometown. He and Cleo went to load the car. I waited with Joy in my apartment. I lived on New York Avenue, right off the boardwalk.'

Ruby's corner. The charged area, where I always felt my mother's presence.

'Jinx wrote about the storm for *The Atlantic City News*,' says Dasha. 'You oughta read it.'

'The worst night of my life. I waited for Cleo and Frank for so long I got worried. I carried baby Joy through the storm to the hospital and went to the theatre to find them.' A hush broken by Jinx's cracked voice. 'I saw Morelli shoot Frank. I heard Cleo scream.'

'You were there,' I breathe.

Jinx's eyes meet mine. They are deep and dark, as if she saw me there too. 'You know what happened.'

I hear the rustle as everyone turns to me.

'I left before the end.'

Stormie grips my arm. 'What are you talking about?'

Auntie Maze's eyes glow. 'Ah, Lucy, you went through a thin place.'

'I did.' I turn back to Jinx. 'Jimmy the Crab said someone is watching. It was you. Couldn't you stop it?'

Her eyes fill with tears. 'When Dirty Hand shot her and shoved her inside the sawing box, I felt like my life was over. But I was holding baby Joy inside my coat. Cleo told me, "Her life will be different." I had to make sure of it. I kept Joy alive – for Cleo.'

'How did Frank get blamed for Cleo's murder?' Elvis asks.

'Morelli and Jimmy the Crab changed the story. A doctor heard the shots and came in. Jimmy and the doctor carried Frank's body out on a stretcher as if he were one of the patients. They carried

Morelli too. His story was that Frank shot him in the arm, then he shot Cleo, and finally turned the gun on himself. In the chaos of that night, no one checked on his story. And soon after, Morelli disappeared.'

'Members of the Mob came to see Jinx,' says Dasha. 'If she wrote the truth, they'd kill her.'

'Did Morelli know you had Joy?' asks Da.

'He didn't ask about her,' says Jinx. 'But just in case, I wanted to keep her out of his sight.'

Da says, quiet, 'I recall rumours that your husband died in the war and left you with a wee girl.'

'Dasha and I spread those rumours,' says Jinx. 'We kept track of news and gossip to watch out for Morelli.'

Dasha nods. 'We were hoping he'd died.'

'He didn't die,' I say. 'He transformed himself into Nicodemus Cray and lived in the Pine Barrens with his grandson Little Nick, who became Charlie Becker. And he killed Joy, my mother.'

I lean toward Jinx over the sawing box. I sense she's leaving out something. 'You did this alone.' I grope for what I'm missing. 'You helped Cleo and Frank. You raised Joy. You became her mother.'

She's silent. Then: 'I made mistakes. The worst, telling her about Morelli. Poisoned her life. I didn't want you to grow up with that kind of bitterness and need for revenge. That's why I thought of Declan, the man with the great heart. Was I right?'

Through a veil of tears, I look at my father, his own cheeks wet. 'You were right. Yet you did give me the rose and the note.'

'The rose was your legacy, and the note connected you to your mother. One day you might need to know the truth. If you were like Cleo, you'd find a way to open the door.'

'But Jinx, I don't think it was a mistake to tell Joy about Morelli. After all, she needed to know who her father was.'

'Dirty Hand?' Jinx spits the name. 'Joy's father was Frank. Morelli found out the baby wasn't his. That's why he killed Cleo and Frank.'

'Oh my God. Oh my God.' Stormie pokes my side. 'Oh jeez, Lucy.'

Jinx lifts her cane and points it at me. 'Child, your grandfather is Frank Weir.'

I can't see Jinx through the blur of tears. Just the red jewel of her cane, blinking furiously.

81

On the corner of New York Avenue, Ruby wails her favourite blues about a town that will be the death of her – but not for a long, long time, I hope. Scents of pizza, salt-water taffy, and cotton candy mingle with salt, sand, and sea. Drunk and laughing, a costumed group – a devil, an angel, a witch, a walking shower curtain – staggers past DiBruni's. A man in a top hat twirls a woman in a strapless evening gown past Central Pier. The Bee Gees are stayin' alive while Sinatra praises his kind of town. This is *my* kind of town: tacky and grand, Jersey shore and Camp Boardwalk, strippers and magicians.

I cross the boardwalk and climb down the steps to the beach and the underside of Central Pier. The two greybeards are back, watching from the shadowy pillars. I move beneath the pier to the rafters. Shut my eyes and breathe in. No burning peat. No big-band music. Just the waves breaking behind me. Cleo and Frank are gone. But I'll carry them, and Joy, with me always.

When I open my eyes, a man is watching me. The grey hoodie tugs at me again. Okay, girl, time to show what you're made of. I came prepared. I dig into my purse, get what I need and move toward him. 'Do you believe in magic?'

He tilts his head to the side. 'You're here, aren't you?'

I catch my breath. Oh yes, this man understands.

'I believe we can create something real from magic, something as real as a black rose. Do you want to try?'

'I do.'

I hold out my hands and show him they're empty.

'Press your palms together as if you're praying.' When he does, I press my palms over his hands. They're so warm. I press harder, squeezing my hands against his. 'We can do this together, create magic in the real world.'

I lift my hands from his and stare at his hands.

After a moment, he parts them. A small gemstone glows red between his hands. His gasp warms my heart. He lifts his head. 'Ah, Lucy.'

'It's a love stone,' I say, breathless. 'It will keep you safe. Maybe even give you hope.'

He smiles. 'Hope is all I want.'

My wings, those tender shoots, quiver. Trained, not tamed.

The man has promise.

So do I.

He drops the gemstone in his pocket and tucks my hand in his.

We head north to Midnight. Anywhere else, heading north to Midnight would sound like a fairy tale. In this town, the road is the Atlantic City boardwalk, and Midnight is a casino, and the odds are a gambler's nightmare. But if you're a dame, you pick yourself up and start over. After all, if you can't have hope in a city that dies and rises with the tides, then you can't have hope anywhere.

82

Wednesday evening
Halloween, Samhain

A few hours later, Elvis and I meet Stormie at the Golden Nugget marina, our arms filled with orange daylilies. Stormie and I are dressed to celebrate, both wearing dresses from Red Light Vintage that brush against our ankles. She is a goddess in a rich burgundy gown that clings to her breasts and hips, and I'm in golden amber silk that shivers down my arms and legs. We both painted our lips Carmine Red.

Detective Torres returned my mother's rose, and I pinned it to my hair.

Captain Tom ushers us aboard his gleaming yacht, Lady Luck, her deck twinkling with fairy lights. Jinx and Dasha are settled safely on deck. Misty helps Ruby install herself next to Jinx. Da, moustached and bearded, in full velvet regalia like a modern-day Henry VIII, and Auntie Maze, draped in layers of brocade and lace, help Dom carry bottles of champagne on deck. Tal, our original mysterious loner dude, is all in black. I catch him stealing glimpses of the goddess, Stormie... and her, as flushed as her deep wine-red dress, pretending not to notice.

Rex Saylor appears in his black leather jacket and jeans. He nods a greeting, but when he spots Detectives Torres and Wax, he scowls at me. I invited them but wasn't sure they'd come. For the first time I see Torres with her hair loose and Wax smiling.

Tonight, Gus styled his hair in Princess Leia side-buns. 'Lady Moon.'

A cocktail waitress from Midnight takes his arm. 'Hey, Gus. Sorry I'm late.'

He adjusts his glasses and smiles at her. 'Hey, yourself.'

We distribute cups of champagne and set sail around Absecon Island, getting a glorious view of the city skyline. Three miles out at sea, east of Atlantic City, we stop.

Auntie Maze speaks first. 'My friends, tonight is the actual night of Samhain, which marks the Gaelic new year as well as the end of summer and beginning of winter. But truly, Samhain is an entire season. We've been feeling it creep up on us, haven't we? Longer nights, the moon lowering to connect with us while the sun retreats. Voices and smells from the past remind us that we're all here together sharing our fair earth. This is the season when spirits of the dead visit the living, the perfect time to send Van off. Declan, please come here.'

Da moves to her side. Their coppery hair glows against the fairy lights and red-gold rays of the setting sun. 'When a magician dies, our community mourns their passing in a traditional ceremony we call the Broken Wand. A couple of weeks ago Lucy broke Van's wand to mark the end of her magic, and this evening she will scatter her ashes to mark the end of her life.'

He gestures to me.

I raise my cup. 'Everyone, please join me in sending Van off on her voyage.'

We drink to her, and the group gathers near the railing while Ruby sings, 'I'll Be Seeing You,' adjusting the lyrics for Van: 'We'll be looking at the moon, but we'll be seeing you, Lady Miss Van...'

I open the plastic bag filled with her ashes and toss them overboard. We watch the ashes scatter in the waves. Then the lilies, flickering like sun rays on the water.

'Good night, sweet Van. We love you.'

Elvis wraps his arm around me, Stormie leans against me, and together, we sail back to shore.

Acknowledgements

"Magic is a house with many rooms," wrote my friend, the late great magician and philosopher, Eugene Burger, and to my everlasting joy, I was welcomed inside that amazing house of secrets and wonder. Thank you, Eugene. And thank you, Larry Hass, for being a true mentor and friend, and for sharing your wisdom and insights with me for years (Hofzinser!... and so much more!) I'm grateful to the brilliant shaman, Jeff McBride, and to Abigail McBride, for your generous spirits. To Luna Shimada for trusting me with your experiences as a magical woman. To George Parker (The magical gemstone!), Bob Neale, Connie Boyd, Kenton Knepper, Kayla Drescher, Carisa Hendrix, Tobias Beckwith, and so many others, including Teller, who once said, "I love to wallow in magic." Me too, Teller.

This story couldn't take place anywhere but Atlantic City—that grand old dame with her own gritty magic and secret history under the boardwalk. I was lucky to have Susan West as a guide—you're the best, Sue! Thanks to you, and to Reggie Ballard, for taking me through the haunted theatre and showing me the ghosts of Atlantic City.

Thanks to Charlie Love, former captain of criminal investigations in the Atlantic City Police Department, for his expert advice.

And I couldn't have navigated the New Jersey Pine Barrens without the incomparable Jeanie Roy Collins, whose legends and tales brought that eerie world to life.

Thanks to my editor, the brilliant crime writer Luca Veste, for your vision and faith in my book, and to Todd Swift, director of Black Spring Press, and to Evie Rowan, Edwin Smet, and the wonderful cover designer, Matt Broughton.

I'm grateful to the writer's colonies that helped nurture me and my work—I began this novel at the Virginia Center for the

Creative Arts, and after ten residencies, it feels like a second home. Thanks also to Hedgebrook, the very first colony I attended, and to Yaddo, MacDowell, and Highlights.

Thank you, Sarah Hilary, Bill Boyle, Richard Kahan, Gar Anthony Haywood, Amy Tipton, and Russel McLean for your support and insights. Thanks also to Curtis Brown Creative and Sisters in Crime.

I'm honored that *Zigzag Girl* won the Grand Prize in ScreenCraft's Cinematic Book competition and First Prize in the Daphne du Maurier Awards for Mystery/Suspense.

Every magician knows that the true magic begins backstage. I'm fortunate to have wonderful writers in my corner who have offered years of support, encouragement, critiques, food, wine, and laughter, and who've let me dream aloud, and on the page: my writing group, Joyce Hinnefeld and Virginia Wiles; Judy Lasker, Kit Grindstaff, Katherine Ramsland, Kate Brandes, Irina Reyn (plot walks!), Miryam Sivan, Ann de Forest, Sharon James, Joyce Woollcott, Elaine Wolff, Stephanie Powell Watts, Janice Eidus, Kathryn Craft, Laura Olson, Donna Galanti, Tori Bond, and Janice Gable Bashman. You've all profoundly enriched my writing—and my life.

I am also incredibly lucky to have a supportive family—my husband Jojo (Joe's Java every morning, and the best listener!), my children, Ishai, Arielle, and Avi—and their partners— Liz and Tanya—and the youngest members, Margot, Leo, George, and Cosmo. I couldn't have carried on without you. My amazing mother Rosine, my sister Danielle and my brother Jerry, and their families. And the extended Setton clan in Israel, Costa Rica, and the US, including my dear sister-in-law Lynda (We haven't stopped talking since the day we met!)...

I believe in magic—Jersey Girl magic—the kind that zigzags from me to you, and all the way back to a nine-year-old girl who wrote in her first diary, "I want to be a writer," and watched in wonder as her pen transformed into a wand. *Abra Cadabra*!

The Black Spring Crime Series

Curated and edited by the best-selling author Luca Veste, and endorsed by the likes of Lee Child, Mark Billingham, and Val McDermid, the Black Spring Crime Series is filled with fantastic reads, waiting to be discovered. From psychological thrillers, to historical crime novels, to classic noir, we have something for everyone, with many, many more to come . . . some of our selection are listed below!

***A Crime in the Land of 7,000 Islands,* Zephaniah Sole**

This psychological literary fiction tells the tale of Ikigai Johnson, a Special Agent working out of the FBI's Portland, Oregon field office, who pledges to bring justice to children abused by a monstrous American in the Philippines. Amidst an expertly accurate police procedural, Ikigai recounts her tale to her eleven-year-old daughter through fantastical allegory.

This is a powerhouse crime thriller written by a serving FBI agent fused with folk tales and the influence of anime. Described by bestselling author Stuart Neville as 'an extraordinary feat of storytelling'.

***Jasper's Brood,* J.K. Nottingham**

It Takes a Killer, To Raise a Killer, To Raise a Killer . . . Jasper is a killer. Raised by a man who is not his father, but a serial killer to become just like him. Only, he is different. He wants to help people. The only way he knows how. To be just like him.

Cormac McCarthy meets North-East England in this unforgettable novel, with a fresh and exciting voice from a debut author.

The Salt Cutter, **C.J. Howell**

Bolivia. 1991. A soldier arrives in the small town of Uyuni. A place people endure rather than enjoy. The soldier knows they're coming for him. Hunting him down so they can deal their own brand of justice. He needs to get out. To make it to the border and escape what is waiting for him. He's prepared to do anything to survive. Even kill.

This is noir fiction at its finest. With characters that you will root for, heartbreak, and breathtaking writing, this is a story that will linger in reader's minds long after you've turned the final page.

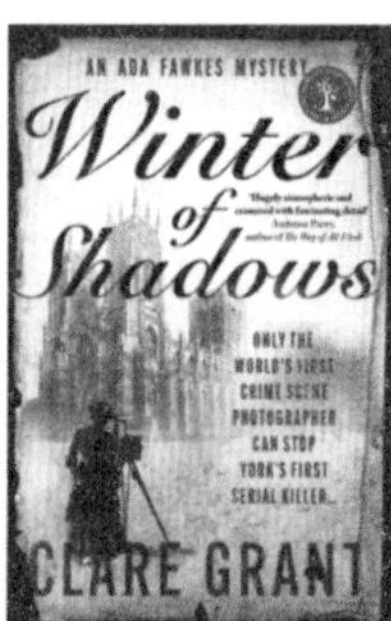

Winter of Shadows, **Clare Grant**

In the midwinter of 1862 in York, a young woman is found dead by the river, her body marked by a sinister act of mutilation. The mysterious death spreads fear, for this is not the first corpse to be discovered. Speculation grows there is a killer stalking the city's medieval streets.

This glorious historical crime thriller, described by Ambrose Parry as, 'hugely atmospheric', introduces the character of Ada Fawkes, the country's only crime scene photographer, who you won't forget in a hurry.

The God Secret, **Yves Laliberté**

When a deadly biological attack is narrowly thwarted by Royal Canadian Mounted Police agent Kristen Vale, she uncovers a chilling pattern of crimes. Joined by medieval historian Quentin DeFoix, Vale follows a trail of cryptic symbols, ancient torture devices, and forgotten iconography from the Dark Ages. As the body count rises, the pair must decipher a centuries-old mystery known only as The God Secret – before the next wave of terror is unleashed.

For the first time in English, Book One of the best-selling French-Canadian literary phenomenon, *The God Secret.*

***The Scotsman,* Rob McClure**
Chic Cowan will do anything to find his daughter's killer…even sacrifice his own sanity…and maybe he wasn't all that sane to start with…

Set during the turbulence of a divided America, a plot that engages with what 'woke' means, and the realities of policing, *The Scotsman* is the blistering debut from a new Tartan Noir talent. This is *Rebus* meets *Taken.*

***Cast No Shadow,* Nick Quantrill**
Podcaster Yaz Moy is stuck in small town purgatory with no way out. That is until someone approaches her with a story that could be the key to fulfilling her big city dreams. Yaz is forced to decide what matters more – her safety or the truth. And she's willing to risk it all…

"Hull's answer to Ian Rankin" – Hull Daily Mail

***CrimeBits: 100 Opening Gambits for Great Thrillers & Linked Mystery Puzzles,* selected and introduced by Lee Child & ed. Luca Veste**
A unique, interactive puzzle book including 100 first pages of thrillers, the best selected by the world-famous crime author Lee Child. Each page is linked to a puzzle, ranging from crosswords to wordsearches to mystery logic puzzles created by a *L.A. Times* puzzle setter Robin Stears.

***CrimeBits 2: 100 Opening Gambits for Great Thrillers & Linked Mystery Puzzles,* selected and introduced by Val McDermid & ed. Luca Veste**
The sequel to Lee Child's *CrimeBits* but this time selected by Val McDermid. A unique, interactive puzzle book including 100 first pages of thrillers. Each page is linked to a puzzle, ranging from crosswords to wordsearches to mystery logic puzzles created by a *L.A. Times* puzzle setter Robin Stears.

The Wykehamist, **Alexandra Strnad**
Lucian is The Wykehamist, a bright, handsome, charming, and privately educated young man, who glides through life effortlessly. But when his life begins to unravel following his arrest in Hong Kong, journalist Clementine cannot resist the urge to rediscover the man who has been her obsession for so long. . .

Saltburn meets *American Psycho* in this shocking debut crime novel from Alexandra Strnad.

Liar Thief, **May Rinaldi**
Ginnie says she is a serial killer who kills people who have wronged her. No one believes her. Author Fiona Taylor is writing Ginnie's memoir, The Killer Inside, trying to understand why Ginnie should still insist that she's a killer. She recruits ex-DI, Tom O'Brien, to examine the evidence. As Ginnie's oldest friend, Tom has his own insights into her story.

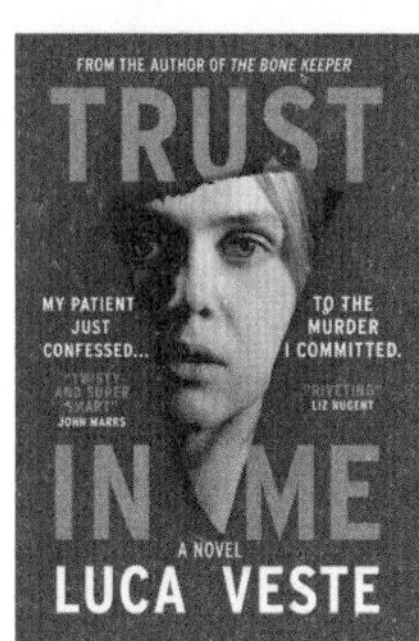

Trust in Me, **Luca Veste**
Sara seems to have it all – a thriving practice as a trauma counsellor, a comfortable home, a loving husband and two children. She's the only one who knows that her entire life is built on a lie. Until a new patient confesses to a crime that Sara knows all too well – because it's the one Sara committed many years earlier. How can this person know about Sara's past? What does this patient have planned? And how can Sara stop her telling anyone? One thing is certain: Sara will go to any lengths to keep her secret and her family safe ...

ABOUT THE AUTHOR

Ruth Knafo Setton is the award-winning author of *The Road to Fez* and *Zigzag Girl*. Her work has received fellowships and prizes from the National Endowment for the Arts, PEN, and Writer's Digest. *Zigzag Girl* won the Grand Prize in the ScreenCraft Cinematic Book Competition and First Prize in the Daphne Awards, while her pilot adaptation won the 2024 Los Angeles Crime and Horror Film Festival. A student of magic who has been sawed in half and thirds, locked in straitjackets, and managed to break free, Setton brings firsthand knowledge of illusion to her fiction. Born in Morocco and raised on stories of wonder, she has taught creative writing at Lehigh University and with Semester at Sea.